INDIAN PRAIRIE PUBLIC LIBRARY DISTRICT
3 1946 00038 0052
W9-BYT-772

Hangman

Also by Christopher A. Bohjalian
A Killing in the Real World

Hangman

Christopher A.
Bohjalian

Carroll & Graf Publishers, Inc.
New York

First Carroll & Graf edition 1991

Carroll & Graf Publisher's, Inc.
260 Fifth Avenue
New York, NY 10001

Library of Congress Cataloging-in-Publication Data

Bohjalian, Christopher A.
Hangman / by Christopher A. Bohjalian. — 1st Carroll & Graf ed.
p. cm.
ISBN 0-88184-685-6 : $18.95
I. Title.
PS3552.O495H36 1991
813'.54—dc20 91-4506
CIP

Manufactured in the United States of America

For Annalee and Aram, my mother and father,
and for Cassandra,
the little girl with the greatest potential

Acknowledgments

The author wishes to thank the Vermont Council on the Arts for their support of this book, as well as Sergeant Emmet B. Helrich of the Burlington, Vermont, Police Department, and Dr. Paul Morrow, Chief Medical Examiner for the State of Vermont.

I would like also to thank my agent, Mary Jack Wald, for her continued encouragement; friends Linda Kelliher and Yoram Samets; and Victoria Blewer, my wife, for her insight into my writing and her patience with my words.

It is better to be half-hanged than ill wed.
Vermont Proverb

". . . there'd be no complications—except in her dreams."
John Irving

Prologue:

Ten Years Earlier

It was like driving through a tunnel, J. P. Burrows decided, a tunnel made up of thousands upon thousands of oncoming darts. Small, white specks that shot through the black at his windshield, missing it—narrowly—but unceasing.

Still, he felt safe. He had grown up driving Vermont roads in the winter, and the illusion—snowflakes cascading upon him like darts —never interfered with his ability tc navigate through snowstorms. He knew by the way people would doze in his car at night that most passengers had plenty of confidence in his driving.

Despite the storm, he was able to pick up the New York City news station WCBS on the car's radio. Regardless of how dense the cloud cover or how heavy the snow, as long as the temperature remained below freezing, he had always been able to find the station. There was a bit of static tonight, but no serious interference.

He tuned in to a traffic report about the highways six hours south of him. "Traffic is down to one lane on the northbound Major Deegan, the result of a stalled vehicle in the righthand lane. There's especially slow going at the exit to the George Washington Bridge, where a jackknifed tractor trailer truck is clogging both entry on and off the bridge. Avoid that one if you possibly can. And if you want to be home for Christmas, at all costs keep away from the Lincoln Tunnel. Last minute Christmas shoppers have traffic at the tunnel backed up across the island to Queens."

The best part of the traffic report was the sound of the helicopter's propellors in the background. It wasn't snowing in New York City, and Chopper 88 was in the air.

Burrows wasn't sure why he enjoyed listening to news from Manhattan, but he always had. It certainly wasn't because he had terrific memories of the place. He had visited New York City twice as a child, once for a Yankee game when he was eight, and once for the Macy's Thanksgiving Day Parade when he was nine. Both expeditions had been unequivocal disasters. He and his father had gotten into a fistfight with three city kids at the Yankee game after they had called his five-year-old brother, Simon, a retard, and then a year later Simon had disappeared on Broadway for three hours when he ran into a crowd after someone shot a BB through Underdog and the massive, inflated crime fighter collapsed atop two police officers while emitting the loudest—there was no good word for it—fart in the history of public ritual.

Nor did he believe his affection for the radio station was driven by any sort of conventional interest in faraway places: there was nothing particularly romantic to him about police corruption, traffic jams, and homeless people on sidewalks.

And while there were moments when he feared he appreciated New York City news radio because he had some grotesque personality disorder that took pleasure in the nonstop litany of subway decapitations, child murders, and fired baseball managers, he believed —he hoped—there was a deeper reason.

No, he was sure of it.

He listened to News Radio 88 because of Simon. When his parents were gone for the evening and he was home alone with his brother, he had always listened to the news station. The voices were adult and protective and serene, and—perhaps most important—they too were awake. As long as he listened to the news announcers from New York, he wasn't alone.

He checked his watch and saw that it was just about a quarter to eight—meaning that next up on the news station would be the two-minute sports report—and wondered if Simon would like the Christmas present he had brought. He hoped he would. He hoped it with a sigh so deep that it sounded almost like a gasp, because as sure as sap ran sweet in March, Simon was going to hate his news.

Christmas was supposed to be a time of good news and good cheer, a time of miracles, Burrows thought wistfully, parking his decade-old Falcon beside the barn. He pulled in between his uncle's and his cousin's pickup trucks, one silver and rust, the other blue and rust. This year, however, he was coming home to the family farm in West Gardner with an announcement that would be greeted with nothing but sadness. Especially by Simon. Which was too bad, because his announcement was exciting, perhaps the most exciting thing that had ever happened to him. In most homes, his good fortune would be greeted with toasts and well wishes and perhaps just a bit of awe. But then—and the bitterness behind the thought worried Burrows—most homes didn't have a Simon.

When he turned off the headlights, he noticed the moon was so full he could have driven the last hundred yards or so solely by the light in the sky and wished that he had. He liked driving the empty back roads at night without his headlights on. It was like being invisible.

Perhaps it was just as well, however, that he had kept his headlights on. One of these days he was going to glide down a road in the dark and smash into another car or person. He could just see the headline the next day in the *Burlington Free Press:* ROOKIE COP ARRAIGNED ON MANSLAUGHTER. EARLY REPORTS INDICATE VEHICLE LIGHTS WERE OFF. He could live without that news story on Christmas Day.

In his family's house, the tree was trimmed on Christmas Eve, when everyone returned home from the candlelight service at the church in the next town. J. P. recalled once remarking to his father that he couldn't think of anything scarier than giving Simon a lit candle in a crowded, confined space, and his father had chastised him, telling him that he didn't have enough faith in his little brother.

His father was right; he never seemed to have enough faith in Simon. But the flip side of that skepticism had been the fact that he had always been there for his brother. Until now.

Simon was the first to greet J. P. as he walked in the front door, shuffling into the front hall and hugging him with the tremendous hams that passed for hands.

"Howdy, Simon," J. P. said, noticing immediately the candle wax on his brother's shirt. "How was church tonight?"

"We all went to church tonight," Simon said, grinning madly.

Clearly, church had been fine. "You want to put these under the tree?" he asked, motioning toward the bag of wrapped packages he had brought with him from Montpelier.

Simon looked down at the presents, wide-eyed, nodded frantically, and then ran with the bag into the living room, an already balding, overweight eighteen-year-old who would never—ever—quite grow up. Of the fourteen or fifteen people waiting for him in the next room, J. P. knew that Simon would take the news hardest that he was moving out, and moving a good two hours away to Burlington.

He couldn't imagine how he was going to tell him, how he was going to explain to him that becoming a cop really was good news.

"The point is, you've always been there for him," his father said, slowly, thoughtfully, when the two were alone. J. P. had decided to tell people individually that he was leaving West Gardner, beginning with his father, rather than make an announcement while everyone was gathered around the holiday table. Yes, it was an honor that he had been given an assignment in Burlington straight out of the state police academy, and, yes, his family would be proud. But they—Simon—would also be painfully aware that this honor meant he was moving out.

"You've always been there for him," his father said again, refilling the copper kettle that sat atop the small wood stove in the den. Thomas Burrows was the sort of tall, white-haired Vermonter from whom only the most aggressive down-country leaf peeper would ask directions. The irony was that he talked more than any male in his family—with the exception of J. P. himself—a quirk of personality that J. P. could attribute only to the work his father did part-time assisting other farmers as a county extension agent for the state university.

"I know that," J. P. said, nodding.

"Maybe you been too good to him. Maybe that's the problem. Pure 'n' simple, he couldn't a had a better brother. Stayin' home with him as much as you do, takin' him to Montpelier two, three times a month. Simon ain't spoiled, but he's got himself a routine now."

"He'll find other routines," J. P. said, regretting the remark immediately. He had meant it as merely a casual affirmation that life was indeed a transient, linear thing, but he could tell that he had disappointed his father. He had sounded callous.

" 'Course he will," Thomas Burrows said, folding his arms across his chest. "But things come a might harder to Simon than to most of us." J. P. watched him shrug, stare for a moment at the snow piling up on one of the ash cans out back, and then turn back to him.

"You remember Christmas thirteen years ago? You were seven at the time. Maybe eight, but I think you were seven."

"The year we went slidin' at the Bascombs?"

"Nope. Year after."

J. P. remembered the Christmas well, dreading the fact that his father had brought it up. "I was eight that year. Simon was five. It was the Christmas after we went to Yankee Stadium." In the living room, he heard the Ray Coniff Singers murmuring "Silent Night."

"Only one Simon would listen to was you."

J. P. shook his head. It was crazy, that whole afternoon had been crazy, and his family had virtually canonized the eight-year-old J. P. Everyone in his family recalled the incident differently, and so all that remained now for Burrows were random details—nothing exactly chronological. A small, white candle on the Christmas tree, no wider than a pencil, burning, falling. The drapes on the bay window on fire, then disappearing as the flames climbed upward, devouring the sheer, lacy fabric. The room became dark, his eyes burned as if his mother had dumped Mercurochrome in them, and the air tasted like a barbecue grill. It was as if the entire dining room floor were a mass of burning leaves, and he was trapped inside it, small and sweaty and scared. While his father and Uncle Orvis emptied fire extinguishers and sap buckets of water onto the flames—onto everything—and his mother and Aunt Catherine searched the house for Simon, he found his brother hiding in the breakfront and coaxed him outside to safety. Even then, J. P. knew it wasn't so much that he had any special power over his five-year-old brother, as that he had an eight-year-old's intuitive understanding of where the best places to hide were.

"Dad, this is an opportunity I can't pass up. You have to know this is what I've wanted."

"I do. I'm right pleased for you. I made my peace long ago with the fact you wouldn't be takin' on the farm someday. But at the same time, I got to be concerned for my other son. That's all."

Near them, perhaps as near as the hallway, Simon laughed at something Uncle Orvis had said or done. Probably that thing he did with his hands, making animal silhouettes against the wall.

"You're gonna love what Simon got you this year," his father said, trying to lighten their mood.

"Want to tell me what it is?" J. P. asked, knowing that his father would refuse.

"Can't, 'cause I don't know. That's truth. All I know is Simon picked it out by himself the week before last, and he told your mom it's the best gift he's ever got for you. He says it's just the thing."

His father picked up the glass coffee cup of eggnog he had placed on the oak table. "You gonna tell your mom next?"

"Yup."

"She'll be a tad concerned, like me. But don't read her wrong. We're both real proud of you. That's truth too."

His mother hugged him, and he could feel the weight of her arms —weight new with age—through her red plaid dress. Her Christmas dress, worn once a year for every Christmas he could remember. He wondered suddenly if she took the hem up or down as fashion dictated, and couldn't imagine on second thought that she did. He had never seen *Vogue* or *Redbook* or *Cosmopolitan* in this house.

When she pulled away, she asked him, "Now you've thought this whole thing through?"

"Yes, of course," J. P. said, smiling.

"Heck of a day for an announcement like this. But I guess Christmas Eve is as good as any."

"It's the time the whole family gathers."

His mother raised an eyebrow above the rim of her eyeglasses. Like her dress, J. P. believed his mother had worn that specific pair of glasses for as long as he had been alive. Gray tortoiseshell frames, little tin diamonds at the joints. She then turned from him to pull the turkey halfway out of the oven, holding the pan—a cast-iron roaster that with the bird in it may have weighed close to thirty-five pounds—with one hand, while basting the turkey with the other. It was one fluid, almost habitual movement. She had probably cooked a hundred turkeys in her lifetime.

"Looks good," J. P. told her, his attempt at positive reinforcement.

"I guess I shouldn't be surprised," his mother said, ignoring him, "because I know how much you want to live in Burlington. And how hard you worked at the academy."

"Nah. Not all that hard."

"Hard enough to get this—what's it called, appointment?" Before he could answer she handed him two potholders—red with Christmas bells—and asked, "Would you mind drainin' these?" referring to the sweet potatoes that had been boiling on the stove.

He lifted the pot off the burner and poured the water through the colander in the sink, the steam stinging his face and blinding him for just the slightest moment. "I'd call it a job. That's all, a job. 'Appointment' makes it sound more important than it is."

"What are you gonna tell Simon?"

J. P. grimaced reflexively. Simon. "I'll tell him I'll be a little further away than usual, but I'll still see him. I'll still visit."

"When you tell him, don't forget how much he needs you."

"I won't." He heard the front door open. Laughing, commotion, people kicking off their boots. His cousin Sherry and her husband had returned from town, where they had been caroling with a group of people from the church.

"He needs you more than you know. He still talks about the Christmas you and that Avery girl—Patience—took him on a sleigh ride."

J. P. stared down into the sweet potatoes, little rust-colored footballs, unwilling to look at his mother. Another misshapen memory. Another odd opportunity for his parents to cast him—this time as a fourteen year old—in the role of Simon's guardian angel. He remembered the plan, plotting with Patience how to steal a few moments alone on Christmas Day, and deciding upon a sleigh ride. Taking advantage of the Avery's tremendous gray and white Appaloosas. Patience's ability with horses. The day so cold it simultaneously burned and soothed his cheeks, his forehead, his eyes. Someone—his father—suggested Simon go along, suggesting that he too might enjoy a sleigh ride. J. P. dreaded the idea, but he knew it was impossible to argue. Of course Simon then loved the ride; he loved it more than he loved anything he had found in his stocking; he loved it more than he loved the G.I. Joe Frogman he had found under the tree.

Motives. Intentions. Yes, it had been impossible to argue with his father, but J. P. wondered now if perhaps there weren't other currents there. Maybe it was an unwillingness to argue. Maybe he had been afraid to be alone with Patience. Maybe—just maybe—he had liked the idea of having Simon with him. Simon simplified things. Like a chemist, Simon distilled things down to their basics. Hot and cold. Light and dark. Good and evil. There were no grays for Simon, because he didn't overcomplicate issues or intellectualize them. He didn't waste gray matter justifying decisions, or—as J. P. knew he himself did—rationalizing them. Simon did what came naturally, what came from the heart. He hugged you when he saw you. He asked you how you felt, and actually listened to your answer. He told you he loved you, without inhibition, without shame, without any hidden meanings or agendas.

"This is gonna sound wicked—wicked," his mother said, looking up from the carrots she was slicing into the boiling water, "but I hope Simon doesn't quite understand what your going to Burlington means. 'Cause if he does, it may hurt him more than we'll ever know. And you don't deserve that."

Simon's fingers were too big for the bows, his joints insufficiently nimble. It was like tying his shoes, but worse because the ribbon was slippery, fat, uncooperative.

Moreover, the box was perhaps a foot and a half high and a foot and a half wide, and Simon had to set it between his knees on the step below him.

But Simon didn't seem to be frustrated. He continued gamely, methodically, pulling one end of the ribbon and then the other. Once he looked up at J. P., sitting beside him on the top step of the stairs, and smiled.

Downstairs, J. P. heard his mother, Aunt Catherine, and Sherry washing the dinner dishes. Normally there was some peculiar female camaraderie that led them to laughter when they did the Christmas or Easter dishes. Not this year. At one point he heard Aunt Catherine raise her voice with a question, followed by his mother hushing her, telling her that he—J. P.—was probably telling him right now.

Finally Simon discovered the secret, the move that with one deft tug untied the ribbon, causing it to fall away from the sides of the package.

The package itself—wrapped in the paper J. P. saved exclusively for his kid brother, cartoons of bears hibernating in a forest of brightly trimmed Christmas trees—was much easier. No knots, just Scotch tape. He sliced open one seam, pulled the tape off another, and gingerly—with a gentleness reserved for the bears—peeled the wrapping paper off the box.

He knit his eyebrows, deepening the two long wrinkles across his high forehead. J. P. knew Simon had never seen the word on the box before, but he may have understood the concept from the photograph.

"Pull—" Simon started awkwardly.

"Phil," J. P. said, correcting him softly. "*Ph* makes an *f* sound. Phil-a-telic. Philatelic."

"Stamps?"

"Right, stamps. It's a book to help you start collecting them. As a hobby."

"As a hobby." Simon smiled, raising his voice just the slightest bit. "I want a hobby!"

"I figured. There are some other things that go with this which you can open tomorrow."

"Tomorrow?" Simon asked, still staring at the picture of the small boy surrounded by a magnifying glass, acetate sheets, and multicolored stamps from Malasia.

"Yes, tomorrow. When we exchange our Christmas presents."

Simon rested his hands on the top of the box. "Tomorrow's Christmas. Tomorrow. Why'd you give me this now?"

The way his mother talked, it would be a miracle if the news didn't devastate Simon. He wondered if a stamp collection was the stuff of miracles. It had seemed so at the time, when he had stood in the hobby store. Now? Now he wasn't so sure.

"Because I wanted you to have it now," J. P. explained.

"That's all?"

J. P. shrugged without commitment.

"Why didn't I open this by the tree?" Simon asked.

"Because I have something to tell you. And stamps are part of it. Letters are part of it."

Simon frowned, not following this line of reasoning. J. P. could almost see the questions forming like flash cards in Simon's brain: why couldn't his older brother tell him something about stamps by the tree? Was it something to do with the tree? Or was it something to do with the stamps? Or was it something else, something to do with whatever it was J. P. was about to tell him? Simon just couldn't be sure.

Finally he turned away and ran one pudgy finger over the vines in the wallpaper pattern. Could he sense it would be bad news—rather, could he sense it would be news he would dislike? J. P. cautioned himself not to view his assignment as bad news. People grew up and left home all the time. His leaving for Burlington wasn't bad news, no matter what his family thought; it just wasn't.

J. P. lifted up the stamp collecting kit and placed it on the landing behind them. He then put an arm around Simon's shoulders. "What I'm going to tell you is pretty terrific. Pretty good stuff."

Simon didn't look at him. "What?" His voice was filled with suspicion, fear.

"You remember the time we went to Burlington this summer?

There were a couple of buildings I was real interested in—one was white, one was brick?"

Simon looked at him blankly.

"That was the Burlington Police Department."

Simon showed no sign of recollection, just dread. J. P. could smell the stuffing from dinner on his breath.

"Well. Those two buildings are right around the corner from the pizza parlor you like. The one with all the different toppings."

"I know where that is!" Simon boasted, his eyes brightening abruptly.

"Of course you do."

"I've been there!"

"Of course you have," J. P. said, smiling.

"Is that what you wanted to tell me?"

"No, there's more," J. P. continued, watching the relief melt from his brother's face. "Burlington is a big place, a growing place. It's a place where they need some more policemen."

Behind him, the windows in Simon's bedroom rattled in the wind. Once, many Christmas Eves before, J. P. remembered telling Simon that the windows were shaking because of reindeer on the roof.

"Anyway—and you're supposed to be smiling, Simon, because this is good news—I've been asked to go to Burlington to become one of those policemen."

Simon pushed his tongue into his cheek, billowing it out like a squirrel. A nervous habit. "But you don't live there."

"No, I don't. Not now, anyway." He inhaled deeply and looked down the stairs and away from Simon. He rubbed his brother's back as he spoke. "But I'm going to have to start spending a lot more time there. And pretty soon, I'm going to have to move there."

"You're moving? You're moving that far?"

"Burlington's not that far—"

"You're moving!" It was no longer a question, it was now an exclamation, perhaps even an indictment.

"Yes, but Burlington's only two hours away, so I'll still be in West Gardner a lot. And I'll write lots of letters—"

Simon stood up and pulled away from him in one movement, a movement that was almost graceful it happened so quickly. He rushed down the stairs, past his mother who had run from the kitchen, a plate and drying towel still in her hands, and past Uncle

Orvis, who evidently had been toying the whole time with the jigsaw puzzle his father had begun on the table by the front hall. He ran into the living room.

"Simon!" J. P. called, standing up. He considered racing after his brother, running down the stairs behind him, but he was unable to move. His muscles seemed to freeze, his knees to lock. He could feel his hand gripping the banister so tightly he was bruising the bone at the base of his own thumb, but he couldn't stop. He wanted to call Simon again, but he was incapable now even of that. So he remained alone at the top of the stairs, a statue, his mother looking up at him sadly, as sorry for him as she was for Simon.

From the living room, J. P. heard the sound of his brother rifling for something under the tree, tossing the packages around the room like spare socks. When he had found what he was looking for, he ran back past Uncle Orvis and his mother, and up the stairs to J. P. He tripped slightly on one step, but caught himself on the next.

When he reached J. P. he handed him the box, commanding urgently, "Open it! You have to open it now!"

Sheepishly, J. P. finally released the banister and took the package from his brother. "As you reminded me, Simon, Christmas is tomorrow. Why now?"

"Because you're going to Burlington," Simon told him with more insistence in his voice than J. P. had ever heard.

"I'm not leaving tonight, Simon. I'll be here tomorrow—"

"Open it!" Simon commanded again.

J. P. nodded. "Okay." He could tell by the gift's impeccable presentation that it had been wrapped at the store where Simon bought it. Red Victorian paper, a gold bow. It may have been a book, given its shape, but it didn't feel quite heavy enough.

He looked up at Simon as he unwrapped the box, trying to understand the intensity in his brother's face. He had never seen anything like it. It appeared to be neither anger nor sadness nor hurt. If anything, it looked to J. P. like excitement.

When he pulled the top off the box, he understood, and in the dim light in the hallway he saw his brother smile. Lying flat in the box was stationery, a light blue bond with a gray cursive flourish, stationery with his name on it: "From the desk of J. P. Burrows."

The Story:
The Present

1.

Chapter 1

Lymon Hollis told the North American moving van where to go.

The rig pulled up outside his general store one Wednesday morning in early November, and he knew right away that it had to be looking for the Finch place. Or what had been the Finch place for forty-plus years. Ernest and Edna had moved out about three weeks ago. And so he pulled on his red plaid hunting jacket and strolled out to meet the truck.

"Hello!" the driver shouted before Lymon could open his mouth. "This Deering?" He was hanging his arm out the truck window, tapping his fist distractedly against the door.

"Far as I know," Lymon answered. "You lookin' for the Finch place?"

"We're looking for the yellow house on the Haverill Gap Road. It's got itself a yellow barn, and it's next to the church." He sounded like he was in a hurry.

"Yup, that's the Finch place," Lymon said, nodding.

"Well, do you want to tell me where it is?" the driver asked, with more irritation in his voice than Lymon thought necessary. Clearly these fellows were from down country. Perhaps even New York.

"I could be persuaded," Lymon said thoughtfully. "Not sure as I do right now though."

The driver paused, and then looked at his partner. When he turned back to Lymon he was grinning. "Could you please tell me where the Finch place is?" he asked.

"Sure can. Go round that corner and past the fire department. It's 'bout a half mile up the road, next to the church. Not far. It'll be on your left."

The driver tipped the painter's cap he was wearing and began the laborious task of turning his rig around on the thin country road, a maneuver further complicated by the fact the road was bordered on one side by the steep embankment that rolled into the Deering River. Lymon watched the driver struggle with the truck for a few moments, moving it a foot forward then a foot backward, until the young man stuck his head out the cab window and hollered, "Don't you got better things to do?"

Lymon answered honestly that he didn't, but he could sense the driver's frustration and decided to head back inside. He hoped the new folks weren't in as big a hurry as their moving company.

CHAPTER 2

Sarabeth Nash was at the church Wednesday morning because Dottie Cornwall was sick. Not real sick, perhaps not even ill. Just feelin' poorly sick. Sick enough that Sarabeth's weekly lunch for the Deering Seniors couldn't be held at Dottie's home. So Sarabeth called the minister and arranged at the last moment for the lunch to be served in the Sunday school room below the church. It wouldn't be as cozy as eating in Dottie's living room, but it wouldn't smell like Ben-Gay either.

She was spreading out the crazy quilt tablecloth (hand sewn the last winter by four children in a local youth group) when she saw the rig back into the Finches' driveway, missing by inches the lawn jockey thermometer the Finches had left behind. Both movers then jumped from the cab and knocked on the front door. When nobody answered, they wandered back to their van: the one who had been driving opened the back door, while his partner—a teenager, really—climbed inside the van and began throwing onto the driveway large burlap blankets and furniture pads. They both looked annoyed, and Sarabeth feared they might actually unload those poor people's furniture right there on the driveway.

Unsure of exactly what she expected to accomplish or what she would say to the men, Sarabeth buttoned up her cardigan sweater and strolled over to the Finches' front porch. All she knew for sure was that she was a selectman's wife, and a selectman's wife ought to do something in this situation.

Besides, her husband, Josh, was helping to renovate the house for the newcomers—a couple named Brian and Marcia Middleton. The real estate agent had put him in touch with the people; and he, Dave Dunbar, and that simple one—Simon Burrows—had spent much of the last two weeks Sheetrocking, insulating, and turning what had been Foster Finch's bedroom into a library. The Middletons had asked them to take the day off while their furniture was moved in, but Sarabeth still felt an almost contractual obligation to help out if she could.

"Good morning," she shouted from the edge of the lawn, waving as she walked. When she had gotten a little closer, she smiled broadly and asked, "Is there a problem?"

"We're locked out," the driver said, staring down at the clipboard he had just pulled from a hook inside the van. "We're supposed to move someone in, and they're not home."

"Were they supposed to be?" Sarabeth asked, watching the tiger striped cat that lived in the barn wander over to the burlap blankets.

"No, of course not," the driver mumbled sarcastically, still not looking up at her. "We just figured we'd pry open a kitchen window like we always do, and throw their stuff on the kitchen floor."

"Well I do hope you're not planning on leaving their furniture in the driveway. I'm sure the people who bought the house will be here any minute."

"I hope so," the driver said, finally looking up from his forms. "We got another stop to make today in someplace called St. Albans. Whole back half of this truck. But don't worry, we don't plan on tossing a Barcalounger out on the asphalt here. We're just getting ready is all."

Sarabeth nodded, wondering if the young one could talk. Up close, he looked very young, clean-cut. He was probably eighteen or nineteen years old, perhaps no more than half as old as the driver.

"Well, would you like some coffee?" she asked. "No sense in standing around out here, when I have a pot brewing over at the church."

"What do you think, Warren, could you go for a cup of coffee?" the driver asked the younger man.

Warren started to nod agreeably but stopped abruptly and instead craned his long, thin neck to see behind the truck. Both Sarabeth and the driver turned to see what he was looking at. There, about a hundred yards down the road, a red Saab with New York plates was streaking toward them.

"Looks like you'll have to bring that coffee over here. Or we'll have to take a pass on it," the driver said, putting down his clipboard.

The Saab coasted to a stop in front of the moving van, and for the split second before the ignition died, Sarabeth thought she heard rock music coming from the car radio.

The woman who climbed out of the car looked to Sarabeth to be three or four years younger than she was. The woman was probably in her late twenties and very attractive—which explained why Josh never said much about her, although he had met her at least twice. She was holding a canvas overnight bag, which Sarabeth grabbed from her instinctively, saying, "You must be Marcia, our new neighbor. I'm Sarabeth Nash. Welcome." Despite the twinge of jealousy that passed through her, she was thrilled to see someone roughly her own age moving into the Finch place, almost overjoyed, and she hoped she didn't seem unreasonably enthusiastic.

"Good morning," Marcia Middleton said to Sarabeth, extending her hand as she spoke. "It's wonderful to meet you. I can't tell you how excited Brian and I are about the work Josh is doing on the house. It really looks fantastic!"

She then turned to the movers, adding, "I guess I'm a bit late." She said it casually, without guilt. Her voice was slightly hoarse, but it didn't sound to Sarabeth as if she had a cold; evidently, Marcia's voice was naturally husky.

"A bit, yeah," the driver said to her.

"Sorry, guys," Marcia said to the movers, spreading her arms expansively. She saw the barn cat kneading one of the furniture pads and rubbed its head, and then jumped up onto the porch steps to unlock the door. Sarabeth noted that her wool pants were very stylish, very new, and that her scarf was too filmy to be much use in Vermont. At least when winter really set in.

After unlocking the door, Marcia turned and smiled, saying, "Now I've never moved into a house like this before, so you'll have to tell me how you want to handle it. I've got a list of what's supposed to go where, if you think that will help."

"That'll be just fine," the driver said politely, surprising Sarabeth with his sudden civility. "My name's Todd, and this young one here is my nephew, Warren." He then tipped his hat.

"And I'm Sarabeth," the selectman's wife said quickly, afraid of being left out. She was a little hurt that the movers had introduced themselves to Marcia Middleton, but not to her. It didn't seem fair. But then, she reminded herself, men never seemed to notice her when there were other women around. Casually therefore, as if she were just scratching her neck, Sarabeth brought her hand to the base of her throat and unfastened the top buttons on her sweater and blouse.

"We live in that brick house, about two hundred yards down the road from the church—on the side closer to town," Sarabeth said to

Marcia early that afternoon, over coffee. The movers had left the Middletons' for St. Albans, and the Deering Seniors had left the church for their afternoon naps.

"How long have you lived here?" Marcia asked. "Are you and your husband from Deering?"

"No, neither of us is. Josh is from Montpelier, and I'm from Portland. Oregon, believe it or not. Not Maine. But we've lived here about eight years now."

"That's a long time."

"For a town like this? Not really. To be a local in these little hill towns, your family has to stick around a good seven generations. And stick around on the same piece of land. You cross the street or move 'round a bend, you got to start all over again."

"Sounds intense."

Sarabeth shrugged. "Well, I wouldn't say anything about Vermont is intense. Especially a town like this. All I meant is that Josh and me aren't considered real locals; we're not exactly part of the old guard. Oh, we're accepted enough that Josh won the selectman's election four years ago, and has run uncontested ever since. But we're not locals. Someone like Win Bingham—now he's a local. The Binghams have been at the top of Township Hill since the day this place was chartered. We're talking almost two centuries. Now that's local."

Marcia nodded and went to the stove for a plate of the shepherd's pie that Sarabeth had brought over from the seniors' lunch.

"Make sure you try the ambrosia mold," Sarabeth told her.

"I'll just have a little, if that's okay. I'm not a real fan of Jell-O."

"That's not just Jell-O," Sarabeth said quickly. "It's got cottage cheese in it and peaches and bananas and pears. It's one of Bonnie Boley's favorite recipes!"

Not wanting to offend a selectman's wife (especially the selectman restoring their house), and unwilling to question Bonnie Boley's evident good taste, Marcia smiled and piled onto her plate a wiggly mountain of mold.

Sarabeth walked home with her head down and her arms wrapped around her chest. So that, she thought to herself, was the Finch place. After eight years, she had finally set foot in the house. She had wandered through its rooms with the new owner; she had sat at the kitchen table and enjoyed a cup of coffee. And—rumors and stories be darned—nothing had happened. Nothing at all. Like Josh had said, it's an old house with a history. That's all. Nothing else, nothing more. She certainly didn't need to waste an ounce of pity on its new owners or worry about them. They would do just fine.

If she felt anything toward Marcia Middleton right now, she decided, it was envy. And she didn't like that in herself. So she quickly reminded herself that she had a great many things to be thankful for, a great many reasons to smile. She had a husband who was very kind and responsible, who made a good living as a small building contractor; she had two young daughters who were very pretty and very smart; everyone had their health; and there was plenty of food on the table.

But she was nagged by a frustration so pronounced that it scared her. It upset her, and she didn't view herself as the sort of person who was easily upset.

She and Josh, she realized sadly, had no style. She especially had none.

Her cardigan was almost shabby next to Marcia Middleton's cheerful ski sweater. Her blouse was frumpy. And worst of all, she carried herself like a kindergarten teacher: legs crossed demurely at the ankles, hands perched stolidly on the table (fingers intertwined); always a patient, concerned half smile on her lips. She had just introduced herself to her new neighbor from the city by talking about bingo suppers, quilting fairs, and why Josh had joined the Middlebury Rotary Club. Oh God, she thought, I am dull.

She wished she moved as unself-consciously as Marcia Middleton, as casually. She wished she had Marcia's slender, sexy figure, one not yet ruined by childbirth. She wished she had that mane of auburn red hair; she wished she had money; she wished she had a breakfront as handsome as the Middletons'.

She wished, she said almost aloud when she reached her home, that she hadn't thrown away those catalogs that came out of the blue from Horchow, J. Crew, and Victoria's Secret.

Chapter 3

Marcia Middleton sat down in the middle of the living room on the floor and sipped her instant coffee. She pretended that she was in a television commercial. Somehow, the dozens of boxes seemed less intimidating if she were only in a thirty-second television commercial. Maybe they would go away when she was done with her coffee.

Of course, they didn't. If anything, there seemed to be more of them when she was finished with her coffee—and they seemed bigger too. All together, counting the boxes of books, Marcia knew there were one hundred and eighty-three boxes. It astounded her that she and Brian had somehow managed to cram one hundred and eighty-three boxes of stuff, plus furniture, into a one-bedroom apartment on Columbus Avenue. A one-bedroom apartment with a galley kitchen only thirty-four inches wide once the appliances were in, and only seven feet long. A one-bedroom apartment without a dining room. A one-bedroom apartment with only five windows. The kind of one-bedroom apartment that the Manhattan real estate agents had referred to euphemistically as charming, cozy, and unspoiled.

It was already close to four o'clock, too late really to begin to unpack. The sun was dropping behind the small mountain just west of Deering, and Marcia knew there were too few fixtures on the first floor to get much done at night. So instead of diving into any of the one hundred and eighty-three boxes, she wandered into the kitchen to see if she could find the carton with the corkscrew. Brian and she had agreed that rather than his taking the day off from work when the movers arrived (supervising was really a one-person job), he would instead take the following Thursday and Friday off, giving the two of them a four-day weekend together in their new home. He had said, however, that he would escape work a little early that day and try to be back in Deering by 5:30. If she could find the corkscrew, she could welcome him to their new home with a bottle of wine.

She was also curious how her cats were adjusting. She had let them out of their travel boxes as soon as the movers had left, but so far she had kept them in the kitchen. She didn't want them roaming the house until she herself knew every crevice into which they might disappear, and which rooms had the most dangerous booby traps: exposed knob and tube wiring, old rat poison, or broken glass from cracked windowpanes. The basement and the attic would probably always be off-limits, since there were an infinite number of places in each area where a cat would most certainly get into trouble, (the loose and jagged floorboards in the attic especially scared her), but eventually Marcia did plan on giving the cats the run of the house on the first and second floors.

She saw Chloe right away, lounging casually on the counter beside the sink. Chloe had always been the more intrepid of her two cats, so Marcia wasn't surprised to see her so comfortable so quickly. She stroked the cat behind her ears, listening to the animal's uninterested half purr.

"Where's your brother?" she whispered to Chloe. "Where's your brother?" Undoubtedly, he had crawled behind one of the boxes in the kitchen or was lurking in the plastic trash can on its side in the far corner. Perhaps that monstrous tiger stripe that lived in the barn had peered in a window and scared Solstice into some obscure corner. Solstice had always been a coward.

She dumped the last of her coffee in the sink, watching the small brown rivulet dislodge some peas from the shepherd's pie she hadn't finished. She had never liked shepherd's pie, but she thought it was very sweet of Sarabeth to bring some by.

Clearly that was going to be a big difference between Deering and Manhattan. People cared about people in Deering. Sarabeth had come by with lunch, that Lymon person had given her a care package from his store, and an older woman from the village's senior citizens' group had brought her a plant. A Christmas cactus.

"Solstice?" Marcia asked gently, kneeling so she could peek into the upended garbage can. "You in there?" When he wasn't, she righted the waste basket and stood up. Surveying the room she saw immediately at least two places he could be: behind the pile of boxes filled with kitchen towels and utensils or behind the refrigerator. She hoped he was only behind the boxes, because it was always hell to coax him out from behind appliances. Twice before, in Manhattan, Solstice had spooked himself and burrowed underneath the stove, and both times it had taken Marcia hours of coaxing on her belly to convince him that it was safe to come out.

When the cat wasn't anywhere near the boxes in the kitchen, Marcia stood perfectly still, scanning the room to make sure that every door and cabinet was shut. She saw the doors to the dining room and pantry and front hall were closed; she saw the door to the basement was latched; she saw the cabinets were in perfect order.

"Damn it, Solstice," she murmured softly, "damn it." Frustrated, she went out to the car to get the flashlight from the glove compartment. If Solstice really were behind the refrigerator, he might not come out until Christmas, (and certainly not before Brian returned home from work—that would be too easy).

The Saab was out by the road, where Marcia had moved it when it was time for the North American van to pull out of her driveway and head north to St. Albans. It was across the street, against Obie and Claire Newsome's barbed wire fence.

Marcia's frustration was eased a bit when she saw the crowd by her car: five of the Newsome's cows, black and white Holsteins with eyes as wide as cocktail coasters, had come down off the hill and were standing against the fence, staring at the car. They were not as clean or as crisp as the cow caricatures that graced the containers of the premium ice cream she used to buy in Manhattan, but they were very cute in a basic, unaffected sort of way. When she opened the car door and reached into the glove compartment for the flashlight, in unison they took two steps back.

From her spot across the street from her house, she saw clearly the Nashes' home. It was a brick Cape with white shutters, and flew an American flag halfway down the driveway. She recalled that Josh was a member of the Middlebury Rotary Club, and was pleased. It was not that Marcia had a special fondness or respect for Rotary Clubs, but the fact that Josh—a town selectman and one of its foremost cheerleaders—had a life outside of Deering was a good sign. It seemed to suggest that it was okay for her to work in Middlebury and Brian to work in Burlington. Not that there was anything they could do about where they worked: she could no sooner suggest to the twelve people at the advertising agency she had joined that they move the office to Deering, than Brian could broach the idea to the seven thousand Vermonters employed by IBM. Still, it was reassuring to know that people went to and from Deering daily.

When Marcia returned to the kitchen, Chloe was still half asleep on the counter and Solstice was still in hiding. Before beginning her inevitable struggle with the refrigerator, Marcia once more checked the inside of the waste basket and behind the packing boxes. And once again, there was no Solstice.

Finally, resigned to her fate, she crawled around to the far side of the refrigerator and shined the flashlight into the coils lining the back of the appliance. Solstice wasn't there. Trying to remain calm, she ran the beam of light slowly around each coil and along the base. But there was definitely no sign of a cat. She stood up and scanned the kitchen again, trying to see what she had missed. Because surely she had missed something, because surely the cat was there.

She saw she was wrong, however; she had missed nothing. There were no unchecked nooks or crannies in which the cat could have hidden, no unexplored drawers, shelves, or boxes. It was as an act of desperation, therefore, that Marcia braced her back against the wall and pushed the refrigerator forward. Soon there was enough room behind the Philco for her to literally walk between it and the wall. And still there was no Solstice.

She began to feel nauseous and for a brief moment panicked, thinking that one of the moving men had inadvertently let Solstice outside, and the cat was now lost in the hills. But no, she knew that wasn't possible, because she hadn't let the cats out of their travel boxes until after the movers had left. And Solstice couldn't have run out of the house when Sarabeth Nash went home either, because she remembered distinctly seeing Solstice atop the dishwasher when she had opened the front door.

It was clear that Solstice was somewhere in the kitchen. It was not possible that he could have gotten out; it was just not possible. There was only one thing to do. Start over and once again comb systematically every inch of the kitchen. She opened every single cabinet. She looked inside the oven, the dishwasher, and the refrigerator. She ran her hand over every inch of the tile, looking for a loose piece, and over every inch of exposed wall, looking for a gap or a hole.

And when she was completely finished, there was still no cat.

"Chloe, where is your brother?" she asked the yawning calico, aware that her voice was quivering. "Where is he?" she asked again.

She tried to convince herself that there was no reason to panic. The cat simply could not have gotten outside the house. Evidently he had escaped the kitchen, but that was as far as he could have gotten. He was somewhere in the house. He had to be.

Careful to shut the door to the front hall behind her so Chloe wouldn't disappear as well, Marcia began to search the rest of the house. She moved with a determined efficiency, closing off each room once she was positive Solstice wasn't inside. She began with the den, one of the rooms being renovated, and peered behind the leaning slabs of Sheetrock, underneath the sawhorses, and inside the closets. She then moved swiftly through the living room and the dining room, pushing the boxes flush against the walls when she was sure there was no cat behind them.

"Solstice?" she would call every few moments, "Solstice?" Periodically she would shake loudly a box of Bonkers, his favorite cat treats.

When it was clear that Solstice was not on the first floor, she started on the second. It was almost dark now, and Marcia realized with some irritation that she was scared. Not just scared for the cat, but scared for herself too. Suddenly she didn't like being alone in an old house. She didn't like being alone on the second floor or alone in the dark. She felt tiny, and wished that Brian were with her now, instead of at work at IBM.

She began searching the second floor in the one room that had a working light fixture, the one she and Brian had chosen as their bedroom. When she had combed it thoroughly, without success, she moved on to the bedrooms without lights. Nervously she shined her flashlight in every corner and in every closet, trying to convince herself that the ivy and butternut wallpaper was not actually moving and that the ladder Sarabeth's husband had left behind was not really a living thing. At one point she bolted upright and let out one small, short whimper, when the furnace kicked on with a thud in the basement.

"Solstice, please, baby, come on," she pleaded when she had examined all four bedrooms and the upstairs bathroom. She realized she had begun to cry, and wiped her eyes with the bottom of her sweater. "Solstice, come out!" she said insistently to the empty house.

She leaned against a hallway wall and stared down the stairs, hating the house for its size. For being big enough to swallow up her cat. Her stupid, neurotic, defenseless, overweight cat. This wouldn't have happened on Columbus Avenue, not in a manageable one-bedroom apartment.

Angrily she banged the wall with one of her fists, and heard some plaster crack inside. And then she heard the yowl. The cat yowl, the Solstice yowl, the yowl of a trapped, overwrought cat. It was so high and prolonged, it sounded almost alien. But it was definitely Solstice.

Quickly she ran to the sound of the cries. The cat was on the far side of the house, on the second floor. She knew he wasn't in either of the bedrooms on that side, because she had checked every inch of both of them.

Solstice screamed again, one long, panicked cat bellow. Marcia whirled to her left, the direction of the whine, and dropped her flashlight when she saw that between her and her cat was the attic door. A door that was shut tight. A door that was warped, a door so gnarled with time that neither Marcia nor Brian could open it easily. The flashlight bounced once on the linoleum tiles the Finches had placed over the hardwood floor, its beam skirting the walls and doorways like a strobe light.

"God, Solstice," Marcia murmured, "God, how?" Nervously she wedged her left foot against the frame and pulled at the doorknob with both hands, yanking the door open abruptly.

Solstice, crouching on the third step to the attic, jumped past her the moment he was free. For a brief second Marcia considered peering into the attic, looking up the stairs into the living blackness above her, but she stopped herself.

Like a small, scared child she slammed the door shut behind her and raced with her cat down the hall.

Chapter 4

When thirty-five-year-old Foster Finch mentioned to Grace Macknight that his parents were putting their house up for sale and heading west to Arizona, Grace feared that it would be a good long time before the right buyers appeared. Anyone who knew anything about Deering would sooner live in the cemetery than that house.

And people who didn't know anything about Deering just didn't walk in off the street every day wanting to move there. The town was too small, too cold, and too far from civilization. Middlebury was thirty minutes away and Burlington an hour, and that was a lot by Vermont commuter standards.

Still, as a realtor she didn't mind listing the Finch place, because when it did sell, it would sell at a fair price. A high price. If it wasn't actually the largest house in Deering, it was among the largest, and its views of the Newsome's farm and Mount Stillman were picture-postcard pretty—the sort of views that in and of themselves commanded a pretty steep price tag.

She therefore surmised that its buyers would be city folk, city folk with money, (since God knew no one in Deering would pay anywhere near what the Finches were asking); the sort who thought they wanted a taste of the country, who would see an acre and a half as just about the right size, and who would think it right quaint living next to a church.

And although Ernest and Edna Finch hadn't kept their home in perfect condition the last few years, they hadn't let it fall to pieces either. Besides, it took more than three years of semineglect to undo thirty years of care.

Certainly the second floor needed a good deal more work than the first, but a lot of it was minor: some new Sheetrock in one or two of the bedrooms (followed by some wallpaper that wasn't ruined by decades-old water damage and mold), perhaps a couple new window frames with modern storms, and maybe a new railing for the banister. All told, it needed about one or two good weeks of work from an outfit like Josh Nash's—maybe three or four weeks if the renovations were a little more elaborate.

The outside of the house needed work too, but as with the inside, it was mostly cosmetic. It was mostly painting: the outside of the home was four shades of yellow, and no two walls were quite the same. Toward the end, Ernest had simply wanted to patch things, not repair them, and that attitude was manifested no more clearly than in the exterior painting. Whatever yellow the Middlebury Aubochon had in stock, that was the yellow he would buy. The front of the house was a straw yellow, and by far the warmest of the four yellows. It was also the prettiest. The ugliest yellow was probably the south wall, the side opposite the church. That yellow resembled sandwich mustard, and was applied with just about the same care that one reserved for sandwiches. Ernest's son, Foster, had slapped on that particular yellow the day after the house went on the market.

Grace also knew that the house could use about double its number of electrical outlets, although what wiring there was was sound; that some of the shutters hung improperly but none was close to falling off its hinges; that the roof needed a dozen or so new slates, but only in one far corner of the attic could a prospective buyer stand and stargaze; that the basement needed proper insulation, but it was nothing a few panels of rigid blue board couldn't tidy up; and that the barn was no longer a working barn, but it was a first-rate garage for a couple of city slickers.

What Grace didn't know for sure was which stories about the property were true and which were the inevitable exaggerations that cling to every ninety-year-old house. She had heard some people say that the place had been built at the turn of the century by a wealthy railroad attorney who had murdered his own daughter under its roof. She had heard others talk about the basement, one group claiming that the little girl's body was walled up there, another absolutely sure that the railroad man had left his fortune—and a sizeable one at that—hidden behind those beams.

She considered asking Ernest himself about the rumors, but decided in the end that she didn't know him well enough to bring them up. It was gruesome stuff, and pretty crazy when she really thought about it. And she had to admit that as a realtor, she didn't want to know for sure what was true and what wasn't.

* * *

The house had been for sale for five months, and had only been seen by two people when a pretty young thing from New York City wandered into Grace's office and said she was looking for something "charming but expansive," something with a view of the mountains. It was late August. The woman saw the picture of the Finch place hanging on the wall and whirled toward it, exclaiming happily, "That's it! That's what I'm looking for! I feel like I know that house!"

Chapter 5

Brian and Marcia Middleton had flown to Vermont for three days in early October, when the foliage was peaking, to close on their new home. Although they weren't planning on moving to Deering permanently for almost another month—they both planned on working in Manhattan until Halloween—the Finches wanted to start their cross-country drive to Arizona before the winter kicked in.

It was during the preclosing house inspection that Grace Macknight turned to Brian in the room that Brian hoped to make his library and asked, "You plannin' to fix this place up yourself?" Marcia recalled that in addition to herself and Brian and Grace, Ernest and Edna Finch were there, following the three of them around the house as if they expected one of them to start spray-painting graffiti on the barren walls.

"There's an awful lot to do," Brian had said, offending Mrs. Finch especially. "So if you know a good designer—"

"I know a good renovator. I'm not sure what you mean by a good designer."

"You speakin' about Josh?" Mr. Finch had asked Grace.

"Yup. He's doin' some real nice work right now at the town hall in Middlebury."

"Indeed he is," Mrs. Finch had said, affirming the quality of a local artisan.

The Middletons sat down with Josh Nash the very next day, right after the closing, and discussed their plans for the house. What they wanted to do with the upstairs bedrooms, the banister, the work that needed to be done in the den, the kitchen, and the basement. Two and a half weeks later, toward the end of October, Josh, his partner David Dunbar, and their assistant—a retarded fellow named Simon Burrows—had been able to start working on the house.

It was at the Middletons' closing, when all the mortgage and turnover documents had been signed and there was no turning back, that Grace Macknight turned to Brian Middleton and said with a disarmingly cryptic smile, "Betta get to know your neighbors right quick." Both Brian and Marcia understood the remark as a warning, although their Burlington loan officer—an expatriate from Pittsburgh—told them they were reading far too much into the comment.

Nevertheless, they vowed to heed the woman's advice. They would meet their neighbors, and they would meet them quickly. Brian, who could vacillate wildly at times between frantic enthusiasm and an almost immobilizing depression, switched into high gear with Grace's remark. He said he would begin right away to show his neighbors that he was no slick know-it-all from the city. Although he had retained a contractor to do much of the renovation—even some of the cosmetic renovation, such as the wallpapering in the den and the library—he would demonstrate for the town that he wasn't the sort who was afraid to replace a few clapboards, build his own hearth, or climb out onto his roof and fix a few slates. He had no idea how to do any of these things, but at least he wasn't afraid of them.

And so the two days after they moved in, the Thursday and Friday that Brian took off from work, Brian immersed himself with Josh and David and Simon in the renovations on the house. He learned from David Dunbar how to use a miter box to make a perfect cut across a two-by-four; he learned from Josh Nash how to tape Sheetrock; and he learned from Simon Burrows—slow, unknowing, but uncommonly sweet Simon—how to strip wallpaper with Metylan.

It was odd, but Brian took an immediate liking to Simon. Marcia had never seen anything like it in Brian. Around this lumbering retarded fellow almost exactly his own age, Brian grew patient. She watched—if not in awe then at least in wonder—at the way he would sit cross-legged on the floor beside Simon, paying careful attention to every word Simon said about his stamp collection, his brother, the policeman, or his father, the dairy farmer.

Thursday night she asked Brian why he found Simon so interesting, and Brian had answered simply, "He's so trusting. How can I not listen?" And then on Friday morning he had insisted that she rush off to the grocery store to get the makings for beef stroganoff, because Simon had said in passing that his mother made the best beef stew in the world.

Brian was becoming, suddenly, the world's friendliest fellow, all part of his plan—Marcia assumed—to win over the town as quickly as possible. On his first Saturday in Deering, in what he perceived as a perfectly reasonable way to meet his neighbors, he went to the town dump seven times, insisting that Marcia come with him. The dump, Sarabeth Nash had told Marcia, was only open on Saturdays and consequently served as an informal town meeting place. Sometimes the lonely old man who looked after the dump, a bankrupt dairy farmer named Delbert Hawkins, would even brew a couple pots of coffee for the townspeople to sip as they emptied their rusting pickup trucks.

The Middletons did not actually have enough garbage for seven trips, despite the fact that Marcia had spent all of Thursday and Friday unpacking boxes; but by stretching four carloads into seven, Brian reasoned they would meet three additional people. When they returned home from the dump for the last time that day, close to three o'clock, Brian surveyed the tremendous number of cartons still remaining and commented with what Marcia thought was unreasonable joy, "We might have nine or ten trips ahead of us next week." He concluded that with a little help from his red plaid jacket and her L. L. Bean duck boots, they had made a favorable first impression that day at the dump. Moreover, they had learned who they could turn to if the furnace exploded, who they could call when their pipes needed thawing, and exactly who it was who plowed the church driveway—and who could therefore plow theirs.

Brian's only disappointment, he said, was that they hadn't met any other "young" people with whom he thought they would ever become friends. Good friends. Close friends. The sort of friends who might have shared their interest in movies, or picnics, or—just maybe—gourmet cooking. But this wasn't a big disappointment for Brian, because he hadn't expected to find aficionados of Thai cuisine in Deering. It just would have been a nice, pleasant, unexpected extra in moving to Vermont.

More important than good friends, Brian said to Marcia that afternoon, they had found good people. Honest people. Upfront people. People Marcia could turn to if she was ever in need or ever in trouble. People without malice or hostility or hidden agendas. People who had never even visited New York City, much less lived there. Good, basic people.

* * *

Good, basic people, Marcia thought to herself, repeating the words over and over in her mind. Good, basic people. Wasn't that one of the main reasons Brian had talked her into leaving New York City? To find good, basic people? Decent people?

People in New York City were too harassed to be good, he had said in one of his more impassioned late-night dialogs, too harried to be decent. They were too busy jostling for space in sweaty, over-crowded subway cars, or shoving their way down packed sidewalks, angrily swinging their briefcases and handbags and umbrellas for interference. People in New York were constantly snapping at each other. They snapped at each other from behind delicatessen counters, supermarket conveyor belts, and the bulletproof glass windows at banks; they yelled at each other across cabs, in restaurants, in galleries. New Yorkers, Brian had insisted, were just not very nice people . . . and they should know, having both lived there almost their entire lives.

Of course there were other reasons for leaving Manhattan—another reason, actually. It was not so much the people as it was the person. One person. Marcia recalled Brian's peculiar confession and his self-righteous preamble: he had never, he began, viewed himself as the sort of man who would have affairs, the sort who would let himself become involved with another woman. He had always thought he had too much self-control for that sort of thing, that he was above it. There was something squalid about illicit sex, something vaguely pathetic—meeting in dark bars, obscure restaurants, hotels far from midtown. In his eyes, he had claimed, there was nothing particularly appealing about a clandestine tumble in Eighth Avenue sheets.

Besides, he had a beautiful wife. He knew that. An intelligent wife. He knew she was a loving, caring woman, a woman to whom he had been married for five years, a woman he had known for eight. He knew he had no reason to have an affair; he was denied nothing.

And yet he had. He said it evenly, as if admitting stoically for the first time that he had an inevitably fatal disease, as if his affair were an illness that hurt only him—not her, not them. When he tried to analyze what had happened (never what he had done—Marcia thought—it was always a passive analysis), consistently he was unable to pinpoint an exact cause. Never at any moment had it crossed his mind that he wanted to leave her, he told Marcia, never had he feared that she wanted to leave him. There was no rift that he was aware of in their marriage, no unspoken anger, no unhappiness. He was more or less satisfied with his job; he was more or less satisfied with his home; he was—more or less—satisfied with his life.

No, the fault wasn't his; it wasn't Marcia's; it wasn't their marriage's. It wasn't even Joyce's fault, though Brian did believe—no, Brian had said he was sure of it—that she was the one who had actually initiated the affair, who had forced into the open whatever attraction he felt for her by strolling downstairs to their apartment one evening when Marcia was away on business. No, if the fault belonged anywhere, it belonged to New York City. To Columbus Avenue. To the way Manhattan took people and dangled before them fantasies they had no right pursuing.

In Manhattan, Brian explained, people were deluged with visions of the things they couldn't—perhaps shouldn't—have. Fifth Avenue had become a row of opulent Babels like Trump Tower and opalescent baubles like Bijan; Avery Fisher Hall was less a center for the performing arts than a runway for the latest fashion furs; and Forty-second Street, despite AIDS and herpes and home VCRs, seemed to have more live sex shows than ever. It was conceivable, Brian tried to convince Marcia, that everyone in Manhattan had affairs, because everyone there was subjected to the same unrelenting barrage of images of excess. Manhattan, he had told her when he suggested they start over away from the city, simply had too much money, too much power, and too much sex. It corrupted people. He would never have had an affair if they hadn't lived in Manhattan, he had insisted.

It had taken some convincing to bring Marcia around to the idea of leaving Manhattan. She agreed completely that they had to find a new apartment building ("Any one without Joyce will do nicely," she had said), but a new town was a harder sell. After all, with the exception of four years at college, she had never lived anywhere else. And she and Brian both had good jobs in Manhattan, and their friends and families lived in the area.

But there were other reasons Marcia was hesitant to leave: what if she discovered hundreds or thousands of miles from home that the wounds from Brian's affair wouldn't heal? What if she found that she just couldn't forgive him, that she just couldn't love him as she once had? She would have uprooted her life for nothing. Absolutely nothing.

Moreover, Brian seemed to be growing more restless each year, his periodic mood swings more pronounced. The moody young man she had married five years earlier struck her at times these days as downright unstable, capable certainly of other affairs in other towns. As she said to Dr. Michaels, the psychiatrist she saw for three short months after Brian's confession, leaving the city instead of just Columbus Avenue seemed to be a rather extreme risk, an attempt at saving a marriage that Marcia wasn't sure should be saved.

But Brian was persistent and Brian was eloquent, assuring her hourly of his love for her and his dedication to their marriage. And besides, he reminded her, hadn't they always fantasized about New England, moving there someday, perhaps when they were forty-five or fifty? Virtually every spring and every fall, hadn't they visited obscure inns in obscure Vermont villages, savoring the quiet and the pace and (inevitably) the tremendous brass beds? Hadn't they?

Marcia loved New England; she had to admit it. Occasionally she would waver, reminding herself that three brisk days with the trees an endless panorama of reds and yellows and oranges was very different from three months when the trees were bare, the sky was gray, and the ground was rock-hard mud. But Brian was absolutely sure that moving to New England was right, and he made sure that his enthusiasm was infectious. Marcia remembered that he had sold her first on the idea of a home instead of an apartment and real trees outside of their windows instead of just more buildings. She recalled his babbling about Independence Day picnics, town meetings, and victory gardens. Maybe someday, he had said, they would even get a couple of horses.

Sure, they would be sacrificing large New York City salaries, but they wouldn't need as much money. How expensive were string bean seeds and playing cards? If they lived in the country, Brian had assured her, he would become the good, basic person he believed he was meant to be, both publicly and privately. If they could find the right town, he had insisted, and the right house, they could begin together a new life—a simpler life, a slower life, a better life. A life without Joyce.

Initially, two New England cities held promise for them: Portland, Maine, and Burlington, Vermont. Both cities were big enough to have advertising agencies where Marcia could work and computer or software manufacturers for Brian. Yet both cities were also small enough that the Middletons knew they could find a small, rural village to call home within commuting distance.

They visited Portland first, over the Memorial Day weekend, and were disappointed. The city was too close to Boston, and felt in fact like a little Boston. Boston North, Marcia had called it. They found the waterfront restoration, with its resemblance to Faneuil Hall and Manhattan's South Street Seaport, especially distressing.

Burlington, however, seemed to have real potential, especially since the Middletons discovered it by the light of July fourth fireworks, visiting the small city over the Independence Day weekend. In Burlington, they found no buildings taller than seven stories, yet the downtown shopping district was sufficiently sophisticated to house Laura Ashley and Ralph Lauren. Despite the fact they were visiting Burlington in the summer, the place felt to the Middletons like a college town, with a university and three separate colleges lending an air of academic propriety to the community from the hills overlooking the city. And its outlook over Lake Champlain was at least as pretty as Portland's Atlantic waterfront, while Burlington also had a magnificent view of mountains that Portland lacked: the Adirondacks across the lake in New York and the Green Mountains to the east.

So Brian sent resumes to IBM and GE and every other high-tech abbreviation the Chamber of Commerce said was in the Champlain Valley, and Marcia contacted the four ad agencies in Burlington and two in Middlebury. IBM, unreasonably overjoyed at the prospect of hiring a new sales manager without having to pay any transfer or relocation costs, grabbed up Brian quickly. Marcia, forced to choose between an ad agency in Burlington and one in Middlebury, finally picked Middlebury because it had the same sorts of clients as Burlington, but its offices were in a restored 1790 colonial. Her own office, while lacking some of the basics New York City account executives took for granted—long, wide windows that cut glare, an automatic sprinkler system in case of fire, an unlimited supply of Pendaflex and manila folders—had one accoutrement few Madison Avenue cubicles could boast: against the west wall, underneath the hand-colored nineteenth-century Wallace Nutting photograph, was one of the largest fireplaces Marcia had ever seen. And, the owner of the agency assured Marcia, it worked.

Chapter 6

The Dunbars could have been the aficionados of Thai cuisine for whom Brian was searching. Both Marcia and Brian sensed it immediately, the moment they met David's wife, Carrie, and saw David at his own home, away from his plaster and drills and tape measures. They went there for dinner their first Saturday night in Deering, the day after David had asked them—awkwardly, almost shyly—if they would like to have dinner with him and his wife, Carrie. Carrie, he had said, was an excellent cook, and he thought it would be real nice if they could all get together sometime soon.

Since they had no plans that Saturday—they had no plans any Saturday in the foreseeable future that Marcia knew of—David suggested that they drop by the very next evening. And it was clear to both Brian and Marcia as soon as they arrived at the Dunbars' that these people would be their best shot at close friends.

After all, David and Carrie were the only other married couple in Deering who didn't have children. Instead they had dogs, three tremendous golden retrievers, distinguished by the different colored scarves they wore around their necks. At home, away from Josh and Simon, David reminded Marcia of an assistant professor she had known at college, a closet poet who taught freshman English to support his wife and baby son. There was a rough, unfinished quality about David, but underneath the surface it was clear was a tender—if eccentric—man. (It didn't surprise Marcia when he confessed early in the evening that as a teenager he had hitchhiked to Martha's Vineyard to voluntarily help build a summer home for James Taylor and Carly Simon.) It was clear also that Carrie, the manager of a surprisingly elegant little clothing shop in Middlebury, had a history of dancing at local weddings and birthdays with a tad more enthusiasm than her elders thought seemly. They were an attractive, imaginative couple in their early thirties, who insisted that Saturday night that Marcia finish the last of the pâté mousse Carrie had made and Brian get the last piece of chicken in maple butter.

"The reason you'll like this place," David told them when they were seated in the Dunbars' living room after dinner, "is that people here help each other. I guess it's 'cause the winters are so long, somethin's bound to go sour, and everyone's bound to need a little help. So if somethin' breaks and there's anything I can do—off the clock—you just let me know."

"Oh, David loves to fix things," Carrie said, sipping her coffee and rolling her eyes. "Especially if he gets to break them first. His favorite kinds of home improvements are the kinds that begin with destruction. I don't think I've ever seen him happier than when he got to cut a hole through the house for the wood stove. Except maybe the time he got to tear up all the floorboards when we were redoing the kitchen."

David Dunbar smiled. "She's right. Fact is, I'm better at breakin' things down than I am at puttin' 'em up. But you know, that wood stove's a good example how people in this town help each other out. Josh Nash and Pete Banyin helped me punch in the wall, and Mort Hollis and me put in the bricks around the stove."

"How did you find the house?" Carrie asked, directing her comment at Marcia specifically. "Had you heard of Deering?"

Marcia shook her head. "It was all just luck. We knew we wanted a small town somewhere between Burlington and Middlebury, and the man who hired Brian had a half-dozen suggestions. Deering was one of them."

"And Grace Macknight thought of the Finch place?"

"She probably would have," Marcia answered, "but I beat her to it. She had photographs of fifteen to twenty houses on her wall, and the picture of the Finch house—our house—jumped out at me. It was almost as if I had seen the house before, it was so perfect."

"But you are redecorating the house substantially," Carrie continued.

"Just the inside," Brian explained. "And we're not planning on breaking down walls or pulling up floorboards, at least not right away. But we are going to make a lot of cosmetic changes. Some now, some we'll get to next summer. But it's going to be a long process. We'll probably be wallpapering for the next ten years."

"Is that because the wallpaper is old or because it's unattractive?" Carrie asked.

Marcia paused. Should she tell Carrie Dunbar the hard truth that walleyed six year olds had better taste in wallpaper than Edna Finch, or should she say simply that the paper was just a little tired looking? She glanced again around the Dunbars' living room, and decided that her first impression was accurate: the room was a stunner, with hand-stenciled walls and a warm hardwood floor. The Dunbars had style; they knew what they were doing.

"I think Brian's and my taste is a little different from the Finches'," she said. "Some of Edna's wallpaper is a little loud, don't you think?"

"I don't know. I've never been inside your house."

"Really? I got the impression from Sarabeth Nash that everyone visited everyone in Deering."

"Most people visit most people," David said. "But the Finches weren't most people. I've lived in this town all my life, and I'd never been inside your house until Josh and I started working on it last month."

"Don't get the wrong idea," Carrie said quickly. "It's just that the Finches kept to themselves a bit."

"Well, we'll have to have you over real soon, Carrie," Brian said. "Give you a tour of the place."

"Except the attic," Carrie said.

"Especially the attic," David said.

"What's so interesting about the attic?" Marcia asked uncomfortably.

David leaned forward in his chair, a half smile on his face. "You been up there?" he asked.

"Of course we have," Brian told him. "A number of times."

"Then you two haven't looked around real carefully."

"You make it sound like there's a ghost up there," Brian said, a slight edge to his voice.

"Could be," David said, "but that I couldn't tell you. What I can tell you—and you two must know this, this can't be news to you—is that you got yourselves a noose in your attic."

Marcia reached down reflexively and began to pet Sugarbush, the golden retriever at her feet. Scratching the dog behind her ears, Marcia said, "I've been up there three times. At least three times, including once with the building engineer who was inspecting the place. And I've never seen a noose."

"There is a piece of rope up there," Brian told Marcia, his voice even. "But I certainly wouldn't call it a noose. It's just a piece of rope."

"Hey, I don't mean to upset anyone," David went on, "but the fact is, it's not just a piece of rope." He turned toward his wife. "I've seen it; I've touched it; I've held it. It's a noose. Plain and simple, it's a noose. Ernest Finch kept a noose up there, and when he went out west, he left the noose behind."

"I don't get it," Marcia said. "Why would anyone keep a noose around the house? Did Ernest ever talk about using it?"

David shook his head. "Ernest Finch hang himself? Not a prayer."

"Then why?"

"Word is, because he was superstitious. At least that's what my daddy told me when he first said there was a noose in Ernest's attic. He said Ernest was afraid to take the thing down. Ernest musta figured takin' it down would be like openin' up a jack-in-the-box—just imagine the kinda nasty stuff he mighta unleashed if he ever gave that rope one good yank!"

"Why did he put a noose in his attic in the first place?" Marcia asked.

"I can't believe no one told you any of this," Carrie said, genuine concern creeping into her voice.

Brian smiled sarcastically. "I guess you two get the honor."

"I don't think we want it," David mumbled.

"So why did he hang a noose?" Marcia asked again.

David took a deep breath before beginning. "Ernest Finch didn't put the noose up," he said finally. "Edna Finch didn't put the noose up. And Foster Finch didn't put the noose up. Fact is, no Finch put the noose up. It was from the first people who lived in the house. The people who built it."

"And they were whom?" Brian asked.

"Jeez, I don't even know their names anymore," David said. "You remember, Carrie?"

Carrie nodded. "Barrington, I think. And I believe the little girl was named Adelaide Thistle Barrington."

"That's right, and her nickname was Thistle Peep."

"Thistle Peep? That's almost pretty, it's so quaint," Marcia said.

"Yeah, I guess," David said, " 'cept is, little Thistle Peep Barrington hanged herself at the ripe old age of six or seven, and her parents took down the body and left behind the noose."

"David, that's just a story," Carrie told her husband, chastising him. "You're going to give Brian and Marcia completely the wrong idea!"

"Yeah, it's just a story all right," David added. "But I've seen the noose."

If the rope in their attic really was a noose, Brian and Marcia wanted to examine it alone—that is, without the Dunbars present. They would be happy to show it to Carrie Dunbar once they had established for themselves that without question it was a noose, but they wanted first to study it on their own. And so that night, as soon as they had left the Dunbars, they scaled the stairs leading to their attic, despite the fact it was almost midnight and they should have been in bed with a book or curled up in front of a late-night movie on the one television station Deering received.

Both Brian and Marcia had forgotten how cold the attic was. When Brian opened the door to the attic stairs on the second floor, bracing his foot against the frame and pulling the knob with both hands, they were greeted by a blast of air from above every bit as cold as their refrigerator. It was in fact almost like opening the refrigerator door, Marcia thought, except that the attic air smelled tired—a combination of damp wool insulation and the piles of the thirty-year-old magazines the Finches had left behind. She wondered briefly if it wasn't the smell that had prevented her from venturing up into the attic after she had liberated Solstice and not the dark, but she didn't recall being especially bothered by the smell at the time.

Initially Brian had stood back on the upstairs landing, allowing Marcia to go first. It was a reflex born of courtesy, but Marcia wanted no part of decorum. "You first," she said.

The moon, though not quite full, was large and round enough to shine some light through the attic windows—enough to make out vague shapes—but it was still dark, despite the flashlight Brian angled before them. What may have been worse than the dark, Marcia decided, was the silence. Unlike the rest of the house, where windows shook and storm doors rattled on their hinges, nothing moved in the attic, nothing settled. It was as if the attic were holding its breath, waiting for them.

"I wanted to get up here this weekend anyway," Brian said as they reached the top. "I wanted to get another look at the insulation situation."

"In the middle of the night?"

"Well, no. But I figured I might come up here tomorrow to see if there was anything we could do quickly—before winter really sets in —to make the house more energy efficient. Maybe throw down a few rolls of fiberglass up here."

"Or we could be real Vermonters, and just layer the floor with these magazines," Marcia said, pointing at one of the piles of *Look* magazines from the nineteen fifties.

Brian ran the flashlight along the north wall, spotting a line of old electrical wiring at the base.

"Let's also keep our eyes open for a hole or something in the floor," Marcia added. "I want to know how Solstice got up here the other day."

"I will," he said, "but I don't think we'll see anything with a flashlight. Besides, I'm sure all that happened was a mover opened the attic door by accident."

"I told you, I didn't let the cats out of their boxes until after the movers had left."

Brian shrugged. "As I recall, I saw the rope—and honest, that's all it is, a piece of rope—hanging from a horizontal beam by the old chimney."

Slowly Marcia's eyes adjusted to the dark, and she became less dependent on the flashlight. She saw the rows of shutters lined up against the south wall and the large window vents above them; she saw an antique high chair, Foster's perhaps, in the far corner; and then she saw the old chimney, the chimney that long before had been used with a coal furnace that no longer existed.

She felt Brian take her elbow and guide her. Together they stepped over one of the piles of magazines and walked gingerly over a rotting pair of floorboards, their destination the three-foot space between the old chimney and the wall. The roofs slant in that space didn't leave much room between the floor and the eave, perhaps not more than five or six feet, but how much room did a seven-year-old girl need? Marcia tried to recall how tall she was at seven, and thought she was well below four feet.

"I don't believe a seven-year-old would hang herself," Brian said softly. "Even if it is a noose there, that doesn't mean it was ever used for anything."

If it is a noose, Marcia decided, she wouldn't wonder whether it had ever been used in the past so much as whether Grace Macknight's head would fit through it in the future. The whole idea that the woman might have sold them a house with a noose in it infuriated Marcia.

Because Brian was a step ahead of Marcia, he was able to wedge himself behind the chimney first. But they actually discovered the noose together. Or what might have been a noose. In actuality, Marcia told herself, trying to calm the nausea in her stomach, it really was just a piece of hemp—a piece of hemp tied in a circle, hung perhaps ten inches to a foot away from one of the ceiling boards. It certainly wasn't the sort of thick rope she normally associated with a noose. . . .

But the cord *was* tied in a hangman's knot. She couldn't deny that. And it was hung from a cross beam. . . .

It was a noose. There was no mistaking it for anything else; there was no denying what it was. It was a noose.

"My God," she whispered, her breath visible in the flashlight beam.

"But it's not a noose," Brian said quickly, more for his own benefit than for hers, she thought.

"It's not?"

"No, of course not," he said, raising his voice slightly. "It's a piece of cord tied in a loop, but it's not a noose—look at the rope, for crying out loud!"

"That's a hangman's knot, isn't it?"

"But the rope, look at the rope. It looks nothing like a noose," he insisted. "It looks nothing at all like a noose." He wrapped his free arm around her shoulders and suggested quickly, "Let's go back downstairs. It's too cold to be up here in just a sweater."

Did he really believe it looked nothing like a noose? Marcia wondered. Could he really believe that? Or was he just trying to reassure her? She couldn't tell. All she knew for sure was that they had just bought a house with a noose in it, and that they were sleeping in a bedroom below an attic with a noose in it. She tried to keep her voice calm, even, but she knew the result was a hiss, a cornered, panicked hiss. "It's a noose, Brian; it's a goddamn noose."

"We can talk about this downstairs," he said, barely audible. "But I'm telling you, they probably used the rope to hang a light on or something. That's all. When they were doing some repair work, perhaps." She felt his arm around her back, rubbing her side, moving her slowly toward the stairs as if they were waltzing.

"But honest, sweetheart," he said again, "it's not a noose."

CHAPTER 7

Sarabeth Nash was wrapping a Muppets green Band-Aid around her thumb when Brian Middleton knocked on the Nashes' kitchen door—which was also their front door—early Sunday afternoon. She had cut her thumb peeling apples for three separate pies: one for the new folks, the Middletons; one for the Historical Society supper; and one for her own family. As someone in Deering once said—and she had no idea who—"You don't stop baking till the bushel's 'bout bare." She figured if she didn't say anything about the apples, Brian wouldn't guess that she was making him and his wife a pie.

"Hello, there," she said cheerfully, opening the storm door and waving him into the kitchen. "Hello, there," she said again. When he was inside, standing before her in what looked to be a ridiculously expensive ski jacket—it had zippers everywhere, down the front, on the pockets, along the sleeves—she realized that he was upset, that something was wrong. His glasses sat on his nose as if he had been punched, he was sweating (she looked over his shoulder at the thermometer on the porch and saw that it was only twenty-five degrees outside), and his hands were covered with dirt. There was even dirt in his hair, specks of brown clay that almost—but not quite—blended in.

"Hi, Sarabeth. Afternoon," Brian said, breathing heavily.

"You look like you've been in a train wreck. You all right?"

He tried to smile, and adjusted his glasses. "Sure, I'm fine. I guess I got a little messy working around the house a bit."

"You're sure?"

"Of course I'm sure," he said with more vehemence than she thought necessary. He almost sounded angry.

"Okay. Well, what brings you by on a Sunday afternoon? It's too soon in the season for cabin fever."

Behind her, in the living room, she heard Josh say something to Allie, their eight-year-old daughter. Evidently, Josh was trying to watch the football game, and Allie was trying to get him to watch her. It sounded like she was offering to show him a somersault.

"I'm here to see Josh. Is Josh here?"

Sarabeth folded her arms across her chest and leaned back against the counter. "Yup," she said slowly, dragging out the one syllable as long as she possibly could. Either this man was a lot more rude than he had seemed when she first met him the other day, or he was having a devil of a time getting used to the cold. Was he shivering?

"Can I talk to him?" After a moment he added, "Please?"

"I don't see why not," she said. "Can I get you something? I brewed a pot of coffee about an hour ago, and it would just take a minute to heat it up again."

He blew on his fists, seeming to notice for the first time the mud on his fingers. "No, I've had a couple cups today already," he answered, putting his hands in his pants pockets.

"You ever had coffee with maple syrup in it? Instead of sugar?"

"No."

"It's really something."

"No, I'm okay."

"You're sure?" She liked slowing him down. Nothing could be so urgent on a Sunday afternoon that this fellow from the city couldn't take the time to—as the saying went—sit down and smell the coffee.

"I'm sure."

"Seems like I'm always offering people coffee and they're always saying no. The two fellows who moved your furniture in didn't want my coffee either. Think I make a bad pot?"

Brian nodded without listening. "Do I hear Josh in that room? Looking at a football game?"

"That's the living room, and that is indeed Josh. He's watching the Patriots, I believe."

"My boots are a little muddy. Should I leave them here before going in?"

She looked down at his boots and saw that they really did have mud on them. "Well, I'll be darned. The ground is frozen solid, and you managed to get mud all over those nice new boots. Where did you find it?"

"The mud?"

"Yup."

"Around the basement, I guess," he said, kneeling down to untie his laces. "I was working down in the basement, where the floor is still dirt. I was trying to figure out what we need to do for insulation down there."

"Rotten day for it. Cold, clammy. Just yucky."

Brian didn't say anything. When his boots were off, Sarabeth noticed that his socks had diamonds on them, blue and green diamonds running up the sides in an argyle pattern.

"This way?" he asked rhetorically, nodding with his head toward the living room.

"That way," Sarabeth said, following him as far as the doorway and then leaning there against the frame. Immediately Allie, her younger daughter, sat up on the floor. Confronted with a man she had never seen before, she became rigid, nervous.

Quickly Sarabeth said to her little girl, "Allie, this is the man who lives in Mr. and Mrs. Finch's house. Want to say hi to him? His name is Mr. Middleton."

"Hi."

"Hi," Brian said, not really looking at her. He then stepped around the child, missing her knee by inches, and said to her father, "Hello, Josh. I'm not going to shake your hand because mine is covered with dirt." Perhaps it was a good thing he and Marcia didn't have any children, Sarabeth decided. Clearly he had no interest in them.

Her husband stood up and took the man's hand, despite the dirt on it. "Don't see that a little mud makes a man more dishonest," Josh said.

"You got a minute?"

"Seem to. Have a seat."

Sarabeth thought Brian hesitated, but after a brief moment he sat down in the rocking chair beside the television set, leaning forward. Allie meanwhile stood up and ran through the kitchen and up the stairs to her bedroom. She just didn't like strangers.

"So what brings you by? Needed a breath of air?" Josh asked.

"Nope, not exactly." He unzipped the zipper at the front of his jacket.

"Can I take that coat for you?"

"No, I'll just be a minute. I'm sort of here on business."

Josh turned off the television and sat back down on the couch. "Business? Can't be too important. No one does much real business on a Sunday. At least around here."

Brian sighed. "Probably not. But I'll be up in Burlington from tomorrow through Friday, and I wanted to tell you this in person. So I had to come over today."

Sarabeth noted the way her husband became tense, the way his posture became perfect when he was wary of something. He was just like his daughter.

"Go ahead," he said, somewhat crisply.

"Okay," Brian said rubbing his hands together slowly. "Okay. First of all, I think—me and Marcia both think—you and David are doing a fantastic job on the house. Simon too. Everything looks fabulous, and it's all happening in record time. I—we, the both of us—couldn't be happier with the work."

"But . . ."

"But. You're right, there is a but."

"We could see that but coming a mile away," Sarabeth said from the doorway.

Brian tried to smile. "Guess so. But I meant what I said about the work you've been doing. It has all been splendid."

Splendid. Sarabeth didn't think she had ever heard anyone actually use that word outside of public television.

"That's why this has been such a tough decision," Brian continued. "A very tough decision. But I guess it's been something I've been thinking about for a while now. And it was sort of driven home for me today when I was working around the house. I've decided I want you and your people to stop working on the place. At least for now. In three months, maybe four, we'll want you back—I promise—but for right now, I want you to stop all work."

"You mean after we've finished what we've started, right?"

"No, I don't. I mean now. I mean stopping right now. I've discovered two things lately, and they both tell me we need to take a breather. Now. The first is that Marcia and I are thinking pretty seriously about doing the house differently. Very differently. Like that banister. We were thinking we might want to open up the stairway and the front hall, make it more airy. Which means we certainly don't want you and David spending time rebuilding that old banister. The second—and this is less important in the short term but maybe more important in the long term—is that I've found I love to do the stuff you guys are doing. I love it! I've gotten more satisfaction working around the house this weekend than I've gotten doing almost anything else in my life. That's true too, no exaggeration."

"But how can we stop? We haven't finished a darn thing."

"That's okay. You've given me exactly the head start I need to finish up the key things. For instance, now that you're done rewiring the den and you've hung the new fixture—things I know nothing about—I can finish the wallpapering myself."

"This is awful sudden. Awful sudden. You're sure it's not the quality of the work? Something we did or didn't do?"

"I'm positive. The work couldn't have been better."

Josh scratched the back of his head. "Okay. It's your house. Just so long as it isn't the work we've done."

"I promise you, it isn't."

"So when is our last day?"

"For the moment—and like I said, this is just a temporary, three or four-month breather—it already was. It was last Friday. But what I'd like to do is pay you guys for two more weeks worth of work. Just write you a check right now, as if you were going to be working on our house for the next two weeks."

"I couldn't accept that," Josh said.

"Sure you could. You should. Here you've done all this excellent work, and now I'm asking you to stop with absolutely no notice. None, none whatsoever."

"Still, it just doesn't feel right, getting paid for work we're not going to finish."

It amazed Sarabeth what money could do, and she grimaced. When you had it, you could do anything you wanted. Drive that Saab of theirs, own that monster breakfront, hire—and fire—people at will.

"I'm the one who should feel bad," Brian said, "not you. Your accepting this money—and it's fair money, it really is—will make me feel much better." He unzipped another zipper on his jacket, this one along his left sleeve, and removed a checkbook.

Josh glanced up at Sarabeth, and he appeared more hurt to her than angry. After a second he looked back at Brian, asking, "When should we get our tools? Any special time?"

"I'll have them all ready for you first thing tomorrow morning. They'll be in the kitchen before I leave for Burlington."

Marcia knelt on the front porch of their house Sunday afternoon, not far from the front door. She pushed the cat food around in the bowl with a spoon, calling the kitty in a soft voice.

"Come on, sweetie," she tried to purr. "Come on up here."

The barn cat remained four or five yards away from the porch, refusing to move. He would stare at Marcia, and then at the food, but he wouldn't budge.

"Come on, sweetie, I won't hurt you. You know that."

It was strange: for two days now, the cat had let Marcia hold him and pet him in the front yard, and that morning he had even eaten some dry cat food out of her hand in the barn. But he still refused to come near the house.

She stood up and started toward the cat, taking the bowl with her. The cat immediately jumped back, preparing to run away.

Down the street she saw Brian returning from the Nashes, walking briskly with his hands in his ski jacket pockets.

She stood perfectly still, trying to regain the cat's trust. "It's okay, fella," she murmured, "if you don't want to become a house cat, I won't make you."

The cat turned a wary eye toward the sound of Brian's approaching footsteps, and then scampered back into the barn.

"He just won't come in the house," Marcia said to Brian as he walked up the front steps. "He won't even climb up onto the porch."

"I can't say that I blame him," Brian remarked, before adding quickly, "after all, he is an outdoor cat."

Chapter 8

The Federal Express plane circled in low over the university, banked toward Burlington International Airport, tried to glide in above a bridge across Interstate 89, and then crashed. It slid, then rolled, then exploded, parts and pieces and overnight envelopes flying in every direction.

Marcia had had the dream many times before, usually with different airlines and airports and bridges, but it always ended the same way: most often, it was a Continental Airlines jet approaching Newark Airport from the northeast, crashing into the Pulaski Skyway just west of Manhattan. But there were never any survivors, and the dream often signaled bad news.

Marcia had the dream involving Burlington Airport their first Sunday night in their new home. She awoke a little before four A.M., sweating, the sheets damper than if she had wet the bed, her nightgown little more than a clammy sponge clinging to her legs. She rolled over in bed and reached for Brian, but when she opened her eyes she saw he was gone.

Brian, Marcia knew, was a very light sleeper. While she could sleep through anything—including the fire in the Silvermans' apartment their first month on Columbus Avenue—Brian seemed to be up and around at the slightest noise. The elevator doors opening on their floor at three in the morning had often been enough to pull him from a sound sleep.

She, on the other hand, could not recall the last time she had left their bed in the middle of the night. Unless it had been the Silvermans' fire five years ago. But she could not recall ever getting up for a drink of water, to go to the bathroom, or to pace away some nagging fear about work. Sometimes it took her a very long while to fall asleep—occasionally hours—but once she fell asleep she stayed asleep. And once she got into bed, it took a fire to get her out. It amazed her.

Unfortunately, it now appeared that Brian was going to sleep as lightly in the country as he had in the city, a feather-soft sleep that a creaking branch could disturb. Reflexively, to confirm with touch what her eyes were seeing, she reached again across the bed and tapped the mattress: yes, he was gone.

She sat up in bed, astounded by the way her wet nightgown clung to the sheets.

"Brian?" she called softly, not quite loud enough for her voice to carry outside of their bedroom. "Brian?" she called again, slightly louder.

When there was no response, she pulled her legs into her chest and wrapped her arms around them. She then pulled her nightgown over her drawn knees, pressing her naked legs against her breasts for warmth. Suddenly, she felt chilled.

She wasn't sure how long she sat like that, waiting. Five, perhaps ten minutes. She wondered if Brian weren't feeling well and was at that moment in the downstairs bathroom rummaging through the cardboard box marked "Medicine Chest," looking for the Nyquil or Maalox or Bayer.

That was probably it. He was looking for the aspirin. He was beginning to feel the aftereffects of the brandy he had polished off Sunday night, and was trying to find their half-empty bottle of Bayer.

She listened carefully for sounds from the first floor—Brian's measured footsteps, the clinking of a glass, the bathroom door—but the house was silent. No movement, no activity.

"Brian, what are you doing?" She tried to sound commanding, but she knew it was a whine: a soft, plaintive, pathetic whine. It crossed her mind that the house was doing it again, stealing a living thing. It had started with a cat, taking poor simple Solstice for a round, and now it was after her husband. But she managed to convince herself that she was overreacting, panicking perhaps because she was in a strange bedroom in a strange house, or perhaps because she had taken a sleeping pill. She had almost forgotten the sleeping pill. She had swallowed it after she and Brian had fought that evening and she had had trouble falling asleep. And now, perhaps, she was having some sort of reaction to it. Of course Brian was in the bathroom. Where else could he be?

"Brian, are you all right? Are you?" When he didn't answer, she murmured softly to herself, "If this is your idea of a joke, you're wrong. This isn't funny."

Brian, of course, knew that. Marcia was confident that the last thing Brian would try to do right now would be to scare her. Not when she had been so visibly shaken by that piece of rope they had found in their attic.

That noose. That's what it was, after all, a noose. There was no mistaking it for anything else. And so she hated it, just as she suddenly hated the house. Two people and two cats didn't need a house this big, they just didn't.

"Solstice? Chloe?" She realized abruptly that neither of the cats was with her either. Normally the cats slept at the foot of their bed, fighting for a spot on the quilt. But not tonight. At least not now. The cats had jumped ship too.

She considered staying in bed. She could wrap the quilt around herself and stay right where she was, warm (at least warmer) and unmoving. It would be light in two, two and a half hours, and she could then search the house.

Search the house. What a horrid choice of words, she thought. It suggested that her husband and cats had to be found, that they were lost or trapped or hurt. Or dead. And that certainly wasn't the case. They were fine. They were just, well, missing. And they would turn up any second. She didn't have to search the house. She just had to be patient.

But she couldn't just sit there in a corner of the bed, listening to a house full of dead air. The place was absolutely and completely silent. She and Brian had both commented their first night in Deering how quiet the country was in comparison to Columbus Avenue, but this was different even from a Deering quiet. The house wasn't settling; the radiators weren't clicking; the shutter over the screened porch wasn't thumping. There was no furnace, no water pump, no hot water heater. Nothing.

No, she couldn't stay in bed. If she stared at Brian's closet door long enough, it seemed to move; if she watched the mirror on his armoire, shadows lurked in its reflection. She imagined hands reaching up from under their bed from Brian's side, from under the covers at its foot; she saw the window buckling, the glass pane pressing in and then expanding out, always in danger of shattering; she could feel drafts of ice-cube-cold air cutting across the room from under the bedroom door.

She had to pull herself together. She was too old to be scared of the dark. She was too old to be frightened of inanimate objects like closets and houses and nooses. After all, the Finches had lived in the house for decades, and nothing had ever happened to any of them. At least nothing she knew of. Nevertheless, it took all of her courage to free an arm from underneath the quilt and reach across the bed to turn on their reading lamp.

With the lamp on, the closet door stopped moving and the windows stopped breathing. But Brian and the cats were still gone. She would have to find them. She would have to climb out of bed, put on her robe and slippers, and walk around the house at four in the morning. Four-thirty, really, and that made it a little better. Because four-thirty was almost five, and didn't people in Vermont wake up at five?

She wrapped her robe around her, pulling the belt tight at her waist, wondering if this was her new life: roaming alone around a haunted house in search of her family. First her cat, now her husband. It would have been monotonous if it weren't so scary.

Of course, everything had turned out all right with Solstice. Solstice had just been trapped in the attic.

But Brian wasn't a cat. As she walked downstairs, after seeing no lights on upstairs, she realized that there had to be a more complex explanation for his disappearance.

Or did there? Perhaps the country air affected him exactly like city air and kept him up at night. Perhaps the insomnia that had begun to plague Brian more and more often in New York was continuing now in Vermont, and he was at that moment walking around the yard or the barn. Yes, it was early November, probably fifteen or twenty degrees outside, but it was possible. It was, in fact, likely. Because where else could he be?

"Brian?" she called, opening the kitchen door and turning on the light. "You down here?" She wandered from the kitchen to the dining room, and then to the bathroom. There were no lights on downstairs, and no sign of Brian once she flicked some on.

Surely he was outside somewhere.

But that wouldn't explain the cats. Brian would never have taken Solstice and Chloe with him if he went outside, not two city slicker kitties like that pair. They would panic, run away, disappear. They couldn't be trusted outside, especially in early November at four in the morning. Four-thirty, she reminded herself.

No, the cats weren't outside.

The cats were in the attic. They had to be. That's where Solstice had been once before; that's where he was now. Except that now he had taken his sister with him, and his father. Her husband.

She was sure of it: Brian was in the attic with that goddamn noose. She could search the house, she could search the grounds, but she would never find her husband if she didn't climb those long dark stairs to the attic. Because that's where he was.

She couldn't explain why he hadn't answered her cries a moment earlier; rather, she could explain it, but she wouldn't. She would not articulate even in her mind the reasons why a thirty-one-year-old man would be unable to answer his wife from behind an unlocked door.

She wondered if she had the courage to go to the attic right now. She wondered if she should call the Nashes or the Dunbars. She wondered if she should call the police.

But what would she say to them—to Sarabeth Nash or Carrie Dunbar or a state trooper? Would she tell them that her husband had disappeared, that he had been in bed with her only five hours earlier, but now he was gone? Or would she assure them that he was in the attic behind the door that was warped shut, and that she was simply afraid to go up there alone?

She would tell them—could tell them—no such thing. It sounded ludicrous. She had to go to the attic alone.

Solstice raced into the light when Marcia opened the door to the attic, with Chloe close on his heels. Oblivious of their liberator, they ran past Marcia and down the stairs to the first floor, the fur of both cats ramrod straight like spikes. They looked almost like porcupines.

"Brian, you up there?" Marcia called. She wasn't surprised when there was no response. Brian would have answered her calls much earlier, if he were capable. So she pointed her flashlight beam up the stairs and began to climb. She tried not to think morbid thoughts, but she did: she envisioned her husband curled up in a ball in a corner, scared to death by something he had seen or lying facedown by the shutters, choked somehow by the rat poison left behind by the Finches.

Amazingly, the most likely vision—and the one that greeted Marcia when she finally stood upright in the attic and began to spray the area with light—never occurred to her. She screamed when she saw her husband, and fell back involuntarily against a box of old magazines, but for all her horror and fear and sorrow was the realization that she should have expected this. It was obvious; the pieces all fit.

Brian had taken the noose down and moved it. He had hung the rope from the highest beam in the attic, and there, with his two cats for company, hanged himself.

2.

Chapter 9

J. P. Burrows threw darts two nights a week at Bosox Bar in downtown Burlington in an organized league, and five days a week in the detectives' office around the corner from Bosox. At Bosox he threw at a dart board; in the large office he shared with six other detectives, he usually ignored the department dart board and threw instead at photographs of whoever looked most foolish in that morning's edition of the *Burlington Free Press.* His targets on any given week, therefore, ranged from Liza Minnelli to Imelda Marcos, from the mayor of Burlington to a state senator.

He was in the process of clipping a picture from that Monday's paper of three hockey players from the university who were brought in the night before for brawling in the town commons and then resisting arrest, when the phone rang just before eight-thirty. He immediately recognized the voice of Dr. Patricia Lange, head of the state coroner's office.

"Morning, J. P.," she said. "Finished your coffee?"

"Just starting it," he answered, wondering if the kids in the picture could be of any help in his drug investigation at the school. He was looking for a student willing to go undercover for him; and one of the athletes, a rich kid from a Boston suburb, might be willing to nose around a bit in exchange for having the disorderly conduct and resisting arrest charges dropped. He would have to see.

"Well, if you could put a lid on it and bring it here, I'd appreciate it. Or I'm sure I could round up another cup for you."

"Where's 'here'? You in your office?"

"Nope, I'm up the street," she said, referring to the Medical Center Hospital of Vermont.

"Then I think I'll bring my own coffee, thank you very much. No living person can stomach that stuff you people brew up there in the morgue." He finished cutting the photo from the newspaper of the "tag team wrestling match in the commons," and decided to keep the caption. "What do you have?" he continued.

"White male, thirty-one years old, found by his wife at four-forty this morning. Cause of death appears to be asphyxiation."

"Where did she find him?"

"In their house's attic. She says it was a suicide. She says he hanged himself."

"That's nasty. But why do you need me?"

"You should see for yourself."

"Sounds pretty darn cryptic, Patricia."

"My life is cryptic," the coroner said.

Thirty-one years old, Burrows thought to himself, throwing on a windbreaker over his bulky ski sweater. The dead man was a year younger than he was. It always disturbed him when people younger than he was died. It seemed to disrupt the natural order of things, the way things were supposed to be.

It also disturbed him that the man was married. He knew that probably half the adult males in the state younger than him were married, but that didn't make it right. He too should be married. He wanted to be married. He was sick of living in a lonely guy apartment filled with the smells of lonely guy pizza, lonely guy socks, and lonely guy soap. He wasn't a sloppy person—his apartment was actually rather tidy. When he did bring an occasional date back there, they never seemed to notice the distinct lonely guy stench the way he did—but he believed he was a disorderly person, and he was absolutely positive that marriage would provide his life with the exact order he was looking for.

He wasn't sure why he wasn't married. Women seemed to think he was handsome in a boyish sort of way; he had blue-green eyes and curly—but short, always cut short—light brown hair. Until joining the police force ten years earlier, he had spent all of his life on the family farm in West Gardner, so his skin was rugged and weathered. And more important, Burrows thought to himself as he drove the mile uphill to the Medical Center, he was a nice enough sort. No major vices, no major character flaws—at least none that he was aware of.

Nope, Burrows concluded, there was no one reason he could think of to explain his self-proclaimed status as a lonely guy. His luck was due to change. It had to.

* * *

The Medical Center Hospital of Vermont was the pride of the Vermont medical community. No hospital had more space, better equipment, or cleaner rooms. Certainly everyone was aware that there was no air-conditioning in the oncology wing, but after all, how often did you need air-conditioning in Burlington? One, maybe two weeks a year?

And, at least in the eyes of Patricia Lange, the pride of the Medical Center was its morgue. Not only was it every bit as antiseptic as the operating rooms scattered across the floors above it, it was filled with the latest in forensic equipment: cryostats that froze and cut tissue, Zeiss photomicroscopes, and a state-of-the-art autopsy table that allowed the examiners to move bodies to and from the sink without touching them.

Lange met Burrows at the entrance to the morgue, sipping coffee that Burrows was positive tasted like formaldehyde, and led him into the small blue tiled room in which Brian Middleton lay naked beneath a sheet.

"What's his name?" Burrows asked.

"Middleton. Brian Middleton. He's not from around here."

"No?"

"He's from New York City. He and his wife—woman named Marcia—just moved here."

"To Burlington?"

"Nope. Deering."

"Deering, really? My kid brother is helping to fix up a house in Deering. By the church, I think."

"I don't know exactly where these folks lived. Could be by the church, but you'll have to ask Floyd Dempsey from the state attorney's office or Rudy Thomas from the state police. I wasn't on call last night."

"Any idea why they wound up in Deering?"

Lange shrugged. "Not a clue."

"Who pronounced him dead?"

"A local doctor. Ted Dial. Nice old guy from around Middlebury. Wins the Fishing Derby almost every year."

"I thought I knew the name."

"Ted pronounced him dead at the scene, called it a suicide, and sent him up to us for the official autopsy."

"And the autopsy held a surprise or two?"

"It hasn't been done yet. But Hank is convinced it will," she said, referring to her assistant, a French-Canadian doctor named Henry Tillier. She never called him Hank to his face. "Hank viewed the body about an hour ago when he first got into the office, and he had some questions right away. He scheduled the autopsy for ten o'clock: by then he should be finished taking a look at a crib death that occurred upstairs in the hospital nursery."

"Swell."

"Ready?" Lange continued, reaching for the top of the sheet.

"Yup, go ahead," Burrows mumbled, before taking a deep breath. He always became slightly dizzy, slightly nauseous when he had to view a corpse. Unquestionably, this was the worst part of his job.

Lange slowly pulled the sheet down as far as Brian Middleton's chest, exposing the rope marks around Middleton's neck. Someone had once told Burrows that dead people looked peaceful, but Burrows disagreed: he thought they just looked sad. Dial—or Tillier, perhaps—had shut the man's eyes.

"Have you ever seen a hanged corpse?" Lange asked evenly.

"No." Lange amazed Burrows. This middle-aged woman with elegant cheekbones and silver hair was one of Burlington's leading citizens—a member of the Lake Champlain Chamber of Commerce, twice a state senator, a trustee for the state university medical school —and yet she spent her days staring at dead people. And it didn't bother her.

"Normally, there is a distinct rope burn about two inches above the larynx. It should look almost like a line of welts, and it should cut into the skin just above the thyroid cartilage. The face should appear congested, and the lips and tongue should look as if they were covered with blue Magic Marker."

Burrows studied the marks around Middleton's neck, and then looked closely at the man's lips. He could tell by Lange's voice that something was wrong. "Okay, I give up," he said finally, looking away. "What's wrong with this picture?"

"Look at the marks on the neck."

Burrows continued to stare at the tiles across the table. "Do I have to?"

Ignoring him, Lange explained, "First of all, the burns on his neck do not look deep enough to me to be antemortem—before death. They don't look like welts, they look like one long hickey. Secondly, the marks are not above the epiglotis, they're below it."

"Meaning he didn't hang himself?"

"That's what Hank thinks. Hank took a look at our friend here, and thought it all looked real suspicious."

"Any special reason that Hank is doing the autopsy instead of you?"

"Hank's our resident expert on asphyxial death. He published a paper on hangings just last year. I'd like to save this one for him."

"But you do think the actual cause of death was asphyxiation."

"Maybe. Maybe not. Don't get me wrong, J. P., it could be a simple case of suicide by a man with very thick skin. It probably was: Brian Middleton probably hanged himself, and that's all there is to it. But Hank thinks there's at least a chance that the man was dead before his head was even stuck in the noose."

"Any marks on the body to support that?"

"None that are immediately apparent. No wounds, no bruises, no sign of trauma. Nothing."

"Then how might he have died?"

Lange shrugged. "That's why we do autopsies."

"Any guesses?"

"Hank's guess—and it's just a guess—is that he was smothered. But there's nothing yet to support that."

"Wouldn't there have been a struggle if he were smothered? Wouldn't there be bruises or something?"

"You would think so, wouldn't you?"

Burrows nodded. "Unless he were smothered in his sleep."

"Exactly."

"So when you open him up, you'll be looking for signs that he was drugged or poisoned?"

"Among other things," Lange said, pulling the sheet back up over Brian Middleton's face.

"Thank you," Burrows said.

"No problem."

"Have you established time of death?"

"Looks to be between two A.M. and three A.M. But Hank will confirm that during the autopsy."

"Does that fit with the widow's story?"

"More or less. She found him at four-forty. He could have been hanging there an hour and a half."

"Who did she call first? State troopers or an ambulance?"

"She called the state police in Middlebury. She found the poor guy strung up from a beam in the attic and knew there was no need for a doctor."

"Any note?"

"Nope."

"Isn't that a little fishy?"

Lange frowned. "Not at all. Only about fifteen percent of all suicides leave behind notes."

"Did anyone say how the widow was doing?"

"She was doing badly. Anything special behind that question, other than a little human compassion?"

Burrows put his hands in the pockets of his windbreaker. "I have to ask, don't I? A man's found hanged in his house in the middle of the night by his wife, and the state coroner tells me it might not be the noose that killed him. . . . I have to wonder."

"According to Doc Dial, Sergeant Thomas, and Floyd Dempsey, the widow was grieving. According to all of them she was pretty busted up. It never occurred to any of them that this wasn't a suicide."

"So why do you think I'll be involved?"

"As you put it so eloquently, J. P. . . . I have to wonder."

Chapter 10

It's not very cold in New York in November, at least in the city. Marcia recalled believing as a child that from Halloween to Easter the temperature never rose above thirty degrees, and there was always snow in Central Park. But that was incorrect. It is actually not uncommon, Marcia thought to herself, for the temperature to rise into the sixties as late as Thanksgiving. It probably would this year.

"Warm enough?" Jennifer asked Tuesday afternoon, as she drove Marcia's Saab down the Major Deegan Expressway past Yankee Stadium. It was probably forty-five degrees outside.

"Yes, I'm fine," Marcia told her younger sister. "I'm plenty warm." Jennifer had flown to Vermont the day before, as soon as she had heard about Brian's death, to help Marcia pack and bring her home to New York. A police officer from Burlington had met her at the airport and driven her to Deering.

"A week or so in Vermont really thickened the blood, eh?" Jennifer commented.

"I guess," she answered, staring out the window at the billboards and housing projects bordering the expressway. Vermont had absolutely no billboards, and few—if any—housing projects.

She wondered if Brian was back in Manhattan yet. The funeral was scheduled for Friday, so he was probably en route also, somewhere between Deering and New York City. Unless he was flying, in which case he might already be there.

"Dad said he would be happy to speak to some realtors in Vermont for you, if you don't feel up to that sort of thing," Jennifer said, trying to sound casual.

"Oh?"

"He said he'll take care of everything—if you want him to. I know he'll tell you all this tonight, but I thought I should probably warm you up first."

"Thank you."

"You are going to sell the house, aren't you?"

Marcia closed her eyes and leaned back against the headrest. Her sister had been trying desperately to make conversation throughout the six-hour drive from Deering, talking about everything from her job—her first job—as a research assistant for a downtown bank, to their mother's plans for redecorating the apartment. Twice, when Marcia began abruptly to sob, little hiccups of sadness pressing her against the seat belt, Jennifer had gone so far as to talk about the Thanksgiving cotillion their mother was planning. This, however, was Jennifer's first foray into Marcia's future plans, and Marcia wasn't sure she was ready.

"I don't know," she said distantly. "I probably will."

"Well, you know if you want a place to live in the city and don't want to stay with Mom and Dad, you can move in with me. I'd love it."

"Jenny, that's sweet, but two people can't live in a studio."

"Sure we could. You could have the pull-out, and I'd get a futon or something."

"You're not in college anymore, sweetie; you can't sleep on a futon night after night," Marcia said, reaching across the seat and patting gently her sister's knee. Jennifer was slightly heavier than she was, and her hair was sandy brown. But like Marcia she had their mother's small, soft nose, and their father's sky blue eyes.

"I assure you, I've slept on much worse."

"I don't doubt it. But I'll probably get a place of my own fairly soon anyway. But thank you."

"Okay. But if Mom or Dad begins to drive you wild, let me know. You're always welcome."

Get a place of her own. She hadn't lived alone in years, and the idea scared her. And after selling their apartment on Columbus Avenue and buying a new home in Vermont, the actual logistics of real estate horrified her as well. She couldn't cope, not yet.

Jennifer double-parked in front of their parents' apartment building on Seventy-eighth Street, as the doorman came out to help them with their boxes. They didn't have suitcases, they had boxes. Jennifer had packed for her sister, and rather than worry about overnight bags and suitcases, she had taken advantage of some of the empty moving cartons still scattered around the house, and thrown whatever sweaters and skirts and lingerie she could find back into them. When the boxes were unloaded on to the sidewalk—Marcia counted six of them, not including the pair of animal carriers with Chloe and Solstice inside—Jennifer said she would go find a parking garage for her sister's car, and drove off around the corner. The doorman, an older fellow who must have joined the staff recently because Marcia had never met him, then said that he would handle the "luggage," adding awkwardly that he was sorry to hear what had happened.

Both Marcia's mother and father greeted her when the elevator doors opened on the fifteenth floor. The doorman must have called ahead. Her father, a large man who became clumsy when he tried to be gentle, inadvertently knocked over the umbrella stand in the hallway when he went to hold her. Her mother meanwhile massaged her back, then kissed her cheek. They looked terrible to Marcia, old and depressed and frightened. Her mother's hair was pulled tight and looked grayer than she had remembered, and her father seemed to have lost more hair. And yet it had only been three or four weeks since she had seen them last. She wondered if she looked as bad, and realized that she probably did.

Together her parents steered her into the apartment, her father taking her coat, her mother continuing to rub her shoulder.

Finally Marcia asked the question that had been on her mind since the elevator doors had opened. "What are you doing here, Dad? Aren't you supposed to be at work?" She wasn't surprised that her mother was home (on the phone the night before she had said that she would be), but her father had never before been home at three in the afternoon on a weekday, at least not in her lifetime. William Hampton had worked for thirty-five years for Richmond-Tremont Foods, the last seven as its chief executive officer. She didn't think the company doors opened unless he was there. "Don't you have a meeting or something you're supposed to be at?"

He looked hurt. "I wanted to see you," he said. "I wanted to be here for you."

"Thank you," she said, nodding. She began to realize that in the eyes of her parents she was now an invalid. The idea had begun to take shape in her mind when her sister had arrived in Deering to get her the day before, (arriving less than seven hours after she had found Brian). But it was only now becoming clear to her exactly what the ramifications of being an invalid were: she didn't have to do anything; she didn't have to think for herself; she didn't have to make decisions. She didn't have to cope: all of a sudden, she was again six years old.

Jennifer decided to spend the night at her parents' apartment, keeping her sister company. They went to bed early, in the bedroom Marcia had lived in for seventeen years before college, and for three months after. Marcia slept in her old bed, and Jennifer curled up beside her on a cot.

"Really, you don't have to do this," Marcia insisted, as they turned out the lights. "I appreciate it, but no one should have to sleep on a forty-year-old cot. I'll be fine."

"I know that, but I want to do this. I like slumber parties."

Marcia sighed, staring up at the ceiling.

"Would you rather be alone?" Jennifer asked.

Marcia thought for a moment. "No," she said finally. She was developing a litany of words that depressed her. *Alone. Tomorrow. Sorry.* "No," she continued, "I'll have plenty of time to be alone."

"Is that such a bad thing? I've been living alone since June, and I find it rather pleasant."

"You're twenty-two. You've just spent four years living with people you didn't even know five years ago. When I was twenty-two, I also liked living alone."

"When I was twenty-two," Jennifer said, mimicking her sister, "they didn't even have automobiles. Nope, the horseless carriage was a thing of the future. Along with flush toilets, little double-A batteries, and those newfangled word processors. That's how old I am."

Marcia came as close to smiling as she had in two days, the sides of her mouth at least quivering. "I don't mean to sound like the sage of the century. But I do feel old. Old and beaten."

"You have every reason to be depressed right now. But you shouldn't feel old."

"I'll be thirty next spring."

"Oh, I forgot. I guess you are over the hill. Thirty. I know if I were that old and decrepit, I'd buy myself a walker and a couple cases of Metamucil, and pack it in."

"You can't know how scary the future is, Jenny. Not because I'll be thirty. That really has nothing to do with it. But look at how my life has been upended in the last six months. Six months ago I had a good job, a nice little apartment, and a happy marriage—more or less," she added, referring to Joyce. She had never spoken with Jennifer in any detail about Brian's affair, but she had alluded to it, and she knew that her sister was aware of it. "But at least I had a husband, and Brian and I would have worked things out. No, as a matter of fact, we had worked them out. We had . . .

"But now—God, I just don't know what will happen now." She thought for a moment that she might again cry, but she took a deep breath and the feeling passed.

"Can I ask you a question?"

"Go ahead," Marcia said, not quite sure what to expect, but knowing it would be about Brian.

"Did you love Brian? At the end, I mean."

"You mean after his affair?"

"Yes."

Marcia thought for a long moment. "I wanted to love him. At least I wanted to try," she answered, turning her head toward the pillow as her eyes began to tear after all.

"Can I ask you something else?"

Marcia nodded, not wanting her sister to hear the tremor in her voice. It crossed her mind that Jennifer might not be able to see her nodding in the dark, but she didn't care. If her sister wanted to pursue this line of questioning, she would.

"Why did he do it?"

"His affair, you mean?"

"No," Jennifer said, in almost a whisper. "That other thing. Sunday night. Mom told me there's a history of it in Brian's family—his uncle and one of his cousins, both on his father's side."

"That other thing," Marcia murmured softly, thinking about the expression. She had heard paramedics and ministers, the Burlington police and the pastor's wife all refer to Brian's death with one euphemism or another, but no one had yet been as delicate as to refer to it as "that other thing."

"Was it because of that other woman?" Jennifer continued, still whispering, but whispering now with more urgency. "Or did it have something to do with Vermont?"

Marcia burrowed further into the down pillow, the cold, clean cotton of the pillowcase almost stinging her face. Here was yet another first for her kid sister: asking the unaskable and asking it without ever using the words *suicide* or *hanging* or *death.* "I'll tell you what I told Sergeant Rudy Thomas of the state police," she said slowly, thinking. "Thomas asked me that same question yesterday morning, and I told him what I know is the truth, even though I knew he wouldn't believe me. He nodded when I told him, but I could see in his eyes that he had written me off as some loony grieving widow—some poor woman completely out of touch with reality. And now I'll tell you, even though I know you won't believe me either."

"I've never doubted anything you've told me. Why wouldn't I believe you?"

"Because it sounds crazy. But you asked, so I'll tell you. I don't think Brian killed himself. I don't think it was suicide."

"Then what?"

"Then what happened? I don't understand it exactly—and, oh God, how I wish I did—but it has something to do with that house. From almost the moment we moved in, I felt something . . . something dangerous . . . about that place. Something shameful. And I don't understand it—at least not yet—but that house killed him. It took him, just the way it tried to take my cats. It took him, and then either it told him something or it showed him something. But I'm telling you, Jenny, it killed him," she said, her last words lost in a series of soft, angry sobs. "That house killed him."

CHAPTER 11

Gerald Montgomery had been chief of the Burlington Police Department for over fifteen years, or five years longer than Burrows had been a cop. Approaching fifty-five years old, Montgomery looked to Burrows exactly as he had the day he greeted the young police academy graduate a decade earlier: muscular, clean-shaven, and bald. While his two sons had grown from small boys to a teenager and a young man, and his wife had grayed and grown wrinkles, the chief had remained unchanged. Given an earring and placed on a plastic bottle, Burrows had thought the day he met Montgomery, he could have passed for Mr. Clean; ten years later, the likeness hadn't waned.

As soon as Montgomery opened his door and hollered for him to come into his office Tuesday afternoon, Burrows knew what Montgomery was going to tell him. Henry Tillier, the deputy medical examiner, had just dropped off the results of Brian Middleton's blood test, the last detail of the autopsy.

"Let me guess, Gerry," J. P. began, closing Montgomery's door behind him and sitting down in the swivel chair before his desk. "I'm the lucky winner of the Middleton Murder Sweepstakes."

Montgomery didn't smile. "I wouldn't consider this a lottery, Burrows, because there's not going to be a winner." Montgomery was the only person Burrows knew who refused to call him J. P. Nothing personal, Montgomery claimed, but he said that until Burrows told him what his parents had in mind when they put J. P. on the formal birth certificate over thirty years earlier, he would never use the name. And as long as the mystery frustrated Montgomery just the slightest bit, Burrows had no intention of attaching any names—real or fictional—to his initials. He liked Montgomery, but he liked keeping his name a mystery even more.

"Good enough." Burrows shrugged. "Am I the loser?"

"Yup. As far as the state attorney is concerned, there is sufficient reason to investigate this death as a homicide. The case is yours."

"That's fine."

"I'm glad you're happy. Because that also means I'm taking you off the university drug investigation. I'm reassigning that case to Anderson."

"What for?" Burrows asked, sitting forward in his chair and leaning over Montgomery's desk.

"I want you to concentrate on this homicide."

"Oh, come on, Gerry, I think I'm a big enough boy to handle both of these investigations at the same time."

"There's no reason you should have to—not when Anderson's spending most of his time these days tracking down kids stealing toasters."

"Then give the Middleton investigation to him, Gerry. For God's sake, I've spent the last three weeks talking to almost every deadhead and down-country hustler on campus. I've trailed more dumb-ass jocks than I care to admit, and I've watched at least a half-dozen fraternity brothers puke their guts out on their front lawns. And now that I'm finally getting close, you're taking me off the case!"

"I know you're close. I know that. That's why I want you to make sure that you spend a good long time bringing Anderson up to speed. Be thorough."

"Why don't you just flip our assignments?"

Montgomery leaned back in his chair and placed his hands behind his head. "You and Anderson are good, Burrows. But—and you know this as well as I do—you're better. You're the best we got when it comes to dead things."

The dart whizzed past Detective Sherman Anderson's eyes, missing his nose by centimeters, and smacked into the Styrofoam coffee cup on his desk, spilling his last sip of coffee onto the magazine he was reading.

"Well done, Hank," Anderson said irritably, without looking up. "At least I'm on the same side of the room as the dart board."

Burrows wandered out of Montgomery's office, surprised to see that Tillier was still there, and retrieved the dart. "Gently, Hank, gently," Burrows said patiently, handing the coroner the missile. "Don't go for velocity, go for arc."

Henry Claude Tillier was the only man in the city of Burlington who wore suspenders and bow ties. Always. He had moved his family to Burlington over two years earlier, but still dressed as he did in

Montreal. He had, in Burrows' estimation, the worst eye-hand coordination of any doctor—any person—he had ever met, and so Burrows dreaded the moments he spent visiting the detectives' office. Tillier insisted on tossing darts with Burrows whenever he dropped by, an exercise Burrows once likened to giving a blind terrorist an Uzi in an airport.

"I throw it like a baseball," Tillier said defensively, pronouncing his *s* like a *z*.

"You throw it like a girl," Anderson mumbled, just loud enough for Tillier to hear.

Ignoring Anderson, Tillier asked Burrows, "So tell me, J. P., have you been assigned to this investigation?"

"I have indeed," Burrows said, imitating Tillier's French accent. He then turned to Anderson, continuing, "You're next with Mr. Clean. He's on the phone right this second, but as soon as he finishes, he wants to see you."

Anderson looked up from his magazine. "What for? You just said you were the one assigned to the Middleton case."

Burrows moved a small pile of manila folders off to the side of his desk and leaned against the edge. "Yup. But you're getting the university drug probe."

"Oh boy, a lot of little rich kids playing with cocaine."

"They're probably more interesting than the kids you're chasing down right now—ratty teenagers who break into appliance stores."

Anderson didn't smile. "If there's a collar, I'll be sure to share it," he said sarcastically. He flipped shut the magazine he had been reading, a month-old *Sports Illustrated*, and tossed it into the trash can. "What about your new case? Do you really think this flatlander killed her husband?" he asked.

Burrows shrugged. "I have no idea. All I know right now is what the good doctors Lange and Tillier told me and Montgomery—and that is that Brian Middleton may not have died by hanging."

Tillier threw another dart, missing the photograph of the game show host Burrows had pinned to the wall by about two feet. "You can say 'may' if you like," Tillier said. "But if I had to bet, I would bet 'did.' "

"Well, Pat isn't quite so sure, Hank," Burrows reminded Tillier.

"Pat may be right. But Pat has not seen so many hangings."

"What makes you so positive?" Anderson asked Tillier, standing up and moving to a safer seat behind the medical examiner.

"Reason number one," Tillier began, "there wasn't a well-developed rope abrasion on the neck. Put a noose there on a living person, pull it tight, suspend him, and most of the time you will get a prominent rope burn. Not always, but most of the time.

"Reason number two, I did find a small bit of hemorrhaging on the inside of the man's upper lip and around his upper gums. There were these tiny little cuts that might have been caused by someone pressing something hard against the man's mouth and holding it there. You know, smothering him.

"Reason number three," he continued, circling a finger into the air, "the fellow's blood alcohol content was point two oh. Point two oh," Tillier repeated for emphasis. "That's a lot of alcohol."

"You think the guy was murdered because he was drunk?" Anderson asked, joking. "I know little towns like Deering don't approve of alcohol, but don't you think murder's a bit excessive?"

"One of the reasons Pat isn't as confident as Hank here that the man was smothered," Burrows answered, "is because you would expect to find traces of a struggle on the body. Even if Middleton were smothered in his sleep, he would probably have woken up and fought. But there isn't a bruise on the guy anywhere, no lumps, nothing to suggest that someone had forcibly held him down and smothered him."

"But if he were intoxicated when someone suffocated him," Tillier continued, "well, he might not struggle quite so much, because he might be in a much deeper sleep."

Burrows reached for a pair of darts and tossed the first one through the talk show host's microphone, missing his nose by a fraction of an inch. "The thing is, Hank, do you honestly believe this woman is so dumb that she would believe she could smother her husband and make it look like a hanging?"

"I have never met the lady, so I do not know."

"You know what would burn me up?" Burrows said suddenly. "I'll tell you: you'll see me get nastier than a bull with the epizootic if this lady did kill her husband. Can't you just read her mind? Slick city gal wants to off her husband, so what does she do? She convinces him to move to the country, some hick state like—oh, I don't know—Vermont. Then she finds a little town where they don't know their forensic ass from their elbow, like Deering. And then, when she thinks she's two hundred miles from civilization, in a place where we're all hicks and rubes and farmers, she murders the poor guy and tries to make it look like a suicide. She's afraid she couldn't get away with it in New York City, but in Vermont? Hell, we're all a bunch of dumb-ass dairy farmers up here she thinks! In her mind, we're all so goddamn stupid we can't tell the difference between a hanging and—what's the word, Hank, a smothering?—a smothering!"

Burrows heaved his second dart as hard as he could at the newspaper clipping, missing it but splintering the seam in the paneling beside it. "If she came to Vermont just to kill her husband," he added softly, "she's not just a witch, she's a stupid witch. The kinda witch who ain't fit to root with pigs."

Chapter 12

J. P. sat on the living room floor in his parents' house Tuesday night, watching Simon rub Formby's wood oil into the handle of his hammer. He treated that hammer—all of his tools, really, but especially his hammer—as if it were a piece of antique furniture, polishing it, preserving it, placing it each night in the special leather holster J. P. had given him one year as a birthday present. It was a ritual for his brother, something their father had told J. P. that Simon now did every Tuesday night of his life.

In the kitchen, he heard their mother listening to the radio while she washed the dinner dishes and scrubbed the massive roasting pan. She had made J. P. his favorite dinner, the dinner she always served when he visited: roast chicken. She was listening to the public radio station broadcast a special fiddling concert out of St. Johnsbury. His father was still closing up the barn for the night, where he had been since they finished dessert.

J. P. had offered to help his mother with the dishes and his father with the barn, as he did every time he dropped by for dinner, but as always they had declined. "If a boy comes home to wash dishes, he must have somethin' awfully dirty under his fingernails," his mother had said.

After they had been sitting there a short while J. P. asked his brother, "Are you going to miss working on that house up in Deering?"

Simon placed a few more drops of wood oil on the rag he was using, careful that none splashed on the rug. Finally he shook his head up and down, signaling that yes, he would miss it.

"I'm going there tomorrow," J. P. said, "so I'll check out your work and let you know what I think."

"It's not done," Simon said, his voice dulled with sadness. "We still had lots to do."

"Does your boss have another job lined up? Another house or something to work on?"

Simon shrugged his shoulders, and with his thumbnail tried scratching a chunk of caked sawdust off the hammer. "Don't know."

"You like your new boss? What's his name, Nash?"

"Nash is all right. He's okay."

"Only okay?"

"No, really okay," Simon answered, finally looking up. "I like Mr. Nash. He shows me how to do somethin', and then he lets me do it!"

J. P. nodded approvingly. That was good to hear. The mental health department in Waterbury had fixed Simon up with perhaps a half dozen carpenters and building contractors over the last few years, and none had worked out once they discovered that Simon could not be sent to a building site alone. He was an excellent handyman with proper supervision, but he needed direction; he needed to be told what to do. Perhaps this Nash fellow would be different. He hoped so.

"Mom tells me that you liked the Middletons—the people whose house you were fixing up."

"Oh, yes. Last . . . last Friday, we were there and they had moved in, and Mrs. Middleton made us all lunch. A big lunch. It was a big, big lunch."

"What did she make?"

Simon concentrated, his lips pursed tightly. "She made . . . she made . . . she made a big plate of food for us. It had onions on it, and peppers and meat."

"Was there a sauce?"

"Uh-huh."

"It sounds like beef stew. A big beef stew."

"Oh no, not beef stew. Mom makes beef stew, and this wasn't like that. This . . . this had spaghetti, and the sauce was white. Oh no, this wasn't beef stew."

J. P. thought for a moment. "This lady made you guys beef stroganoff?" he asked, almost incredulous. "How many of you were there?"

"There was me, the little girl—no the girl didn't come—and Mr. Nash and Mr. Middleton and Dave, a course. Dave is Mr. Dunbar. He works with Mr. Nash, and he lets me call him Dave."

"What little girl?" J. P. inquired. He hadn't realized that the Middletons had a daughter.

"The little girl who lives there," Simon answered, his shoulders twitching just the tiniest bit—a sign that he was getting nervous.

"The Middletons' child?"

"I don't know. I guess she is."

"Do you know her name?"

"No. She never told me," he said, shaking his head.

J. P. felt himself becoming angry, partly at Montgomery and Lange for failing to tell him that the Middletons had a child, and partly at the Middletons themselves: either one was a murderer or one was a suicide, and neither alternative suggested particularly strong parenting.

"Was the only time you met the lady—Mrs. Middleton—the time she made you lunch?" J. P. asked, as much to change the subject as to learn about Marcia Middleton.

"Nope. She was there other times. But only a couple other times, 'cause they just moved in, you see."

"Oh, okay," J. P. said, forcing himself to smile for his brother's benefit. "Thank you."

"Welcome."

He watched Simon reach behind him for a clean cloth and begin wiping the excess oil from the hammer. In the other room an announcer said something about the renaissance of fiddling in the Northeast Kingdom. "And you also met the man who owned the house? Mr. Middleton?"

"Uh-huh."

"Just once?"

"No, lots. He was there more than Mrs. Middleton, see, 'cause he had to tell Mr. Nash what to do. And he was there helping a lot himself."

"Helping?"

"Uh-huh, helping."

"Was he a nice man?"

"Yup. He called me partner. We were partners."

"Partners?"

"When Mr. Nash showed me stuff, Mr. Middleton wanted to be showed too. So we were partners," Simon explained, smiling.

"What sorts of things was Mr. Nash showing you guys?" J. P. asked, stretching his legs.

"You know, stuff. Just stuff."

"Just stuff," J. P. repeated, before catching himself. Whenever he spoke with Simon for more than a few moments, he had a tendency to mirror Simon's own speech patterns, which meant repeating words. "But you really liked him—Mr. Middleton."

"Yup. We were partners."

"Was he a happy man?"

"Happy?"

"You know, happy. Like you or me."

"I guess he was. I never saw him cry."

"Did you ever see him laugh?"

"I guess. I guess he laughed sometimes."

"Can you remember when?"

Again, that concentration. "Nope. But everybody has to laugh sometimes."

J. P. sat back against the base of the couch. "Do you know what the word 'depressed' means? The word, 'depressed'?"

Simon shook his head that he didn't.

"It means being sad," J. P. explained. "But it means being real sad for a real long time. Did Mr. Middleton ever seem that sad to you?"

Simon put down the hammer and opened his toolbox, inspecting the contents. It was immaculate inside, perhaps the most orderly toolbox in Vermont. J. P. noticed immediately that his brother had even categorized his nails and screws by size in the small compartments in the toolbox's shelf.

"I don't know," Simon answered. "But I don't guess he was sad. We were partners." He then handed J. P. his hammer. "Pretty spiffy, huh?"

"Spiffy? Where did you learn a word like 'spiffy'?"

Simon opened wide his eyes. "Is it a bad word?"

"Oh no, not at all," J. P. quickly reassured his brother. "It's a good word, all right. It's just a new word. I was just wondering where you heard it, that's all."

"Maybe I learned it from Mr. Middleton?"

"Maybe?"

"Sometimes he tells me new words. Like 'spiffy.' He said I keep my toolbox spiffy."

J. P. hammered the air a few times, banging an imaginary nail. "Did you ever see Mr. and Mrs. Middleton together? Maybe that day you all had the big beef stroganoff?"

"Together? You mean at the same time?"

"Yup. At the same time."

"Oh sure."

"Did they like each other?"

Simon scratched the back of his head. Clearly he had no idea. J. P. tried a different question. "Did you ever see them fight?"

Simon continued scratching. "I don't know."

"Can't remember?"

"Can't remember."

J. P. stared up at his imaginary nail, envisioning the two-inch wood nail he stepped on as a little boy that had gone clean through his foot. It amazed him that with all the time his brother spent around tools and construction sites, Simon had never once hurt himself. Never once. His brother was either very lucky or very good, and J. P. was fairly confident that it was the latter.

"Did Mr. Middleton ever talk about Mrs. Middleton? Maybe to Mr. Nash?"

Simon shrugged. "Maybe he did and I didn't hear it. That could happen."

"Sure it could. What about the other way around: did you ever hear Mrs. Middleton talk about Mr. Middleton?"

"Nope."

"Didn't think so."

Simon closed the lid on his toolbox and put his hammer in the leather carpenter's holster. "How come you want to know all about these people?" he asked. "Did they do something bad?"

J. P. saw his mother appear in the doorway with a dish towel in her hands, shaking her head at him. Evidently, because Simon was Simon, no one—not Mr. Nash, not their mother—had told Simon that Brian Middleton was dead. "No, they probably didn't do anything bad," J. P. told his brother. "I guess I just wanted to know if they were sad."

J. P. wandered out to the barn before leaving that night, and stood by the door smelling the hay and mud and the breath of the cows themselves. The herd was down to nine animals, down from a high of thirty-seven when he was a small boy. Soon there would be none. It was only a matter of time. Like many of his neighbors in West Gardner, his father would eventually auction off the remaining Holsteins, and sell the land to a developer to subdivide. The acreage extended south from the barn, enough land for twenty-five properly zoned West Gardner two-and-one-half acre lots.

His father would probably make more money off the land in one morning than he had earned from it over the entire last decade.

J. P. reached into his jacket pocket for his car keys and turned away from the barn. He wished he had it in him to be a farmer.

CHAPTER 13

Perhaps it was easiest Wednesday morning to just lie in bed. Jennifer had gotten up and showered over forty-five minutes ago, and her father had been awake and out the door for almost two hours. It was peaceful in her room, quiet except for the distant mumble of her mother and Jennifer in the kitchen. Occasionally a bus backfired on the street below her or an ambulance or police car tried fruitlessly to wind its way down Lexington Avenue, but those were noises from another planet. Her room was warm, a sanctuary removed from the violence and chaos around her; she needn't leave it, ever.

Marcia rolled over so she could face the wall, pulling the quilt up over her shoulders. Twenty-five, twenty-six years ago, the Weesimmos had lived in that wall. Never harmed anyone, never spoke to anyone but Marcia, they were her four in the morning friends—miniature humans, little bigger than puppets. The perfect nuclear family for the Kennedy years, the Weesimmos included a father and mother and sister and brother. The father always wore a white V-necked tennis sweater, and the children wore striped tee shirts. Mother Weesimmo looked exactly like the crisp, tidy brunette on the Betty Crocker cake mixes. Marcia could no longer remember what she would tell the Weesimmos or what they would say to her in return; all she could recall now was how they dressed and when they came and the fact that they left her for good when Jennifer was born.

She wondered who among her and Brian's friends now knew Brian was dead. She hadn't spoken to anyone, but she was fairly sure that Jennifer had. People by now probably knew. Word gets around. All it would have taken was one judicious phone call from Jennifer to her closest friend, Susie Crenshaw, or from Mr. or Mrs. Middleton to Brian's old roommate, Duncan Towers. Surely that one phone call had been made. Between all the other logistics Jennifer and the Middletons were coordinating, someone surely had thought to call Susie or Duncan.

It was just after nine o'clock in the morning when the phone rang, or—as Marcia had begun to tell time—fifty-three hours since she had found Brian.

Without ever speaking about it, Jennifer and her mother had concluded separately that Jennifer would answer the phone for the next few days. Mrs. Hampton wasn't sure how well she would hold up. So when the phone first rang Wednesday morning, it was Jennifer who tossed one of her sister's cats off her lap and climbed around the kitchen table to get to the receiver. Immediately she recognized the soft, perpetually tired voice of Brian's father—a voice, Jennifer realized, that sounded no different in tragedy than it did in joy.

"Hello, Jennifer?"

"Hi, Mr. Middleton. Good morning. How are you feeling today?"

"Not great, but I'm forging ahead. I'm sleepwalking through the details, I think."

"How's Mrs. Middleton?"

"She's still sound asleep, so right now she's fine."

"Marcia's in bed also."

"Good."

After a long pause, Jennifer asked, "Have you spoken to Mr. Anchor—about Friday?" Jennifer had learned from Brian's father that Anchor and Bouyea had buried three generations of Middletons.

Mr. Middleton cleared his throat. "Just now. And I don't want to upset you or Marcia or your family, but there seems to be a problem."

Jennifer started to ask him what kind of problem, but saw her mother listening intensely from her place at the table, and said instead, "Oh?"

"Yes. Bill Anchor couldn't give me any of the details yet, but the Vermont state attorney's office refused to ship him Brian's body yesterday."

"Was yesterday the day they were supposed to?"

"Yes."

"Will he be arriving today in that case?" Jennifer asked, allowing her brother-in-law the dignity of a pronoun. She couldn't yet refer to him as simply the body.

"Bill's not sure. But he doesn't think so."

"Then how can we have the funeral on Friday?"

"We can't. That's the problem."

Jennifer saw her mother's back already was arched, and she was tapping her butter knife nervously. There was no point now in discretion; this sounded like a very big problem. "Why won't Vermont let us have Brian?" she asked, anger beginning to creep into her voice.

"I don't know. Bill doesn't know. He thinks there must be some difficulty with the autopsy."

"Like what? I don't know a whole lot about these things, but I would be willing to bet it didn't have to be the most complicated autopsy ever conducted!"

"I wish I had some answers for you, Jennifer. But I don't. All I know right now is that it's unlikely we'll be able to have the funeral on Friday."

"Should I tell Marcia?" she asked, trying to calm down.

"Yes, definitely. You might also want to call anyone you've already told about the funeral that it will probably be moved."

"I will," Jennifer said, and then added, "I'm sorry if I snapped at you, Mr. Middleton. I didn't mean anything by it, I'm just edgy."

"I understand," Brian's father said. "Don't think anything of it."

Marcia vaguely remembered dreaming of her house, but she could only recall select details. She knew that her house had been a different color in the dream, white with brown trim, instead of yellow, and she thought there were horses in the barn. It may even have been the Weesimmos' house that she had conjured up from her past.

There was also a child in the dream, a little girl in a Victorian smock standing alone in the front yard with a jump rope. She—Marcia—may even have been that little girl. But she wasn't sure.

Jennifer knocked gently on the bedroom door, whispering just loud enough for her voice to carry into the room, "Marcia, you awake?"

"Uh-huh," Marcia said, still staring at the wall. She wasn't positive that Jennifer heard her, but her sister came in anyway.

"How did you sleep?" Jennifer asked, sitting at the side of the bed. Although the shade was pulled down, Marcia could tell by the light in the room that it was sunny outside.

"Okay."

"Sweet dreams?"

"No dreams," Marcia lied, rolling onto her back so that she could face her sister.

"That's probably good. Would you like some breakfast?"

"I'm not very hungry."

"You should probably get something in your tummy," Jennifer said, smiling.

Marcia stretched her arms, looking up into Jennifer's eyes. "You're taking such good care of me. Thank you."

"Look how many years you took care of me," Jennifer said, taking her sister's hand and holding it. "It's time I returned the favor."

"I think you always took pretty good care of yourself."

"Nah. Besides, you're avoiding my question right now."

"You really want me to eat something?"

"I think you should. I'll be happy to make you breakfast in bed."

"Fine, if that's what's best."

"What would you like? Toast, cereal, eggs? All of the above? I think Mom even has some English muffins in the house."

"All I want is toast, I think."

"Tea?"

"Sure. I'll sip some tea. Invalids are supposed to sip tea," Marcia said, smiling just the slightest bit.

"Okay. You stay right here, and I'll be right back," Jennifer said, rising. She decided to wait until after her sister had eaten something to tell her about the problem with the funeral.

"Have you had a chance to call Susie Crenshaw?" Marcia asked, pushing the breakfast tray down to the bottom of the bed.

Jennifer nodded that she had. "The flowers on the breakfront—the arrangement with all the iris in it—are from the Crenshaws."

"Was that Susie who called?"

"When? A few minutes ago?"

"Around nine."

"No. Susie called once last night just to see how you were. So did John and Melissa Weber and Jill Thorpe and her fiancé—Ted. Everyone, obviously, is worried about you. And everyone sends his love."

"Did Duncan Towers call? Or Carl Maggio?"

"Those are two of Brian's friends from college, right?"

"Right."

"No, I don't think they called. They probably called the Middletons."

"Have you ever realized how much this is like a wedding?" Marcia asked thoughtfully.

"No, I can't say that I have."

"It is, you know. People who were my friends before we got married have called us, while people who were Brian's friends have called the Middletons. Who knows: perhaps in church on Friday, someone will be asking whether guests are friends of the bride or friends of the groom."

Jennifer smiled. This was Marcia's first attempt at humor since Brian had died.

"So who called this time?" Marcia asked again.

If there was a good way to break the news to her sister, Jennifer couldn't imagine what it was. So she decided simply to present it as factually and succinctly as she could. "That was Brian's father on the telephone," she said. "There's some sort of problem in Vermont, and the police haven't sent Brian back to us yet. That means the funeral won't be held on Friday. It will probably have to be on Saturday now."

Marcia opened her mouth into a small O and started to speak, but only air came out. She closed her eyes and took a deep breath and tried again. "What kind of problem could they be having?" she finally was able to gasp.

"It's probably just paperwork," Jennifer answered, keeping her voice calm and assured. "It's probably one of those things that gives a state computer hell. After all, Brian and you had only lived in Vermont a short while, and you had just last week moved to Deering. And Brian still had a New York State driver's license. I'm sure it's a combination of all those circumstances."

It's not the state, Marcia thought to herself, it's the house. This too probably had something to do with that house. She turned away from Jennifer and stared at the wall, her eyes following the series of small bows that comprised the wallpaper.

"Everything will be fine tomorrow," Jennifer went on. "It will probably be all cleared up this afternoon, in fact."

"No, it won't be," Marcia mumbled. "This is just the beginning."

Jennifer reached for the breakfast tray and placed it on the floor, and then sat on the bed beside her sister. She wasn't sure what to do with her hands, and tried to recall what her mother would do. Her mother would stroke Marcia's hair in this situation, she decided, so awkwardly Jennifer began to pat her sister's red hair. "You're past the beginning," she said quietly, almost whispering. "The worst is over, I promise."

Marcia shook her head. Her sister didn't understand. She ran the tip of her finger along the bows and lines in the wallpaper, trying to push away her memories of her house in Vermont, trying to drown them if necessary with visions of the Weesimmo family: with V-necked tennis sweaters and striped tee shirts, with barbecues and board games and a house that . . .

"Oh God," she said, sitting straight up in bed, taking and squeezing Jennifer's hand. "I know where I saw my house before!"

Marcia's grip was so tight that Jennifer felt the bones in her fingers press against each other, and she wondered if her sister needed a stronger tranquilizer.

"Jennifer, my God," Marcia continued. "My house in Vermont . . . it's the exact same house I made up over twenty-five years ago for the Weesimmos!"

Chapter 14

It was overcast Wednesday morning, the kind of gray November day that makes the deer hunters stay in camp extra long and the cows huddle far from their water. There was a good chance, the weatherman had said on the morning radio, that northern Vermont might get three to five inches of snow before nightfall, with a couple more inches up in the mountains.

Sergeant Rudy Thomas of the Vermont State Police met Burrows at the Deering general store just before lunch on Wednesday. Thomas had arrived there first, and was chatting with Lymon Hollis when Burrows pulled up in his Ford Bronco.

"Don't believe Deering's had a hanging in a good twenty-five or thirty years," Hollis told Burrows after he had introduced himself.

"Whole county only has 'bout one or two every decade," Thomas added.

Hollis was leaning against the rack of chewing tobacco behind the counter, and Thomas was sitting on the small stool before it. Burrows noticed the shotgun Hollis had leaning near an unpacked case of Pepsi, and asked how the hunting had been.

"I'm still out there, so I don't guess it's been real good," Hollis answered. "You hunt?"

"Used to," Burrows said. "My daddy does."

"I'm the first to admit pity's a right poor plaster, but there's just nothing to hunt this year," Thomas said, raising his voice slightly. "For two years runnin', Montpelier has just plain mismanaged the herd, and now there's nothing out there but fisher cats and rabbits!"

Hollis nodded. "The snow will help some."

"It would be nice. Only goddamn thing I've shot all week is a little bull," Thomas continued.

Burrows bought a five-stick pack of Juicy Fruit, tossing a quarter onto the counter. "So tell me, Lymon, did you get a chance to meet the Middletons? Either Brian or Marcia?"

"Met 'em both."

"What did you think of them?"

"Didn't know 'em well enough to think much."

"Ever talk to them?"

" 'Course."

Hollis reminded Burrows of his Uncle Orvis. If he didn't want to talk about something, he would answer your questions in as few words as possible. As his uncle had once chastised him, "Talk less, boy, and say more."

"What did you talk about?"

"Not sure I remember. Couldn't have been real important."

"When did you meet Marcia?"

"Wednesday, the day she moved in."

"How come? Did she come by to buy something?"

"Nope. Don't think she ever made it in here."

"Then how did you meet her?"

"The missus thought it would be right neighborly to bring her over a care package. Some flour, a gallon of milk, butter. That sort of thing."

"She appreciate it?"

"She did."

"What did she say?"

"Thank you."

Burrows nodded. "Well, I think we've established the fact that the woman was polite."

"Politer 'n her moving company, anyway. 'Course, that wouldn't a taken a whole lot."

"When did you meet Brian?"

"Saturday."

"He came by the store?"

"Yup."

"What did he say?"

"Which time?"

"How many times did he come by?"

"Four or five. Word around town is, he spent every waking moment Saturday either goin' to the dump or comin' here."

"How come?"

Hollis shrugged. "Maybe he was disorganized."

"Why did he come to the store? Was he buying things?"

"He sure wasn't comin' here to talk 'bout huntin'."

"What did he buy?"

"He bought one thing each visit. He bought a Pepsi without caffeine once, a newspaper once, a piece of maple candy once. It was like he couldn't wander in here often enough."

Burrows tore open the gum wrapper, offering pieces to the storekeeper and the sergeant. Only Thomas accepted. "Can I ask you another question?"

"Sure."

"Did you hear anything around town about their marriage?"

"Brian's and Marcia's?"

"Yup."

"Nope."

"Not a word?"

"Not a word."

"Do you think they had a good marriage?"

"If it was a dunghill, they never told me."

Burrows smiled and thanked Hollis. He then turned to Thomas and said they should probably get moving up the road to Marcia Middleton's house.

"You got the warrant?" Thomas asked.

"Yup," Burrows answered. "Didn't leave home without it."

"I have to tell you, J. P.," Thomas said as he opened the front door to Marcia Middleton's house, "I find it real hard to believe that the sad little lady I met Monday morning killed her husband."

"I haven't met her," Burrows said, watching a huge tiger striped cat race around the house and toward the barn, glancing back at them only once.

"Real pretty redhead. Sorta elegant. She coulda been on television, you know?"

Burrows looked around for the light switch, running a palm down a wall in the front hall.

"Even at five A.M., she looked real pretty to me," Thomas continued, "even when she stood like a robot against the attic door."

"There we go," Burrows said, flicking on the light.

"Not too shabby, is it?" Thomas said, glancing around the hall and up the wide stairway. He then mumbled, "And it's a damn shade more cheerful today than it was before sunrise last Monday."

"Seems pretty depressing right now."

"Stand here at five A.M., J. P., then you'll meet depressing. Where do you wanna begin?"

"The attic."

"I was afraid you'd say that," Thomas said. "Well, follow me."

They stepped around books unpacked and piled along the stairs, and over boxes lining the second floor hallway. In some of the boxes Burrows could see the Middletons' summer clothes: tennis shirts with different monograms, V-necked sweater vests, about eleven pairs of sneakers, each with a different kind of puma or tiger or panther along its side.

"Why would three people want a house this big?" Burrows asked Thomas, as they walked down the corridor of bedrooms.

"Maybe they were gonna have a big family," Thomas started to answer without thinking, but then caught himself. "Three? There were only two of them living here."

"The Middletons don't have a daughter? A little girl?"

"Not as far as I know. I didn't see one Monday morning or hear about one. Where did you get the idea they had a child?"

"Simon."

"Oh. Well, maybe the kid lives with her grandparents or something," Thomas said quickly. "Maybe she's at a boarding school or something."

"And maybe I just misunderstood Simon," Burrows admitted, shaking his head. "That the attic door?" he asked, motioning toward the door on Thomas' right.

Thomas nodded, stepping aside. "I'll let you lead the way for the next couple minutes," he said, tossing Burrows his flashlight.

"Don't tell me a little hanging has given you the jitters," Burrows said, smiling.

"How much have you heard about this little piece a lumber we're in?" Thomas asked, a touch of irritation creeping into his voice.

"Not a thing. Was there something I was supposed to hear?"

"I don't have what you call real hard evidence, real good proof . . . it's hearsay is all. But let me tell you, everyone in this here town believes this house is weird."

"Weird?"

Thomas paused. "I don't wanna say spooked or haunted. Maybe that's too strong. But everyone from here to Middlebury who knows 'bout this house is sure as it snows in January that it's big trouble."

"Rudy, don't tell me you believe in ghosts."

The sergeant shrugged. "Fine. I won't tell you. In any case, you go first."

Burrows turned the knob and pulled, and felt the door stick, almost pulling against him. "Warped shut," he murmured to himself, before bracing a foot against the frame and pulling again. This time the door opened, pulling free of the frame with a squeal that sounded almost human to Burrows. "Onward," he said to the sergeant, starting up the stairs. "Onward and upward." He stopped the moment his body broke the plane of the doorway, however, even stepping back slightly.

"Jesus Christ, you feel that?" he asked Thomas.

"The cold?"

"Yes!"

"It's somethin', isn't it? You shoulda felt it Monday morning."

"The attic must be twenty degrees colder than the rest of the house!" he said, watching the smoke from his breath climb gently up the attic steps.

Thomas smiled. "I told you, it's a weird house."

Burrows leaned against the door and tried to regain his composure. He looked at the sergeant and rolled his eyes. "There's nothing weird about an attic being colder than the house below it. Attics are always colder than a house in the winter and hotter in the summer."

"Then why'd you just jump like a buck in headlights?"

"I was caught off guard. I didn't expect it to be that much colder."

"Damn right. Sure, attics are colder 'n a house in the winter, but I'm telling you, that attic's colder right now than it is outside! It's probably thirty-five degrees in the driveway down there, but I'd bet it's not more 'n twenty right now in front a your nose! That's why you were surprised, J. P. It's goddamn cold up here!"

"It's not that cold, Rudy," Burrows said evenly. "It's probably colder than I expected because the heat's been way down since yesterday morning when the widow left for New York, and because these houses have crap for insulation."

"You were scared, J. P. I'm tellin' you, this house'll spook the best of us, and you were scared."

"I was surprised, Rudy. That's all. I was surprised." Burrows turned away from the sergeant and started up the steps. He knew, however, he had been scared, and he didn't like the idea. It was one thing to be scared of a living, breathing killer: he would be the first to admit that he had been terrified when they were running around Powder Peak Mountain in the dead of night, chasing down the maniac who had killed the little Mallorey girl. But it was another thing to be scared of a house. Houses, after all, didn't kill people.

"Be careful on the steps; they're pretty run-down," Thomas warned the detective.

When he reached the top step, Burrows paused, waving the flashlight along each attic wall. He saw there were two windows, but with an overcast sky, they didn't help much. "This whole attic is pretty run-down," he said.

"Supposedly, the Finches never came up here."

"They were the people who left the noose Middleton used?"

"Yup."

"That was a dandy house-warming present," Burrows said, wandering past an old high chair to one of the piles of thirty-year-old *Look* magazines.

"Well, it was useful."

Burrows pushed aside the magazines and shined his flashlight on the electrical wiring running along the lower foot of the walls, trying for a moment to distance himself from the idea that a man had been found hanged in this attic, hanged with a piece of rope between eighty and ninety years old. "Look at that," he said, "knob and tube. Probably forty years old, and still in good shape. Best kind of wiring there is, in my opinion."

"You come all the way down here to see wires or where Middleton did himself in?" Thomas asked, sounding just the tiniest bit nervous to Burrows.

"If I thought Middleton did himself in, I wouldn't have come here at all," Burrows said, standing. "Why so edgy, Rudy?"

"I'm not edgy, just like you're not scared," Thomas said. "It's just that we have a job to do, and I wanna do it and leave. I got things to do."

"I'll bet you do," Burrows said, envisioning Rudy lying in wait for out-of-state drivers by the long straightaway on Route 7, just north of Middlebury. "Why don't you show me where Marcia Middleton found the body."

"Happy to," Thomas said, smiling. He led Burrows to the approximate center of the attic, beside the stairs from the second floor, and just below the house's highest peak. "Gimme the light," he said, taking the flashlight from Burrows and shining it almost straight up. "See that cross beam? The one with the pair of knots? Right there. The rope was strung right between the knots, and we found him hanging about three feet off the ground. He wasn't dangling all that far from the stairs."

Burrows blew into his hands, wishing his gloves weren't sitting on the dashboard of his truck. "Where's the ladder?" he asked the sergeant.

"Over there," Thomas said, pointing. "We leaned it up against the wall. Middleton kicked it so it fell a good three or four feet away from him."

"How was it found?"

"What do you mean, how was it found?"

Burrows wandered over to the ladder. "Which way did it land? Was it found step-side up or step-side down? Or was it completely on its side? That sort of thing."

"I don't remember how the steps were. All I remember is that the thing was kicked over, a good three or four feet away from the body. Why does all that matter?"

He picked the ladder up to feel its weight. It was heavy, an old wooden monster perhaps left behind by the Finches. "It might not matter. Might not matter at all. But I want to recreate what happened the other night, and how the ladder fell could be real helpful, Rudy. Especially if it fell at an unrealistic angle."

Thomas shrugged and turned toward one of the windows.

"You really think the ladder was three or four feet away from Middleton?" Burrows asked.

"Closer to four, probably," Thomas answered without facing Burrows.

"Middleton was found in his slippers. Seems to me that if he kicked a wooden ladder four feet in his slippers, he might have a bruise somewhere. On the bottom of a foot if he pushed it, and on the top if he kicked it."

"And?"

"And Hank Tillier said he couldn't find a bruise on Middleton, not a one. And he checked."

Thomas picked one of the old magazines off the floor and held the cover up to the light from the window.

"Has somebody dusted the ladder for prints?" Burrows asked when Thomas said nothing.

"No, not yet."

"Terrific."

"Oh, come on, J. P., give me a break. Until that hot-shit frog up in the coroner's office did an autopsy, we all thought it was a simple suicide. No need for prints and shit, it was all cut and dried!"

"Well, I want this house sealed off until Waterbury can send in the state crime van. They promised me they could be here by tomorrow morning."

"I got news for you, the widow and her sister spent a full day in here packing stuff up! If you really think the widow did kill her husband, don't you also think any evidence went with her to New York City yesterday?"

Burrows looked at Thomas angrily, angry at the officer for no other reason than the fact that—like himself—he was a Vermonter. No wonder Marcia Middleton thought she could get away with killing her husband in Vermont. They were all idiots up here, they really were.

Chapter 15

Marcia Middleton climbed out of bed Wednesday afternoon, and went for a walk. She went alone, despite Jennifer's offer to go with her, because she wanted to be alone.

Initially she started west on Seventy-eighth Street, planning to walk around Central Park, but she was afraid that the trees would remind her of Vermont and the park would remind her of the West Side and her old apartment, and so she started south when she reached Park Avenue. When her mind began roaming too close to ideas that frightened her or memories that saddened her, she would stare up at the Pan Am building directly before her but over a mile and a half away, and calculate the number of blocks between her and the structure.

She estimated that every three blocks she passed as many people walking on the sidewalk as there were residents of Deering, Vermont. She estimated that just about every apartment building she passed had more residents than Deering, Vermont. And the Pan Am building? Well, at that very moment, a little before three-thirty, it too had far more people inside it than had ever stood in the town square of Deering, Vermont.

It astounded her how much her life had changed in eight days. Eight days ago they hadn't even moved into Deering. She and Brian were staying in the Econo-Lodge on Williston Road in Burlington, two people, two cats, and a litter box in a motel room as small as the library would be in their new home. But it didn't matter, Brian had said, it didn't matter: the very next day they would be starting a whole new chapter in their lives. They had bought an old farmhouse they would restore, revise, and make their own. They would cross-country ski out their back door in the winter, and swim in the river down the road in the summer. They would have surprisingly interesting jobs, despite the fact they were two hundred miles from Boston and three hundred and fifty from Manhattan.

Moreover, they had left behind everything that had made their lives unhappy in Manhattan: their closet of an apartment on Columbus Avenue; the constant degradation and petty frustrations of day-to-day living in New York City; and—perhaps most important—Joyce Renders.

Joyce. There had been no question in her mind, moving to Vermont was a gamble: she was gambling that there remained enough love in their marriage to overshadow Vermont's shortcomings. And Vermont would indeed have shortcomings, there was no doubt about it: there would be months, perhaps years, of loneliness while they assimilated into small town life, while they wove their lives into the centuries-old fabric of the lives around them. There would be a loss of anonymity, the fact that in New York she could go about her business, her life, without being watched, discussed, judged. And there would be, she assumed, the day-to-day difficulties of simply managing an old house: leaky faucets, frozen pipes, peeling paint.

No, Vermont would be far from perfect; she had probably known that all along at some level. Nevertheless, she had managed to approach the move with joy and confidence and optimism: a week ago, it had seemed, she had a life that was filled with—if nothing else—promise.

The phone was ringing when Marcia returned to her parents' home, and she decided she would answer it. She hadn't touched a phone since early Monday morning, when in rapid, shocked succession she had called the state police, her parents, and Jennifer. Without taking her coat off she jogged into her father's study, the nearest extension, and beat her sister to the phone by seconds.

"Hello, Ms. Hampton?" an unfamiliar male voice began.

"There are two Ms. Hamptons here right now," Marcia said. "Are you looking for my sister, Jennifer, or my mother, Grace?"

"My name is Detective J. P. Burrows, with the Burlington, Vermont, Police Department. I'm actually calling to speak with either Marcia Middleton or her sister, Jennifer Hampton."

Marcia fell against her father's desk, losing her balance slightly. "This is Marcia," she said, her mouth becoming dry.

Burrows paused a moment. "Well, Ms. Middleton, I'm real sorry about your husband. If there's anything I can do, or the department can do, just let me know."

"Thank you," Marcia mumbled. "Thank you very much." She

wondered if it was the tone of Burrows' voice or her own paranoia, but the man almost sounded sarcastic to her.

"How are you holding up, ma'am? Your family taking good care of you?"

"Yes, they are," she answered. Her sister hovered in the doorway, evidently surprised that she had been willing to answer the telephone.

"Good. The reason I'm calling, Ms. Middleton, is because some questions have arisen in your husband's death."

"Oh?"

"Yup. There's no good way to couch this, so I'll just come right out and say it. There's a chance that your husband didn't kill himself. There's at least a chance that your husband was murdered."

If only she could tell him that she believed that too, Marcia wished, almost aloud. She wanted to. She wanted to tell him that yes, he was absolutely right, her husband had been murdered. Moreover, it wasn't an issue of chance, it was one of certainty: Brian had been murdered as surely as if she herself had found a gun and shot him or had taken a pillow and smothered him. But what would be the point? He wouldn't believe her. And he certainly wouldn't do anything about it. Because there was nothing to do. He couldn't arrest a house or a noose or the ghost of that little girl who had hanged herself—Thistle Peep Barrington.

So instead she asked simply, "Why do you think that?"

"Well, the medical examiner is not convinced that your husband died by hanging," Burrows said, hoping to avoid discussing with a possible suspect the exact status and details of the investigation. "And we—me, mostly, if the truth be told—are having some trouble recreating the suicide."

Recreating the suicide. Of course they were having trouble recreating the suicide; Brian hadn't killed himself! The whole situation was ludicrous. She wanted to tell this sarcastic detective he could spend his life in that frigid attic and he would never be able to recreate the suicide, because her husband had simply not killed himself! Instead she just put her hand over the mouthpiece and mouthed the word "police" to her sister, answering the questioning look on her sister's face.

"Do you understand what I'm suggesting, Ms. Middleton?" Burrows continued, when Marcia said nothing about his explanation for calling.

"Yes, I think I do."

"Do you understand what it means?"

Marcia began to feel dizzy and leaned forward, hoping the sensation would pass. "I imagine it means my husband's funeral will be postponed at least another day."

"Maybe. But it also means that I've had to have your home sealed off, pending a full investigation by this department, and by the state's Bureau of Criminal Investigation."

"How does that affect me in New York City?"

"While you're there, it doesn't affect you at all. However, you will not be allowed into your house in Vermont unless accompanied by a police officer until the investigation is completed."

"But it's my house," she said softly, swaying slightly.

"And of course you'll be allowed access to everything you own."

"So long as a police officer is with me . . ."

"Right."

"And that's legal . . ."

"Of course it is. What you must understand is that your home may have been the site of a murder. As a result, anything in it could be a piece of evidence, so everything in it must be examined."

It was like sitting on the bottom of a pool, Marcia decided, that's what it was like. She felt tremendous pressure building up all around her head, pushing in on her skull and down behind her eyes. It hurt. And when she tried to breathe, her chest was tight, as if no matter how hard she tried to inhale, not enough air would get in.

"Are you all right, Ms. Middleton?" Burrows asked after a moment.

"No, I don't think I am," she said, sliding off the desk and into her father's heavy leather chair. She handed the phone to Jennifer, only half listening as her sister introduced herself to the detective and heard for herself the idea that Brian Middleton had been murdered.

"You have to listen to me," Jennifer said again to her sister as they lay in their beds in Marcia's bedroom that night. "You have to stop saying that Brian was murdered."

Marcia saw that her kid sister was close to tears, and reached over to her cot and ran a finger gently along Jennifer's arm. "You think I'm crazy, don't you, sweetie?"

"No, I think you're upset, that's all. And I'm scared that you're saying things that will get you in trouble. Things you don't really mean."

"Like what?"

"Like Brian was murdered!"

"But he was."

"You don't know that. You can't really believe that!"

"I can and I do. That house is a living, evil thing." She spoke as evenly as she could, hoping to drive the point home to her sister.

"What you really mean is that the house drove Brian to kill himself. But it was Brian who walked up to the attic and moved the noose and hanged himself! The house itself did not actually hang him!"

"I'm not sure how it happened."

"Is what I said possible?"

"It's possible, but it's too simple," Marcia said, staring up at the ceiling. She wondered what Thistle Peep Barrington had looked like. She wondered whether the little girl had showed herself to Brian before he died.

"But it is possible, you'll admit that? It is possible that Brian hated himself so much for having that affair that he hanged himself? Or that he was so restless—you told me he couldn't even sleep through the night without getting up—that he hanged himself? Or that he was just plain depressed, so depressed that he hanged himself? It is possible, isn't it?"

"Brian was restless, Brian could be moody, but—"

"Or maybe he just decided he hated Vermont! But it is possible that he hanged himself. That's all I'm saying. Tell me you believe that it's possible!"

Without looking back at Jennifer, Marcia asked, "Why are you doing this? Whether the house killed him or he killed himself, what does it matter? My husband is dead either way."

"It makes all the difference in the world!" Jennifer answered, raising her voice. "Don't you understand what's happening?"

Marcia shook her head that she didn't. Why *was* her sister doing this to her? Had the whole world gone mad?

"This afternoon you told Susie Crenshaw and Jill Thorpe that Brian was murdered! You've been telling me and Mom and Dad that for almost two days now!"

"So?"

"There's a detective up in Vermont—my God, not just one detective, a whole goddamn police force—who believes that yes, Brian was murdered, but he doesn't think the house did it."

"I wouldn't expect him to."

"Marcia, he thinks you did it!"

Marcia rolled over to face her sister. "Me? Now that's crazy. Why would anyone think that?"

Jennifer climbed off her cot and sat on the bed beside Marcia. "You should have heard the questions that detective was asking me this afternoon. What kind of marriage did you and Brian have? Were you two happy? Did you ever fight?"

"What did you tell him?"

"I told him you had a wonderful marriage!"

"Thank you."

"But don't you see what he's thinking? A man and a woman move into this quaint little town in the mountains. Five days later, the man is found hanged in the middle of the night in his own attic, except that the hanging doesn't look like a suicide, it looks like a murder. The body looks suspicious, there's no note—"

"Brian would never have left a note," Marcia said quickly, interrupting her sister. "Even if he did kill himself, he would never have left a note. Not after his uncle's experience."

"The one who killed himself?"

"Yes, of course. His Uncle Howard. Aunt Susan was devastated by the note Howard left her. It was mean and angry and—supposedly—it said some terrible things about their marriage. Aunt Susan told Brian's father that finding the note was worse than finding Howard. It destroyed her in ways more horrible than just finding him alone would have."

"Okay, that's fine," Jennifer said carefully, trying to steer the conversation back to Brian's death. "That's fine. There's nothing suspicious about Brian not leaving a note. But something else about his death is. And the fact that practically the only soul in town Brian knew was you—his wife—doesn't help matters much. As far as that detective is concerned, he has exactly one suspect. One."

"Me?"

"Yes, you! And now you're going around saying that, yes, Brian was murdered, except it was an inanimate object that did it!"

"I did not kill my husband, Jennifer, it's that simple."

"I know you didn't. But look at how all this must look to that detective. Burrows. When he hears you've been saying that Brian was murdered—"

"I didn't tell Burrows that, because I knew it would sound ludicrous to him—"

"But you've told other people that! And when he hears that you've been saying it, he'll either think that you killed your husband and then lost your mind, or that you killed your husband and are trying to appear insane! Either way, you're in trouble!"

Marcia saw that Jennifer had begun to cry, little rivulets of tears that rolled down her cheeks. She wiped them away with the sleeve of her cotton nightgown, wondering if maybe—just maybe—she really was losing her mind.

Marcia turned to the wall in the middle of the night and was relieved to find that the Weesimmos had returned. She was relieved because it was dark and because she was scared, despite her sister's even breathing just a few feet away.

For a change father Weesimmo wasn't barbecuing in a suburban backyard, and mother wasn't baking a cake. They had moved to Vermont, and father was standing on the back of a Chevy pickup, banging an eight-foot fence post into the April muck surrounding the Weesimmo farm. Mother Weesimmo was on the ground holding the fence post steady while her husband—her man—swung a sledgehammer in great, majestic arcs onto the top of the post, slamming it inch by inch into the mud. Father was wearing a pair of brown overalls, and mother was wearing jeans. As far as Marcia knew, it was the first time mother had ever worn anything but a print dress.

She wondered where the children were, and after waving at their parents, she wandered past the truck and up toward the house. It was strange for her to stand outside the Weesimmo home, knowing now that the actual house existed in a small town in Vermont, and that she had actually purchased it.

She knocked once on the house's front door, but there was no answer. That shouldn't have surprised her, she decided: on a beautiful spring day like this, the children were probably outside playing. Perhaps they were in the barn stroking the goat's forehead or feeding him bubble gum. Nevertheless, she did holler hello once before venturing inside.

She noted that the Weesimmos had changed very little about their kitchen since coming to Vermont. The Philco refrigerator was in the same corner in which it had always been, and the white egg timer sat in exactly the same spot on the gas range. The only difference she could see was that tollhouse cookies weren't baking: instead, the sap that father Weesimmo had tapped from their maple trees was being boiled down in a long lasagna pan. On the floor beside the oven were four large metal buckets filled with sap.

She walked through the kitchen and into the dining room, hoping to find the children coloring, but they weren't there. Nor were they on the floor in the living room, lying on their stomachs with their heads in their hands, watching television. She called them once again, but they didn't answer.

She ventured upstairs and saw that the second floor hadn't changed much either. The same beige rug covered the hallway floor, the same rose-patterned wallpaper covered the walls. The only difference appeared to be where the bedrooms were placed: there were four or five bedrooms, instead of three, and the doors were different. They were older, Marcia noticed, and they were coated with so many layers of varnish that the wood was dappled different shades of mahogany.

She paused, running her fingers over one of the bedroom doors. Of course the doors were old. These were the doors to her house in Vermont. This was the second floor to her house in Vermont—hence the increased number of bedrooms.

Almost instinctively then she knew which bedroom would belong to the little boy and which would belong to the little girl, and which ones would be empty. With a chill she understood that one of the doors would lead to the attic.

She turned back toward the stairs, planning to leave, but she stopped herself: how could she leave without checking the children? After all they had done for her over the years, how could she leave them alone in the cold of her old evil house? Yes, she was scared, but she was also worried. She would therefore open the bedroom doors, find the children, and make them bring whatever games they were playing outside.

As she had surmised, the little girl's room was the one facing east, the one that got all the morning sun as it rose over Mount Stillman. She saw the child's collection of Barbies, her Betty Crocker playtime stove, and her little blue rocking chair. But the child herself wasn't there.

She found the little boy's room directly across from his sister's, a room somewhat darker than the first, but slightly larger. She saw his plastic Mercury space helmet, his baseball cards, and the pieces to his electric football set scattered across the floor; but the children were not here either.

Nervously Marcia peered into the other bedrooms, throwing open the doors and flicking on the lights quickly, but as she had expected, the rooms were empty, cold, and uninviting. The children weren't there.

The children, she understood with a mixture of frustration and fear, were in the attic. The house wasn't satisfied with kidnapping cats and husbands, it ate children too. And now it had taken the little Weesimmo boy and the little Weesimmo girl, little kids in striped tee shirts who didn't know any better than to stay away from ice boxes that posed as attics.

She stared at the attic door, knowing that she had to open it. She had to wedge her foot against the frame and grasp the white porcelain knob and pull it open with all the strength she could muster. She had to get the door open and free the Weesimmo children from the attic. That, after all, was the whole reason she had been dragged to the Weesimmos' farm, and upstairs in their house. She alone knew about the attic and the cold and the noose. If she didn't free them, who would? Who would?

As she had expected, the door was warped shut; only when she braced both her shoulder and her foot against the wall beside it was she able to pull the door open.

"Hello?" she called up the attic steps. "Hello?"

She had hoped the children would race past her when the door was opened, but clearly they wouldn't. She would have to go get them. Like Brian.

Like Brian. She walked up the stairs, careful not to fall through the rotted steps midway up, fearful that one of the two children might be hanging from the noose. Fortunately, there was only one noose, so the house could only take one at a time.

In the attic—an attic still filled with old *Vermont Life* and *Look* magazines, with shutters that had sat there for who knew how long—she saw the shadow of the swaying body, suspended only inches above the ground. She could not tell if the shadow wore pants or a dress, but she could see it bob, almost as if it were floating on water instead of suspended by a rope from a rafter.

She wandered past the bag of blown wool, the attic's insulation, and around to the rear of the chimney. She saw that the hanged child was the girl, but as she got closer she saw that it wasn't a Weesimmo. The hair was too long, and it was parted evenly in the middle; she wore a dress that fell almost to her ankles; and the shoes she wore were boots, really, mid-calf boots with a Victorian array of hooks and clasps and lace.

She understood that she was staring at Thistle Peep Barrington, a little girl with the palest, fairest skin she had ever seen on a person and the reddest hair. Hair as red as autumn leaves, hair as red as a sunset. Hair as red as her own. The little girl's eyes were closed, and she looked almost as if she were sleeping.

Marcia stepped up onto the pile of magazines below the little girl, and reached up for the child's neck. Gently she wedged her thumbs underneath the rope, trying to pull it away from the girl's delicate skin, hoping she could pull Thistle down without allowing the rope to further disfigure the child's neck. She looked up again into Thistle Peep's face, astounded by its contentment, when the eyes abruptly opened. The lids pulled back and the eyes became wide, and the little girl began to smirk.

She was not holding Thistle Peep in her hands, she realized, gasping in horror; she was holding herself: she was clutching the little girl she once was, that small, frail first grader. She tried desperately to pull away from the child, sobbing, but her hands were caught under the rope and pinned to the child's neck. She began to scream, in part at the child and in part at the house, long, piercing, uncontrollable sobs—"Let go!"—but the rope just pulled her hands tighter around the girl's neck and drew her closer to the swaying thing above her.

"Let go!" Jennifer screamed as her mother switched on the light and her father raced into the room. "Let go, you're hurting me!" she screamed again, her voice hoarse and throaty.

Marcia was vaguely aware of her father grabbing her by her shoulders and pulling her off her sister's cot. She looked up at him, surprised by his strength, and then back down at her sister, quivering in a ball below her. "My God," she murmured, staring at the deep red marks along Jennifer's neck. "My God, what have I done?"

Chapter 16

Homicide was losing to the Four Taps—four sales reps from Green Mountain Maple—in a Thursday night league game at Bosox Bar in Burlington, and they were losing because J. P. Burrows was tossing his darts like fastballs—fastballs that were always just missing the dart board's strike zone.

"Wound pretty tight, tonight, eh, J. P.?" Detective Sherman Anderson commented, when another of Burrows' blue Assassins ripped across the bar and into the outermost circle on the dart board.

"Yup, I am." Burrows shrugged, leaning back against the bar. It was ironic, but most of the time it was Anderson who was wound tighter than fishing line; it was Anderson who was edgier than a bear in April. This was perhaps the first time that Burrows had ever seen Anderson trying to lighten a mood. Ever. The man had a short fuse, a reputation on the force for inflicting exactly as much pain as he thought he could get away with on an arrest, for exerting exactly as much physical pressure—jabs, punches, slaps, shoves—as a suspect would tolerate. Everyone knew that one day he would go too far, that it was only a matter of time before the man's natural orneriness got him in trouble. Tonight, however, Burrows thought he seemed almost sympathetic, almost concerned.

"You realize, don't you, that tonight you're tossing those things only slightly better than Hank does," Anderson added.

Burrows smiled and reached for his beer. He noticed two blonde women rolling up literally millions of points on the Trivial Pursuit video machine at the end of the bar, and decided they were probably students from the university. Judging by their cashmere sweaters, he decided they were probably moneyed out-of-state students, perhaps from New York City. And then, because all women from New York City were on his shit list at that moment, he decided he hated them on sight and stopped smiling.

"You talk to those two?" he asked Anderson facetiously, referring to the two women by the video game at the end of the bar.

"About what?"

"The college drug investigation, what else?"

"Sorry, J. P. I guess I missed those two."

"You any closer to an arrest?" he then asked more seriously.

"Who knows? I sure don't."

"Well, it's only a matter of time. Think of me when you're on the front page of the newspaper: 'Sherman Anderson Uncovers University Drug Ring.' "

Anderson ran his finger over the label on the beer bottle before him. "It's only a matter of time for you too, J. P. I know it is. You'll nail that Middleton woman. There's bound to be something incriminating in the lab reports."

"Not enough to arrest her, Sherman," Burrows said, shaking his head in disgust. One of the two blondes was actually clapping at her score in Trivial Pursuit.

"You don't know that."

"I do, and you do. It will be a miracle if Waterbury comes up with a reason to arraign her."

"Yo, dart art!" one of the maple sugar salesmen shouted, when one of the detectives managed to surround his target on the dart board without actually hitting it.

Anderson took a sip of his Rolling Rock. "What the hell happened, J. P.? When you came back from Deering this afternoon, you thought you might have something. You did; those guys from Criminal Investigation did. What happened?"

"We spoke to the state attorney."

"Floyd Dempsey or Terrance Beech?"

"Terrance Beech."

"And?"

"And nothing. Seems every cider apple's got a goddamn worm these days."

"What did Beech tell you?"

Burrows rolled the tip of the dart between his fingers, pricking his thumb slightly. He was always surprised by how sharp his darts were. "In a nutshell, he said it is entirely possible that Marcia Middleton killed her husband. He also said we have absolutely no case."

"Right now, that is."

"Right. Right now."

"I'm telling you, that will change. Once those guys in the lab are done with the stuff you took from the house this afternoon, they'll find enough evidence to arrest *and* convict her. Hell, they'll probably find proof she was laundering money for Columbian drug dealers!"

"Beech doesn't think so."

"Terrance Beech is just covering his bottom. You know what a thorough guy he is; you've seen him work."

"Not this time. This isn't just an overly cautious prosecutor. We'll have two new pieces of evidence when Waterbury is through, a photo and a ladder, and even I have to admit they're both pretty weak." He watched one of the maple sugar salesmen stagger to the baseline for his turn, knocking over a chair and spilling half his beer on the way, and then hit the inner circle of the dart board four consecutive times. Even blind drunk these guys were good, Burrows decided.

"I don't agree. I heard about that note on the photo, and it sounded to me like a pretty damn good motive for murder."

Burrows rolled his eyes. "It doesn't prove anything: it sure as hell doesn't prove that Marcia Middleton killed her husband."

"No, but it does suggest that her husband had an affair with another woman last spring. And that could be a motive."

"But it's not enough for an arraignment."

"What about the ladder? This afternoon you thought there was a pretty good chance the widow would snag herself on the ladder."

"I was wrong. Even if the ladder has her prints on it," Burrows said, exasperated, "it won't prove that Marcia Middleton murdered her husband. The ladder was in her house; she most likely had to touch it sometime. For all we know, she was using it to stack boxes in some empty bedroom closet all weekend."

"Yo, dart fart!" another of the maple sugar salesmen shouted when he wasted his own turn by failing to hit his mark.

"Well, there's still the rope," Anderson said, trying to be helpful. "I'm sure that can be linked to the woman."

"Probably. But it's like the ladder: it had been in her house; she could have touched it or handled it anytime over the five or six days that she lived in the place."

"Okay. But what—"

"Sherman, I like you," Burrows said, cutting his friend off as he reached for the rosin bag to dry the tips of his fingers, "but don't go dippin' your lip in my porridge." He then took a sip of his beer and returned to the dart game, hurling his darts as hard as he could at the wall.

Burrows wandered over to the police station when he left Bosox a little before eleven o'clock. He wasn't drunk, but he was—as his mother put it—a smidgen too happy.

"You win tonight?" Molly Branigan asked him as he walked in the door. Branigan, a recent mother who had returned to active duty only the week before, was running the graveyard shift that night.

"No, but we lost to the best—a bunch of sugar salesmen. How's Helen?" he asked, referring to her baby girl.

"She's gonna be a heartbreaker, J. P. She's already got her daddy and two granddaddies wrapped around her pinky."

"Got any more pictures?"

"Are you kidding? Mike must be supporting the Kodak Colorwatch System. I got more pictures than Lake Champlain's got trout." She reached behind the counter for her purse and pulled out a gold and white envelope overflowing with snapshots. "In this here packet are photographs of the cutest little baby Milton's ever seen, 'cept for me twenty-five years ago."

Burrows smiled politely as he flipped through the photos. Helen certainly wasn't grotesque, but her head did look a bit like a turnip. She was also too little to be called Helen. Helen was an old person's name, he thought to himself; people should not be referred to as Helen until they were at least fifty.

"She's a cutie," Burrows told Molly, returning the photos.

"We think so," Molly said.

"You got the keys to the vault tonight?" Burrows then asked.

"Yeah. What do you need?"

"The photos we took from the Middleton house this afternoon."

"Ah, exhibit A. Or is it B?"

"Don't know."

"Well, I don't think they're here at any rate, J. P. I think they're all down in Waterbury."

"They should be here, Molly. The only things I tagged for Waterbury were the ladder, the rope, and some clothing. I logged in the pictures here."

"Let me check for you," she said, packing her snapshots together like a deck of playing cards. "Want to keep an eye on the desk for me?"

"Why sure."

Molly was only gone a moment. When she returned, she had with her a large Ziploc bag. Burrows could see the photographs he was looking for through the clear plastic.

"You were right, J. P.," she said, tossing the bag onto the counter. "Want to sign 'em out?"

Burrows nodded, reaching behind her for a requisition form and a pen.

"What do you need 'em for?" Molly asked.

"No real reason. Curiosity, I guess," Burrows said, taking the pictures with him to his desk in the detectives' office.

Her hair was described as red, but that was too easy. Red was shorthand—a shortcut, really—for such bureaucracies as the police department and the department of motor vehicles. Red was comprehensible; red was convenient; red was short. Red had just three letters and so fit easily on forms.

But Marcia's hair wasn't red, not really. It was rust; it was ruddy; it was faintly ruby. It was a simmering, shimmering mane the color of hot coals in a wood stove. It was full and long and lustrous and every other adjective Burrows had ever heard in commercials for hair conditioners and shampoos. He had had just enough to drink, he decided, to fall in love with the woman's hair. At least for now.

He put the photographs of Marcia Middleton and the woman named Joyce side by side on his desk. Joyce was not unattractive, but comparing her to Marcia Middleton was like comparing a sow and a filly. It was just that simple. Burrows hadn't seen many redheads in his life, but he couldn't imagine there was one anywhere more beautiful than Marcia Middleton. Hell, he thought, blondes and brunettes included, there probably weren't many women in the world more beautiful than Marcia Middleton. This woman was a stunner, no doubt about it.

He assumed the photograph of Marcia was taken in her old apartment in New York City. In it she was sitting Indian-style on a couch, reading a newspaper, a cat on either side. She was wearing jeans and a tee shirt that matched the blue in her eyes, and her hair—that wonderful, flowing, fire-red fleece—was cascading down her shoulders and across her breasts. It was the sort of casual picture snapped on a Sunday afternoon.

The photograph of Joyce was taken on a beach somewhere, somewhere south, judging by the palm trees in the distance. In it Joyce was wearing what Burrows classified as an R-rated bathing suit: a one-piece maillot that was cut up the sides to the woman's rib cage. Joyce had nice legs, a nice body, but one of the sharpest, harshest faces he could remember seeing. Her smile wasn't as soft as Marcia's, nor her eyes as gentle. She had dark brown hair, cut short like a boy's.

He turned over the photograph of Joyce and read again the inscription she had written Brian:

> *I know it's stupid and wrong to write you, my love, even at your office, but I want you to know what you're missing. You should know I stripped this suit off about an hour after this picture was taken, when Louise and I found a secluded little cove. And because you were so far away, I had to rub in my Coppertone all by myself! Your loss, sweetheart . . .*

The photograph was eight months old, based on the date Joyce had scribbled above her inscription. It had been taken the previous March.

Burrows reached into his jacket pocket for his leather pouch of Assassins, and sat back in his chair, idly lofting the darts in high arcs at the dart board across the room. His aim, he discovered, was every bit as poor that night whether he hurled the darts like fastballs or tossed them gently into the air, whether he aimed at an official North American Dart League dart board or a photograph of rowdy college kids.

He wondered what it was that had driven Brian Middleton into an affair with a woman named Joyce. It certainly wasn't beauty, because God knew he had enough of that in his own bed at home. He couldn't imagine that Marcia Middleton was an impossible to live with bitch, not with those eyes and that smile (and she certainly hadn't sounded bitchy on the phone that afternoon—if anyone had, it was him . . .).

No, whatever it was that had led Brian Middleton astray was probably some character flaw of his own, some inherent idiocy or impulse toward self-destruction.

He stared down again at the photograph of Marcia Middleton, trying to find in the woman's face a trace of the calculating killer she was supposed to be. It just wasn't there. It just didn't seem possible to Burrows that a woman who looked as warm and sweet as Marcia Middleton could kill her husband on a cold November night in Vermont.

Chapter 17

Betrayal. That was the word that came to Burrows' mind when he was dialing Marcia Middleton in Manhattan Friday morning. Betrayal. The woman was perhaps a murderer, but she was also a victim. A person betrayed.

Did betrayal change much? It shouldn't. Homicide was obviously a crime of far greater consequence than adultery. Even in staid Vermont, adultery had never been a capital offense.

But it did change something. Marcia Middleton had been betrayed. Isn't that what the picture of Joyce somebody said?

Burrows watched Anderson tack to their corkboard a photo from the *Free Press* of the university's dean of students, claiming in a speech to the alumni that they were doing everything possible to combat drugs at the school. He wondered how his supervisors would feel if he were to post on the wall that picture of Joyce instead.

"Hello?" It sounded like Jennifer Hampton's voice on the telephone, Marcia Middleton's sister.

"Good morning, Ms. Hampton. This is Detective Burrows in Vermont. How are you feeling today?"

A pause. Then: "I'm feeling fine. Is there a problem?"

"No, not really. I just have a couple of questions I wanted to ask your sister."

"Brian's body . . . Brian has been returned, hasn't he?"

"Far as I know. He should have arrived in New York early last night."

He heard the woman exhale over three hundred miles away, and could almost feel her relief at the other end of the wire. "I don't know if I could have told Marcia that the funeral was going to be postponed again," she said.

"You won't have to."

"Thank you. I'm very glad."

"Well, is your sister available? Like I said, I have a few questions I'd like to ask her."

"She's here, but can they wait? Do you really have to ask them right now?"

"They'll only take a minute."

"Can you ask me, and I'll ask her? With the funeral tomorrow, I'd rather wait."

"No, I'm sorry, Ms. Hampton, but if your sister is home I would like to speak to her directly."

"All right," Jennifer said, irritated, before dropping the phone onto a table or countertop with more force than Burrows thought necessary.

Outside his window a jet flew by, perhaps one of the fighter planes from the air force base across the lake. He swiveled his chair around to see, but by the time he faced the window only the sound was left.

"Hello," Marcia said, picking up the receiver.

Betrayal. Things had changed, Burrows thought to himself, but he was kidding himself if he believed it was that picture of Joyce alone that had changed everything for him. That picture of Marcia, that picture of the woman at the other end of the telephone, had changed something too.

"Good morning, Ms. Middleton. This is Detective Burrows. I appreciate your taking the time to speak with me right now."

"That's okay. What do you need to know?"

She sounded tired, more tired today than Wednesday afternoon.

"I need to know a couple of things," he said, wanting suddenly to stall. He wished there was a diplomatic way to approach these questions, another way to get the information he needed. "And I'm real sorry to be asking you about them right now."

"Go ahead. You're just doing your job."

"I am indeed. What I need to know," he said slowly, "is whether your husband knew a woman named Joyce."

Marcia was silent, and Burrows could almost imagine her wincing at the sound of the name. After a moment she said in almost a whisper, "Yes. He did." He wondered if she were about to cry.

"Do you know Joyce's last name?"

He heard her take a deep breath, gathering herself perhaps. "Yes. Her name is Renders. Joyce Renders."

"Where does she live? New York City?"

"Manhattan. She lives in our—my—old building. Three-forty-five Columbus Avenue."

"Can you tell me where she works?"

Again, that pause for breath. With the image from her picture in his mind, Burrows could almost see her slouching forward, sagging beneath the weight of the memories.

"Powell and Time. They're a big architectural firm," she answered, her voice breaking just the slightest bit on the last word.

Burrows phoned directory assistance in Manhattan as soon as he said good-bye to Marcia, and then Powell and Time, never stopping to return the receiver to the cradle. He did not want to reflect a moment longer on Marcia Middleton, on the sound of that low, tired voice.

"Good afternoon, this is Powell and Time," the switchboard operator assured him.

"Joyce Renders, please."

"Thank you."

Barely a split second later a second Powell and Time female voice came on the line. "Good afternoon, this is personnel."

"Joyce Renders, please," Burrows said again, surprised. He hadn't envisioned Joyce Renders working in personnel. He had assumed that she was an architect or a financial something. But not personnel.

"Thank you," the second woman said, and transferred him to another phone.

"Good afternoon, this is Al Terkel," a man said, answering his phone with what was apparently the requisite Powell and Time greeting.

"Good afternoon, this is J. P. Burrows," Burrows said, imitating the Powell and Time phone manner. "I'm a detective with the Burlington, Vermont Police Department. I'm calling to speak with Joyce Renders."

"Is there something perhaps I can help you with, Detective?"

"I don't think so. I believe I should speak directly with Ms. Renders. Is she there?"

"No, she's not."

"Will she be back soon?"

"Not likely," Terkel said. "She left the firm about three weeks ago."

Burrows hung up the phone after calling Joyce Renders at her home, and thought about her voice. It wasn't evil. It wasn't the voice of some sleazy home wrecker. It was a nice voice, perfectly nice. It may not have been as husky or as sexy as Marcia Middleton's, but it was perfectly pleasant. There was even something lilting about the cadence of her speech, something almost comforting.

He smiled to himself. Modern technology, it was amazing. He had already formed in his mind at least a dozen preconceptions about Joyce Renders, all from a thirty-second tape on an answering machine.

CHAPTER 18

Marcia lay on her bedroom floor with Solstice beside her, and stared into the cat's eyes. All cats' eyes looked alike. Solstice's looked no different from Chloe's, not really, and the eyes of her two cats looked no different from the eyes of that cat who lived in their barn. Her barn. The tiger stripe.

What a strange cat that was, she thought. He would let her pet him; he would let her hold him; he would even eat dried cat food from the palm of her hand. And yet he had absolutely refused to set foot inside her house or even sit for a moment on the front porch.

Solstice stretched, his paws widening into a web, and he yawned, breathing cat breath onto Marcia's face. He seemed to smile at Marcia; he thought this was a pretty comfortable way to spend a Friday afternoon.

Tomorrow, Saturday, Brian would be buried. Finally. What had those people in Vermont done to him? Marcia wondered. To his body? She had been told it could still be an open casket, so he could not be too terribly disfigured.

She wondered what they had discovered. If anything. She tried to recall the words of that detective, Burrows: "I'm having some trouble recreating the suicide." Something like that. Had they found therefore that he hadn't died by hanging, that perhaps he had died of a stroke or from some sort of wound? Had they found a clot in his brain, or—and with this thought her breathing changed rhythm and Solstice grunted once beside her—had they found Joyce in his heart?

Joyce. Brian had insisted that Joyce meant nothing to him, that it was long over. And she had believed him. She wouldn't have left for Vermont, after all, if she hadn't believed him; she wouldn't have left behind her family and friends and a life that was—if nothing else—comprehensible to her. She had lived in New York almost all of her life, so she understood the city; she knew always what to expect. But Vermont? God, Vermont was a wild card, an infinite series of unknowns that more times than not would probably disappoint her.

Clearly, however, Brian had been wrong about Joyce. Or lying, lying at the very least to himself and perhaps to her as well.

What did it mean that Burrows was now interested in Joyce? Was she too a suspect? How ironic: she and Joyce Renders, both suspects in the murder of Brian Middleton.

Or was Burrows merely looking for a motive to confirm in his mind once and for all that she herself had murdered her husband? That was the more likely scenario. Jealous wife kills husband in insane rage.

Actually, the real irony was the fact that Burrows was still talking to the wrong women. Especially since he shouldn't even be talking to women; he should be talking to a girl, a little girl. A six- or seven-year-old girl with the reddest hair and the wildest blue eyes she had ever imagined—ever seen—on a child. She was the one with all the answers; she was the one who could tell him about the house and why Brian went to that hushed, frigid attic to die.

But what brought that little girl to the attic in the first place? What could possibly be so horrifying as to drive a small child to suicide? A very small child? What could be that sad?

Marcia rolled closer to her cat to face him. Solstice had extended his front legs straight before him like a sphinx. She wished he could talk. She wished he could tell her what he had seen in the attic their first day in the house; she wished he could tell her what had frightened him.

"What did you see, sweetheart?" she asked Solstice. "What was up there?"

She started to ask aloud if the cat had seen a sad little girl, but she stopped herself. Thistle Peep's eyes had been dark and wide in her dream, but they hadn't been sad. That was where she was wrong. Thistle Peep's eyes were evil; they were wicked; they were—if eyes could really be so—possessed. They were eyes that had laughed at her.

She stared into Solstice's eyes. Perhaps all cats' eyes were not alike. Or at least not identical. From a slightly different angle, with the light from the window, it was not impossible to see in the eyes of her cat the eyes of that dead little girl, the eyes of Thistle Peep Barrington.

Burrows was surprised to find selectman Joshua Nash home Friday afternoon, since there was no car in the driveway or the garage. But when he rang the doorbell, a tall, wiry fellow in a navy blue tee shirt answered it, smiling.

"Afternoon," the fellow said to Burrows. "Can I help you?"

"Afternoon," Burrows said. "My name is Detective J. P. Burrows. I'm with the Burlington Police Department. Are you Joshua Nash?"

"Last time I checked. 'Course, I like people to call me Josh. Josh sounds less formal. Less biblical," Nash said, and then asked, "You're Simon's brother, aren't you?"

"I am indeed."

"Let me tell you, you got yourself one hard-working brother. One nice brother. It's real helpful having him around."

Burrows smiled, pleased. "Well, we—my family and me—are grateful that you can use him. He speaks highly of you too."

"Yup, he's a real good worker," Nash concluded, nodding. "You here about Simon?"

"Nope, not at all."

"Didn't think so."

"You got a minute?"

Nash rubbed his bare arms. "Sure, if you'll take that minute inside. Either that or I got to get me a jacket."

"Inside's fine."

Nash smiled and pushed open wide the glass storm door, waving Burrows inside. "You want some soda or something? A Pepsi?"

"Sure, why not?" He followed Nash through a short hallway that smelled of dog and into the kitchen. He moved the Hostess cupcake refrigerator magnets and leaned against the freezer, noticing the Middleton house in the distance from the kitchen window. Spread out on the dining room table in the next room, Burrows saw at least a half dozen mail-order catalogs from stores he had never heard of. Places called Ghiradelli Chocolate, the Nature Company, and Fogal caught his eye.

"You're the first person I've spoken to since lunch," Nash volunteered, holding the large two-liter bottle of Pepsi with two hands as he poured. "My wife's out visitin' Meg Hollis—she's laid up at the hospital with a bum knee—and my girls went right out sellin' raffle tickets for the historical society the minute they got home from school."

"Deering has an historical society?"

"You bet." Nash sat down at the kitchen table and motioned for Burrows to join him. "A real active one! But I'd be willing to bet you're not here to buy a raffle ticket. I'd bet you're here 'cause of the new folks," he said.

"That would be a good bet."

"Damn shame what happened to 'em."

"How well did you know them?"

"Me? I knew 'em a bit, especially Brian. You probably know we were fixing up a good piece of their house."

"I also heard that Brian asked you to stop working right in the middle of the job. When was that?"

"Sunday. Sunday afternoon. He came by right about the time I was giving up on the Patriots."

"The day he died?"

"Yup."

"How come? He gave you any special reason?"

"Not really. He said somethin' about he and his wife changing their minds about the place—exactly what they wanted to redo and how they wanted to redo it. He may also have said somethin' about what a handyman he had become himself—overnight, a course."

"That was it?"

"That was it."

"Why do you think he changed his mind so suddenly?"

Nash shrugged. "Like he said, he and his wife probably just figured they wanted to do things differently. The fellow always seemed to be wound a little too tight to me anyway."

Burrows nodded. "You like them?"

"I liked 'em fine."

"What do you mean when you say Brian was wound too tight?"

"Not mean or gloomy, nothing like that. Edgy, maybe. Or frustrated. Everyone from New York City is probably like he was. It just seemed like things couldn't happen fast enough for him. It just seemed like he always had so much on his mind that he was always a little angry underneath. Just a little. Maybe a little unhappy. Don't get me wrong, I was probably as surprised as the next person by what happened. He had just seemed a mite tense to me a lot of the time."

"Can you think of any examples?"

"Of him being tense?"

"Right."

Nash thought for a moment. "Every time I saw him. I can't tell you any one thing, 'cause it was just the way he was. His nature. He just always seemed a little short with people. Except with Simon—your kid brother."

"Really?"

"Yup. I couldn't tell you why, but Dave—Dave Dunbar, we work together—Dave noticed it too. Brian got a real charge out of Simon. He used to teach him words; he used to tell him stories about New York City. Simon loved hearing about the trains that run underground. And then a lot of times, Brian would let Simon show him things: Simon taught Brian how to peel wallpaper; he taught Brian how to use a cat's paw to pull out nails. It was almost like they were brothers."

The word "brothers" hit Burrows like a cold wind in January. It stung. And though he knew in his head it made no sense to be jealous, he was. He was jealous of a brief relationship a dead man he probably wouldn't have liked had once had with his brother. "Did Middleton ever talk about his wife?" he asked Nash, consciously changing the subject.

"Nope, 'cept when we were talking about the renovations. Sometimes he'd say 'we want such and such,' or 'we were hoping to do such and such,' and I knew the 'we' was him and Marcia. He mentioned Marcia mostly when he was showing me the wallpaper or paint colors, 'cause Marcia picked most of those out."

"You must have seen the Middletons together a number of times."

"Yup."

"What were they like together? Did they make a good couple?"

"I guess so. Good enough, anyway. But I did see them have one dandy little tiff together," Nash answered, smiling just the tiniest bit at the recollection.

"What about? Why did they have this tiff?"

"Wallpaper. What does every married couple renovating a house quarrel about? Wallpaper, a course. Marcia wanted these bows for the den, see, and Brian wanted stripes. He was actually sort of mean to her. Like I said, edgy."

"Who won?"

"You know, I don't remember. I think they said they'd make a decision later. I wouldn't be surprised if the wallpaper they ended up buying is still in clear wrappers in the den, still all rolled up."

"Did you ever get a chance to talk to Marcia? When Brian wasn't around?"

"She made me and Dave and Simon lunch last Friday. Week ago today, as a matter of fact. We talked a bit then, while she was in the kitchen preparing it."

"Just the three of you and her husband?"

"Yup."

"What did you talk about?"

Nash rubbed his chin, trying to remember. "Plowin' mostly," he said finally.

"Plowin'?"

"Plowin', yup. The roads and all."

"That's it?"

"I told her 'bout the times Orville Beanman got himself stuck. See, Orville maintains if you don't get yourself stuck once in a while, you're not gettin' your road out as far as you should."

Burrows grinned. That flatlander from New York must have loved listening to Joshua Nash chew her ear about Orville Beanman for God knew how long her first Friday in Deering. "What else did you talk about?"

"Their barn cat. They got this big 'ol tiger stripe that lives in their barn, and Marcia really took a liking to it. Said she wanted to make it a house cat someday."

"Anything else?"

"Nope, that was about it. If you want to know more about Marcia, I'd talk to Sarabeth. Sarabeth knew her better 'n me."

"Is Sarabeth your wife?"

"Yup."

"And you said she isn't home now?"

"Yup. She's in Middlebury this afternoon, watching Meg Hollis' knee mend. She's real important to the Deering Seniors, see."

"Did she ever say anything about Marcia?"

"Oh, Sarabeth liked Marcia. But I guess she's learned now that women are a lot like cows."

Burrows had heard his uncle use the expression once or twice before, without knowing exactly what the words meant. "I don't get it," he said to Nash. "I'm not sure what you mean."

Nash rubbed his arm again. "You know. You can't judge a cow by her looks."

Burrows thought for a moment. "Marcia Middleton was a deceptive cow?"

"Well, she didn't look like a cow. Just the opposite, really. She was pretty. But Sarabeth also thought she was this nice city gal. She thought Marcia was this sweet thing who'd come here with her husband to start a family. She never woulda picked her to kill him."

Burrows placed his Pepsi down on a place mat on the kitchen table. "What makes you think she killed him? I never said that. Far as I know, no one has ever said that around here."

"No one had to," Nash said carefully, quietly. "A lot of folks heard all about those questions you were asking Lymon Hollis at the store last Wednesday. And a lot of other folks saw all those police officers at the house on Thursday—yesterday. Even up here, detective, we can put two and two together and get four."

"You don't have to say 'up here' to me, Josh," Burrows said evenly. "I'm from a little town just like Deering. West Gardner. My daddy's a dairy farmer."

"And you decided to get out of dairyin' while the gettin' was good?"

"Something like that."

Nash was silent for a long moment, evidently weighing Burrows' answer.

"You should know, Josh," Burrows said, breaking the silence, "that we have absolutely no evidence linking Marcia Middleton to her husband's murder."

"But the man was murdered?"

"He might have been."

"So who do you think did it?"

"I don't know. That's why I'm talking to you," Burrows said, staring up the hill at Marcia Middleton's empty house.

Marcia looked once again into Solstice's eyes, looking so deeply that the cat turned away. Just a cat's eyes, she tried to tell herself, but she knew that she was seeing in them something more. The pupils were round, rounder than a cat's, and for just the slightest second the eyes had looked more white than green.

She inched closer to the cat's face, but Solstice closed his eyes and drowsed, seemingly oblivious of Marcia's interest. She rubbed the top of the animal's head, massaging the fur between his ears, and whispered his name.

"Solstice."

The cat opened one eye, and Marcia relaxed. Yes, it was just a cat's eye. She laid her head on her arm and tried to drowse too, to forget for one moment how very sad her life had become.

And then she heard someone say softly, "Don't leave me."

She rolled over, expecting to see Jennifer behind her, perhaps in the doorway, perhaps in the hall.

But she saw no one there. The room and the hall were empty. "Jennifer?" she asked quietly, as quiet as the voice she had heard. "Jennifer?"

Had she made the voice up? Had she dreamt it?

She looked back at Solstice to see if the cat had heard it too, had heard what sounded more and more in her mind like the plea of a scared little girl.

David Dunbar was splitting wood in his side yard using an Omark brand wedge known as a "Wood Grenade" when Burrows drove up to his house. Burrows recognized the wedge immediately as the same kind his family used on their own farm. Dunbar looked up when Burrows arrived, but he didn't stop slamming the wedge into the wide log before him until it split cleanly in half.

"Nicely done," Burrows said. "You David Dunbar?"

"Yes, sir, I am," Dunbar said cautiously, carefully dropping his sledgehammer behind him. "Can I help you?"

"Hope so. My name is J. P. Burrows. I'm a detective with the Burlington Police Department."

"That explains it," Dunbar said happily. "I was just thinking how I knew I'd seen your truck someplace before, but I couldn't begin to place where. Now I can; now it fits. You were in Deering twice this week, on Wednesday and Thursday. Right?"

"Right. You have a good memory."

"Nah. It's just that this last week has been the most excitement Deering's had in a real long time. I was home part of Wednesday and Thursday, and must have walked past the Middleton house 'bout a dozen times while you folks were checking it out."

"Couldn't have been very interesting from the street."

"Didn't have to be. I didn't have much else to do."

Burrows bent over and picked up the wedge from the grass. "You probably know why I'm here," he said, estimating that the wedge weighed a good eight or nine pounds.

Dunbar shrugged. "No, can't say that I do."

"I want to ask you a few questions about the Middletons."

"I don't believe I could tell you much about them. Me and Carrie —my wife—really only spent one evening with 'em, and most of the time we had on our good neighbor smiles. That was last Saturday. I mean, I spoke to the two of 'em a bit now and then when we were fixing their place up, but nothing real major. If you wanted, I could tell you a good bit about their house, but I don't guess you're real interested in that."

"No, not a whole lot. But I would be interested in anything you could tell me about the evening you spent with them."

Dunbar scratched the back of his neck and thought for a moment. "I could tell you 'bout that. You got a minute, Detective?"

" 'Course."

"Let's go sit down," he said. "Me and Carrie already brought the porch furniture into the barn for the winter, so we'll have to sit on the steps. That okay?"

"That's okay."

"Like I said, I don't know much about the Middletons. I know he did something with IBM, and I know she was supposed to start working for some Middlebury advertising agency. And they had a couple of cats, I know that. But that's about it."

Somewhere in the woods behind the Dunbars' someone fired a gun, the report echoing across Deering. Burrows noticed Dunbar flinched at the sound.

"I hate hunting season," Dunbar explained. "I'm always afraid some nearsighted rookie will mistake one of our dogs for a seven-pointer and turn it into venison retriever."

"What kind of dogs do you have?"

"Golden retrievers. 'Course this time of year my wife makes 'em look like pure orange retrievers. She covers 'em from snout to tail with orange scarves and red bandannas."

Burrows stretched out his legs onto the ground before the bottom step. "So what did you talk about when you all got together?" he asked.

Dunbar sighed. "I've been feeling a little weird this week, Detective, a little guilty. I really have."

Burrows nodded without looking at Dunbar.

"There's no reason I should feel guilty, don't get me wrong. I mean, I didn't kill Brian or anything like that."

"I didn't think I was about to get a confession out of you," Burrows said lightly.

"Good, 'cause there's nothing for me to confess. But the thing is—and this might sound crazy—the thing is, I think I might have been the one to put the whole idea into his head. Or Marcia's head, I guess."

"You told Brian to hang himself?"

"No, I wouldn't tell anyone to do that. But I was the one who told him about the noose and about Thistle Peep Barrington."

Burrows turned to Dunbar. "I know about the noose. But who is Thistle Peep Barrington?"

"No one told you about her?"

"Not yet."

"Jeesum crow, I'm tellin' two in a week. I must be on some kinda roll," Dunbar said, raising his voice and laughing just the slightest bit. "I can't believe it," he said again. "I'm tellin' two in one week."

"Do the Barringtons—or at least Thistle—live in Deering?"

"I can't believe this. I just can't believe this! I'll tell you 'bout her, Detective, but don't you go hangin' yourself like poor ol' Brian after I do. Okay?"

"Trust me, Dave; it's not in my plans."

"Good, 'cause I don't want to see a pattern here. Know what I mean?"

"I think so."

Dunbar leaned forward, putting his elbows on his knees and resting his head in his hands. "Like I told the Middletons last Saturday, I don't have all the details. What I said to 'em is that there was a noose in their attic. A real old one, supposedly one that had been hangin' there for a good eighty years at least."

"The Finches didn't put it up?"

"Ernest's a strange one in his own way all right, but he just kept the noose there once he found it. He didn't hang it."

"So who put it up?"

"The story goes that a little girl named Thistle Peep Barrington put it there . . . and then used it."

"How little?"

"Six or seven."

"You're telling me that you believe a seven-year-old girl hanged herself in that house eighty years ago, and no one ever bothered to take the noose down?"

"Well, that's the story, at any rate."

"I suppose the Barringtons were the people who lived in the house before the Finches?"

"You got that right."

"Why didn't Thistle's parents take the noose down?"

Dunbar shook his head. "Don't know that. But I do know why Ernest Finch kept the noose up. He was afraid. He was afraid to take it down."

"Afraid? What was he afraid of?"

"That's a very strange house, Detective. You should talk to Ernest Finch or his son, Foster. They can tell you."

"I still don't get it. What was Ernest afraid of? Did he think the house was haunted?"

"I don't know if 'haunted' is the right word. I think he just thought the house was a little strange, and takin' the noose down might be just the thing to set it off. Unleash all kinds of nasty stuff."

"And you told Brian and Marcia Middleton all this last Saturday night?"

"Yup."

Burrows turned to Dunbar. "What do you think about the house, Dave? Do you think it's haunted?"

Dunbar sighed. "I think all old houses have got their share of history, and some of it's bound to be kinda raw. Kinda messy. And I guess it's possible some of it's bound to stick to the woodwork here 'n' there."

"Did you ever see anything strange in the house?"

"Detective," Dunbar said carefully, "I went to school with Foster Finch. I went slidin' with him in the winter and swimmin' with him in the summer. I went to twelve years of school with him. But the first time I set foot in that house was the day I started renovating it after the Finches had moved out. In all the years I knew Foster, not once—not once—did he ever let me or anyone else into that house. Not once!"

The cat had heard it! Oh God, Marcia thought, the cat heard it too! She had looked at Solstice, she realized, hoping to see in the cat's placid gaze, proof that she had dreamt the scared little voice after all. But no, the cat's tail was fluffed to twice, perhaps three times its normal size, and he was up and alert and staring at . . . at nothing! The cat was staring in rapt attention at an empty doorway!

Marcia sat up on her knees and rubbed her eyes, reaching gently for her cat.

"What do you see, sweetie? There's nothing there," she whispered, more for her benefit than for the cat's.

But the cat continued to stare, his tail swatting rhythmically the legs of the bureau beside her, stopping only when the plea returned once more: "Don't leave me! Please, don't leave me tonight!"

Ernest and Edna Finch had already gone west for the winter to a small condominium they had bought near Phoenix, but Foster Finch and his wife, Shirley, lived in a charmless log cabin in Dresden. Dresden was an old hill town like Deering, ten minutes from Deering in the summer, forty in the winter when the Deering Gap was closed.

Burrows decided it was too late in the season to chance the gap that afternoon, and so took the long way around the mountain, arriving at the Finches' near sunset. Through the window on the front porch he could see the couple hunched over a table, watching television.

"How do you do?" Burrows said to the woman who opened the door, a tremendously thin, tremendously pale woman in her early thirties. She was at least six and a half feet tall, and towered over Burrows like a giraffe. She wore blue jeans and a print blouse that was so many sizes too small it looked like a halter top. "My name is J. P. Burrows. I'm with the Burlington Police Department. I was hoping to speak to your husband for a few minutes."

"Foster! You feel like speakin' to anybody?" the woman yelled into the living room.

Foster snapped, "Nope!"

"It's a po-lice officer, Foster!"

"What's he want?"

Shirley Finch turned to Burrows. "What do you want?"

"I want to ask your husband a few questions about the house he grew up in," Burrows said patiently. "You may have heard, there was a death there last week."

"He wants to yak about the feller who done himself dead in yer daddy's house!" Shirley hollered to her husband.

"Tell him I never met him!"

"Foster never met him," Shirley told Burrows.

"I figured as much," Burrows said. "Like I said, I only want to talk to your husband about the house itself."

"He only wants to yak about the house!" Shirley yelled.

Burrows heard Foster Finch grumble, and then slide his chair away from the table.

"We're doin' a pitcher puzzle," Shirley told Burrows, as if to explain Foster's grumpiness.

"What is it?" Foster said, joining his wife in the frame of the front door. Foster was a good seven or eight inches shorter than Shirley, but just as thin and pale. Although he too had been sitting inside, he was wearing a blue Snoopy sweatshirt underneath a plaid flannel jacket. When Foster leaned across the front door, Burrows saw that Snoopy was surfing on the sweatshirt and shouting "Cowabunga!"

"How do you do?" Burrows said again, this time more firmly. "I'm J. P. Burrows. I'm a police detective out of Burlington. I'm here about a homicide," he then added for emphasis.

"What, do you think I killed that fool flatlander in my daddy's house or somethin'?" Finch asked, half smiling.

"No, that idea never crossed my mind. I'll have to give it some thought now, though."

"You do that."

"I will," Burrows said, trying to muffle the tension creeping into his voice. It wasn't so much the Finches' evident hostility that was disturbing to him, as it was the fact they represented in his eyes the worst in Vermonters. It was people such as the Finches who gave hill towns a bad rap. "In the meantime, let's talk about your parents' house. Did you have a noose hanging in your attic?"

"Come again?"

"Did you have a noose in your attic?"

"Like to hang people with?"

"Like that. Yes."

Finch grinned. "When my daddy sold the place, there mighta still been a loop hanging by the old chimney. It had been there all my life, and I don't recall him takin' it down. But to me, it was the kind of loop you stick a lamp in, not a person's neck."

"Why wouldn't your father have taken it down when he moved?"

"Why would he have bothered?"

"Did your father put it there?"

"Nope. It came with the house. Like a 'fridgerator," Finch said sarcastically.

"Do you know who put it there?"

"The railroaders who lived there 'fore us. The ones who came to Deering from the city—from Boston."

"The Barringtons?"

"Yup."

"Do you know about their daughter?"

"I know she died young."

"Do you know where she died?"

"Some people say the attic."

"What do you think?"

Finch leaned against his storm door and stared over Burrows' shoulder at Mount Ellen. "I don't think I care, Detective," he said tersely. "I don't think I care one little bit."

Burrows followed his eyes briefly, and then turned back to him. "Did anything strange ever happen to you while you lived in that house?"

"Like what?"

Burrows realized he was at a loss and regretted asking the question. He was conducting a homicide investigation, and he had now managed to set himself up to ask a curt Vermonter if a house were haunted. "Anything unusual, anything you couldn't explain," Burrows said sheepishly.

"Don't tell me you believe any of that Deering bullshit 'bout the house bein' haunted. It's all 'bout this much manure," Finch said spreading his arms as far apart as he could.

"No, I'm not one to put much stock in haunted houses."

"Then whacha need to know?"

Burrows rocked back on his heels, frustrated. "How come you never invited people into your house when you were growing up?"

"What kinda question is that?" Shirley asked angrily.

Finch put his hand on his wife's elbow, calming her. "It's okay," he told her, before turning to Burrows. "Far as I know, we had plenty a people in our house. At least I never recall bein' lonely. And even if we did keep to ourselves a bit, I don't believe that's a crime in this here state. Now you can tell me if I'm wrong 'bout that, but I don't believe I am."

"No need to get defensive. I was just asking," Burrows said.

"Well, are you all done 'just asking' now?"

Burrows shrugged. "Guess so."

"So we're all through?"

"For now."

"Then good-bye," Finch said, reaching around his wife and closing the front door. "Good-bye!"

"Were you and Solstice taking a nap on the floor?" Jennifer asked, wandering into the bedroom. The sun had almost set, bathing the Manhattan bedroom in shadows of blue and gray.

"No," Marcia said.

"You were in here so long. Daydreaming? Reading?" She sat on the bed, above her sister.

"Not exactly." Marcia stood up and went to the window, staring out at the rows of windows on the building across from her. What was it the little girl had said? Don't leave me?

"How are you feeling?"

She felt Solstice rubbing up against her ankles, wishing to be held. Scaredy-cat. Scaredy-cat. Who—what—would scare a little girl the way Thistle Peep had been frightened? Who would do that?

"Marcia? Are you all right?"

She glanced back at her sister and nodded. "Fine. I'm fine." It wasn't the little girl who was evil, she thought to herself, at least not in the beginning. It was something in that house. As she had feared all along, it was something in that house.

It was dusk by the time Burrows reached the interstate to return to Burlington. Before rolling on to the highway, however, he decided to pull into the gas station beside the interstate and use the pay phone to see if Joyce Renders was back in her apartment. She wasn't, and as a result Burrows left yet another message—his third that day—on the woman's answering machine. He wondered if she had landed a job with another architectural firm, and hoped she would be home later that evening. Because it was a Friday night, however, and because Joyce Renders wore R-rated bathing suits, he doubted it.

He was only one exit north of Montpelier, the exit for the long road to West Gardner and his parents' farm, and so he briefly considered driving by and saying hello. But he knew his family would already have sat down to dinner. He hoped they were playing cards that night at the town hall, military whist perhaps, but he imagined that his father had spent twelve hours that day getting the barn buttoned up for the winter and was probably exhausted.

Burrows hadn't believed Dunbar's story about Thistle Peep Barrington when Dunbar had first told him about the incident, but alone in a dark car on the highway, it seemed somewhat more plausible. Although he couldn't imagine a seven-year-old girl hanging herself, that didn't mean it couldn't happen. There was a lot of gray in Vermont, probably more gray than green—at least for the real Vermonters, at least for the farmers and loggers and carpenters who lived there all year. For most real Vermonters, the state colors were a good deal more drab than the neon parkas New Yorkers would wear on the ski slopes or the fluorescent purples and pinks that Canadians would wear on the golf courses. Burrows sometimes wondered if there was a more depressing place in the world than Vermont in January. It was hard to be cheerful when for weeks at a time the sky was a bleak and sunless gray sheet that smothered 'most every town in 'most every valley. On those rare January days when the sun actually did shine, it was usually so cold that people remained in hibernation, curled up by the wood stoves that prematurely wrinkled the women and dried out the eyes of the men.

The idea of a little girl killing herself seemed especially possible to Burrows in a hill town like Deering. Deering was the sort of Vermont village with an awful lot of history for so small a place. One myth every Vermont Cub Scout heard around camp fires was the story of a Deering farmer named Casey. Casey was so poor, the story went, that sometime not long after the Civil War he was finding it impossible to feed all the mouths in his household during the winter. He became so desperate one December that he tried to freeze solid his crippled parents and little daughter, with the intention of thawing them out after sugaring season—late March or early April. He buried the three people in huge tombs of snow behind his barn the day after Christmas, promising them that they'd keep just as well as a frozen ham hock or a side of beef. Of course they didn't.

And then there was the story of the nineteenth-century New York state liquor salesman, who brought whiskey over and over into Deering when not just the town but the whole state of Vermont was dry. The town council asked him to cease, and he refused; the state authorities asked him to stop, and he ignored them. Enraged, the town reverend and some of the deacons asked the salesman to attend a special meeting one morning before church. The fellow agreed. No one ever saw the salesman leave the parsonage; moreover, much of the congregation insisted that the communion wine was thicker than usual that day, and tasted very peculiar.

Burrows wondered all the way back to Burlington whether Thistle Peep's story was fact or just one more example of Vermont hill town fiction. He decided he would have to find out.

Chapter 19

Marcia Middleton stared down into her husband's face at the church Saturday morning. She hadn't seen him in almost a week, the longest separation they had ever endured in their marriage. She saw that the mortician had pulled the collar of his shirt up almost to his chin, covering the rope burns along his neck. She wondered if she were allowed to pull open his lips and examine for herself the cuts the detective had said were there, but decided she was afraid in any event to touch his skin. It would be too cold now to touch.

She felt the presence of Brian's parents behind her, as well as her own mother and father. How much did they know, she wondered, and how much did they believe? Did they believe there was even the slightest chance that she had murdered their son?

Her sister came up to her side and gently squeezed her elbow. "Would you like to sit down?" Jennifer asked. "People are beginning to arrive."

She turned around and saw the Crenshaws and Brian's aunt and uncle filing into the back of the church. She then turned back for one last, long look at her husband. He looked to Marcia neither contented nor at peace. He looked merely like a wax model of himself, like the life-size mannequins that stood in wax museums of the grotesque in London and Lisbon and Atlantic City. She wanted to ask him why it had happened: why he had let the house take him, seduce him, kill him. She wanted to ask him how he could have left her alone, how he could have left her a widow. There was no reason to give himself up to the house; there was no reason to feel guilty. Not anymore. She had forgiven him for Joyce. She had.

Marcia realized early into the service that she was playing two roles: widow and murderer. It was evident by the way Brian's mother was keeping her distance that the Vermont police had told the family they were having trouble "recreating the suicide." At one point she went to hug Mr. Middleton, and the man almost reflexively cringed, as if he were being approached by a leper. And Brian's aunt, an unstable woman who Marcia knew had never much liked her in the first place, had been glaring angrily at her throughout the service, the woman's face a mask of pure hate.

Marcia had not cried during the service, and she wondered if she should—if only for appearances. She knew that her sister would probably recommend it, and Jennifer was fast becoming her counselor on these matters.

But she was finished crying, at least for the moment. After over five days of weeping, crying, sobbing, and whining, the tear ducts were dry. There was just nothing left.

Marcia felt a chill. She felt it as she was filing out of the church between her parents, her mother holding her left elbow, her father her right. She felt the chill despite the fact the sun was quite warm for a November morning, and despite the heavy overcoat she was wearing. She felt the chill because Brian's aunt was waiting for her. The woman was standing alone at the base of the church steps, watching her descend the stairs.

For a brief second neither Marcia's parents nor Brian's aunt spoke, and Marcia felt as if the older woman were trying to read her mind. She thought the woman looked tired and aged and drawn. Her hair was disheveled, as if she were unable to cope with anything more complex than simply washing it, and the lines around her eyes looked especially deep and dark. She also looked deranged. Even through the softening web of her black veil, she looked demented.

Marcia opened her mouth to speak, but nothing came out. She had planned on telling Brian's aunt how sorry she was, but she recalled her sister's advice that morning: say nothing under any circumstances that could be construed as a confession or admission of guilt. The word "sorry," therefore, was out.

When Marcia was silent, Brian's aunt filled the vacuum. She filled it easily, abruptly, with one staccato burst of venom.

"I don't know if you're insane," she said quietly, "or cold-blooded. But it doesn't matter, because everyone knows you did it."

Marcia didn't respond, expecting that one of her parents would answer for her. She turned to them, confident that—as they had all week—they would shelter her, shield her, protect her. She was, after all, now their daughter the invalid.

Her father looked down at the cement steps for a brief moment, gathering his thoughts. He then looked up at the woman and said simply, "You don't mean what you're saying. Let us by."

Her mother appeared for a moment as if she wanted to add something to her husband's thought, looking back and forth between Marcia and Brian's aunt; but it wasn't a word that finally came from her mouth, it was a sob. It was a two-syllable cry of anguish, something that may have started as an articulate "Oh God," but finished as an instinctive, almost primordial gag. She then let go of her daughter's elbow and fell against her husband's chest, forcing Mr. Hampton also to release his daughter's elbow as he wrapped his arms around his wife.

"I know what you did," Brian's aunt hissed again at Marcia. "I know what you did."

Marcia stood alone and unsupported, watching her father comfort her mother. She grew angry, wondering where her sister had disappeared to when she needed her most. When she was unable to find Jennifer in the rows of curious and appalled faces surrounding her, she took her defense into her own hands and told Brian's aunt in a voice so furious that she barely recognized it as her own, "I didn't do anything: I didn't hurt Brian; I didn't kill Brian; I didn't drag his body up to the attic! I didn't put a noose around his neck! If I've done one insane thing in my life, it was letting him drag me to Vermont in the first place!"

Brian's aunt started to cry too, wailing something about her nephew. She might have fallen to her knees had her husband not run up behind her and caught her sagging body, literally ramming his hands under her armpits like a forklift and hoisting her body erect. "She's been under a lot of strain," he said softly to Marcia and her parents, before steering his wife away from them and toward the car that would take them to the cemetery. "A lot of strain," he mumbled again to no one in particular, "just a lot of strain."

CHAPTER 20

J. P. ran a few feet to his side Saturday afternoon and caught the football, tossed by his brother like a table lamp. Simon would master many things in his life, many things the doctors had never expected, but the spiral pass would probably never be one of them.

He gripped the end of the football and threw it back to Simon, hoping to indicate to his brother that a football should be thrown with one fluid motion. Simon's eyes followed the flight of the football from J. P.'s hand into the air, and then from the sky down to—and then off—his chest. Unconcerned, Simon shuffled over to the patch of hard ground by the fence post where the football had come to rest.

J. P. glanced at his watch and saw that it was a little after four o'clock. He and Simon had told their mother they would meet her at the town meeting house by four-thirty, to help out with the West Gardner Volunteer Fire Company's annual turkey dinner.

"Come on, Simon," he called. "We should bring it in."

Simon chugged over to J. P., his legs pounding the ground awkwardly as he tried to jog. When he reached J. P., he stopped to catch his breath, and J. P. put his arm around his brother's shoulders.

As they walked in from the field, J. P. said casually, "I've been wanting to ask you something for the last day or two."

"Yeah?"

"Yeah. I have indeed. Did I understand right when you told me the Middletons had a little girl?"

J. P. felt Simon's shoulders become tense. "I don't know."

"Well, what I thought you said to me was that there was a little girl at the Middletons' house, but she didn't join you and the rest of the gang for that big lunch last Friday—the last day you worked on the house."

"I guess."

"You guess?"

"I guess that's what I said."

Wrong answer, J. P. thought to himself. He realized as soon as he asked the question that the only correct answer—the answer he hoped his brother would offer—was that Simon had made the child up. He realized that he wanted his brother to tell him there was no little girl, that—for whatever the reason—he had lied.

"Who was this little girl?" J. P. asked.

Simon stopped walking and folded his arms across his chest. "I don't want to talk about this."

J. P. bounced the football between his hands. "How come?"

"I just can't."

"Do you think you'll get in trouble if you talk about it?"

"I don't know."

"But you think you might."

"Uh-huh."

"Is that because you made the little girl up?"

"I didn't make her up!" Simon answered, raising his voice.

"It's okay," J. P. reassured him quickly. "I was just making sure, that's all. You see, the Middletons don't have any children."

"I didn't make her up!"

"I believe you, Simon, I believe you. I promise I won't get mad if you talk about her."

"I know you won't," Simon said, calming down.

"In that case, will you tell me about her?"

"Will you tell anyone else?"

J. P. thought carefully about his answer. He had never lied to Simon, and he wasn't about to start now. "That all depends. But let me ask you a question: have you ever gotten in trouble for telling me anything? Anything at all?"

Simon didn't have to think about that question. "Nope."

"Okay then. We're brothers, right? And brothers don't have secrets, right?"

"Just don't tell her I told you! Okay?"

J. P. shrugged. "Okay." He patted his brother on the shoulder. "So tell me about this little girl. Do you think she was the Middletons' child?"

Simon slowly scratched the top of his head, rubbing the balding patch on his scalp. "No. She already lived there."

"In Deering?"

"In the house. She lived in the house before the new people. She lived there first."

Another wrong answer, J. P. thought to himself. "You mean she was a neighbor?" he asked, trying valiantly to find explanations for Simon's answers.

"No. She lived in the house!"

"How old was she?"

"I don't know. She was little."

"Six or seven, maybe?"

"Uh-huh."

"Did she tell you her name?"

Simon shook his head, indicating that she hadn't.

"And you didn't ask?"

"No. I guess I didn't think of it."

"When did you meet her? Was it as soon as you started working on the house?"

"No. She didn't visit me till after the new people moved in."

"So you only saw her a couple of times?"

"Yup. Three times, maybe."

"Where did you see her?"

"In the house."

"I mean, where in the house? In which rooms?"

"I think in a bedroom."

J. P. stared at his brother, almost struck dumb. No one would believe what Simon was telling him, not a soul in the world. It would be hard to believe coming from an adult who wasn't retarded; coming from Simon, the story didn't have a chance.

"Did anyone else see her?" J. P. asked, but with little hope. "Mr. Nash, maybe? Or Mrs. Middleton?"

"Nope. Just me."

"You're sure?"

"Yup. She said she was hiding. That's how come she didn't have lunch with us."

"Who was she hiding from?"

"I don't know."

"What else did she tell you? What did you two talk about?"

"I don't know. Just stuff."

"What kind of stuff? Did you talk about the house? Did you talk about games? You must have talked about something."

Simon reached into his pants pocket. "She gave me this. She said not to lose it." He placed into J. P.'s hand a small pewter skeleton key, adding, "She said it's good luck."

* * *

It wasn't merely a turkey dinner that Saturday night, it was—as Lorna Proctor's handmade posters boasted—a "turkey dinner with all the trimmings." Five dollars (two-fifty if you were under ten), and you got turkey and ham and a vegetable medley, small finger rolls and mashed potatoes, and for dessert a choice of deep-dish pies. Apple pies and pumpkin pies and even a chocolate pie with coconut slivers from a recipe Rhonda Thrip had found in the *Ladies Home Journal.* It was an all-you-could-eat affair.

The dinner was an annual event, held in the town meeting house. It was sponsored by the ladies' auxiliary of the volunteer fire company, of which Mrs. Burrows was a key member even though Mr. Burrows had retired from the company two years earlier and was now only an honorary chief. All the proceeds from the dinner this year were going toward the Official West Gardner Volunteer Fire Company "Prime the Pumper" Fund.

J. P. had driven down from Burlington earlier that afternoon, to help his brother Simon take tickets at the door. It had become something of a tradition for J. P. and Simon to stand at the front door of the meeting house, taking people's tickets or money, and then seating them. People in West Gardner just expected to see the two Burrows boys—though one was now thirty-two years old and the other twenty-nine—standing together at the entrance to the meeting house, J. P. suggesting gently to Simon where some people might like to sit, Simon instinctively taking the arms of the older ladies and guiding them to their tables, both men getting slightly windblown from standing so long just inside the building's entrance.

The dinner was supposed to begin at five-thirty, but by the time J. P. and Simon arrived—a little before five—the first small groups of people were lining up on the meeting house steps. Their mother handed them the gray metal cash box, explaining to J. P., "There's about a hundred dollars in change inside, including about ten dollars in quarters. You may need that for the children under eight."

"Ten," Simon corrected her. "Children under ten."

J. P. smiled at his brother. "Mom's just trying to make an extra buck or two, Simon. She knows the age break."

"Whatever. There's also a list of names on the back of my grocery list. Those are people who should be admitted for free tonight, because other people have already paid for their tickets."

"Do they know that?" J. P. asked.

"Some do, some don't."

"Oh good, nice and simple."

His mother ignored him. "You should also know that the Messiers —all six of them—Mr. and Mrs. Douglas, and Mrs. Foreman will be arriving at the same time, and they all want to sit together. So make sure you keep a table of nine empty until they arrive."

"You got it," J. P. said, holding one thumb up. "Me and Simon are up to the task."

The worst crunch came at about quarter to six. All ninety-two seats in the meeting house were taken, a dozen people were waiting just outside the kitchen to be seated, and people were still arriving.

"I hope there's enough food," Simon said to J. P., shaking his head.

"Me too."

"Mom said she would save us a piece of the chocolate pie."

J. P. glanced quickly at the dessert table, and was pretty sure that the white porcelain pie tin, the one that now was empty, was the one that fifteen minutes earlier had held the chocolate pie. "I hope so," J. P. said, counting out the Monroes' change. "There you go, Mr. Monroe, a five dollar bill, five ones, and my partner here, Simon, will seat you in about five or ten minutes."

"Ten," Simon said, holding up all the fingers on both his hands, and then, after surveying the room, added, "Fifteen."

Everyone looked so old this year. Not just a few of his neighbors, not just the older folks who seemed to deteriorate with increasing speed every year, but everyone. There were wrinkles all around Rhonda Thrip's eyes, deep black ones that looked almost as if they had been drawn on with a felt-tip marker, and Luther Grant needed Simon's arm to steady him as he walked ever so slowly across the meeting house floor. J. P. wished he saw most of these people more than once a year; it would make some things easier. Seeing them every day or every week or every month, their gradual declines and decay would be less noticeable. Less affecting.

He watched his father, washing dishes with some of the active volunteer firemen in the kitchen, and noticed a large wet spot on the back of his shoulder. Evidently, he had been rubbing his bursitis between plates. He glanced at his mother, racing between the tables with other women in the auxiliary, depositing bowls of vegetables, replacing platters of turkey, resetting the tables after groups finished and left. She looked so tired this year, not a little pale, and not particularly happy. Most years she seemed to enjoy this lunacy.

"Should I seat the Johnsons?" Simon asked, motioning toward Jane and Homer Johnson. "I think the Larches are all done."

J. P. looked over at the Larches and nodded, wondering when Cynthia Larch, a once-dignified old lady from Boston who with her husband had retired to West Gardner, had started to wear macaroni jewelry. "Yup, that's a good idea."

In some ways, Simon was almost fortunate. Though J. P. knew he would never understand exactly how Simon's mind worked or what sorts of things his brother thought about when he was alone, J. P. was fairly confident that Simon never thought about Cynthia Larch's macaroni jewelry. He never thought about his father's bursitis, and he never thought about his mother slowing down. He could appreciate loss and he could experience sadness and he could fear death, but he didn't, J. P. believed, agonize on a daily basis over Rhonda Thrip's wrinkles, and what those wrinkles really meant.

And he didn't panic when a dead little girl said hello to him in the bedroom of a century-old house.

Yup, in a lot of ways Simon was almost fortunate.

The dinner was over by eight o'clock, and J. P. wandered back into the meeting house's kitchen to help his father and Norm Grismon wash the tremendous roasting pans that stunk of hardening turkey fat.

"We made close to fifteen hundred dollars, your mother tells me," Mr. Burrows said to his son.

"Well, that was the total I counted in the cash box," J. P. answered, "not including the one hundred dollars we started with for change. You must have made something less than that, depending on your expenses this year."

"Ah, our expenses are nothing. You know the supermarket donates most of the food, 'cept for the desserts, and the women make those."

"You must have paid for something."

His father grinned. "We paid for nothing."

Outside the kitchen there was the crash of breaking plates and falling silverware. Everyone who remained in the meeting house, perhaps a dozen men and women clearing and cleaning, turned at once.

"Uh-oh," Simon said softly, nervously, bunching up his shoulders. Below him on the hardwood meeting house floor were the shards and pieces of the dirty dishes he had been carrying.

His mother put down the platter she was holding and went quickly to her son, but it was too late. He had already sat down on the floor by the piles of broken place settings and begun to sob.

Chapter 21

"You're being foolish," Jennifer told her sister. "This is just plain foolish!"

Marcia snapped the suitcase shut Sunday morning and glanced again at her watch. It wasn't quite eight-thirty. She hoped to be on the road by nine o'clock, so she would be in Deering before dark. "Everything I've done this year has been pretty foolish," Marcia said evenly. "I see no reason to stop now."

"I just don't understand why you have to go to Vermont! You keep telling me that the house is haunted and that it scares you, and now you're going back to it. I just don't see why!"

"I'm not going to go back to the house, at least not at night. I told you, I'm staying with neighbors. Or people who would have been my neighbors—a very nice couple named Josh and Sarabeth Nash. I called them and they said they were happy to have me. They understand completely. So you don't have to worry. I have no intention of going anywhere near that house except in broad daylight."

"It just seems foolish to go back now!"

"You know who you sound like?"

Jennifer shook her head no.

"You sound like Grandma. 'This is foolish. You're being foolish.' What's next, 'No good comes from fooling'?"

"This isn't funny," Jennifer insisted. "Don't you understand, the police think you killed Brian! They might not even let you into the house."

"They said they would. They told me on the phone last night that they had finished examining the house, and 'unsealed' it. Or whatever they call it. But they assured me I can come and go in the house as I please."

"I just don't understand why you have to go back now! Can't this wait a few more days?"

"Of course it could. But I don't want it to."

"Why won't you at least talk to Dr. Michaels?"

"I did talk to him. I called him. I spoke to him for about twenty minutes."

"And?"

"And I'm seeing him as soon as I come back."

"Why wait?"

"Because I don't feel like seeing him right now. I'm not ready."

"What about the other night?"

"You mean my sleepwalking?"

Jennifer nodded, unconsciously rubbing her neck.

Marcia sighed and sat down on her bed. She reached down to the floor and picked up Solstice, putting the cat in her lap. Solstice purred and pushed his head into the palm of her hand. "I was having a bad dream. Given everything I've been through lately, that shouldn't surprise you."

"It surprised you."

It had, that was true. Marcia glanced briefly at the wallpaper, and then glanced away.

"I want to go with you," her sister then said. "If you insist on going, I'll go with you."

"You can't, Jennifer, you know that. You just took an entire week off from work for me. You can't take another; they won't let you."

"Then I'll take a leave of absence."

"I don't think investment banks give twenty-two-year-old research assistants leaves of absence."

"Then I'll get another job!"

Marcia reached up and took Jennifer's hand, pulling her down onto the bed beside her. She had already told her sister that she was going to Vermont to pack up her house and put it on the market, certainly two critical reasons for her trip. But there were other reasons, reasons she knew she could not adequately explain to Jennifer. Don't leave me, the child had begged, don't leave me. Whether the child was begging her, Marcia Middleton, to return or whether it was a plea made eighty years earlier to a parent or neighbor or cousin, Marcia didn't know. Either way, she had to see Deering again. It was a quest of sorts, perhaps even an obsession, but she had to learn—if she possibly could—what would drive a little girl to hang herself in that cold and silent attic.

And there was no possible way to explain any of this to Jennifer—that is, if she wanted to return to Vermont alone. Mentioning once more to Jennifer her interest in the dead girl was the surest way to compel her sister to join her.

"You can't revolve your life around me, sweetheart," Marcia reminded Jennifer. "You just can't. I appreciate what you want to do for me, but I won't let you. I'm not an invalid, not anymore."

"It just seems to me it's too soon for you to go back to that town."

Marcia scratched Solstice between his ears. "Maybe. But I'll only be there for a few days. I'll be back here by Friday or Saturday, I promise."

"Is that why you're not taking Solstice and Chloe?"

Marcia shook her head. "How can I take the cats? I'm a guest in the house of some people I barely know."

"It's not because you're afraid for them?"

"No, it's not. If I'm afraid for anyone, I'm afraid for me."

"Then why go? Why go?"

"Because I want to get my life in order!" Marcia told her sister, raising her voice. Startled, Solstice jumped from her lap. "Vermont was a digression, and I want it straightened out and behind me. I want it behind me now! I want every loose end up there cleaned up, so I can start over and never think about that place again!"

"You can't do that over the phone?"

"How? Can I pack up the house over the phone? Can I go through my things up there over the phone? Can I put the house up for sale over the phone? Use your head, Jenny. For crying out loud, use your head!"

"If you have to go, then let me go with you!"

"Stop it! Just stop it, will you!" Marcia snapped at her sister. "I'm going, I'm going alone, and I won't discuss this anymore!" When she stopped speaking, she realized that both she and her sister were quivering. She couldn't remember the last time they had fought.

The key felt cold in Burrows' hand, regardless of how long he held it. He leaned back in his desk chair in the detectives' office late Sunday morning and studied it, trying to imagine which lock in Marcia Middleton's house it would open. Judging by the key's size, perhaps an inch and a half in length, it might open anything from a bedroom door to a blanket chest.

Away from West Gardner, away from his brother, it seemed less likely to Burrows that a spectral little girl had handed Simon the key. His brother may have found the key in the Middleton house himself, but no one—no thing—had given him the key. It just wasn't possible. Burrows couldn't imagine why his brother would make the story up, but he couldn't accept the story as truth either.

It just wasn't possible.

Nevertheless, he found himself fiddling with the key while he was on the telephone, unable to put it away. It was almost like holding an ice cube, and it became a game to Burrows to see how long he could keep the key in his hand before the cold forced him to put it down.

Meanwhile, he continued to look for Joyce Renders. By noon, he had called twenty-six of the thirty-one Renders listed in the New York City, Westchester, Fairfield, and upper New Jersey phone books. After leaving messages on Joyce Renders' answering machine since Friday morning, he had decided it was time to try reaching her through her family.

There had been no answer at eleven of the twenty-six numbers, two had been disconnected, and the other thirteen were no relation to the Joyce Renders who lived on Columbus Avenue. The twenty-seventh call was the charm. An older woman answered the phone listed under the name T. Jefferson Renders of Ridgewood, New Jersey. She became flustered when Burrows told her he was a cop from Vermont.

"Joyce is my daughter," she said to Burrows. "Is something the matter?"

"Probably not, Mrs. Renders. As far as I know, your daughter is fine. But I need to talk to her, and I was wondering if you knew where she was working these days."

"May I ask why you're looking for her?" Mrs. Renders asked.

"Sure you can," Burrows said, pushing the pewter key across the phone book with the eraser at the end of his pencil. "A man was murdered last week in a little Vermont town called Deering, and I was hoping your daughter could tell me a little about him."

"Joyce doesn't know anybody in Deertown. I don't think she's ever even been to Vermont."

"This gentleman lived for a couple of years on Columbus Avenue in the same building as Joyce. He moved to Vermont very recently."

"Oh."

"I know Joyce left Powell and Time. Where is she now?"

"She doesn't have a new job yet. She's still looking for the right opportunity."

"Do you know why she left Powell and Time?"

"She said she was bored there. She was tired of designing executive washrooms. She wanted more challenging assignments."

He picked up the key with his free hand, pressing it flat between his thumb and forefinger. "Is she still in New York City?"

"Yes. But she's gone away now for a vacation with a girlfriend, Louise Curry. She and Louise travel together a lot."

"Where did they go?"

Mrs. Renders clicked her tongue against her teeth. "Nowhere specifically. They rented a car and said they were just going to drive around, see New England."

"New England? Like Vermont?"

"No, she said Boston. Portland. Maybe—maybe—up into New Hampshire."

"I see." He dropped the key back onto the phone book. "When did she leave on this trip?"

"A week ago Friday. Nine days ago."

"Have you heard from her?"

"Yes. Jeff—Jeff's her father—Jeff and I have gotten two or three postcards from her. One from Boston, one from Kennebunkport, one from Boothbay."

"Do you know where she is right now?"

"Right this second? Of course not. Joyce is a big girl; I don't watch her every move."

"When is she due back?"

"Tuesday or Wednesday. She plans to resume her job search later this week."

Burrows thanked Mrs. Renders and hung up the phone, scribbling down the name Louise Curry, and the names of the towns from where Joyce had sent postcards. He then reached into the manila file folder with the photograph of Joyce Renders on the beach in it, and looked again at the image of the woman's face. It was a crisp, clear picture, certainly good enough to show people in and around Deering to see if they had ever seen the woman before.

He then grabbed the small key Simon had given him and decided to take a drive to Deering. He had no idea what kind of door the key would open, but he had a whole afternoon to find out.

* * *

Houses breathe in Vermont. They're built to breathe, to give when the harsh cold insists upon it, contracting and expanding with occasional cries and rumbles.

The Middleton house breathed differently, Burrows thought, standing on the bottom step of the stairway in the front hall; it breathed in a way he could not quite put his finger on. It breathed with a series of small gasps—gasps that he felt, rather than heard. When he was perfectly still, he could feel tiny air currents puff all around him.

He was glad it was sunny outside.

Holding the key in his gloved fist, he wandered up to the second floor. He was fairly confident that the key would be too small for the locks on the bedroom doors, since it had been too small for all of the doors on the first floor. For one brief moment he had thought the key might fit a pantry off the dining room, but the key was a hair too small for that particular lock.

He tried the door to Marcia Middleton's bedroom first, discovering immediately that this lock also demanded a key substantially larger than the one in his hand. He glanced across the hall at what he assumed would have become one of the guest bedrooms, noting that its door was identical to the door before him.

He felt a draft rise up the stairs and graze past him, and then, almost immediately behind it, a second, small gust. The house didn't really breathe, Burrows decided, it rasped. It choked, as if it were constantly struggling for air.

He entered the main bedroom, scanning the room for doors and locks. There were two closets, but neither door had a lock. The upstairs windows, like the ones on the first floor, were sealed without locks and keys. And the dresser and the armoire, brought to Vermont he believed by the Middletons, didn't have locks either.

He wondered if it were possible that the key opened some secret passageway. Scratch away the wallpaper, perhaps, and there would be a tunnel connecting two bedrooms, or a bedroom and the living room. It was possible, he decided, but it wasn't very likely. Not in a house like this, not in a house like this in northern Vermont.

It suddenly seemed rather silly of him to have thought for one moment that he might actually have been able to find the lock that matched this key. No doubt, the key belonged merely to an antique blanket chest, long sold, or a century-old desk that had disappeared years ago.

Above him the house sighed in the attic, and Burrows jumped just the slightest bit. It was almost as if the house were watching him. It was almost as if the house were seeing through him.

He closed the bedroom door and started toward the attic, gripping the key so tightly that he could feel its chill through the leather of his glove.

At the door to the attic he stopped, prepared for how difficult the warped door would be to open. He planted a foot against its frame and reached for the knob, planning to turn the knob and yank the door open with one fluid motion. Before he could even begin the process, however, he could feel something different about the knob, a pure white globe with a trace of ivy molded into its edge.

The knob wouldn't turn; it wouldn't budge at all. It wouldn't move, not to the right nor the left.

He backed away to view the entire doorjamb mechanism, noting that this particular door did not have a lock. Without pulling the door toward him, he tried simply to turn the knob, trying to turn it first clockwise, then counterclockwise. He tried jiggling it, jerking the knob up and down. Again, the knob behaved as if it were cemented in one place.

He wondered if he could break the door down, and—then—whether he should. Technically, he had no legal right to be in Marcia Middleton's house right now. Destroying the door would certainly not endear himself to the police chief or the state attorney.

Still, this was odd. The doorknob had worked fine just the other day, first on Wednesday and then again on Thursday. Perhaps he could kick the door hard enough to jar the knob loose, yet still keep the door on its hinges. It was worth a try. He put the key in his pocket so he wouldn't lose it and took a step back.

As he was about to step up toward the door, however, he felt the house lurch, and he stopped. The house—the attic, if he was going to be literal—had exhaled a gust of frigid air underneath the door, freezing instantly the cuffs of his blue jeans.

It was somewhere just south of the Vermont border, after she had been driving a good four hours, that Marcia became fixated by her hands. At first she was just glancing at them, letting her eyes drop off the road for only a split second at a time. Soon, however, the looks grew longer, and she was actually staring at her hands. She became oblivious of the farmhouses and rest stops she passed periodically along the way, and was virtually unconcerned with the highway. At one point she veered into the passing lane, almost sending a station wagon on her left off the road.

She had lovely hands, she decided. Long, lovely, sensual hands—especially her fingers. Her fingernails, though not long, were clean and well-manicured, and there was something very sexy about the immaculate sickle moons at their tips.

She noticed that if she squinted, she could make the steering wheel look like a snake. A beige snake. Especially if she gripped the steering wheel in her fingers, rather than in the palms of her hands. If she had not been alone in the car, she would have commented to whomever was with her on how overtly phallic her daydream was; even alone, however, she laughed out loud.

She wondered if she would ever have noticed how sexy her hands were if not for her sister. If not for her sister's neck. After all, the night she had seen them around her sister's neck was the first time she had ever really looked at her hands and noticed how beautiful they were.

She wished she knew what her sister truly thought about the incident and what her parents thought: were they still as sure as she was that she hadn't killed Brian? Or had her sleepwalking planted in their minds just the shadow of a doubt that maybe—just maybe—she had murdered her husband?

She knew she didn't believe it. She couldn't believe it. How could she go on living if she thought there was even the slightest chance that she had murdered Brian? What was the expression Dr. Michaels had used? A fugue state? People, supposedly, could do things in a fugue state and not recall them. Not recall even a single detail. A fugue state, he had said, was similar to a trance, a very deep trance.

No, she couldn't have murdered Brian, not even in the deepest trance. Perhaps she was falling out of love with him, perhaps the scars left by his affair were deeper than she had ever realized. But she still couldn't have killed him. And not just because he was her husband—she didn't believe she was capable of killing anyone. She simply couldn't believe such a thing, she couldn't. Because if she had murdered her husband—if she had murdered anyone—how could she herself go on living?

The answer was, she couldn't. She wouldn't.

3.

Chapter 22

Burrows was not exactly nervous—that was too strong a word for what he was feeling—but he was uncomfortable. He had known since Saturday night when he had heard that Marcia Middleton had phoned the station that he would eventually see a red Saab parked somewhere in Deering. But he had not expected to see the car so soon, and certainly not in Josh Nash's driveway. It was only Monday morning. The woman had not yet been gone a week.

He considered pulling into the Nashes' driveway and talking to her that very moment, but he decided he was unprepared—not from an investigative perspective, from an emotional one. He wasn't sure he was ready to stand in the Nashes' doorway or sit at their kitchen table and ask Marcia Middleton questions about her husband's murder. He knew he would find her eyes too pretty, her smile too soft.

But he was also unsure he was ready to tell her—to tell anyone—that only the day before the doorknob of her attic had refused to budge, as if it had been cemented in place, or that he had at that very moment a small pewter key in his pocket, a key that his brother insisted was given to him by a mysterious child who lived in the house.

So instead of stopping in at the Nashes', he drove another quarter mile to the Deering town clerk's office as he had planned. He figured he could visit with Marcia later that morning, when he had finished investigating the history of the house. Nine o'clock on a Monday morning was probably too early for Marcia Middleton anyway. Especially these days.

The history of Deering, Vermont—births and deaths and budgets and tax rolls—had been entrusted to Nathaniel Nester for close to sixty years now. So far, three generations of Deering citizens had come to Nate for their hunting licenses and dump permits, and the hope was that three more generations would follow. Nate was past eighty, but how far past was anybody's guess. Some people said town clerk was the only job Nate had ever held, but others were positive he had gone to Boston for a short time and done something with the theater. Of course no one had any idea what that something was, except Nate himself, and he wasn't about to tell anyone.

In the two-hundred-plus-year history of Deering, the building that housed the town records had at various times served also as the town hall, the town clerk's home, and even for a short while as the parsonage. It was a two-story clapboard structure that had been renovated often, and—at least for the sixty years Nate had run the place—was always kept an immaculate, pristine white. In the summer and fall, Nate would carry a pair of rocking chairs out on to the front porch, and sit and rock with whoever felt like dropping by.

Burrows was prepared for a man like Nate as soon as he wandered into the town clerk's office. Nester was a short but robust fellow wearing a gray work shirt and an orange hunting cap with the flaps pulled down over his ears. Like Burrows' own grandfather, Nester evidently thought it made more sense to wear his hat indoors—at least while the wood stove was firing up—than it did to simply turn up the dial on the thermostat.

Burrows was not prepared, however, for Nester's comment after he showed the clerk his badge. "If you're goin' to do any shootin'," he said, "I suggest you take it outside."

Burrows dropped his badge back into his windbreaker pocket. "Why would I do any shooting?"

"I suppose you're here to arrest the lady upstairs."

Burrows leaned across Nester's desk. "What lady?" he asked quietly. "I didn't see any other cars in the parking lot when I pulled in."

Nester folded his hands across his desk blotter and looked up at Burrows with an ironic smile. "I guess that's 'cause she walked—she bein' the new gal in town. The one whose husband passed on."

Burrows felt just the slightest flicker of panic cross his stomach. "Ms. Middleton?" he asked anxiously.

Nester nodded. "Yup."

"What's she doing here?"

"Says she came here to learn 'bout her house. Its history. Was camped out on the porch when I got here 'bout quarter to nine."

"And she's upstairs right now going through the records?"

"Yup."

Burrows took a deep breath, trying to compose himself, and stood up straight. He put his hands in his jacket pockets. "Well, could I talk you into showing me exactly where those records are? And how to use them?"

"You're not goin' to arrest her?"

"Nope. I'm not going to arrest her."

"Oh. If you'd gotten here ten minutes ago, you know, I coulda shown you and the lady how to use the records at the same time."

"Sorry."

"No need to apologize." Nester stood up slowly, gripping the armrests of his chair for balance, and waved his arm toward the stairs over Burrows' shoulder. As he wandered past the wood stove, he bent over to close the flue. "The town insisted we get ourselves one of those catalytic combusters last summer. Supposed to make wood burn longer. But at one hundred and seventy-seven dollars and sixty-five cents, seems to me the wood didn't have to burn quite so long."

Burrows wondered whether he should proceed to investigate the history of the house as he had intended, sharing the tax records and title documents with Marcia, or whether he should ask her his questions right away. He decided he would wing it, do whatever came naturally when he met the woman face-to-face.

"You from 'round here?" Nester asked, climbing slowly the thin stairway.

"West Gardner. Other side of the mountain and up the road a bit."

"Pretty country, West Gardner. I been there once."

They reached the top of the stairs, and Burrows could see the small room in which the Deering historical records were kept. And then over the bill of Nester's cap he saw Marcia Middleton, hunched over a card table with two thick brown and gold ledgers on either side of her. When she heard their footsteps and looked up and Burrows could see her face, the small eddy of hesitation he had experienced downstairs returned as a tremendous wave of anxiety. He shuddered when he saw her. Yes, the woman looked tired and there were small, fine circles under her winter blue eyes, but she was beautiful, every bit as beautiful as the picture that was still sitting on his desk in his office.

He asked himself how he could possibly have thought this woman was a murderer. Murderers, after all, were supposed to be ugly. They were unshaven, smarmy, scary—they looked dangerous. But this woman? This lady? She was too lovely to be a murderer, too gentle to plan—much less, implement—her husband's execution. And yet she was his principal suspect.

She was wearing a black crew neck sweater over a white turtleneck, and Burrows noticed that the sweater's sleeves extended well past her wrists. Her hair—the hair that red didn't begin to describe—was pulled back, with a tortoiseshell barrette keeping it off her shoulders. He was struck by how long and slender her arms appeared, and was reminded of Henry Tillier's observation about Brian Middleton's body. Tillier had said that if Middleton had been murdered, his killer would had to have been fairly strong: not because it would have taken such strength to smother him, but because whoever had smothered him had in all likelihood then carried him upstairs into the attic. And "carried" was the key word, Tillier had explained. Given the fact there were almost no bruises or scrapes on the body, he did not believe it was likely that Middleton's killer had dragged the corpse up into the attic, letting it bounce and smack into each step. The corpse had been carried. Lifted, hoisted, carted maybe—but almost definitely not dragged.

"You got yourself some company," Nester said to Marcia, reaching behind the door for a second gray folding chair.

Marcia smiled politely. Burrows realized that she had no idea who he was.

"What we have here," Nester continued, "are ledgers. Lots of 'em. The brown ones—like the ones Marcia here is goin' through—are what I call the 'come and gone' books. In 'em is everyone who's ever been born or died in this here town. The red ones—those over there—are the ledgers listing property titles. I call those books 'dates 'n' deeds.' "

Burrows nodded, although Nester wasn't looking at him. Marcia had resumed flipping through the pages in one of Nester's "come and gone" ledgers.

"Now I don't imagine you two know each other," Nester said, turning back toward Burrows. "Marcia, this fellow here is a police officer—what did you say your name was?"

"J. P. Burrows."

Nester raised an eyebrow. "J. P., huh? That your idea or your daddy's?"

"My daddy's."

"Uh-huh. Well, Marcia meet J. P. J. P. meet Marcia Middleton."

Burrows watched Marcia's mouth open just the slightest bit when he was introduced as a police officer. He wasn't sure if she looked betrayed by the news or just hurt. "We've spoken on the phone," she murmured after a moment, so softly Burrows initially hadn't understood what she had said.

"That's right, we have," he agreed, trying to smile. He had almost decided that she looked hurt, and only hurt, when abruptly her eyes widened and she stood up to face him, extending to him her hand.

"Are you here to arrest me?" she asked, her voice almost ironically light.

"No. I hadn't planned on it," Burrows told her, holding her hand a moment longer than he should have. He liked the fact that she had soft skin but a firm grip. "I'm just here to do a little research."

"So you two know each other," Nester mumbled. "Guess with all that's been goin' on in this town lately, I shoulda figured that."

"What are you researching?" Marcia asked.

He didn't smell perfume, at least he didn't think it was perfume. It wasn't that pronounced or affected. But he thought he smelled lilac, as if she had bathed in lilac soap. He answered, "Your house."

"Really?"

"Yup."

"Me too." She folded her arms across her chest, and Burrows was struck by her wedding ring. It was a plain gold band. For some reason—perhaps because she came from the city—he had expected something more elaborate.

Nester reached across the table for an unopened "come and gone" ledger. "You'll see that the 'come and gone' books work chronologically. Some books have two years, some have three or four. Depends on how many people got themselves hitched in a year, and how many got themselves a family," he said to Burrows. " 'Dates 'n' deeds' is a little trickier. Some of it is listed by lot—the newer volumes—and some of it is alphabetized by the name on the deed."

Nester paused, staring back at the "come and gone" ledger, and then scratched the back of his neck. "Normally we got old newspaper clippings taped or patched into the ledger by year," he continued, sounding irritated. "Looks to me like someone managed to lose a lot of 'em from the early part of the century."

"May I ask why you're interested in my house, Officer?" Marcia asked Burrows, her tone more curious than defensive.

"Detective. I'm a detective."

"I'm sorry," she said, sounding very sincere to Burrows. "I didn't mean anything by that."

"There's nothing wrong with being an officer. I wasn't offended. I was just setting the record straight." He tried to smile, but he was sure the smile looked forced to her. He felt pretentious.

Nester tossed the ledger he was holding back onto the center of the table, annoyed. Burrows figured he probably thought they hadn't heard a word he had said. "I'll be downstairs if you got any questions," Nester mumbled in Burrows' general direction, and then turned and left.

"So why are you interested in my house?" Marcia asked again. "Are you allowed to tell me?"

"I probably shouldn't."

"Because I'm a suspect?"

"Partly. Partly because it's just plain stupid."

Marcia nodded and sat down.

"What about you? Would you tell me why you're researching your house?" Burrows inquired.

She rested her chin on her hand, and for one brief second looked straight into his eyes. Then she turned her gaze toward the window. "I imagine I'm here for the same reason you are," she said, her voice thin. "I want to know who murdered my husband."

It was Marcia who found the listings, both of them, but it was J. P. Burrows who was able to decipher the penmanship of one of Nester's early predecessors. The 1903 record stated that on November 12, to Everett and Belle Barrington was born a daughter, christened on the Sunday before Thanksgiving by the Reverend Thomas Whitcomb as Adelaide Thistle Barrington.

Furthermore, in the 1910 ledger, among the three pages listed as "The Deceased," was a line for Thistle Peep Barrington. The child had died in October. And while the cause of death was recorded as "injuries to the neck sustained in a home accident," how the accident occurred was not explained.

"Do you have coffee with everyone you suspect of murder?" Marcia asked, pouring the hot water for the instant coffee into the two mugs. She noticed he was watching her again as she walked across her kitchen, and wondered if he had taken his eyes off her for more than fifteen seconds that entire morning.

"Not everyone. But I have in the past."

His look did not seem particularly lecherous to Marcia, but neither did it appear driven solely by investigative curiosity. It was a look that almost reminded her of the kind of lovesick gaze she had once given her older boyfriends when she was in college. "What do you take in your coffee?" she asked him.

"A little milk is all."

Marcia glanced quickly at the refrigerator behind her, but knew that any milk in it was over a week old. "Wrong answer. I don't have any."

"Black will do," Burrows said, sipping the coffee. "It's a real pretty house you got yourself here," he then added.

"I thought so. Once. If you'd like, when you finish your coffee I can give you the nickel tour. One of the bedrooms upstairs has a view of Mount Stillman that will take your breath away."

"Yup, the bedroom with the wallpaper with the gray stripes. It's a wonderful view, all right."

Marcia sighed. "Ah, yes. I'd forgotten. You've been here before, haven't you?"

"Yes, ma'am."

She felt exposed, naked almost, and wondered just how thoroughly he had gone through the house. Only a moment before she had thought that she was in command, that his puppy dog gaze had given her some advantage over him. She realized now that she was mistaken. For all she knew, the man had gone through the cedar chest and read the diary she had kept when she was ten years old; he had examined her folders of pictures from *Country Living* magazine and her scribbled pages of decorating ideas; he had opened her dresser drawers and handled her lingerie. Suddenly she looked at his hands and compared them to her own: God but they were dark by comparison.

"I guess you know me fairly well," she said, gazing down at the blue swirls on the coffee mug at the end of her fingers.

"Fact is, I don't," Burrows said, grinning. "That's why I'm here."

"What exactly do you know about me?" she asked, aware that her question had betrayed a hint of desperation.

"I know that you and your husband moved here from New York City. I know he had just started working at IBM just outside of Burlington and you were going to work for an advertising agency in

Middlebury. I know he died a week ago last night and you found the body."

He knew more, Marcia could tell. Lots more. He had spoken slowly, calculatingly. He was keeping his knowledge to himself.

"That's all?" she asked.

"I know—as you told me—he was involved with a woman named Joyce Renders."

"And?"

"And that's all I know about Joyce Renders," he said quickly. He then added lightly, "But I do know you have two cats, plus one you seem to have inherited in your barn."

"The tiger stripe."

"Right, the tiger stripe. And I know you and your husband had about eleven pairs of sneakers."

She tried to smile back at him. "How many are mine, and how many were his?"

"You want an honest answer?"

She nodded.

"In what Nate Nester would probably refer to as the 'sneaker file' —that potato box at the top of the stairs—there were two pairs of sneakers that I'd guess were yours: the pink Reeboks and the white Keds. The other pairs belonged to your husband. And then, of course, you own at least one more pair of sneakers, the Nike running shoes you're wearing this very minute."

"You know a lot about me."

"I know a lot about your sneakers. I know hardly anything about you."

Marcia tried to read his smile, and decided it was forced. He was forcing a smile, probably to put her at ease, to relax her. But no, there was something more behind it. Was it guilt? Was he actually feeling guilty because he was keeping things from her? For a moment their eyes met, and she noticed for the first time the color of his eyes. They were blue, but not blue like hers: there was a tinge of green to them that she had seen before in the eyes of women but never in men. She had never before met a man with eyes she would describe as blue green.

"What do you want to know?" she asked, her voice trembling just the tiniest bit.

"I want to know what happened Sunday night."

"I told the trooper everything I know."

"I'd like you to tell me."

"I'm not sure I'm ready."

"I can wait." Burrows leaned across the kitchen table, folding his hands together and entwining his fingers. He looked at her with more intensity than she had seen in the face of anyone else she had met in Vermont. "I can wait," he said again.

This is wrong, Burrows thought to himself, this is all wrong. Marcia Middleton was showing him her bedroom, retracing for him her steps eight nights earlier, and he was aroused. Looking at the bed in which Marcia Middleton slept—wearing any one of the Lanz nightgowns he had found in her bottom dresser drawer—excited him. He envisioned her sleeping stretched out on her side, a strand of that lovely red mane falling leisurely over her eyes. He took a sip of the instant coffee he had carried with him from the kitchen, hoping its bitterness would calm him.

"I usually sleep on the side of the bed farthest from the door," she said evenly, "so when I discovered that Brian wasn't beside me, I had to reach all the way across the bed for the lamp."

He wished he hadn't suggested that she literally walk him through what had happened that Sunday night and what she had done. Wasn't it cruel of him to put a woman through this exercise only a week after her husband had died? Couldn't he have learned as much merely by listening to her talk in the kitchen?

He tried to convince himself that the reason he was doing this was to see if her story deviated now in any way from what she had told Thomas a week earlier: making her act out the steps instead of simply repeating a story by rote would be more likely to expose an inconsistency. But he knew that this wasn't the only reason: he enjoyed standing with Marcia Middleton in the woman's bedroom.

"I was very surprised when I discovered he wasn't there. Brian was a light sleeper most of the time, but I was still surprised. I just felt something was wrong."

"Really?"

"Really. Something had happened. I was sure of it."

The longer Marcia spoke, the more her voice became a monotone. It had no inflection, emphasized nothing. It sounded almost trancelike to Burrows.

"I called for Brian a couple of times before getting up. I think I may have called for him before I even turned on the light. I'm not sure now."

"Where did you think he was?"

"I hoped he was looking for aspirin. But I really had no idea."

"Why aspirin? Why would he have been looking for aspirin?"

"He had had a lot to drink Sunday night. I thought he might have been getting a hangover."

"Was your husband a heavy drinker?" Burrows asked, aware that Tillier was fairly confident he wasn't. There were absolutely no signs anywhere in the man's body of any physiological deterioration that even might have been caused by alcohol.

"No."

"Any special reason in that case he had so much to drink Sunday night?"

"No," Marcia said again, staring intently at a closet door.

"Were you scared?"

"When Brian was gone?"

"Yup."

Marcia nodded. "Especially when it dawned on me that my cats were gone too."

Burrows followed her gaze, wondering what she saw there. "Your cats had disappeared?"

"Solstice and Chloe. My cats. They're not with me now. I left them in New York with my parents."

"And they disappeared that night also?"

"They did. They always slept at the foot of Brian's and my bed. And then that night—the night Brian died—I woke up and first found Brian was gone, and then I realized the cats were gone too."

"Why did you wake up?"

"I don't know. I just did."

"Do you recall a loud noise that may have woken you?"

"No," Marcia answered. "I think the house was especially quiet that night. I think that was part of the reason I was so scared. No radiators, no furnace, nothing."

Burrows wandered slowly to the closet door and shut it, hoping to break whatever spell it held over Marcia. She seemed startled by the gesture.

"And this was about four-thirty in the morning?"

"Yes. About four-thirty," she said, sitting on the edge of the bed and resting her shoulder against the headboard.

Burrows had seen people manifest their grief in different ways, but never with an almost catatonic numbness. But clearly it was grief he was witnessing, Burrows decided; this woman was definitely grieving. This woman hadn't murdered her husband, not a chance. He tried to will his erection away, guilty about his desire for a grieving widow who—for all he knew—was on the verge of some sort of breakdown. It just wasn't natural to stare at a closet door the way she had. Unfortunately, it was likely that as long as she sat casually on her bed, her body relaxed and yielding, his erection wasn't going anywhere.

How ironic, J. P. thought to himself, that the first time he met a woman from New York City that he was attracted to, she was a murder suspect.

"What made you think to look for Brian in the attic?" he asked, trying to focus on his investigation.

"I didn't think of it. At least not at first."

"When then? When did you think of it?"

"After I had checked the rest of the house."

"And you hadn't found him . . ."

She nodded. "Or the cats."

"Tell me about that," Burrows said softly, afraid she was falling deeper into her trance. He began to fear that she might actually have that breakdown any minute now. The Marcia Middleton who sat before him that moment was very different from the strong woman who had stood to face him in Nate Nester's office only a few hours earlier. "Tell me about searching the house."

"I didn't see any lights on upstairs," she murmured slowly, "so I went downstairs. But he wasn't there either. Not in the kitchen, not in the bathroom, not in the living room. He just wasn't there."

"And then what?" Burrows asked when her voice trailed off. He had planned on having her walk him downstairs when they got to this point, retracing exactly her every move. But he couldn't do that now, not while she was in this state. Instead he put down his coffee on her dresser and sat down beside her on the bed, his desire finally losing itself in his concern.

"I hoped he was outside. I hoped they were all outside. Brian. Chloe. Solstice. I may have opened the front door and called for them, but I don't remember. I probably didn't. It wouldn't have made sense for Brian to go outside with the cats. Chloe and Solstice are city cats; they've never been outdoors. And I think I knew Brian wouldn't have taken them outside in the middle of the night in the middle of November."

Her eyes rolled slowly toward the window, and she glared at it with the same intense fixation with which she had stared at the closet door a moment earlier.

"So you didn't go outside?"

She shook her head no.

"Did you check the basement?"

"No."

"Why not?"

She got up from the bed and went to the window, pressing her palm against the lower pane and holding it there.

"Why didn't you check the basement?" Burrows asked again.

Without turning to him she answered, "I knew they weren't there. When they weren't downstairs, I knew they were in the attic. I knew it."

"How?"

She ran her hand with a slow fanlike motion across the window.

"How did you know that?"

"Would you like to see the attic?"

Burrows stood up. He started to tell her that visiting the attic now was impossible, unless she wanted him to kick the door open or remove it from its hinges. He stopped, however, because he suddenly had a feeling that the doorknob would now turn easily. The door itself would still be warped, but the knob would turn. He was sure of it. "Yes," he said. "I'd like to see the attic very much. But first I want you to tell me how you knew they were there—in the attic."

Marcia turned to him, her eyes blank. "Because," she said quietly, "when the house wants you, that's where the house takes you."

Where has my strength gone? Marcia wondered, as she walked with the detective down the upstairs corridor to the attic door. She had felt such confidence only the day before—as recently, in fact, as earlier that morning—but it was gone now, completely gone. She felt again like an invalid: tired, beaten, unable to cope.

Was it possible that the house had stolen her strength away, sucking it from her the way a leech sucks blood or a tapeworm gnaws at one's intestine? No, the house wasn't a parasite, she realized; that analogy was wrong. The house was bigger than that: it didn't nibble or gnaw or suck at its victims, it simply ingested them whole. It ate them, swallowed them up intact. She was in its belly at that very moment, and the weakness she felt stemmed not from some parasitic invader within her, but because she herself was a part of the house's natural, organic process of digestion.

Marcia was glad to have this detective with her as she walked toward the attic. She would have been afraid to go up there without him.

She gave the detective her hand as they approached the attic door, aware that some men would misinterpret the gesture, but confident that J. P. wasn't one of them. She felt intuitively that she could trust him.

She realized that her hand was still cold from the windowpane in her bedroom by the way the man flinched when she touched his palm and wound her fingers through his. With her other hand she switched on her flashlight, watching the beam reflect off the empty picture frame on the floor at the end of the corridor.

"This'll probably take two hands," the detective said awkwardly when they reached the door, gently releasing her hand. He placed his left foot against the door frame and wrapped both hands around the doorknob, and pulled it open with one colossal squeal from the warped wood. He seemed surprised that it opened.

The icy November downdraft from the attic greeted them immediately, and she wished suddenly that she had never returned to Deering. She wished she was not returning to the attic now. She wished she had stayed in New York. What, after all, had she proven by returning to Vermont? Was she showing the locals that she was innocent, that she had nothing to be afraid of? Perhaps, but why should she care what Lymon Hollis or Joshua Nash thought of her? She was just going to put the house up for sale and return to New York City as soon as possible. She was never going to live in this town, never.

By returning she may also have discovered that a family named Barrington really had lived in her house before the Finches and that they had had a daughter named Adelaide Thistle; she had even learned that the little girl really had died of a broken neck just before her seventh birthday. But what did this accomplish? Had she ever doubted that the story was true from the moment she had found Brian dead? No, not for a second.

Was it possible, she wondered, that the house's grip was so strong that it held her even when she was hundreds of miles away in Manhattan? Had the house itself brought her back, literally summoning her north to join her husband in the attic? To join her husband and Thistle Peep and who knows who—or what—else there?

She felt the detective take her flashlight from her and replace it with his hand. "Now you opened the door," she heard him saying someplace far away, "and you shone the light up the stairs. Right?"

"First the cats came out," she mumbled.

"Ah, yes, I'd forgotten about that. And then you shone the light up the stairs?"

She nodded, following the beam as it skirted up the steps and then along the brick chimney that came into view near the top. She felt a slight tug on her arm as he started to climb up into the attic.

Evidently noticing her resistance, the detective asked softly, "Now, you're sure you want to go up there? I can understand if it's too soon. I really can."

"No. It's not too soon," she answered. She would not, after all, have to look at that godforsaken little girl's noose, the noose that Brian had used. She knew the noose had been taken away by the police the week before.

"You're sure?"

"I'm sure," she answered, as the haze from her breath wafted up through the flashlight beam. She noticed that the detective was shaking his head skeptically, but he nevertheless started up the steps.

She decided that she did indeed like this detective. Like her sister, he was good with invalids. He was patient.

"So you walked up the steps," he was saying, leading the way a step ahead of her.

She nodded. As they reached the top she looked up at the beam from which Brian had hanged himself, noticing how coarse and aged the wood suddenly seemed.

"And this is where you . . . you found your husband?" the detective asked, choosing his words carefully.

"Yes."

"And then what? You called the police?"

"That's right." She saw that the piles of *Vermont Life* magazines had been disturbed and the shutters rearranged, in all likelihood by the police when they had searched the house the other day. Even that old high chair was now on the other side of the attic.

"Not an ambulance?"

"No. Not an ambulance." There were dozens of dead, half-frozen flies caught between the attic's screens and storm windows.

"Where was the ladder?"

One of the flies was actually alive, moving in slow motion up the screen. "Over there," she said, pointing to a spot about three or four feet from the top of the stairs.

"How had it fallen?"

She looked up at the beam, aware for the first time of just how high it was. Twelve feet, perhaps. "Fallen?"

"The ladder. How had it fallen? Did it fall with the steps facing up or the steps facing down? Was it completely on its side, maybe?"

She tried to recall the details, but was having trouble concentrating as long as that one poor stupid fly staggered upward along the wire mesh of the window screen.

"I can't remember," she said finally, looking into the detective's face. She wanted to see his eyes, but was unable to in the dim light.

"But it was a good four feet away from him."

"Yes, it was. A good four feet."

Burrows nodded. "How do you think the ladder got there—four feet away?"

"I assume he pushed it with his feet. Kicked it, I guess." She remembered that Brian was wearing his slippers, and the slippers were dangling almost directly above the stairway.

"How long did you stay in the attic?"

"After I found Brian?"

"Yup."

"Not long. I was too scared. And I needed to do something. *Anything.* I couldn't just stand there and watch him . . . hanging."

"So you went downstairs?"

She wondered what Thistle Peep had used to stand on, and guessed it depended on how tall the child had been. There certainly wasn't much room between the roof and the floor behind the old chimney. "Then I went downstairs, yes," she said, wandering away from the detective to the spot where Thistle Peep had hanged herself. She heard Burrows walking behind her, stepping carefully through a mound of unused wool insulation.

"Which phone did you use? The one in your bedroom or the one in the kitchen?"

"The kitchen. I knew that was where the phone book was."

She paused. For one moment what she saw behind the chimney

might have passed for a shadow, a spectral presence Marcia conjured from her own mind and let free to roam her attic. It swayed, but was not even that explicable in her house of dingy, vague, half-lit shadows?

It was on the second look, the look she shared simultaneously with the detective, that she knew it was not a shadow she saw; it was real. She knew it was real because of the way the detective cut in front of her, reaching for it with one hand while balancing himself against the chimney with the other. She knew it was real because she knew now how the house operated, unashamedly telegraphing its intentions, however evil, to whomever it wanted next.

And now it wanted her, she realized, sliding to the floor with her back against the chimney. The house wanted her; that's why it had brought her back to Vermont, that's why it had brought her upstairs now to the attic.

Almost unaware of what the detective was saying, something about it not being the same one, something about someone hanging it as a fake, she watched him frantically untie the knot along the beam and pull from the wood the noose that had been rehung in her house.

Chapter 23

"You didn't find out why the guy was so drunk?" Anderson asked Burrows later that afternoon, incredulous. It was almost five o'clock, and he was on his way out the door to stake out the small park behind the university's science library, the site of a drug deal Burrows had witnessed three weeks earlier. Burrows had returned from Deering only minutes before.

"I couldn't, Sherm," Burrows said, aiming a dart at a photograph of the inventor of the biodegradable comb. "I couldn't do it."

"You should have."

"I know."

"After all, she didn't tell Thomas a week ago that the guy was drunk."

"I know."

"I mean, if they'd had a fight or something—"

"If they'd had a fight or something," Burrows said, cutting Anderson off, "I'd be no better off than I am right now. All that would give me is one more circumstantial motivation."

"It's something you need to know."

Burrows glanced out the window and watched the streetlights automatically click on. It wasn't even Thanksgiving, and already it was dark by five o'clock.

"I'm serious, J. P.; it's something you need to know," Anderson said again. "The state attorney's going to ask, mark my word."

He knew Anderson was right. But how could he have asked Marcia the question again? She was close to a breakdown as it was. And after they had discovered that noose, he had ended up spending the afternoon with her, consoling her.

"Who do you think put the new noose there?" Anderson asked after a moment.

"Don't know."

"Know what I think?"

"Do I care?"

"I think the widow put it there herself," Anderson continued, in spite of Burrows. "To deflect us. Throw us off the track."

"Well, it will be analyzed tomorrow. I came back here via Waterbury, and dropped it off with the state lab people myself."

Anderson pulled the darts out of the corkboard and took them with him to the door. The last thing he did every day before leaving was to throw one final round from the exit. "You spent a lot of time with the lady today, didn't you?" Anderson asked, trying to sound casual.

"I did indeed."

"Any special reason?"

"She was upset."

" 'Bout the noose?"

"Right. About the noose." Burrows didn't look up at Anderson.

"Where is she now?"

"With some neighbors. A family named Nash."

"She staying with them?"

"Yup."

Anderson was quiet for a moment, staring intently at the dart board. "You do know what you're doing, don't you, J. P.?"

Burrows noticed a small cut on the back of his wrist. He wondered how Marcia had been getting by since he had left. Leaving had been so awkward. "I think I do, Sherm," he said quietly. "I think I do."

Marcia helped Sarabeth Nash chop the broccoli for dinner, while Josh played Parcheesi with his two daughters in front of *Wheel of Fortune.* She felt very safe.

"It's just the strangest thing," Sarabeth was saying. "I have no idea why they keep coming, the postman has no idea why they keep coming . . . but they're unstoppable! Just unstoppable!"

"Do you buy a lot of things through the mail?" Marcia asked.

"No, never. Josh once bought some seeds from a mail-order company; but they weren't very good, so he hasn't done that again. And that was years ago."

"Well, maybe the catalogs are an omen. Maybe it's time you gave mail-order another chance."

"Oh no, I don't think so. Everything's either too expensive, or too . . . too impractical."

"Impractical?"

Sarabeth took Marcia's elbow and pulled her close. She then

whispered urgently into her ear, "I get at least one catalog every month that has nothing in it but French underwear!"

Burrows called the Nashes from the pay phone at Bosox, astounded that it cost a dollar and thirty-five cents to call Deering from Burlington. It was around seven-thirty, so he was fairly confident the Nashes had finished dinner, washed the dishes, and settled down in front of a *M*A*S*H* rerun.

"Hello, is this Ms. Nash?" he asked the woman who answered the phone, trying to sound friendly. He was fairly confident it was the voice of the woman he had met that afternoon.

"Sure is. How are you, Detective Burrows?"

"It's J. P. As I said this afternoon, call me J. P."

"All right, I can do that. How are you, J. P.?"

"Okay. How's your neighbor doing?"

"She's doing okay too."

"Can I speak to her?"

"Not this second. You just missed her."

"I missed her? She didn't go back to that house, did she?"

"No, I don't think there's any chance of that. She just went out for a walk."

"Know where to?"

"Just around. No place special."

"Well, I was just calling to see how she was doing. I'm glad she's feeling better."

"I guess she was a little quiet during dinner," Sarabeth then added. "But she seems to be doing as well as can be expected."

"How about you, Ms. Nash?"

"Oh, I'm just fine."

"You know where to reach me if you need to, right?"

"Yup. Sounds to me like all I have to do is call the noisiest bar in Burlington," Sarabeth said with a slight edge in her voice.

Burrows rolled his eyes. He had forgotten that much of Deering—including, evidently, the Nashes—didn't drink. He had probably just appalled a selectman's wife.

Marcia had her hands in her pockets when she stared up at the sky, and so lost her balance for a brief moment. She thought she could decipher Aquarius from among the clusters of stars over her barn, but she wasn't sure. For all she knew it was the Big Dipper.

She leaned against one of the Newsome's fence posts across the street from her house and thought back to her day with the detective. She wondered why it hadn't occurred to her until that afternoon to tell anyone that Brian had been drinking Sunday night. Drinking a lot. But then she realized that it couldn't have occurred to her to tell anyone: until that afternoon, when Burrows was questioning her, she hadn't even remembered the drinking. Or the bickering. Or the fighting. Evidently she had managed to repress the whole pathetic, stupid scene. And that frightened her. She wondered what else she had repressed.

She held her hands up before her face, and as she had the day before in the car, examined them. They were even lovelier against the night sky than they were in the daylight, she decided. And they weren't a killer's hands. They couldn't be.

She told herself again that she didn't buy Dr. Michaels' conjecture about fugue states and selective amnesia. She would have to be completely mad to have murdered her husband and then forgotten it. And she wasn't. She wasn't.

It might have seemed as if she was going mad the night Brian died. The night they had the fight. But hadn't she read somewhere that domestic fights were always the most irrational? The most emotional? The most insane? Yes, she had read that somewhere, in a magazine in Dr. Michaels' waiting room, perhaps. *Mademoiselle* or *Psychology Today.* It was true.

And when she really thought about it, had she acted irrationally that night? Perhaps not. It might have been more irrational, more indicative of insanity, to have done nothing. Even the sanest person is bound to respond violently when presented with select stimuli. When presented with photographs of another woman one thought were long gone. When hurt.

And Brian had hurt her that day and night; he had hurt her badly —perhaps worse than the night in Manhattan when he had confessed his affair with Joyce Renders in the first place.

"You really think this is smart?" Josh Nash whispered to his wife in the kitchen, folding a dish towel.

"I don't know if it's smart or dumb. And I don't see why it matters," Sarabeth answered.

"Let me rephrase that: do you think this is safe? I worry about Gail. I worry about Allie."

"What about us? Don't you worry about us?" Sarabeth asked sarcastically.

"Of course I worry about us."

"I just don't see what you're afraid of."

"I don't want to wake up tomorrow morning and find that something has happened to one of my daughters. That's what I'm afraid of."

Sarabeth noticed again the rust marks along the bottom of their percolator. They could use a new one. And the catalog she had received that afternoon from some San Francisco department store must have had ten or fifteen different ones. Ones for espresso, ones that ground beans, ones that brewed coffee a cup at a time. Some of them looked so complicated they belonged on spaceships. "You think she killed her husband?" she asked Josh.

"I don't know. But if she did, I sure don't want her sharing the same roof as Allie and Gail."

"And Sarabeth."

"Right. And Sarabeth. I just don't think she's completely right in the head."

"Maybe she isn't. But I don't think her husband was completely right in the head either."

Josh nodded. "Brian was a strange bird."

"I will never—and I mean never—understand what was going through that fellow's brain when he stampeded in here a couple Sundays ago and told you to stop working on the house. I will just never understand that!"

"Nope, I won't either. . . ."

She adjusted one of the plates in the drying rack by the sink, standing it upright. "But I still don't guess Marcia killed him," she said after a moment.

"So you think it's perfectly safe?"

"I think it's safe."

"But not perfectly safe?"

"I ask you, Joshua Nash, is anything in this world perfectly safe? Is anything?"

The selectman thought for a moment, folding his arms across his chest. "No, I guess not," he said thoughtfully. "But there are degrees. You can't make a crooked stick lay straight, you know."

"The girls will be fine, Josh," Sarabeth said, rolling her eyes. "The girls will be just fine."

* * *

Marcia zipped up her jacket and wandered over to the church steps to sit down. She couldn't really see her barn from the church, but she could see her house, and that's what interested her that night. She stared up at the attic windows, half expecting to see movement.

Thank God the detective had been with her that afternoon when she had found the noose. She couldn't imagine how she might have reacted if he hadn't been there to take command of the situation. Alone, she might finally have gone over the edge once and for all.

She liked the detective. J. P. She liked J. P. a lot. He was such a basic person, so unaffected. She tried not to think of him in the context of Brian, but that was impossible. It was only natural to make comparisons. They were so different. Part of it was simply Manhattan versus Vermont, but part of it went deeper than that. J. P. seemed to be a stronger person than Brian; he seemed to have more character. J. P., after all, didn't seem to be the type who would have extramarital affairs.

She imagined also that J. P. was less calculating than Brian, less concerned about public appearances. He probably didn't worry all the time about what people thought of him the way Brian had; he probably wasn't the type who would think about what clothes to wear to the dump, whose first concern after confessing he had a lover would be that she not tell their families.

She sighed. She was probably being too hard on Brian. There had been very many wonderful things about him. He had taken care of things; he had taken care of her. He'd made brunch every Sunday, always elaborate productions for just the two of them, things like eggs Benedict or fresh pears in a ginger sauce.

But he had hurt her, and now she had to fight to remember those good things. That was the legacy of Brian's affair. For the rest of her life she would have to concentrate very hard on very specific details to recall the good things in Brian Middleton.

She wondered if J. P. were angry with her for not telling the police earlier that Brian had been drinking the night he died. Surely they had known it from the autopsy. She wondered if she were actually in trouble for failing to provide them with that information immediately. It might look to the police as if she were withholding evidence. Evidence that was somehow incriminating, though she wasn't sure why.

Well, she could live with that. But she hoped suddenly that J. P. wasn't mad at her. Suddenly it mattered to her very much that J. P. wasn't mad at her for failing to tell him earlier about the drinking. Or the fighting.

Of course, she hadn't yet told him about the fighting. She probably should, but wouldn't that confirm in his mind once and for all that she had murdered her husband? Surely it would. And that was the last thing she wanted. No, she couldn't tell him about the fight. She couldn't tell anyone about the fight. She would have to live with that burden alone—that too would be a legacy from Brian's affair.

Marcia was still outside when Josh sat on the side of Allie's bed and tucked his younger daughter in. Allie was eight, but she was very small for her age. Until she spoke—and the irony was, she spoke like a ten year old—people often thought she was only five or six years old. Josh noticed immediately that she was cradling in her arms Meow Frog, a stuffed frog who Allie insisted had been a cat in another life. Hence the name: Meow Frog. Meow Frog didn't riddip, he purred and howled and meowed.

"Mrs. Middleton's weird, daddy," Allie said.

She watched her father nod, as he pushed a corner of the fitted sheet back under the mattress.

"She's really weird," Allie said again.

Her father thought for a moment, and Allie could tell he agreed with her. She was therefore surprised when he asked, "Is that such a bad thing?"

"Daddy! Everyone at school says she's this crazy lady. What she does is she goes all around the country finding people to marry, and then she kills them! That's pretty weird."

"Who is everyone?"

"Everyone in Gail's class. Bonnie Boisclair. Fred Thetford. Cindy Rudman."

"That's everyone, all right. What about in your class?"

"No one talks about her in the third grade. Only sixth graders talk about her," Allie said, irritated with her father's remarkable ignorance.

"I'll bet you're glad you have a big sister," Josh said. "I know I am."

"Gail thinks she's weird too, you know."

"How do you feel about her staying with us for a couple of days?"

"What do you mean?"

"Do you like having her here?"

Allie shrugged. "I don't care. Maybe I'd care if you and mom weren't married. 'Cause then she might try to kill you. But she can't marry you, because you're already married. Right?"

"Right."

"And she wouldn't want to marry me. Or Gail."

"No, I don't think she would," Josh said. "Mrs. Middleton doesn't scare you, does she?"

Allie played with one of Meow Frog's ears. "Sometimes, she does."

"When?"

"When she doesn't say anything. When she doesn't say anything and she just stares at stuff. That lady can stare and stare like it's nobody's business."

Marcia stared at the rows of bedroom windows facing the church, wondering which had been Thistle Peep's. She assumed it was the one that faced east and got all the morning sun, but she couldn't be sure. She thought that the wallpaper might provide some clue, if she were willing to peel away the layers upon layers that probably coated each wall and find the original pattern. But then again, it might not.

She wondered what Thistle Peep had been like. After all, what kind of six- or seven-year-old girl hangs herself? An unhappy one, certainly. But why? Why was she so unhappy? It crossed her mind that the library might have some answers. The Middlebury Library. Now that she knew the date of Thistle Peep's death, perhaps she might be able to find a newspaper story or two describing the . . . the incident. She decided she would go there the next morning, as soon as she was done meeting with the real estate agent. No, she would go there first thing, even before she met with Grace Macknight.

Marcia glanced back at the house and focused on the window of the bedroom with the gray-striped wallpaper. Her instincts were right, she was sure of it: that room was once Thistle Peep's, it had to have been. Not because of the wallpaper, which Marcia figured was only around twenty-five years old, but because of the amount of sun the room received. Little girls usually had the brightest, cheeriest rooms in the house, didn't they? Of course they did. That was the room Thistle Peep Barrington had slept in for seven years, Marcia was sure of it. One look from the inside would settle the issue once and for all. She reached in her pocket for the keys to her house, and started across the church lawn to her front door.

She stopped midway, the keys falling from her hands onto the walkway. With any other house, it might have been the reflection of the moon or merely a breeze through the attic vents. But not with this house, not here. She saw something move in the attic window. It wasn't her imagination; it wasn't an hallucination, she was sure of that. Something had definitely moved in the attic; something was definitely there; and although she had seen it for only a split second, there was no doubt in her mind what—who—it was.

Without stopping to get her keys, she turned and ran back to the Nashes, unable to push from her mind the image of the little girl's face in the window.

Chapter 24

Chief Montgomery wandered into the detectives' office Tuesday morning shortly before noon and poured himself a cup of coffee. "This is decaf, right?" he asked Burrows.

Burrows frowned. "Has it ever been decaf, Gerry?"

"No."

"Then what makes you think it's decaf now?"

"Hope. You guys drink too much coffee. I keep telling you that."

"And we appreciate it, Gerry, we really do."

"Crap you do," Montgomery said, clearing his throat. "What do you have there, Waterbury's report?" he asked, motioning toward the manilla folder from the crime lab Burrows was skimming.

"Yup."

Montgomery reached for the folder and began to glance through it. "Any surprises?" he asked.

"I think so. It says the noose we found in the house yesterday is made of the same stuff as the noose we found around Brian Middleton's neck. The analysts believe it's probably from the exact same line of eighty- or ninety-year-old rope—something that's been sitting around the Middleton house all this time."

"Why does that surprise you?"

"I guess I figured the lab would come back and tell me the rope could have come from any old hardware store or K-Mart. I guess I expected to see words like 'contemporary origin' or 'modern fabrication' in the report. But I didn't."

"Any traces of human skin or oil on the rope?"

"Nope. Whoever hung it had the common sense to wear gloves. Or something."

"Or something?"

"Even rubber gloves might have left a tiny bit of residue, especially along the slip knot. But there's not even any evidence of that."

"Any idea when the noose was hung?"

"Sometime between Thursday night when the house was unsealed and Monday morning—pretty vague. And that's just a guess on the lab's part. There's no evidence on the rope itself to indicate how long it was hanging there."

Montgomery dropped the folder back onto Burrows' desk. "Not very helpful, was it?"

"Nope."

"Anderson says he thinks the widow hung the noose. Marcia Middleton. What do you think?"

"I think Anderson's wrong."

"Even though the noose probably came from inside her own house?"

"Even though."

"In that case, who do you think hung it?"

Burrows looked briefly at Montgomery, and then away. He couldn't tell him about the key his brother had given him or the little girl his brother had claimed to have met. Not yet. Nor could he explain to him the immovable attic door. He couldn't even explain that to himself.

"I don't know," Burrows said finally, simply. "I think it's possible that someone else hung it, figuring Marcia would find it when she returned home alone to her house."

"Any evidence to back that up? Or is that all judgment?"

"I have no evidence either way, and I wouldn't even go so far as to call it judgment. I'd call it instinct."

"Instinct," Montgomery repeated.

"Yup. Instinct."

Montgomery thought for a moment, sipping his coffee, and then said, "You got good instincts, Burrows. You do. But—for your own sake—don't let your gonads guide 'em."

Burrows swore softly to himself; he should have expected this. Neither the Nashes nor Marcia were home. The girls were at school, Josh was probably out at some building site, and Marcia and Sarabeth could be anywhere. Grocery shopping, for all he knew.

He should have called first before driving all the way to Deering. But he had wanted to see Marcia, and the lab report on the noose seemed as good an excuse as any.

He decided to leave his truck in the Nashes' driveway, and left a note on the windshield explaining that he had wandered up the street to Marcia's house. Assuming that Marcia hadn't been the one who had hung the noose, he should probably look around the house a bit and see if he could get a sense of how somebody had gotten in. It might also be nice to find the rest of the rope—both from the standpoint of his investigation and so he could stop the damn nooses from reproducing.

Burrows began wandering around the outside of Marcia's house, checking the windows. He made sure that the dryer vent was too small for a person to crawl through and that the wheelbarrow ramp from the basement was shut tight. When he had confirmed that none of the first floor windows were broken and all were locked, he walked around the house to the front door.

The front door was open. Not just unlocked, open. Open a good half inch.

"Hello?" Burrows called from the front hall, rapping his knuckles against the woodwork for effect. "Anybody home?"

When there was no response, Burrows walked through the hall into the kitchen. "Marcia?" he called one last time as a courtesy. Although he hadn't seen her car parked in either her driveway or the Nashes', and he was virtually positive that she wasn't home, the last thing he wanted to do right now was to catch the woman off guard and frighten her.

The kitchen was exactly as they had left it the day before. Marcia's coffee mug was still on the kitchen table where she had placed it before starting upstairs with him, and the jar of instant coffee was still on top of the dishwasher. He wandered briefly into the den and picked up one of the unopened rolls of wallpaper leaning against a closet door. Stripes, the pattern was lines of light blue stripes. He was fairly sure that it was Brian who had wanted stripes, (since hadn't Marcia wanted bows?), but he wasn't positive.

He started toward the door to the back porch when he heard a noise above him, a small thump on the second floor. Or the attic. It was most likely just a shutter banging, perhaps that loose one Thomas had showed him on one of the bedroom windows. Or perhaps one of the vertical gutters was rattling.

Nevertheless, Burrows stood still for a moment, listening. He pressed his hand against his windbreaker to make sure he had brought his gun with him, and then remembered he had left it in the Bronco: he hadn't wanted to scare the two Nash girls. He stood up straight and asked himself why in the name of God he would need his gun now in any case. What did he expect to do upstairs, shoot a shutter?

With long, slow strides he crossed the kitchen and the front hall and began working his way up the stairs. He realized he was walking as softly and slowly as possible, and told himself that he was being ridiculous. But he still moved with quiet calculation. He hoped he would hear the noise again, not only so he could pinpoint its origin, but also to reinforce in his mind the idea that it was merely a shutter.

All of the bedroom doors were closed to conserve heat, as they had been the day before. Cautiously Burrows opened each one, turning the handle with his hand, but actually pushing the door open with his toe while he stood away from the frame. He couldn't believe he had left his gun in the truck.

Once inside each bedroom he checked each closet, and in the two rooms where he found beds, he looked underneath them. When he was sure each room was empty, he then checked the windows, both for a sign of entry and for additional loose shutters. He found neither. The second floor was clear.

Which meant he had to climb into the attic.

He paused before the attic door, bracing himself for the cold he had come to expect. It crossed his mind that the thump he had heard might very well have been a small animal in the attic. A squirrel, maybe. Or a bat.

With one good twist he pulled open the attic door and stood back for a moment. If there was a bat awake in there, he wanted to give it ample room to fly past him. When nothing flew past his eyes or scurried past his feet, he climbed the stairs, his eyes darting back and forth in the dim light above him.

At the top of the stairs he stood unmoving and surveyed the attic. There was clearly no one there. And no animal, apparently, at least none willing to show itself to him. He wandered over to a pile of old *Look* magazines and sat down. His heart was racing, he realized, and he smiled to himself. He had let a shutter or drainpipe or squirrel scare him.

When he had caught his breath, he stood up and started back toward the stairs. On the top step he stopped, just long enough to sigh. Even the cold didn't seem so bad once he relaxed, once he reminded himself that he was in an old house and old houses had their quirks. That was all. Old houses had their quirks, and he had let a shutter or drainpipe or squirrel scare him.

In that second, the door on the landing abruptly swung shut, slamming into the frame and shaking the house. He jumped down the stairs toward it, hurdling the steps two at a time. He wasn't sure, but he thought he smelled smoke: the distinctly bitter-smelling smoke he would always associate with one source—the monster wood stove in his family's West Gardner kitchen.

At the edge of the door the odor became worse, and he realized the fumes were coming from the second floor, wafting under the door and up into the attic. He paused, thinking to himself that a draft had slammed the door. That was all; a draft had caught the door and slammed it shut. There was no one out there; there was *nothing* out there.

After all, only a minute or two earlier he had let a shutter frighten him.

He reached for the doorknob, and discovered that—as it had once before—the knob wouldn't move. It wouldn't turn; it wouldn't shake; it wouldn't jiggle. Now, however, he was on the other side of the door: this time he was inside the attic. And outside, he thought, he smelled smoke.

"Hello?" He surprised himself by opening his mouth; he hadn't planned on speaking. But almost reflexively he found himself crying out to the house. "Who's out there?"

He didn't like the sound of his voice. It didn't sound natural to him; it sounded scared. But then, he thought, isn't it natural to be scared? Of course it was. It was only reasonable.

He tried the knob again, trying to shake it loose from whatever was holding it in place, but the white handle wouldn't move.

He took a breath, trying not to inhale the smoke slipping like an invisible mist under the door. And it truly was invisible. He could smell the smoke; he could taste it on his lips; but there was certainly no smoke in the air, nothing burning his eyes.

Rolling his hand into a fist he pounded on the door, slamming his hand into it like a hammer.

"Open up!" he yelled. "Open up!"—aware each time his hand hit the wood that the wood was hot.

Hot, he realized suddenly, like the breakfront in the West Gardner dining room. That was what the smoke smelled like. Not the general and almost reassuring bitterness he would associate always with the kitchen wood stove. No, this was the smoke from the fire that had roared through the dining room when he was eight years old. That Christmas Day fire. He would never forget how hot the breakfront wood had been when he had reached for the handle to rescue Simon. It had felt hot like an oven door.

He pressed his palms now against the attic door, feeling the warmth, his mind finally taking in the obvious: the house really was on fire. The house had exploded into flames like the dining room in West Gardner over twenty years earlier, and he had damn well better find a way out of the attic. Now.

He decided he would kick the door open, breaking it off its hinges. He took a step up the stairs to give himself room, and grabbed a loose floorboard behind him for balance. And then he raised his foot, planning to smash through the century-old wood, when the house lurched again, as it had when the door had first slammed shut. He toppled forward into the door, hitting it with his shoulder, but failing to open it. He collapsed against it, the smell of burning timber engulfing him like fog, and for a split second he thought he heard laughter.

No, he knew he heard laughter. There was no doubt in his mind. From someplace on the far side of the door, someone—*something*—was laughing.

He remembered that Simon had initially refused to take his hand when he had reached into the breakfront, and that his eyes had been shut tight against the smoke. His brother had been—literally—too scared to move.

Reflexively, because the smell and the laughter were on the other side of the door, Burrows climbed to his feet and started back up the stairs. He thought he would break a window. It was that simple. The house was on fire, and he needed air.

And then if he had to, he decided, he would jump. He would not stay in the attic and burn to death, he would not let whoever—*whatever*—was on the other side of the door choke him to death. He would get out, he would get out, he would get out if it meant jumping.

It was, after all, only three floors.

He reached the top of the stairs and stared momentarily at the two windows, wondering which to approach. Perhaps one window was above one of the porches; perhaps one was above some bushes.

It didn't matter. What mattered now was getting out of the house.

He started toward the window nearest the stack of *Look* magazines, jumping quickly over one of the scattered shutters, when he realized abruptly that the smell of the smoke was gone. He stood still for a moment, inhaling slowly, determining for sure that the air indeed no longer tasted like smoke. Not at all. As quickly as the smell had arrived, it had disappeared.

He knew instinctively that whatever was happening with the house was over, and that the door below him would now open. The house had never been on fire at all. He was positive. He turned back toward the stairs, and before he had even started down them the door swung free.

He took a breath. And then he stopped breathing completely. In the light from the second floor, the light shining up the stairs, he could see something on the floor behind the old chimney, something he hadn't noticed only a moment before. He walked toward it, tiptoeing for reasons he could not quite understand, and the thought crossed his mind that it was a sweater—a huge, furry ski sweater.

He had only taken a step or two, however, before he was able to see exactly what was there. Even in the dim light he could see clearly the markings, and the way the animal's chest was heaving.

Somehow the tiger striped barn cat had gotten into the attic and now lay panting underneath the crossbeam of the noose.

Chapter 25

Marcia sat at a pumpkin pine table in the Middlebury Library and rested her head in her hands. Periodically she would look away from the drawing before her, stunned, and stare down at the dust on the tabletop, as thick and light as powdered sugar. If the drawing weren't so morbid, it would be sad. Sad enough to make her cry right there in the middle of the morning in the middle of the library. The drawing, from the October 18, 1910 issue of *The Middlebury Courier,* was an artist's rendition of Thistle Peep Barrington: a little girl whose face reminded Marcia so much of her own as a small girl that she thought she might become sick.

According to the yellowed newspaper clipping, the artist had sketched the picture from a tintype of the child that had been made the day after she died. It seemed the Barringtons had realized while making the funeral arrangements that they had no pictures of their only daughter and had asked a photographer to come all the way down from Burlington to take some. And one did, a gentleman named Ryan Gordon Allen III. He shot Thistle Peep as she was laid out in her bedroom with her dolls and dried flowers in the background for warmth. The bed was surrounded by apples and pumpkins and scattered dead leaves—everything else, evidently, that also had died or been plucked in Deering that day.

And since the newspaper artist had been unavailable to sketch Thistle Peep while she was lying in bed at home (though Marcia couldn't imagine what could possibly have kept him from what had to have been one of Addison County's bigger news stories that year), he had based his drawing of the girl on that last photographic image: Thistle Peep Barrington in her bed in repose, her eyes serenely shut, her lips betraying just the slightest smile.

Although it was impossible to tell from the line drawing whether the child had red hair, there was no question in Marcia's mind that she did. After all, the girl in the picture was dressed exactly as was the child in Marcia's dream, the child she saw hanged in her attic—

the child who could have been Marcia Middleton at age six or seven. And Thistle Peep's long, full hair was parted in the picture in exactly the center, as was Marcia's as a child, and she wore what looked like a very similar bow.

Marcia noted that the article never said that the child hanged herself. At least not explicitly. Nor did the poem that a neighbor wrote about her for the following week's edition of the Middlebury newspaper suggest that Thistle Peep had been a suicide. According to the newspaper, the child had simply "passed on in the night, felled by a tragic accident in the attic of her own home."

Her father, a wealthy lawyer named Everett (wealthy, the newspaper implied, because of his investments in the railroad), told the newspaper's editor that Thistle Peep had gone to sleep that night as she had every night. He himself had tucked her in, he said, since her mother was gone for the evening in Burlington, tending to her own ailing mother. The child had spent her last evening on her father's lap, listening to him read from the Bible, and her last afternoon playing with her cousin at her uncle's farm in Weybridge.

Everett could not imagine "what dreadful influence had led the child to climb the attic steps in the dead of night," nor could he even begin to guess "what charms she expected to find in the blackness above her." As far as he knew, she had never before that night had any interest in the house's attic.

Marcia noticed that the newspaper had at least some doubt as to the exact cause of Thistle Peep's death. The *Courier* said it "appeared" that Thistle Peep had died from a broken neck sustained in a "sudden fall," but added, "Who can really know what forces will take the life of that frailest of creatures, the little girl? Certainly not this writer."

Burrows ran his hands underneath the cat and lifted the animal into his arms, and started quickly down the stairs. He expected the fur to feel warm, as if the cat had a fever, but it was ice cold—as cold as the attic itself.

He wondered briefly if there were a veterinarian closer than Middlebury, but doubted it. He thought he had never seen a cat pant so horribly: the animal's chest was rising and falling with perhaps the speed of a hummingbird's wings, and it was gasping for air with pathetically shallow breaths.

Holding the cat in his arms as if it were a baby, supporting its back and its head with his hands, Burrows stopped for a moment in the second floor hallway and looked down at its face. The cat had eyelashes. He had never noticed it before, but cats had short eyelashes.

He pressed the animal close against him to warm it, and massaged the fur along the top of its head. Abruptly the cat squirmed. It squirmed once, emitting one small, shrill cry, and then died.

Past the Texaco station and the Creemee ice cream stand (now boarded up for the season), Marcia turned off Maple Street and coasted to a stop in the realtor's gravel parking lot. With the exception of Grace Macknight's long brown station wagon, hers was the only car there. Which was too bad, Marcia thought: she hated the idea of being all alone in the office with Grace.

She pulled her key from the ignition and sat back in her seat, steeling herself for her appointment with the older woman. She couldn't pinpoint why, but Grace scared her. She seemed to know more than she let on. She seemed to know more things about the house than she let on.

Marcia glanced quickly, almost unconsciously, into the rearview mirror to make sure she was presentable. She was. She looked fine. But there was something in her eyes that was disconcerting. No, not disconcerting, wrong. Something had been wrong. She sat forward in the seat and looked again into the mirror.

The blue in her eyes was changing, brightening, growing luminescent. It was becoming more of a child's blue than an adult's blue, the kind of vibrant blue found in a little girl's eyes—in her eyes once. Initially Marcia didn't believe it and blinked, expecting that when she opened her eyes their natural color would have returned. But it didn't.

She uttered one small gasp and touched the reflection of her eyes in the mirror. Even their shape was wrong. Those weren't her eyes; they were too round. Too round. Her body shivered and her shoulders collapsed around her neck. There, in the thin rectangular glass before her, were the eyes of Thistle Peep Barrington.

Burrows stood unmoving on the second floor with the body of the cat in his arms, and his eyes began to tear.

He wasn't sure why he was crying. Growing up on a farm he had seen animals die all the time, and he had rarely cried for any of them. He knew he had cried for a pair of sick calves he had found when he was twelve, and he thought he had cried when Lester Tripton had shot a horse with a shattered leg. But those were the only instances he could recall, and they were years ago. He couldn't even remember the last time he had cried or imagine what might have caused those tears.

But this was different. There was no rhyme or reason for this. It was possible that the cat may have discovered a tin of rat poison in some obscure attic crevice, but that didn't make the animal's death any more palatable.

He took off his windbreaker and wrapped it around the cat's head so he wouldn't have to look into the animal's face or see again its strangely petite eyelashes. Although the body was cold, its fur was still soft. Gently he ran his fingers over the cat's rib cage, half expecting to hear a contented rumbling from underneath his jacket.

No, it wasn't rat poison that had killed the cat, he decided, not in this house. He looked briefly back up the steps toward the attic, and then kicked shut the door with his foot.

In the car, the air smelled stale. It smelled stale like the attic.

Marcia closed her eyes, afraid to keep them open. When they were open, she was drawn to the rearview mirror and the vision of the eyes of a little girl long dead.

She sat perfectly still, hoping to compose herself, hoping that if she were delirious, she could almost relax her delusion away.

But this wasn't a delusion; this was something else. A delusion was something that came from inside yourself, something you made up; this, on the other hand, was something—someone—that had come to her from outside of herself. After all, Marcia reasoned, how else could she have known exactly what Thistle Peep would look like long before she had seen the artist's rendering in the newspaper? The house had wanted her to know what its first victim looked like, that was the whole point; the house had wanted her to know that its first victim looked so much like she did as a little girl that the two could have passed for twins.

The house. It wasn't the house that was doing this. Jennifer was right; houses didn't do things. Oh, they decayed, they withered, they aged, just as people did, but they didn't actually do things. People did things, not their houses.

So it wasn't the house that was doing this to her. It was Thistle Peep Barrington.

With the cat still wrapped in his windbreaker, Burrows wandered downstairs and into the kitchen. He noticed the phone on the wall, and wondered for the first time what—if anything—he could tell people about what had happened to him. He had been scared up in the attic, no doubt about it. He had been practically scared out of his mind, scared enough to think seriously about jumping out a third story window onto frozen November ground.

But if he were to try and explain to Sherman Anderson or Gerry Montgomery that the house had a mind and spirit and life of its own and that it had convinced him for one long moment up there that the place was on fire, they would check him for fever. It was that simple. They would laugh and check him for fever and say to him, J. P., do you *really* believe it was anything but a draft that slammed shut that door? J. P. do you *really* believe you smelled anything but mildew and damp wool insulation?

Standing now in the kitchen with daylight streaming in through the windows, Burrows had to admit that it was becoming harder and harder for even himself to believe that he had been frightened enough to consider jumping out an attic window. But he had been. He couldn't forget that feeling of panic: he had been ready to dive out a window.

Although he didn't have to tell anyone about what he had experienced, he decided, he couldn't keep the cat to himself. The idea briefly crossed his mind to give the poor animal a decent burial on his father's farm, but he knew he couldn't do that. He couldn't keep the animal a secret. It was bad enough he was keeping the small pewter key to himself. No, as sorry as he felt for the cat, the cat was evidence, and the cat would have to be offered up to the medical examiner.

Besides, he had to know how the cat had died. How the cat had really died.

He reached for the phone and called Patricia Lange. She didn't say a word while Burrows told her that he had found a barn cat trapped in the Middleton attic, and that the animal had just died in his arms. Poisoned, perhaps. She was even silent for a brief moment when he was through.

"You still with me?" Burrows finally asked, concerned that she had been affected by the cat's death as deeply as he had. "You okay?"

"No, not really," she said softly. "I hate to hear this kind of thing. There's nothing I hate more than seeing an animal die because people are stupid. And leaving rat poison out like that is just plain stupid."

"I don't know for a fact that the cat got into some poison," Burrows said quickly. "That's just a guess."

"We'll know soon enough. You'll bring the animal here?"

"I planned to."

"Well, I'll be waiting," Lange said, and then added, "I want to talk to you about a couple of other things too."

"About this case?"

"Yup."

"Anything specific?"

She thought for a moment. "There's a lot of tongue waggin' going on right now, and I'm sure there's no truth to it. But I think you need to hear about it and deal with it."

"What are people saying?"

"I don't want to discuss this over the phone, J. P."

"It's that bad?"

"No, it's not. I just don't want to talk about it over the phone right now. Not while—" she paused, unsure of the right words "—not while you're holding that cat in your arms."

Marcia opened her eyes for one brief second in the realtor's parking lot and watched her hands grow small on the steering wheel and her nails become as soft as a child's.

Quickly she shut her eyes, this time once and for all, and sat there unmoving. She had no idea how long she had been sitting like that when it happened. When the eyes of Thistle Peep Barrington—the eyes that festered now beneath her own lids—opened in the little girl's bedroom, and she was sure she could see all that the little girl had seen, one night in her house eighty years earlier.

Sitting up in the little girl's bed, Marcia saw in the moonlight that Thistle Peep's mother had meticulously stenciled four-foot-high pine trees along the walls, black silhouettes so close to the real things that the bedroom looked almost like a Christmas tree farm. On the wall directly in front of her Mrs. Barrington had rubbed just a hint of orange into the design, as if the sun were setting behind those pines.

Marcia thought for a moment, trying to get her bearings and determine exactly where Mount Stillman was in relation to the room. Yes, the wall with the orange was the west wall, so that was a sunset. Quickly she looked behind her at the east wall, and sure enough, Mrs. Barrington had painted a bright yellow sun rising between two of the pines.

It was almost as if she were sleeping outside.

The bedroom door was wide open, and Marcia heard someone—undoubtedly Mrs. Barrington—on the floor below her crossing the kitchen. Although there was little sound from the library, she imagined Mr. Barrington was still there, still reading the Bible. She didn't know how, but she knew that the chair—"his" chair—was a large cherry rocker with a crewel pillow that said, "Give neither salt nor counsel till asked."

Above her, she heard the voices. In the attic. At first the sound was so soft that she was unable to make out any actual words; it was just a low, steady murmur. But she thought if she were silent, and concentrated on nothing but the voices above her, she would be able to decipher them. She wrapped the crazy quilt she saw at the foot of the bed around her shoulders and sat absolutely still. She realized she was sitting very much as she had in another bedroom in that house the night Brian had died.

After listening for a moment, she tried to convince herself that the noises above her were different from the noises below. The noises above her weren't real. They weren't as substantial or as pronounced or as tangible. Marcia believed a sound should almost be tangible, if it's real. It should be something you can wrap your mind around, something that conjures up images you can touch. But the voices above her? She couldn't touch them.

Still, they persisted. Almost in response to her questioning their validity, they even became louder. Finally one of the voices rose above the others and sounded familiar to her. It was a man's voice. She wasn't sure where she had heard the voice before, but somewhere, she had.

"Come," the voice said, and then something she could not make out. "Come." It wasn't a command, really, it was a suggestion. It was a proposal from a voice that was protective, soothing, serene.

Downstairs, she expected Mr. Barrington was at that moment closing his eyes and placing the Bible facedown on the table beside his rocker. He folded his hands on his lap and shut his eyes, thinking how hard life was. Mrs. Barrington, meanwhile, was leaning over the rocker and kissing her husband gently on his brow. Marcia could almost hear the kiss.

She thought to herself that she was somehow in tune with the whole house, capable of seeing or feeling everything that occurred anywhere within it.

Except for the attic. There the picture was unclear, as if the attic were a television station her mind's aerial could only partly pick up.

"Come. Come play," the voice seemed to be saying. "Come play. Come upstairs and play."

She knew Thistle Peep didn't like the attic; she knew that the girl found the attic cold: literally cold, in that it would surely raise goose bumps along her small arms, and figuratively cold, in that it was an uninviting, unappealing place for a small child. She knew that Thistle Peep was scared—very scared—of the dark.

But the man above her sounded so warm, so very different from the man below her. Thistle Peep didn't like her father, Marcia realized; he frightened her. He was stern with his daughter, his only child, and distant. Virtually the only time he spent with her were those moments when he would read aloud to her from the Bible.

But the man upstairs, well, he sounded almost playful. He sounded as comforting and unthreatening as the Weesimmo daddy, the father from Marcia's own special four-in-the-morning family. And when she listened more closely and the voice above her became more clear, she knew at once that the voice was in fact that of the Weesimmo father! He was right there in the Barringtons' house, perhaps not more than ten feet away in the attic above her.

"Come upstairs and play. Come play," the voice said again, this time with just the slightest hint of urgency. "Come play!"

She turned her head and looked up toward the ceiling. "Can you come down here?" she said silently, forming the words with her lips but not actually making any sound.

Rather than answer her, the Weesimmo father fell back into the dull chorus of voices around him. She should have expected that. Of course he wouldn't come down from the attic. The whole reason he was in the house now was to lead her up to the attic.

And so she would go. This was her fate; there was no escaping it. One couldn't change history.

She slowly pulled her legs out from beneath the covers and threw them over the right side of the bed—the side farthest from the door.

She knew if she crawled out of bed on the left side the floorboards there would groan and the Barringtons would know she had gotten out of bed.

Still wearing her quilt around her shoulders like a shawl, she tiptoed around the foot of the bed and stood in the bedroom doorway, listening. She heard the sounds of Thistle Peep's father in the library, his rocker creaking gently as it swayed back and forth like a pendulum. The girl's mother was probably sitting on the divan beside him, knitting. She rested one hand on the knob of the bedroom door, astounded for a brief second by the ornate flowers along the brass.

There was almost no light in the hallway, only that which came from the moonlit bedrooms along the south wall. Her feet were bare, and for a moment she was surprised by how coarse and cold the wooden floor was. She had expected to feel the linoleum tiles that would be covering that floor in eighty years.

"Come, come and play," the Weesimmo father said again, his voice rising joyfully from the murmur. His voice was so loud this time Marcia thought for a second that surely the Barringtons had heard it. They must have. Clearly, however, they hadn't: the rocker continued to creak at the same pace it had before.

After shutting the child's bedroom door behind her, a gesture that struck Marcia as more ritualistic than practical, Marcia gingerly placed her fingertips on the wall and used it as a guide as she began to inch her way down the hallway to the attic. Past what in eighty years would become one of her and Brian's guest bedrooms (a guest bedroom they would never have a chance to use), past what in eighty years would become her and Brian's own bedroom for a very short while. She decided to peek inside that second bedroom, curious whether the Barringtons used it as their master bedroom as well.

They did. Her eyes fell first on Mrs. Barrington's dressing table, simple except for the two silver hairbrushes and elegant looking glass that rested on top of it. She noticed that the Barringtons' bed, a handsome four-poster that looked in the dark to be made of a cherry wood similar to Mr. Barrington's rocker, was in the exact spot where she and Brian would place their bed eight decades later.

Above her, a little girl giggled and the Weesimmo father laughed. She had to continue. She closed the Barringtons' bedroom door as she had their daughter's, and then tiptoed down the hall toward the attic.

She recalled making this walk alone in search of her cat on her very first day in the house and alone the night Brian died. She remembered making this walk one Saturday night with Brian and one Monday afternoon with J. P. And each time, no good had come from the walk.

And this time would be no exception. She knew it.

She wondered what would happen if she turned around exactly where she was and tiptoed back into bed. Or better yet, tiptoed downstairs into the protective arms of Mrs. Barrington? She wondered what would happen if she ignored the voices, refused to let them lead her into the attic. Would Thistle Peep live to a ripe old age, perhaps be alive eighty years later? Would the woman perhaps be living still in this very house?

Perhaps. Perhaps. Perhaps she could ignore the voices; perhaps she could change history after all. Perhaps if she never went into that cold, evil attic, she and Brian would still be living in New York City, still be happily married. Or if they had moved to Vermont, perhaps they would not have moved to this town or into this house, and Brian would still be alive. Perhaps.

It was worth trying.

She turned and started back toward the child's bedroom, but stopped when she saw that the door was shut. Shut doors always frightened Marcia, especially at night. Especially now. It didn't matter to her that it was she herself who had shut the door, she was afraid now to touch that frilly, ornate knob and turn it. Who knew what was on the other side? Who knew what was under the bed or in the closet or lurking amidst the stenciled pine trees?

No, Marcia thought, she was better off running downstairs to Thistle Peep's mother. She had a sense that while Thistle Peep was frightened of her father, the girl adored her mother. The child's mother would protect her, the woman who was at that moment stitching or knitting or sewing on the divan.

Without turning back for one last look at any of the doors on the second floor—not the attic or Mr. and Mrs. Barrington's or Thistle Peep's—Marcia raced downstairs on very small feet, the feet of Thistle Peep Barrington.

When she reached the first floor, Everett Barrington whirled around in the rocking chair, and Marcia could see by the anger in his eyes that something was wrong, something was terribly wrong.

She had made some mistake. Mrs. Barrington wasn't sitting on the divan; she wasn't even in the room.

She wasn't even home; that was the mistake. Wasn't that what the newspaper article had said? That Mrs. Barrington had been gone the night Thistle Peep died, that she had been away in Burlington tending to her own mother?

Marcia realized that even a little girl in a small Vermont village in 1910 must have understood intuitively, understood with horror, what she had walked in on. Even if she didn't understand the details, even if she didn't understand the reasons or the urges. The child knew that what she had walked in on was wrong, that what she had walked in on would kill her.

Marcia didn't know who the young woman was on Everett Barrington's lap, or what had possessed her to strip off her blouse and allow Everett to make love to her in the room below his sleeping daughter. She didn't know whether the woman had fainted when she saw the child in the library doorway or whether she had been knocked unconscious when Everett had turned toward his daughter, enraged, and tossed the woman off his lap and onto the floor.

All Marcia knew was that Everett Barrington was so insanely angry, so insanely scared, that he was about to break the neck of his only child.

Chapter 26

The Palms Diner was all metal and glass, an eclectic series of flat, shining surfaces. The place had a sheen to it that was in some ways timeless: long ago Burrows had decided that the diner would look great in a movie, regardless of whether that movie was set in Chicago in 1935 or Mars in the twenty-first century. What a metal diner was doing in the middle of scenic downtown Burlington, however, was beyond Burrows (as it was everyone in the city); he was just glad it was there.

He and Patricia Lange sat across from each other in a booth in the Palms late Tuesday afternoon, the only two people in the diner at that hour. They had been sitting there almost fifteen minutes, sipping coffee and stewing over the barn cat, and still Lange had not gotten around to the tongue waggin' that had prompted their leaving her office in the first place.

Finally Burrows asked, "So tell me, Patricia, what's everybody saying about me that you think I should know?"

Lange raised an eyebrow. "Did I say it was about you?"

"Maybe not in so many words. But you implied it."

The medical examiner nodded. "Well, it is."

"Well, I thought so."

"You've been spending most of your time on the Middleton homicide, haven't you?"

"Investigation. The Middleton investigation. It hasn't been ruled officially as a homicide."

"But that's where you've been spending most of your time, right?"

Burrows ran his finger around the rim of the empty ashtray on the table. He wished he had some darts to throw. "All of my time," he said finally.

"That's what I thought. For a week now that's all you've been working on."

"That's right."

"Do you think you're making progress?"

Burrows pressed his finger down on the edge of the ashtray, causing the far side to pop into the air like a seesaw and then slam back down on the Formica tabletop with a crash. "I see where this conversation's going," he said, becoming annoyed.

"Nope, I don't think you do, J. P."

"I don't, huh? Well, let me save you some breath. Just tell me this, tell me one name: who's going to jump my hide as soon as I get back to my office? Jaffe or Beech?" Burrows asked, referring to the police commissioner and the state attorney.

"Both. But don't forget Montgomery. Sherman told me Montgomery himself is ready to kill you for going to Deering this afternoon."

"Terrific."

"But you don't know why they're going to jump your hide."

"Oh, I'd bet I do."

Lange looked out the window for a moment, watching Mindy Tarbull dole out parking tickets across the street. "You'd lose that bet," she said turning back to Burrows.

Burrows sat forward in the booth, placing his fists and elbows on the table. "Let's just see about that, Patricia. Jaffe is getting ornery because the only suspect I have is the widow, and Beech is getting ornery because I can't give him enough for an arraignment. Did I win?"

"Nope, you lost."

"Serious?"

"Serious."

"I must be losing my touch."

"I doubt that, J. P. But maybe your touch right now is touching the wrong things. Maybe the wrong person."

"I'm not following you at all."

"How many people did you talk to in Deering?"

"Lots. Everyone who even might have known the Middletons."

"Did you talk to Joshua Nash?"

"Yup."

"Did you talk to his wife, Sarabeth Nash?"

Burrows thought for a minute. " 'Course I did. I've spoken with her a couple of times."

"Let me rephrase that question: have you formally interviewed Sarabeth Nash about Brian Middleton's death?"

"I've spoken to Sarabeth twice. Maybe neither time was a 'formal' interview, but the lady certainly would have told me something she thought I should know."

"Don't be certain, J. P. Think about it a minute. When did you talk to Sarabeth Nash?"

Burrows sat back in the booth. "Let's see. I interviewed Josh Nash four days ago, on Friday. Sarabeth wasn't home at the time. I first met her yesterday, after Marcia and I found that noose in the attic. I immediately took Marcia back to the Nashes', where she's staying, and I spent some time with Sarabeth then."

"You said you've spoken to her twice."

"Right. I spoke to her again last night. I called to check in on Marcia."

"Did you interview her at either time?"

"If you mean did I interrogate her, then no, I did not. But, my God, Patricia, sure as sugar'll sweeten snow that lady would have told me something if she had something to tell!"

Lange rubbed her brow. "Sarabeth Nash arrived in Burlington at twelve forty-five this afternoon and gave a statement to Sherman Anderson," she began, keeping her voice even. "In that statement she said that on the night Brian Middleton died, she went to visit the Middletons around seven-thirty P.M., bringing with her an apple pie she had baked them.

"She never gave them the pie, however, because when she arrived at the edge of their driveway she saw them in their living room and heard their voices even though the windows were closed. The Middletons were shouting at each other, fighting about something. It looked—and sounded—like a real nasty affair to Sarabeth. She walked a little closer, trying to figure out whether to leave the pie on the front stoop and go home, or just go home.

"When she got closer, she saw that Marcia was crying. Sarabeth used the word 'sobbing.' So she decided she wouldn't even leave the pie, she would just go. Before she turned, however, she saw Brian raise his hand and hit Marcia. She didn't see exactly where Brian hit her, but it looked to Sarabeth like he smacked her on the shoulder. In any case, he struck Marcia hard enough that he knocked her to the floor.

"At that moment, Sarabeth said she considered ringing the doorbell, just to break up the fight. But she saw Marcia get slowly back on her feet and glare at Brian. Brian glared back, but only for a second, and then stormed out of the living room. That left Marcia alone. So

Sarabeth figured the worst was over and that she should just turn back and pretend she never saw anything. At least for now."

The waitress, an older woman named Arlene, wandered over to the booth and asked if they wanted their coffee topped off. Lange shook her head no, but Burrows nodded and pointed at his cup in slow motion. She then dropped the check on the table, inserting it upright between the salt and pepper shakers.

"Why didn't she tell me any of this?" Burrows asked, his voice sounding to him as if he were in shock. Maybe he was, he thought.

"She says you never asked."

"That's lame," Burrows said, "that's right lame. Why didn't she *volunteer* the information, in that case?"

"She figured she'd seen something she wasn't supposed to have seen, and she should just keep it to herself. Until last night, that is."

"Oh? Well did she say what happened last night that caused this incredible change of heart? What goddamn revelation suddenly came to her out of the clear blue sky?"

"You're angry, and you've got every right to be. But don't take it out on me," Lange said, chastising Burrows.

"I'll rephrase the question: what the heck made her decide last night to suddenly hang out other people's dirty skivvies?"

"Not a what, a who. It was a who that caused her to start talking. Her husband. She hadn't told anybody what she had witnessed a week ago Sunday, not a soul. If Brian Middleton was a suicide—as she had assumed—there was no reason to soil his reputation any further by spreading 'round town the idea that he may have been a wife beater.

"She finally opened up a bit last night when she was talking to her husband, Joshua. It seems Joshua wasn't real pleased with the idea of having Marcia Middleton under his roof in the first place. The woman scared his daughters and even gave him the creeps—"

"That's ridiculous. Marcia Middleton couldn't give a five year old the creeps!"

"I'm just telling you what Sarabeth said."

"Well, it's stupid."

"Fine. But it's part of a sworn statement you never got. Anyway, Joshua and Sarabeth got to talking, and when Josh heard that Marcia and Brian had had—literally—a knockdown fight, he told her to get on up to the police and tell them. Tell them everything, and tell it to them fast. And since you weren't in, Anderson took the statement."

Burrows sighed. "This is all real interesting, but it doesn't prove anything. Fine, Middleton hit his wife. That doesn't mean Marcia killed the guy."

"It helps build a case."

"Swell," Burrows grumbled, reaching for the check. "Let me get this, to thank you for making my evening."

"There's more, J. P."

"Oh? Let me guess: I suppose Marcia Middleton was in the car right behind Sarabeth, got to the station at exactly one-fifteen, and confessed to her husband's murder, as well as to every other unsolved homicide we got on the books. Is that it?"

Lange frowned. "You should never raise your voice, J. P., unless the barn's burning."

"Was I shouting?"

"You were speaking loudly."

"Well, I'm angry."

"Well, take a deep breath, because you're about to get angrier."

"I don't think that's possible."

"You haven't been right once in the last half hour," Lange said lightly, trying to calm Burrows down. "I don't expect your luck's about to change."

Burrows smiled just the tiniest bit. He had to smile, he decided; it was the only thing he could do right now. "Okay, let me have it. What else?"

"Sarabeth happened to say one thing in passing that really hit home with Anderson."

"And that was?"

"She said that when you walked down the road yesterday with Marcia, bringing her over to the Nashes' home, you had your arm around the woman."

"We had just found that noose; the lady was upset."

"Sarabeth said you two—and these were her words—'looked like a couple.' You 'looked married.' "

"And I'll bet that just made Anderson's day."

"Anderson's your friend, J. P. He's concerned. He thinks you're so wrapped up in this lady, you're going to get yourself in trouble."

"Like what? He thinks I'm going to get myself killed?"

"You're not making this very easy for me. I'm only trying to help."

"I know you are, Patricia, and I appreciate that. But this whole thing is verging on the absurd. It really is."

"Maybe it is," Lange said, shrugging. "Maybe it is. But if so, you're making it that way yourself. Anderson thinks you've lost all objectivity on this investigation. He thinks you've stopped using your head, and you're going to get booted in the tail. And I think he may be right."

"Anderson's grandstanding. He thinks Marcia Middleton killed her husband. That's all."

"Well, so does Montgomery, so does Beech."

"I'm sorry, but I don't agree."

"Why not?"

"Because I know what that house can do!" he blurted out. "I was just there, and I know what that house can do!"

Lange stared at him, her brow furrowed in concern. "What are you talking about?" she asked softly.

His hands were shaking, he realized. "I'm not talking about anything," he said quietly, trying to compose himself. "At least anything I understand."

"You just said that you don't think Marcia Middleton killed her husband because you know what that house can do. That's a pretty bizarre statement."

"Yeah, it is. It's a pretty stupid statement."

"What just happened? In Deering? Did something just happen to you in Deering?"

What just happened? Burrows thought to himself. What had just happened? He considered asking Lange if she had ever been scared enough to jump out a window, or whether she would like to see a key given to his brother by a child who had been dead over eighty years. He considered asking her if she believed in haunted houses and ghosts and nooses that grew from rafters, wondering if the medical examiner—if any medical examiner—could have faith in demons or spirits of any kind. He decided it wasn't likely.

"What just happened?" she asked again.

"You know," Burrows said simply. "I found that cat."

"And that's why you don't believe Marcia Middleton murdered her husband? J. P., that doesn't make any sense!"

"All I mean," Burrows continued slowly, "is that I know Marcia. And I don't believe she's capable of killing anyone. Especially her husband."

"That's exactly what Anderson means! Listen to you! You have lost all objectivity on this case!"

"Putting my arm around a distraught woman does not make my investigation suspect. It just doesn't."

"Maybe alone it doesn't. But when you put it together with some of the other things Anderson told me, it does."

"Such as?"

"Such as not probing why Marcia's husband was drunk Sunday night. Such as investigating the history of the house with the primary suspect. Such as movin' slower than molasses in January after this Joyce person—"

"There's no evidence to suggest 'this Joyce person' is a suspect," Burrows explained, cutting her off, "no evidence at all."

"It doesn't matter. You should have gotten to her by now."

"Look, her mother said she was due back in New York today or tomorrow. If she isn't back by tomorrow, I'm planning on putting out a bulletin on her with the state police across New England."

"But the bottom line, J. P., is that it looks like you're missing the small points. And let's face it, a good investigation is nothing but small points. You're as aware of that as anyone. That's why under normal circumstances you're the best we have."

Burrows pulled out his wallet and stood up, starting toward the cash register. He stopped and turned back to Lange. "All this tongue waggin' is great. What am I supposed to do about it?"

Lange reached across the booth for her coat, and stood up with him. "With the statement Sarabeth Nash gave today, Beech thinks we may be able to get a confession out of the woman, if we dangle a plea of second degree before her."

Burrows shook his head in astonishment. "Confess what? Tillier can't even prove the man was murdered! I hear this talk that Brian Middleton was smothered, but I've yet to see a murder weapon—"

"Whose fault is that?"

"I can't find what doesn't exist!"

"Look, J. P., the top brass is not prepared to drop the case for insufficient evidence, at least not yet. They'll sooner drop you from the investigation than they will close the case."

"One swallow doesn't make a summer, Patricia," Burrows said, trying to hide the disgust in his voice, "you—and Montgomery—know that as well as I do."

"Maybe. But you're just about out of time. If you don't give Montgomery a witch to burn real fast, he'll find someone who will."

Maybe Joyce Renders' voice wasn't the voice of a home wrecker, but after hearing the same recorded thirty-five words over and over, it was a voice that had begun to annoy Burrows.

Around five-thirty that afternoon he left one more message on the woman's answering machine and decided that if she weren't home by the time he went to bed, he would release a bulletin on the woman across New England.

Chapter 27

Grace Macknight saw that the light was still on in Dr. Dial's office when she was driving home, and decided to drop in. She told herself she would only stay a minute, because Ted was probably cleaning up and trying to get home himself. It was Dial who had raced over to the realtor's parking lot that afternoon when Grace had called and said something had happened to the new woman.

"Yup, she's fainted," Dial had said to Grace before reviving Marcia. "She's fainted. And after all she's been through, I'm surprised she didn't faint sooner."

Grace, however, was certain it was more than that. By the time Dial had arrived, Marcia looked peaceful, her head resting comfortably against her automobile's headrest. Dial hadn't seen her sitting in her car for ten minutes with her eyes closed, unmoving, and then suddenly twist her neck in the most peculiar—and most violent—manner. Dial hadn't seen the terror in her eyes that one split second she had opened them.

"Evenin', Grace," the heavyset, older man said, opening up the front door and rolling the *Time* magazine on his waiting room table into a tube. He was already wearing his down parka, and was clearly on his way home.

"Evenin', Ted. I see you're on your way out."

"Yup. What can I do for you?"

"Oh, I'm not exactly sure. I saw your light was on, and I was just wonderin' if you'd given any more thought to what happened to Marcia Middleton today."

Dial slipped the rolled-up magazine into the pocket of his parka. "Yup."

"And? You come to any conclusions?"

Dial paused. "Like what?"

"Like what was goin' on."

"She fainted. People faint sometimes, Grace; you know that."

"That's it?"

" 'Sume so."

"You don't think it could be worse than that?"

" 'Course it could be. I asked her to make an appointment to come see me tomorrow or Thursday so we could give her a full physical. Get a blood count, test for iron deficiencies. Things like that. But she didn't go for it."

"No?"

"Nope."

"How come?"

"Said she's got a doctor down country. She'll go see her next time she's in New York City."

Grace nodded. "I'm tellin' you, Ted, it was the strangest thing I'd ever seen. Just the strangest. The way her neck twisted, it was like she'd gone and hanged herself."

Dial frowned. "You're only thinkin' like that because her husband did himself in that way. You've got to stop. It's not good for you."

Grace started to ask the doctor whether he really believed Brian had hanged himself or whether Marcia may have helped the process along, but she caught herself just in time. Dial was the one who had pronounced the death a suicide; bringing it up as a murder would only hurt his feelings.

"Are you done with the peeler?" Sarabeth asked Marcia Tuesday night.

Marcia nodded. She was aware that Sarabeth was trying desperately to sound casual. In the fifteen minutes they had spent in the Nashes' kitchen preparing dinner—breading pork chops, peeling carrots, putting a batch of Betty Crocker double-fudge brownies into the oven—not once had the selectman's wife mentioned the fact that Marcia had fainted that afternoon in the realtor's parking lot.

"Fainted." That was Dial's word, Marcia thought, not the one she would have chosen. She wasn't sure how best to describe what had happened, but "fainted" certainly wasn't right. "Fainted" implied a natural physiological phenomenon. What had happened to her was unnatural, something triggered by a dead little girl. Thistle Peep Barrington had spoken to her, given her a vision of how she had died. Really died. She knew something no one else in the world knew: she knew that Thistle Peep Barrington had been murdered by her own father. She was sure of it.

"I went to Burlington today," Sarabeth said, staring intently at the water she had poured in the measuring cup. It looked to Marcia as if she was consciously avoiding eye contact with her.

"Shopping?"

"A little. I went by that new mall this afternoon, the one out by the airport." She poured the water from the measuring cup into a pot on the stove, and then turned to face Marcia. She still failed, however, to look Marcia in the eye. "Look, Josh will be home from work any minute now, so I better just spit this on out. I have to tell you something. The main reason I went to Burlington today was to talk to the police. I saw them around lunchtime."

"The police? Whatever for?"

"Your husband was not a good man. I know that. I know what he did to you."

Marcia was confused. Was Sarabeth referring to Joyce Renders? And if so, how in the name of God did Sarabeth Nash know about her?

"What my husband did to me . . . ," Marcia said softly, repeating the words. "Help me with that."

"That Sunday night—the night Brian died—I saw something I never should have seen."

"And that was?"

"You poor thing, you don't have to be secret with me. I saw it! I wasn't spying or anything like that, I was just bringing you over a pie—but I saw him do it. I saw Brian hit you!"

Marcia understood. She nodded slowly, becoming angry. Sarabeth had said the night Brian died, not the night Brian hanged himself. Language meant everything. Sarabeth Nash hadn't reported a battered wife; she had reported a murderous one.

She had gone to the police and given them their motive. Here was the one fact Marcia had scrupulously concealed from the police—a fact that to a large extent she had actually concealed from herself—and now they knew. They knew that she and Brian had fought violently Sunday night. And worse, they knew she had concealed the information.

Marcia sat awkwardly in the Nashes' living room after dinner, watching television with Josh, Allie, and Gail. The two girls were playing a board game on the floor called Candyland, and Marcia found herself flinching every time the plastic dice crashed against the game's cardboard box top. Sarabeth was up the street at the town hall at a meeting of the Deering Seniors support group.

Marcia wished she could leave. Neither Sarabeth nor Josh had verbalized their discomfort with her presence since Sarabeth had confessed to visiting the police, but a wall had come between her and the Nashes as soon as Sarabeth had told her. After all, Sarabeth had said in essence that she and Josh believed she may have murdered her husband.

She had therefore considered returning to her home, returning to her haunted palace painted four shades of yellow, but she was afraid. She was afraid to spend another night in that house, now that she knew the truth about Thistle Peep. And it was the truth. It had to be. This wasn't some fantasy she had made up in her head; this was a vision of what had actually happened there over eighty years earlier. And now that she knew, she was more afraid of that house than ever.

She had also considered getting in her car and escaping to the Holiday Inn in Burlington or to any one of the motels that surrounded the airport like bumpers in a pinball machine. But that option struck her as some sort of admission of guilt, some sort of acknowledgment that she could no longer face the Nashes. And now —especially now—she could not give them that satisfaction.

Still, she felt pathetic in the rocking chair in the Nashes' living room; she felt small and unwanted and—although she sat there with three other people—lonely.

J. P. Burrows hadn't spoken to Marcia at all that day when he picked up the phone at his desk shortly before eight o'clock and called her at the Nashes. There was, he thought to himself, a lot he could tell her. If he chose to.

He had wondered all day if he should tell her about her attic and the way it had decided to kidnap him for a short while. He had wondered ever since leaving Hank Tillier's office earlier that evening whether he should tell her that the barn cat was dead and that the autopsy indicated that the cause of death was smoke inhalation. "This cat could not have been alive when you found him," Tillier had tried correcting Burrows. "You must have been mistaken. He was clearly in a fire someplace this morning, and someone put him in the attic after he had died."

Knowing how Marcia loved her own cats, Burrows wasn't sure he could tell her that the animal was dead. But the more he thought about it, the more he realized he had to. He had to tell her about the cat; he had to tell her about the attic; he had to tell her about the key that his brother had given him. He had to tell her everything. For her own sake—for her own sanity—she needed to know these things; she needed to know everything there was to know about that house.

Besides, he wanted to see her. Despite the fact he knew he was setting himself up for a fall, he wanted to see her. It was painfully clear to him that the son of a small town dairy farmer could hold no interest for a woman like Marcia Middleton in the long run. But for now, for the moment, he really didn't care. He wanted to see her.

The older girl, Gail, answered the phone and then hollered for Marcia. Burrows thought the girl hollered exactly as his cousin had when she had spent one summer with them on the farm when they were kids.

"I'd bet you've already had dinner," Burrows began, when Marcia picked up the receiver and said hello.

"Almost two hours ago," Marcia said, leaning over the kitchen table and resting on her elbows. She smiled, and for a moment it surprised her that she was smiling, that she was happy that Burrows was calling. After all, wasn't he the enemy? No, not Burrows. Something vague, something amorphous called "the police" was her enemy. Not J. P. Burrows. She could trust J. P., she was sure of that. "Don't tell me you haven't eaten yet," she then added.

"Nope, I haven't. You folks in the country may take your suppers early, but we cosmopolitan folks up here in Burlington wait till a right civilized hour before eating."

"I'm not impressed," Marcia said.

"Well, I wasn't trying to impress you, so that's okay. All I was trying to do was let you know I was hungry, and I was going to go to dinner. Want to join me?"

"Now? In Burlington?"

"Middlebury. I'll swing through Deering and pick you up. There's a nice burger place just east of Middlebury that the college brats haven't discovered yet. You'd like it: they have California wines by the glass," Burrows went on, teasing her.

"Sounds like a date," Marcia said.

"If your idea of a date is watching me eat a cheeseburger, that's fine. But me, I'd just call it dinner."

"Still, people will talk, J. P."

Burrows leaned back in his chair. Going to dinner with Marcia Middleton was stupid; flirting with her was nuts. He could just imagine Montgomery screaming about "compromised investigations," or Commissioner Jaffe whining in that high-pitched voice of his about "ethical infractions." He sighed. "They already are, Marcia," he said finally. "They already are."

Perhaps not every student at Middlebury College was aware of the Bread Loaf Poets Burger Parlor, but most were. Marcia looked at the men and women—boys and girls, really—sitting in small groups around the restaurant's fireplace and in the large wooden booths surrounding her and Burrows, and decided that she was no longer young at twenty-nine. She and Burrows could have been chaperones for the dozen or so children in bulky ski sweaters and varsity jackets.

She noticed one young thing at the bar wearing clogs over thick wool socks, and recalled how she too had liked to wear clogs in college. She had liked the idea that her heel was exposed, and that with one flick of her foot the clog would fall to the floor, and her foot would be free. There was always something very sexy to her about kicking off a clog. She wondered if they would ever come back in style.

"Now I didn't come all the way down here just because I was hungry," Burrows was saying after the waitress had brought them each a beer. "A lot has happened today."

Marcia nodded. Was he referring to Sarabeth Nash's visit to Burlington or her own experience in the realtor's parking lot? When she thought about it for a moment, however, she decided he had to be alluding to Sarabeth Nash. She could not imagine that Dr. Dial or Grace Macknight would have thought to call him about what they viewed as a fainting spell.

"I don't know what you know and what you don't know," he continued, fiddling with the handle of his beer mug, "but let me start by telling you something right off. I don't think you murdered your husband. I did when I was first assigned to this case, I'll admit that. But I don't anymore."

"I'm glad." *Glad.* It struck Marcia as an odd word for her to use after she had said it. *Relieved* seemed more appropriate.

"I am too. But I do think your husband was murdered. Sort of. I don't believe he killed himself."

"Do you know who might have killed him?"

"Nope. Just that it wasn't you."

"What convinced you?"

Burrows took a long drink from his mug, and then placed it down firmly on the butcher block tabletop. "Getting to know you. That's a big part of it. You could no sooner kill someone than you could teach a cow to fly."

"Thank you."

"But there are other reasons. Like your house."

Marcia sat forward in the booth, suddenly hopeful. "What do you mean by that?"

"I'm not sure."

"But you know something?"

"Sort of, but probably not what you think. I have no idea who—what—killed your husband." He reached into his pants pocket and tossed onto the table the pewter skeleton key. "My brother gave me that."

Marcia picked it up and held it briefly, before dropping it back onto the table. "It's so cold," she said, surprised. "Where did Simon get it, a freezer?"

"Close. He got it in your house."

Was it possible, Marcia wondered, that the house would pick even on Simon? And then she realized that if the house would pick on a little girl just shy of her seventh birthday, it certainly wouldn't spare a retarded man. "Where did he find it?"

"He didn't. Someone gave it to him."

"Brian?"

"Nope. Simon claims—and who knows if he's telling the truth—that a little girl gave it to him. He says the girl handed the key to him as a good luck piece."

She reached again for the key. "That's why it's so cold," she mumbled.

"Maybe."

She felt her fingers begin to sting from holding the key. "What does it open?"

"I don't know. It doesn't fit any of the doors in your house."

"Did you try the attic?" she asked, returning the key to her place mat.

"Yup. My guess is that it opens some old box or blanket chest—probably one that was sold and resold years ago."

Marcia shook her head. "No. It opens something still in the house. The little girl wouldn't have given it to Simon if that weren't the case."

"Maybe."

"You're not as positive about the house as I am."

"Believe it or not, I am. But I also have two human suspects I'm supposed to be pursuing."

"Me and Joyce?"

"You and Joyce." She watched him push the key against his beer mug, and she wondered half seriously if he believed it would chill his glass. "There's something else I have to tell you."

"About the house?"

"Yup. Take a deep breath. I was in Deering today, around lunchtime. I came by to tell you that the noose we found yesterday in your attic was made of the same rope as the noose your husband used. The exact same stuff. You weren't home, but your front door was open. So I went inside, and I ended up wandering into the attic. And I found something."

"Another noose? A note?" Marcia interrupted.

"I wish that's all that was there." He shook his head and sipped his beer, as if stalling. "Somehow the barn cat that lived on your property, that tiger stripe, got into your attic. While it was there, it died. It died in my arms when I was carrying it downstairs."

"My God, how? How did the poor thing die?"

Burrows paused. "The coroner says it was smoke inhalation."

"Was there a fire?"

"No, there was no fire. You would have heard by now if there had been a fire at your house. But while I was in the attic, something did happen—"

The room grew silent for Marcia, and she became dizzy. Burrows continued to speak, but his words and face began to blend into the darkness behind him, and she thought for a moment that she might faint, especially when she felt herself swaying forward in her seat. She was vaguely aware of Burrows racing around the booth and propping her up beside him, wrapping his arm around her shoulders.

In his arms she began to catch her breath. She realized that she wouldn't faint, but she would cry; she would cry for an innocent tiger striped mouser, a cat who could survive outside in winters of forty below zero, but who couldn't make it one day inside that sick, evil house. The cat knew that, the cat understood the house, and that was why he would never come near the place. Of course, the first time he did, the first time he was lured or cajoled or seduced inside it, he died.

Periodically she opened her eyes and looked down at the lines of black and red wool that comprised Burrows' shirt and watched the way her tears spotted the fabric for brief seconds before disappearing. Once she wiped her eyes against his shoulder, and once she reached onto the table for a napkin to dry her face. But she remained flush against Burrows, unwilling to move, unwilling to leave the red flannel cocoon that was at that moment providing the only warmth and comfort and hope in her life.

"This'll pass," Burrows said softly, rocking Marcia. "Even this will pass."

The moon was waning, but it was still round enough to illuminate some of the farmhouses and barns dotting Route 116, the two-lane highway that connected Deering and Middlebury. Periodically Burrows would take his eyes off the road and glance quickly over at Marcia, dozing beside him in the Bronco's passenger seat. He wished they had a three- or four-hour drive ahead of them, instead of only ten more minutes. Montgomery be damned. Montgomery, Anderson, and Beech be damned. He didn't care about them; he didn't care what they thought. He decided he didn't care about anything but his desire to be with this woman, regardless of the fact they had no future together, regardless of the fact that even in the best of circumstances, he would never be able to offer her the sort of life that she probably wanted. As long as the moon was bright and the night was still, all that mattered to Burrows was that he and Marcia Middleton were together.

He couldn't tell for sure, but he thought she might have been smiling in her sleep. He hoped so. She didn't have much chance these days to smile when she was awake.

When they reached Deering and pulled up before the Nashes' house, dark except for the light on the front porch, Burrows started to reach over to Marcia to wake her, but stopped himself. It didn't seem fair to make this woman go back in there. Not now. Marcia had told him at dinner that Sarabeth had admitted to her that she had gone to the police that day. Going back in there now was at the very least awkward for Marcia, and probably something worse. Something like friendless. Or unwanted.

But as she herself had said, it would be much worse for her to stay in that yellow house up the street. They had both agreed it would be downright dangerous for either of them to enter that house alone, given what had happened to Burrows in the attic that afternoon and the vision Marcia had experienced in the realtor's parking lot. Somehow the two incidents were related. Burrows was sure of it. After what he had felt and heard and smelled in the attic that day, Burrows had every faith that on some level Marcia had been given a glimpse into the house's history. It had been no nightmare or hallucination, not in Burrows' eyes. And there was no way he wanted her back in that house now, not under any circumstances.

Gently he reached over and tapped her thigh and gave her leg a small shake.

Marcia stretched, very much like a cat herself, and turned her head toward him with a sleepy smile on her face. "I fell asleep," she said, "didn't I?"

Burrows nodded. A strand of red hair had fallen casually across her forehead. Without thinking, he reached over and brushed it away from her eyes.

"Thank you," she said softly.

"Welcome."

"This is where I get out, isn't it?"

"Yup, it is. But I wish it wasn't."

She sighed. "Me too."

"You know," Burrows began, choosing his words carefully, "if you want to, you could stay with me in Burlington. That's not a proposition or anything like that. My apartment's only got one bedroom, but I would sleep on the couch in the living room. It would be no problem. I sleep there a lot anyway, when I've sent the sheets to the laundry and haven't put clean ones on yet."

When Marcia was silent for a long moment he was afraid he had offended her. But when she looked up at him and he could see her eyes in the moonlight, almost serene, he saw that he hadn't. "I think I was dreaming," she said quietly, her voice content. "I don't remember the dream, but I know it was pleasant."

"I'm glad."

"It may have been the first dream I've had in a week and a half that wasn't a nightmare."

Burrows nodded, unsure of what to read—if anything—into her remark.

"I'd like that," she said finally.

"To stay with me in Burlington?"

"Yes. But first I should leave a note for Sarabeth and Josh—tell them I've gone to a motel or something. I'll only be a minute." She then leaned across the seat and brushed her lips across Burrows' cheek.

"I'm sorry," Officer Molly Branigan told Jennifer Hampton over the telephone late that night, "but I'm not allowed to release the home telephone numbers of any of our personnel. You'll have to call back in the morning." She stared at the three photographs of baby Helen she had placed on the counter before her, trying to decide which one to put in the new frame.

"But I know Detective Burrows will know where my sister is. I just tried to reach her in Deering, and the woman she was staying with—a woman named Sarabeth Nash—said she was gone."

"Gone?"

"Gone! Marcia left a note saying she was going to stay at a motel in Burlington, but she didn't say which one."

"Why do you think Detective Burrows will know where she went?"

"Because he drove her there! He took her to dinner, and then he drove her there!"

Molly Branigan chuckled. "He did, did he?"

"Yes!"

"Well, I'm not supposed to confirm that sort of information either," she said quickly, not quite sure whether she was trying to sound formal or merely cover for J. P. She looked down again at the photos of her daughter, and decided upon the one of Helen on her side in her crib. It made her look like a baby behind bars, the perfect shot for a police station.

"All I want to do is make sure my sister is all right," Jennifer continued. "I haven't heard from her since Sunday night!"

Relieved at having made a decision on the photograph, Molly listened more carefully to the woman on the other end of the telephone. The woman really did sound fairly desperate, even for a New Yorker. "That's all you want to know? If your sister is all right?"

"That's it."

"Well, as far as I know, she is. I believe Detective Burrows has been in contact with her a number of times."

"He may be in contact with her right now, for God's sake!"

"I can't release that sort of information. Sorry."

"But you did say my sister is okay."

"I did. You said your name was Ms. Hampton, right?"

"Right."

"Well, Ms. Hampton, you would have heard if anything at all had happened up here. Honest. Your sister's just fine. So what I would do if I were you is get myself a good night's sleep and call back first thing in the morning. J. P.—Detective Burrows—goes on duty at eight o'clock."

"I can't believe that's all you'll tell me," Jennifer said irritably to Molly.

"I'm sorry."

"Well thanks a bunch."

"You're welcome. I really do wish I could do more for you," Molly said, but she was pretty sure the woman at the other end only heard the first two or three words before she slammed down the telephone.

Burrows felt Marcia's presence beside him in the room before he actually saw her. When he opened an eye she was already there, kneeling beside the couch on which he was sleeping, wearing the Bosox tee shirt he had given her to wear as a nightgown. He started to sit up but she caught his shoulder and held him still, and then crawled up onto the couch beside him.

He started to speak, to ask her something (though what that something was, was unclear in his mind), when she put one finger on his lips, silencing him.

"Shhhh," she said. "Shhhh." She swung her body over him, and resting on her hands and knees slowly lowered herself onto him. Her hair, her mane the color of hot coals, fell about his face like a drape, and he kissed her.

4.

Chapter 28

Marcia rolled over in Burrows' bed Wednesday morning, surprised that he had managed to shower, get dressed, and leave for work without waking her. It was already eight-thirty.

She slid out from underneath his sheets, and took her blouse from the chair by the window. Outside, she saw columns of students walking to their classes across the university campus. They were babies, younger even than Jennifer.

No. No one was younger than Jennifer.

She turned back toward Burrows' bedroom, leaning against the window frame. She felt fuzzy, dazed. Had she really slept with the man who lived in this apartment? Yes, she had, and it astounded her. She barely knew him, this J. P. Burrows; she didn't even know what J. P. was short for. And yet she had needed him; at least last night, she had needed him. She had needed to feel another person beside her, to be held and warmed and heartened by a person she could trust.

And right now, that person was J. P. Burrows.

She stared at the room surrounding her and decided that it was too neat for a single man, too neat for a cop. His change was stacked by coin on his bureau, and the only clothes that were out were hers. She wandered over to the framed aerial photograph of what was undoubtedly his father's farm, noting how small the house was in comparison to the barn. The barn looked like it might stretch for a city block. She noticed that nailed to the wall opposite the bed was an antique dart board, probably—judging by the art deco numbers—sixty or seventy years old. There were no darts in the board right now, but Marcia could imagine Burrows throwing darts from the bed.

She realized with some giddiness how much she wanted to open his dresser drawers and peek inside his closet. She never would, but she wanted to. She wanted to know more about the man with whom she had just spent the night. Not out of guilt, (though she had to admit, there was some of that in her), but out of curiosity: she was attracted to Burrows, drawn to the man in ways that surprised her.

In the kitchen she found that he had left her a short note on the refrigerator, telling her where he kept everything from coffee to Shredded Wheat. He asked her to call him at the station before going anywhere, adding that he would be back as soon as he could, so together they could talk to Simon about his new little friend in Deering.

He ended the note, "Keep smiling."

That was easy today, Marcia thought. Or easier, at any rate.

She made herself a cup of coffee and sat down at the kitchen table with the note Burrows had written. She imagined that Sarabeth Nash was at that same, exact moment reading the note she had left her, wondering at which "airport motel" she was staying. She would have to call Sarabeth that morning.

Sipping her coffee, she decided that Burrows wrote like a little boy. His note was made up of large print letters and lines that climbed up and across the page like ski lifts. That suggested—someone had told her once—that he was an open-minded, accessible sort of person. Receptive to new ideas, willing to listen.

Perhaps that explained why he had believed her when she told him that Thistle Peep Barrington had not killed herself, that in actuality the child had been murdered, her neck snapped by her own father. When he had asked her how she knew this and she described for him her vision in Grace Macknight's parking lot, he had nodded understandingly, as if she had simply mentioned a late April snowstorm—uncommon, perhaps, but not particularly rare.

It was she, in fact, who had asked him if it were possible that what she had experienced was an hallucination of sorts, maybe a nightmare. Or a mirage. It was she who had asked him if maybe, just maybe, she was losing her mind.

But J. P. had put a finger to her lips and whispered, "If it was anything, it was a premonition. I was in that house too, you know. I know what that house can do."

Molly Branigan had scribbled Burrows a note warning him that Jennifer Hampton would be phoning first thing that morning, so he was ready for Marcia's sister when her call came through. He immediately patched the call into Chief Montgomery's office, so he could have some privacy. Montgomery would be down at city hall for the better part of the day.

"Mornin', Ms. Hampton. Detective Burrows here," Burrows said, thickening his Vermont accent for the New Yorker's benefit. He was hoping it would mellow her out.

"Good morning," Jennifer said evenly. "I'm calling about my sister, Marcia Middleton."

So much for a few mellow pleasantries, Burrows thought to himself. "Go ahead," he said.

"I want to know where she is. I want to talk to her. I tried calling her late last night at the Nashes', and they—Mrs. Nash—told me you took her to some motel. I want to know why, and I want to know which one."

On the desk before Burrows was a photograph of Montgomery, his wife, and their two sons, taken on a beach on Lake Champlain. The older boy, Scott, was a senior in some college down south, while the younger son was a high school student somewhere between the eighth and the tenth grade. Montgomery was smiling in the picture, but even smiling and surrounded by his family he didn't look like a particularly charitable sort.

Burrows turned the picture away from him and decided on the spot that he was finished. Or pretty damn near finished. As finished anyway as a pig on the near side of a roasting spit. It was bad enough when Sarabeth Nash had seen him put his arm around the primary suspect in his murder investigation, but this . . .

This was suicide. Career suicide, at any rate. In the natural light of morning, in the light cast by the overhead lamp in Montgomery's office, the lunacy of it all became clear. He had slept with Marcia Middleton. People would find out. He was finished.

Still, there was no doubt in his mind that she was innocent. No doubt at all. He hadn't slept with a murderer, he told himself; he had slept with a suspect who would soon be cleared. He was sure of that.

"Your sister is fine," he told Jennifer, running a finger along the frayed black felt on the back of the picture frame. "She's just fine. But I recommended to her last night that she leave Deering. Which she did. I made this recommendation based on some new developments which evidently she hasn't shared with you or your family."

"And those are?"

"At some point between the time we reopened your sister's house last Thursday and Monday afternoon, someone rehung a noose in the attic."

"Who?" Jennifer asked, raising her voice in a tone that struck Burrows as closer to anger than panic. "Why would someone do that?"

"We don't know who did it, not yet anyway. As for the why, we believe it might have been meant as some sort of signal for your sister. And then Tuesday—yesterday—something else happened. There was a cat that lived in your sister's barn, a real mouser."

"And?"

Burrows paused to catch his breath, and tried to think. He was about to tell Jennifer Hampton that an important new development in a murder investigation was his belief that a cat had died of smoke inhalation in a house that wasn't on fire. He realized suddenly how absurd the idea sounded, and he knew he couldn't continue.

"And nothing," he mumbled. "The cat died is all. Look, I'm going to see your sister in about thirty minutes. Would you like me to have her phone you?"

Jennifer was silent for a moment, evidently trying to understand where the cat fit in. "Did Marcia want this cat?" she asked finally, her voice softening a bit. "Had she brought it inside the house or something?"

"She was trying to. That's all. Will Marcia know where to reach you? Are you at work?"

"Yes. Yes to both questions. I am at work, and Marcia will know where to reach me. But I can call her . . ." Jennifer continued, and then stopped abruptly. "Or I can wait here. I'll be at my desk all morning."

"Good. I'll have her phone you within the hour," Burrows said, adding, "I want you to know, I'm real sorry for any frustration this miscommunication may have caused you."

As he hung up the phone, he understood the break Jennifer had given him. She hadn't pushed for the name of the motel; she hadn't insisted that he tell her where she could reach her sister. Immediately he dialed Marcia at his apartment, planning to tell her exactly what he had told her sister, and then have her in turn phone Jennifer in New York City. Whether she confirmed for her sister that, yes, she had spent Tuesday night with the detective investigating her husband's murder was her business.

* * *

Marcia stared at her hands after she and Burrows had hung up. She wondered if she should let her nails grow long. She never had in New York because long nails seemed unprofessional, unbusinesslike. Feminine in an inappropriate and lascivious sort of way. Besides, long nails were impractical, given the fact that half her job in advertising seemed to be shaking other people's hands.

In Vermont, however, there was no reason not to let her nails grow. Or to paint them. It was not as if she had cows to milk or fence posts to fix. At least not yet, anyway. If she wanted, she could grow her nails long and paint them scarlet. Now *that* would turn some heads in Deering: Marcia Middleton, Siren of the North Country.

She dreaded calling Jennifer. She dreaded calling Sarabeth. But she decided that she dreaded calling Jennifer more. Jennifer would ask more questions, demand more answers. Jennifer would be louder.

She felt bad that she hadn't called her family since Sunday night when she had arrived in Vermont. She should have. But she knew that all that would have been accomplished by phoning them is that she would have given them one more reason to worry about her. And if she had told them what she now knew was true—that a father had murdered his own daughter in her house eighty years earlier—she would also have given them yet one more reason to question her sanity. They would probably have wound up flying Dr. Michaels himself to Vermont.

She decided finally to get Jennifer over with first, and phoned the investment bank where her sister worked. She realized as soon as she heard Jennifer's voice that although she had prepared herself for her sister's concern, she had not anticipated Jennifer's intensity. The woman sounded almost hysterical.

"Why haven't you called?" Jennifer began, spitting the question at Marcia.

"I should have," Marcia said, and started to apologize when Jennifer cut her off.

"Yes, you should have, you should have. You must have known how worried we are about you. Mom and dad are practically berserk, and I don't have a nail left on my body—fingers or toes!"

"I didn't want to worry you, any of you."

"We already are worried. It made it much worse not hearing from you."

"I know that—"

"Then why did you do it?"

"I know that now. I didn't think of it then."

"Are you all right? Really and truly all right?"

"Yes, I'm fine."

"Honest?"

"Honest."

"Do you know what it all means?"

Marcia thought for a moment. It. Her not phoning? "Do I know what what all means?"

"The noose, for God's sake! And the cat! That detective babbled about some cat dying. What was he talking about?"

The cat. She had managed to put the poor thing out of her mind all morning. "How are Solstice and Chloe?" she asked, not answering Jennifer's question.

"They're fine; they're terrific. They're a hell of a lot better than I am, or mom and dad are."

"Is Solstice eating? He wasn't eating much last week."

"Yes, as far as I know he's eating. Mom hasn't said he isn't eating, at any rate."

"He's a good boy."

"You haven't answered my question. What does it all mean?"

Marcia wrapped the phone cord around her fingers. She had never bitten her nails. She was glad; it was a revolting habit. She wished she hadn't caused Jennifer to bite hers. "I don't know. I don't know what it means. J. P.—the detective—thinks someone is trying to tell me something." She smiled just the slightest bit. She hadn't lied; she simply hadn't explained to Jennifer that the "someone" she had in mind had been dead for eighty years.

"But you don't know what that something is?"

"No."

"Or who's doing it?"

"No." She heard Jennifer sigh on the phone. She wished she hadn't put her sister through this. She wished she herself wasn't being put through it.

"Don't the police—don't you—think it's awfully dangerous for you to stay in Vermont?"

"It's awfully dangerous to stay in that house," she said after weighing her answer. "That's why I'm not there."

"I gather your motel has round-the-clock security and barred windows?"

Marcia slouched in the kitchen chair. She couldn't lie to her sister. Not about something like this. It was one thing to withhold a bit of knowledge, a hunch, a premonition. But this? She couldn't lie about this, not to Jennifer. "I'm not staying at a motel," she said, her voice becoming soft.

"No?"

Sarcasm. Jennifer already had it all figured out. "No. I spent last night in Burlington with the detective. At his apartment."

"The detective," Jennifer repeated. "At his apartment. Imagine that. I gather his apartment has barred windows?"

"No, nothing in Vermont does. This isn't Manhattan."

"Can I ask why? Can I ask why you spent the night with him?"

Why. There were a lot of reasons. Because the Nashes thought she had murdered Brian. Because she wanted to get away from Deering. Because she enjoyed being with J. P. Burrows. A lot of reasons, maybe, but they all added up to one thing, one answer. She had stayed with J. P. Burrows because she had needed him. It really wasn't all that complicated. He had offered, and she had accepted. It was simple. "I needed him," she answered.

Jennifer groaned just the tiniest bit. "When did all this come about?"

"Yesterday. Last night, really."

"Is this some new version of police protection?"

Marcia let the comment pass, puzzled by the edginess in her sister's tone. Jennifer had no reason to be angry with her. "He doesn't think I had anything to do with Brian's death, not anymore," she told Jennifer, afraid after she had said it that it sounded almost like a boast.

"That's big of him."

Again, the sarcasm. Marcia started to explain to her sister that it wasn't what it sounded like, that it just wasn't that tawdry, but she stopped herself. There was no reason to become defensive; she had done nothing wrong. "Look, you asked me if it was dangerous for me to be in Vermont. My answer is no, it's not. At least not while I stay at J. P.'s apartment."

"But you do go back to Deering during the day, don't you?"

"I plan to."

Marcia heard Jennifer snort. She had never heard her sister snort before, and it sounded almost chastening. "Don't you think you should come home? To New York?"

"I will. Soon enough."

"What does that mean?"

Marcia paused, thinking. She wasn't sure what it meant. "It means I don't know."

"Have you taken care of the phone? Or the utilities? Have you set a date for everything to be . . . to be disconnected?"

"The realtor said the only thing I should cut off before I leave is the phone. I guess because winter's coming."

"Does that mean you've at least taken care of putting the house on the market?"

"Yes. I think they may begin showing it as soon as this weekend."

"That's a step. Have you packed the place up yet?"

"No."

"Have you begun?"

"No."

Jennifer sighed. "I must sound like a total bitch. I don't mean to, but I know I do. I just don't like the idea of you being up there—even if you are staying with that detective. I don't like the idea of you spending another couple days in that house repacking boxes."

"Sarabeth Nash and Carrie Dunbar will help me," Marcia said, pulling their names out of the air to reassure her sister. She was confident that J. P. would be there, if she needed any help.

"It doesn't sound like you'll be home on Friday at this rate."

"No, it doesn't."

"Then I'll fly up there. I'll fly up tonight, and tomorrow we'll pack up the whole house. We'll get you out of there and home once and for all." Suddenly she sounded almost cheerful.

"Sweetie, I just don't think that's necessary. I'm okay."

"I know you are."

"Please, Jenny. I'm asking you not to come."

"And I'm asking you to let me."

Marcia pressed her thumb against a countertop in the kitchen and then pulled it away, watching the fingerprint left by the moisture on her skin evaporate. "If I promise to spend today packing—today and every waking minute tomorrow—will you relax?"

"Every *daylight* minute tomorrow," Jennifer said, emphasizing the word daylight.

"Fine. Every daylight minute tomorrow. If I do that, will you give up this crazy notion of flying up here on the next plane?"

Jennifer paused, evidently giving the suggestion some thought. "I'll do that," she said finally. "But you know that I'll have to call you tonight to see how you're doing, don't you?"

"I would expect nothing less," Marcia said, relieved. "I would expect nothing less."

Chapter 29

It snowed in Deering Wednesday morning, a half-inch dusting that encouraged deer hunters and skiers alike without bringing out Orville Beanman and his plow or Zeke Crommer with his dump truck full of sand and salt. Gail Nash spent the morning daydreaming and watching the snow through the windows of the Deering schoolhouse.

Initially she had been relieved that morning when her mother had told her and Allie that Mrs. Middleton had gone to stay at a motel up in Burlington. Now, however, she was frightened. When the crazy lady had been under her roof, Gail had been able to take at least some comfort from the idea that her mother and father were keeping an eye on the woman. At least they knew where she was. But now? Now she could be anywhere.

The gruesome poem Bonnie Boisclair had taught her kept running through her mind:

> Lizzie Bordon took an ax,
> And gave her mother forty whacks.
> And when she saw what she had done,
> She gave her father forty-one.

Bonnie was not only the tallest, blondest, and prettiest girl in the sixth grade, she was probably the smartest; and when she had heard that Mrs. Middleton was staying with the Nashes, she had written Gail a special version of the poem:

> Marcia Middle took a noose,
> And hanged her hubby like a goose.
> And when she spent the night with Nash,
> She gave little Gail a great big gash.

Mrs. Middleton wouldn't have been quite so scary if she didn't have that weird habit of spacing out. Gail's mother had insisted it was because the woman was grieving, but Gail put more stock in Bonnie's explanation: the woman was a killer kook. After all, hadn't Gail's own parents said essentially that to each other Monday night? Gail hadn't been able to overhear every word of their conversation, but she had heard enough to get the gist: Mrs. Middleton had killed Mr. Middleton after they had had a colossal fight. It was possible Mrs. Middleton didn't remember killing him, but—and these were her father's words—"she killed him just as sure as good rhubarb will melt vanilla ice cream."

Gail glanced up at the schoolroom clock and saw that it was ten-twenty. Morning recess was ten minutes away. She dreaded recess today, she dreaded it. When she had told Bonnie on the way to school that morning that Mrs. Middleton was up in Burlington, Bonnie had suggested they go by the lady's house during recess and explore it. "Investigate" had been Bonnie's word. Gail had absolutely no desire to investigate Mrs. Middleton's house but had been afraid to say no to Bonnie. She had tried to talk Bonnie out of investigating the house on moral grounds ("We can't just go snoopin' around somebody's house," she had told her friend self-righteously. "It's not right.") and had failed and had tried convincing her friend to stay away on the grounds of simple logistics ("I'm tellin' you, we'll get caught. We can't just break into somebody else's house—'specially if that house is right next to the church!") and had failed again.

During recess, therefore, Bonnie Boisclair was going to race up the street and investigate Marcia Middleton's house. Gail would either have to join her or look like a chicken in the eyes of her best friend. She knew the moment Mrs. Vandersickle looked at the clock, saw it was ten thirty-one, and excused the class for twenty-nine minutes which course she would take. She had no respect for chickens and fair-weather friends.

Gail joined Bonnie, and the two girls raced out of the Deering school and ran up the street to investigate Marcia Middleton's big yellow house, not even stopping to catch the plump November snowflakes on their tongues. They didn't stop until they reached the Newsome's pasture across the street from the house, where they leaned against two of the fence posts and caught their breath.

"She did it to him in the attic, right?" Bonnie said finally, staring up at the small attic window on the south side of the house.

"I guess," Gail answered, shrugging. The lady scared her, but she still thought she should give the woman the benefit of the doubt.

"We gonna go inside?"

Gail saw Bonnie was smiling her intense smile, the smile she got when she was determined to do something and there was just no stopping her. Gail had seen that particular smile on Bonnie's face the time Bonnie had challenged two older kids to a tug of war during Hill Country Holiday the previous August, and the time she had challenged Mrs. Vandersickle on the meaning of the word "rivulet." Bonnie had won both times. "We don't have time," Gail said carefully. "We gotta be back at school by eleven."

Bonnie looked at her watch, a pink and green imitation Swatch. "We got twenty minutes till recess ends. It took us eight minutes to get here, so it'll take us eight to get back. That means we can spend ten minutes or so in the house. In the attic."

Gail watched the fog from her breath rise through the snow. The snow wasn't sticking to the roads, not yet anyway, but it was coating the rooftops like clean sheets. "We can't do much in ten minutes," she said. "It'll probably take us just that long to get in."

Bonnie wrapped the tassle of her wool hat between her fingers. "What do you bet we can push through the wheelbarrow ramp into the basement?"

"You mean break the latch?"

"I mean give the wooden doors a push. If they're so rotted the hooks break off, super-duper. We're in. If they don't, we'll run back to school, okay?"

"What if somebody comes by when we're inside?" Gail asked, staring up at the house. She had heard all the stories of the little girl who had killed herself inside that house, and of the grown-up man who had died there—or been killed—less than two weeks earlier. If houses really could be haunted, that was a haunted house.

Bonnie shook her head. "Gail Nash, you turnin' chicken on me? Why do I think you're gonna start squawkin' any second now?"

"I'm not a chicken!"

"Then let's go!"

"I think one of us should stand guard. Just in case."

"All right, you stand guard," Bonnie said with some disgust. "I'm tired of standin' here wastin' time. If someone comes by, just start squawkin'."

Gail folded her arms across her chest, ignoring the insult. "You're wastin' your precious time," was all she said.

"Okay, here I go. You got a watch?"

"No."

"Then take mine. If I'm not out by ten minutes to eleven, come and get me."

"That might take too long!"

Bonnie rolled her eyes. "Then yell. Yell up through the wheelbarrow ramp."

Gail nodded and looked away, watching only from the corner of her eye as Bonnie ran across Mrs. Middleton's side yard. When Bonnie reached the wheelbarrow ramp, a small pimple protruding from the side of the house, she saw her friend give it one good push with both of her hands. Nothing happened. Bonnie then looked suspiciously from side to side, before raising her right leg and kicking at the door. Judging by the way she had fallen forward, Gail was fairly sure Bonnie had managed to bash her way inside. She considered racing over to the ramp herself to make sure that Bonnie was all right, but the fact that her friend hadn't yelled she was hurt gave Gail sufficient assurance to stay put. She checked her friend's watch and saw that it was exactly quarter to eleven.

She glanced up at the attic window, wishing she had thought to ask Bonnie to wave when she got there—just so she could follow Bonnie's progress, know where she was inside that big old house.

It struck Gail as odd that she had never been inside the Finch place. As far as she knew, she had been inside 'most every other house in Deering. But not the Finch place. Part of that had to do with the simple fact that the Finches didn't have any children her age. They just had Foster, who was practically her parents' age.

But part of it had to do with the Finches themselves. As a pair they were downright unfriendly. Very few people had ever been inside the Finch place.

There was talk around Deering that the Finches actually kept in their attic the noose that the little girl had used to hang herself. Just as the little girl's own family had before them.

Imagine that. Keeping a noose around the house that someone had actually used to hang herself with. That was just plain weird. And spooky. She recalled again the poem that Bonnie had made up:

Marcia Middle took a noose,
And hanged her hubby like a goose.
And when she spent the night with Nash,
She gave little Gail a great big gash.

Gail decided that she would write a poem about Bonnie to get back at her. Scare her for a change. Unfortunately, not much rhymed with Bonnie. Or Boisclair. So she took a different tack, searching for rhymes with house, home, noose, and neck. And finally, head. She smiled slightly, and even shivered a bit, when she said aloud to herself her poem for Bonnie:

Marcia Middle took a noose,
And hanged her hubby like a goose.
And when she caught Bonnie by her bed,
She grabbed the girl and cut off her head.

That would give even Bonnie a scare. Satisfied, she glanced down at Bonnie's watch, and then gasped. She lost all satisfaction with one horrified, abrupt exhale: it was seven minutes to eleven. She looked over at the wheelbarrow ramp, and seeing no sign of Bonnie, raced across the street and started across the yard.

This was just like Bonnie, she thought to herself. They would never get back to school in time, and they would never be able to come up with a good explanation for where they had been.

When she reached the wheelbarrow ramp, however, school became a secondary concern. She stared down into the basement, disbelieving: alongside the small snowy footprints Bonnie had made with her little girl galoshes was a second set of footprints—muddy prints that were perhaps twice as large as Bonnie's. They began someplace around the far side of the basement, out of sight, wandered toward the wheelbarrow ramp, and then followed Bonnie's tracks back across the floor and up the stairs into the house.

Gail rubbed her eyes, trying to decide what to do. She decided she wanted to run away, run away from this house and back to the school. Run back to her own house, maybe. But she couldn't leave Bonnie trapped inside, not if someone—something—was in there with her.

She checked the time and saw that it was four minutes to eleven.

"Bonnie!" she cried finally down into the wheelbarrow ramp, speaking first in a stage whisper. "Bonnie!"

When there was no answer and no sound she called a little louder, a little more desperately, "Bonnie! We got to go!"

Somewhere up in the house she heard movement, activity. A door closing, perhaps, somebody's feet pounding along the corridors and stairs. It was almost like the pounding in her own chest, her own head. That might be Bonnie racing above her through the house, but it might not be. It might be whatever made those other footprints.

A second later she heard the cellar door open at the top of the basement steps, and then the sound of someone dashing downstairs. Convinced suddenly that it wasn't Bonnie, convinced that it was somebody else, somebody dangerous, Gail fell away from the front of the wheelbarrow ramp and curled up in a small ball off to its side. "Let it be Bonnie, let it be Bonnie, let it be Bonnie," she whispered over and over to herself.

She heard the footsteps run across the basement and up the wheelbarrow ramp. Bursting out into the gray day was Bonnie Boisclair. Immediately Gail jumped to her feet, and said, "Come on. We gotta get out of here!" She started to tell her friend about the second set of footprints, and to point them out to her, but Bonnie cut her off.

"I got as far as the attic door," Bonnie said breathlessly, "and just before I opened it, this little girl—for a minute I thought it was Allie, I swear I did—grabbed my hand and knocked it away! I swear it on your life and mine, she just took my hand and knocked it away!"

Chapter 30

Despite the light snowfall Wednesday morning, Burrows didn't think the roads were half bad, and he made the drive from Burlington to West Gardner in just over two hours. On two occasions, when idiots in a Volvo and idiots in a Mercedes (one from Massachusetts, one from New Jersey, he noticed) began tailgating him, he pulled off to the side of the highway to let them pass, but he knew he was being extra cautious. Let them slip and slide their way into someone else's bumper, he said to Marcia. The last thing that he—the last thing that they—needed right now, was to spend a couple hours waiting for a tow on I-89, ten miles north of Montpelier.

Although J. P. and Marcia reached West Gardner just before noon, it was after one o'clock by the time Mrs. Burrows had fed them supper and had gotten to chat for a few minutes with the woman who evidently had such great influence on *both* of her boys.

After supper, J. P. led Marcia and Simon into the living room, sitting them beside each other on the couch, while he sat across from them on an ottoman. He wasn't sure, but he thought that sitting next to Marcia Middleton was causing his brother to blush just the slightest bit. It looked that way, in any case. It sure looked like his brother was blushing.

"This here couch is older than I am," J. P. told Marcia, not because he was ashamed of the couch (although the paisley slipcovers did look a bit tired these days), but because he appreciated the couch like an old friend. For literally decades now he had dozed on that couch, read on that couch, baby-sat Simon from that couch. On two occasions he had even necked with Patience Avery on that couch, long slow adolescent kisses that lasted forever and that ended each time with him upon her, but unsure how to climb off.

After a moment J. P. pulled from his pocket the small pewter skeleton key Simon had given him and tossed it onto the couch between his brother and Marcia. It bounced once, and as it did Simon's eyes widened.

"You know that key, don't you?"

Simon nodded unhappily. He hadn't expected to see it again, at least not with anyone other than J. P. present.

"Well, I need you to help me with it. I need you to help me with it as much as I've ever needed your help with anything. Maybe more."

"You . . . you weren't supposed to show it to anyone," Simon murmured, afraid to look at Marcia as he said it.

"I know. And I'm sorry for that, I really am. But I wouldn't have shared it with Mrs. Middleton here if I didn't think she was supposed to see it too. You have to know that."

"It's for good luck," Simon said, staring down at the key.

J. P. wasn't sure if he was directing the comment at Marcia exclusively or at both of them. "Yup, that's what you told me, all right," he said simply. "It's for good luck."

"I won't tell a soul about the key, Simon. Not if you don't want me to," Marcia quickly volunteered.

J. P. wasn't sure that Simon had heard her. Without reacting, his brother reached into the couch for the key, holding it gingerly between his thumb and his forefinger as if it were one of the antique drinking glasses he lived in constant fear of breaking. After a few seconds, he dropped the key into his lap; and J. P. realized that it wasn't the key's value that had led his brother to handle the object so carefully, it was the fact that holding the key was like holding a piece of Dry Ice. It stung.

"You told me a little girl gave you the key," J. P. continued. "You told me she gave it to you in Mrs. Middleton's house. Is that right?"

Simon nodded without looking up from the pewter key in his lap.

"Well, I have to know what the key opens. It must open a door somewhere, or a box. Maybe even a chest of drawers or a bureau or something. Something like mom's hope chest, maybe. Did the girl tell you anything like that?"

Simon shook his head no.

"She didn't say anything about what the key opened?"

"I don't remember," he answered nervously.

"You don't remember her saying anything about a door somewhere?"

His voice barely above a whisper, Simon murmured, "I don't know. It was a long time ago."

"Yup, it was. And I can appreciate that," J. P. said, trying not to fluster or scare his brother any more than he already had. "It was a real long time ago. Maybe you remember what room you were in when the girl gave you the key. If you could remember that, that might help a lot. A whole lot."

"She said to keep it is all," Simon mumbled.

"When we were tossing the football last Saturday, you told me you saw the little girl in a bedroom. Is that where she might have given you the key? In one of the upstairs bedrooms?"

"I guess."

"Do you remember which one?"

Abruptly Simon stood up, the key falling from his lap onto the floor, and ran to a corner by the door. "I don't wanna do this anymore!" he told them, raising his voice.

J. P. sighed, but remained where he was on the ottoman. "Me neither," he told his brother sternly. "It's hard stuff. But I have to do it, and you have to do it."

"She'll get in trouble!"

"No, I promise you, she won't."

"She will!"

"It's right for you to look out for her, Simon," Marcia said suddenly, surprising both J. P. and his brother. She rose from her spot on the couch and joined Simon by the door. Touching his arm, she continued, "You're doing the right thing. She needs that. She needs a friend like you."

Simon watched her fingers rest for a few moments on the cuff of his flannel shirt, unable to look up into Marcia's face.

"But she also needs me," she went on. "I think I'm her friend too. That's why I want to help her. But I can't do that unless you tell us all you know about her. And about her key."

Simon stood unmoving, considering all that Marcia had said.

"Was it one of the bedrooms you were working on?" J. P. asked.

His brother turned toward him, opening himself up just the slightest bit. "We were in the room with the ladder," he said slowly.

"The room that faces Mount Stillman?"

Simon rubbed his forehead, unable even to guess at an answer.

J. P. looked at Marcia. "Do you know which room they kept the ladder in? Josh Nash and Dave Dunbar, that is?"

She nodded. "You were right: the one that faces Mount Stillman. That was one of the rooms they were working on."

"Is that the bedroom you believe belonged to the child?"

"Yes. I think so." She took Simon's hand and gently led him back to the couch. "This is really good, Simon," she told him, "and it's really important. It means a lot to us."

When they were again seated, J. P. said, "I'm only going to ask you a couple more questions. Just a couple."

"Then can we stop?"

"Then we can stop," J. P. told him, smiling.

"Good."

"Where else did you see this little girl? Did you see her in any rooms other than the one with the ladder?"

"I don't know."

Something in the tone of his brother's voice suggested to J. P. that there was a detail Simon was hiding. "You don't know, or you don't remember?"

His brother remained silent. On a hunch, J. P. asked, "Did you ever see her in the attic?"

"Oh, no!" Simon answered, surprising J. P. with his abrupt certainty on this one issue. "She didn't like the attic! We never went there."

"Is it possible you saw her in other rooms in the house?"

"I guess. Once I saw her by Mr. Nash's drawings."

J. P. turned to Marcia. "Do you know what Simon means?"

"Drawings of my house?" she asked Simon. "Did you see her by the drawings Mr. Nash made of my house?"

"I don't know what they were. They were Mr. Nash's drawings is all."

Marcia glanced at J. P. and explained, "He must be referring to the diagrams Josh made of the banister and the front hall. And of the library, perhaps. They weren't really blueprints; the renovations weren't that extensive. But they were very detailed sketches of what Josh—what Brian and I and Josh—had in mind."

"Where did Josh keep the drawings?"

"I don't know. I assume he brought them wherever he and David were working." J. P. watched her turn her attention back to his brother, and ask Simon with a softness that surprised him, "What was the child like?"

Simon stared at her, trying to understand the question.

"Was she nice?" Marcia went on, asking the question slightly differently. "Was she a nice person?"

"Yup. She was the nicest."

"How do you know?"

Simon thought for a moment, not because the question was so complicated, but—for Simon—because this one was so basic. So simple. "We . . . we were friends," he explained to Marcia, as if she were the one with the mental handicap. "We were playmates. When no one was looking, we were playmates."

J. P. guided Marcia with him into the kitchen, after telling his brother that they were going to make some coffee and would be right back. She liked the feel of his hand on the small of her back, touching her there for just the slightest moment, leading her gently across the living room floor.

"I should head over to Deering. It's about an hour from here," he was saying, reaching up into the cabinet for a tin of coffee. "I want to see Josh's drawings, and then nose around that house of yours a little more before dark."

She tried to pay attention to him as he spoke, trying to follow his thinking. "Don't you want me to come with you?"

"Do you want to?"

"Of course I do."

Carefully he spooned the coffee into the percolator with a plastic scoop. "Sure, it would be great to have you with me. But I think you'd be better off here with Simon."

"Don't you think you need us?"

He folded his arms across his chest, and smiled. "Us? Since when are you and Simon an us?"

"Simon is the only person who has actually seen the child. He's the one she trusts. You have to take Simon with you."

"Oh, Chief Montgomery would get a real kick out of that: J. P. Burrows and his kid brother, Simon, tag-team detectives." He said it lightly, but she could tell it was nonetheless a real fear.

"You know you need him—we need him. The child sees Simon as a friend . . . a peer." All at once the irony struck her, and she smiled excitedly. "Don't you see? For once in his life, Simon's disability is a real asset! He has to come with us!"

He plugged the coffee pot into a socket beside the refrigerator, nodding. "Well, you know you can't come with me when I go by the Nash place to take a look at his drawings."

"Why not?"

He took her hand, rubbing softly her fingers with his thumb. "In the eyes of only every single Burlington cop and state policeman in the county, you are the primary suspect. Remember?"

"Isn't Joyce Renders a suspect?"

"Yup, she is. And I wouldn't stop by to have a chat with Josh Nash with her present either."

"Then we'll wait in the car."

He rolled his eyes. "You really want to do this thing?"

"I think I have to. I think we have to."

In J. P.'s Bronco, driving west from West Gardner to Deering, it astounded Marcia how easily she had said Joyce Renders' name. She had, for the only time in her life, simply blurted the words out. Joyce. Renders. Joyce Renders.

J. P. had told her that morning that he had issued an all-points bulletin on the woman, announcing to the world—or at least New York and New England—that the woman was wanted for questioning in a murder investigation. He had explained that the bulletin meant that police and state troopers throughout seven states would be looking for Joyce Renders or Joyce Renders' automobile. Her sleek little Toyota.

Marcia could just imagine some burly trooper stopping Joyce on the Merritt Parkway, and telling her that . . . an acquaintance . . . an acquaintance had been found dead, an apparent murder dressed up to look like a suicide. Joyce would probably light up a cigarette, one of those grotesque brown things she smoked, and ask innocently why the police were interested in her.

Why. It was Joyce's favorite word. Why are you angry with me? she had asked Marcia in their one confrontation, their unplanned face-off in the lobby of their building. Why do you think it happened? Why are you torturing yourself now—it's over?

It hadn't been over; Joyce had been wrong. That was the problem. At least not for Brian. If it were, Brian wouldn't have saved those photographs or the notes or the phone numbers. He wouldn't have taken them with him to Vermont, and they wouldn't have resulted in the fight she and Brian had the night that he died. Funny, but if J. P. had ever asked, she could have told him not only where Joyce Renders worked, she could have told him her preference in flowers—or at least what Brian had a tendency to send her—and even some of the movies she had seen over the last year.

She extended her arms before her, almost to the windshield, and stretched out her fingers, studying them. Were those a killer's hands? It was possible; it was possible. She knew those were the hands that had wanted to strike back after Brian had hit her. She knew exactly how those hands had fit across Brian's mouth, when for a few horrifying seconds she had actually pressed them over his lips as he slept, ripping them away when he awoke with a start—ripping them away so fast that in his still half-drunken stupor he had never even realized what she had done.

But were those a killer's hands? She just didn't know; she just didn't remember. She didn't believe that she had actually planned to smother Brian; she didn't believe that she had actually planned to kill him.

Nevertheless, she realized that right now she knew more about Thistle Peep Barrington's death than she did that of her own husband.

Chapter 31

Simon climbed into the Bronco's front seat beside Marcia, sitting in the spot vacated only seconds before by his older brother.

He turned to face Marcia, telling her, "I don't drive. I don't do it." He said it without sadness or frustration, without any seeming awareness that this too was in some measure a handicap. "Mom drives me most. Sometimes dad, and sometimes J. P."

They were parked in the small four-car lot across the street from Lymon Hollis' general store, just past three-thirty, waiting there while J. P. walked up the road for a visit with Josh Nash. She smiled at Simon, and then started asking him the questions she would broach if he were an eight- or a nine-year-old boy. She asked him about his favorite sports, what it was like to live on a farm. She told him bits and pieces about her own childhood in a big city, and then listened while he told her about incidents that had happened to him or to J. P. in West Gardner.

Once Simon pretended to drive for her, walking her through the motions he would go through were he allowed to start the ignition and pull the Bronco out into the street. He asked her if she wished he could drive her up the street to her house, and she told him that they would see it again soon enough.

Soon enough.

Burrows saw Sarabeth Nash pulling into her driveway, and began to jog the last fifty yards up the street to her house.

"Good afternoon, Detective," Sarabeth said guardedly, as he approached her car. She then ducked into the backseat of the Dodge, emerging a second later with a brown bag of groceries. He wondered for a moment why she might be angry with him, before deciding that just the opposite was probably true: she wasn't mad at him; she was afraid that he was mad at her. She had, after all, gone to the police station only the day before and volunteered testimony that made him look as stupid as a dog alone in a rowboat.

"Afternoon, Ms. Nash," Burrows said, trying to alert her with his smile that he wasn't mad—at least anymore. "How are you feeling today?"

Holding her groceries with both hands, she said evenly, "Can't complain."

"Nope. Not with Thanksgiving coming."

"Nope."

"Your husband home? I got a couple more questions for him."

She squinted just the slightest bit, as if she thought she could read his mind if she focused more closely on his face. "Nope. He's in Middlebury, estimating."

"A new job?"

"Yup."

"Nice."

"We'll see."

"You want some help with those?"

"What? My food shopping?"

He reached for the bag, taking it from her hands and holding it by the bottom. "How about you? You got a second?"

"Sure. But if you got questions for Josh, don't expect I can answer 'em."

"Nope. I wouldn't do that. Not to you, not to Josh."

"You want to come in?"

"That would be nice."

"The girls aren't home yet. They're playing over at the Boisclairs."

Burrows nodded, unsure of what he was supposed to do with this information. When he said nothing, she reached into the backseat of the car for a second bag of groceries, and then started up the short walk to the house. She said nothing until she put her groceries down on a counter in the kitchen beside the sink and motioned for Burrows to do the same. Turning to him she finally said, "You probably know I went to the police yesterday. I spoke to a fellow named Sanderson."

Burrows nodded. "Anderson. You spoke to Sherman Anderson."

"Oh. So you do know." She sounded defensive, almost hurt. She almost sounded as if she thought Burrows should have begun their conversation by telling her that he knew she had gone to the police the day before. Ironically, the fact that he hadn't told her right away had given him a power of sorts over her, an authority he hadn't expected to have.

"Yup. You should be real proud of yourself," he said, letting her off the hook, "coming forward with information like that. That takes some courage."

"Think so?"

"Yup."

Sarabeth was silent for a moment, lost in the compliment. Finally she said, "So what else do you need to know?"

"I need to know where Josh keeps his plans for the Middleton house. The drawings of his renovations. I want to look at them."

She unzipped her parka and began to fiddle with the top buttons on her cardigan sweater. It looked almost as if she were trying to unbutton the top one or two without him noticing. "Think he'd mind?"

Burrows shrugged. "I don't see why. It's all pretty harmless. 'Course, you know him better than I do."

"They're in the den," she told him. "They're in one of the tubes on the shelf beside the television. It should say 'Middleton.' They've been there since the day Brian stopped by. That weird Sunday."

"The Sunday Brian asked Josh to lay off the house?"

"Yup."

He pushed one of the refrigerator magnets, this one shaped like a Hostess Twinkie, from one end of the freezer door to the other. "Why was that Sunday weird? Was it because Brian came by all of a sudden and asked Josh to come get his tools?"

"Yup. But Brian himself was pretty strange."

"You mean edgy? Your husband told me that he thought Brian Middleton was always wound a little too tight."

She reached into one of the brown bags and yanked out a six-pack of Pepsi. "Well, I didn't see him as much as Josh, so I don't know if he was *always* wound too tight. But he was mighty distracted that afternoon. And mighty muddy. Can you believe it? A Sunday in November, the ground hard as granite, and the man's got mud all over his feet, his hands. It's even all over this snazzy ski jacket he must have got in New York City! Can you believe that? The man actually managed to get muddy in November!" She knelt before a floor-level cabinet and pushed the soda inside.

"Any idea how he did it? Got so muddy?"

" 'Course I do! He told me! He told me he'd been working in the basement. Doing some darn thing with insulation."

"The basement."

"Yup, the basement. He was doing some darn thing in the basement, and then he raced over here like a bat out of—he just plain raced over here!"

Burrows closed his eyes, trying to concentrate. This was something new, something that mattered. "How do you know he went straight to your house from his basement? Did he say that?"

"No, he didn't have to. If you'd seen the man, you'd know he came straight here too. He was sweating; he had dirt from the basement all over him. All over him, I'm telling you! His feet, his hair, his hands—I'm telling you, his hands were covered with dirt! It was like he was a six year old or something. He didn't even take the time before coming over here to stop at his kitchen sink and run his hands under a little warm water. I keep a clean house, Detective, so I notice that kind of thing."

He looked up at Sarabeth, and then around the kitchen. She was right: it was a very clean house indeed.

Marcia closed her eyes for a moment in the Bronco, confident that J. P. was at that same moment discovering one more detail about whatever it was that lived in her house, learning a bit more about the little girl who seemed so important to it all. He had probably been gone fifteen or twenty minutes by now.

When she opened her eyes, she saw that slowly, almost imperceptibly, the general store was becoming fuzzy, as if layer after layer of gauze were being draped upon it. It looked almost as if the store were fading into a rolling fog. And then all at once her vision cleared, the gauze was abruptly whisked away, and she was staring again at the Deering general store. It wasn't, however, the general store exactly as she knew it, exactly as it had existed only seconds earlier; it was, she realized, the general store as it had existed eighty or ninety years ago. The sign over the front door, GENERAL MERCHANDISE, hadn't changed, but the large red and white Coca-Cola signs in the window —for Coke, New Coke, Diet Coke, Caffeine-Free Coke, Caffeine-Free Diet Coke, for Tab—had been replaced by one handwritten sign announcing, HAIRCUT AND SHAVE, 25 CENTS.

She was now sitting on the steps of the town meeting house across from the store, in exactly the position she had been in on the Bronco's front seat. Simon was no longer beside her, however, replaced by a mid-sized gentleman in his early thirties.

"I kept the noose in my house as a reminder of what I had done,"

Everett Barrington told Marcia, leaning forward slightly, not meeting her eyes.

Barrington's face was dominated by a long, aquiline nose and a mustache that made him look like a walrus. Without the mustache, Marcia thought, he might have resembled Brian: same nose, same high forehead, same intense brown eyes. He was dressed in what was probably a very elegant gray suit for Vermont at the turn of the century.

What struck Marcia most, however, was how little he looked like a killer. At least now, sitting casually on the steps of the town meeting house on a quiet afternoon. Certainly he had appeared capable of murder the first time she had seen him, the night he really did snap his own daughter's neck. But now? Now there appeared nothing evil about him, nothing especially cruel.

He seemed no more capable of hurting a child than Brian had seemed capable of raising his hand and striking her. And yet he had. And yet they both had.

"It was a reminder of what I had done," he told her again, emphasizing the word "reminder." "Every time I went up into the attic, the noose forced me to face again the fact that I had killed my own child."

She wondered what it would mean if she were to open her mouth and speak to Barrington. Would it confirm once and for all that she had lost her mind? Or would speaking to Barrington obliterate the vision? Would the sound of her own voice wake her up if she were asleep, would it calm her down if she were hallucinating?

Calm. She couldn't possibly be more calm. She was neither alarmed nor afraid to be with this man. She was no more fearful of Everett Barrington than she was of Brian Middleton, as if she had known him—and trusted him—for years. Not even the fact that he had betrayed his daughter's love, the fact he had savaged that love with an unforgivable crime, frightened her.

If she felt anything, she felt tired. Resigned.

"I don't believe you," she said finally. "I don't believe that's why you kept the noose."

"No?" Barrington asked, turning to look into her eyes. The sound of her voice had made him no less real. He sat beside her as clear in her mind as J. P.'s brother had been only a moment before. "For some, there is no greater hell than one's own guilt."

Marcia turned away from him. Her head was beginning to throb. "Who knows you killed Thistle Peep? Besides yourself and now me."

"No one."

"Her mother never knew?"

"Her mother never knew."

"What about that other woman? That younger woman I saw on your lap?"

"She fainted. She wasn't even conscious when . . . when Thistle Peep died."

"She never suspected anything?"

"Oh, I think she did. I think she did."

She watched a teenage girl in a long brown skirt leave the store with a large burlap bag that held, perhaps, ten pounds of flour or sugar, and throw the bag into a buckboard. The buckboard was drawn by a horse as dark as molasses.

"Why have you come to me?" she asked.

"No, no, no, you came to me first," he answered. "You came to me, my child—and you are in ways you are only now beginning to understand, truly my child—you came *back* to me."

The buckboard pulled out into the road, its heavy wooden wheels bouncing over hard-packed dirt.

"We are, you see, cut from the same cloth," he continued. "We are apples plucked from the same tree; we have minds that run in the same ditch. Choose your analogy, Marcia, they will all fit."

"No," she said, trying to focus upon what he had told her. My child. Back to me. Cut from the same cloth. "I'm not like you. I'm not a murderer."

"I would think you would be every bit as tired of this charade as I am. How else did your husband die?"

"I didn't kill him."

Everett Barrington chuckled. "No? You honestly believe that he killed himself?"

"I don't believe that *I* killed him."

"I see. This is another example of the empty wagon rumbling loudest."

"It's not!"

"Then let me tell you plainly. You are indeed like me, Marcia Middleton, you are indeed a murderer. You killed a husband as I killed a daughter. You did it in the very same house. And you attempted to cover your sin exactly as I did, by portraying murder as sui—"

"Stop it!" Marcia shouted, cutting him off. "It's not true! It can't be true!"

"Look at your hands. Those are the hands of a mur—"

"You're lying!" she yelled. "Just stop it! Stop it!"

"Stop it?" he yelled back. "Stop it? I'll be happy to stop it! Go to your house—go to our house—and see it all for yourself. Right now. See for yourself if everything I've said isn't true." He waved with his hands toward the house and said again, "Go home, Marcia. See for yourself."

Burrows returned to find his Bronco empty, both his brother and Marcia gone. He threw the tube with Josh's drawings into the back-seat and then stood with his hands on his hips and shouted, "Si-mon! Si-mon!" He was dimly aware that a small crowd was beginning to gather behind the big glass window at the general store, but he didn't particularly care. If Lymon Hollis and two or three local fel-lows didn't have better things to do than watch him scream for his retarded brother and a crazy flatlander, that was their problem.

Abruptly, however, he realized where the pair had gone. "God almighty," he said aloud, his voice more numb than annoyed. With a feeling that made his insides hollow, he understood that they had probably gone to her house. Leave them alone in a car for fifteen minutes, he thought to himself, and all hell breaks loose.

CHAPTER 32

Over the sound of the crows that cackled on the barn behind them, Marcia heard the doors in the house click shut, nuzzling against the hard wood frames: the door to her bedroom, the library door, the closet door in Thistle Peep's room. Even the door to the attic moved on its hinges, trying to wedge further still into its cramped frame. She thought for a moment that Everett Barrington might also have heard the noises, a progressive series of little clicks and sighs, but it was clear by the way he stared at everything in the kitchen but the doors that he hadn't.

She considered telling him that she knew the house was waiting for them. It was clear to her the moment they stepped through the front door into the kitchen: the house was waiting for them, poised and expectant. She could feel it. The house had been anticipating their return, the two of them together, and now they were here.

But he probably knew all that. It was, after all, his house. It always had been and always would be his house. That was the real reason he had left behind a noose: so that its owners would never delude themselves into believing that Everett Barrington was gone, that he had relinquished his claim to the beams and clapboards and slate that comprised the place.

Although it was only a few minutes past four, and there was still a half hour of daylight before them, she watched him light a kerosene lamp in the kitchen. "Where are we going?" she asked, as he stared into the dining room.

"Where do you think?"

Judging by the way the branches of the baby maple trees were swaying, thin bare twigs bent back almost as far as they would go, the wind was beginning to pick up. As if to confirm her thought, the kitchen windows that faced the driveway began to rattle. "The attic," she answered.

He turned to her, frowning. "You must know that I never hurt a soul in the attic. You must know that. I brought a little girl there once—" he surprised her by pausing, gathering himself before finishing his sentence "—once she was dead. But that's not where she died."

She thought for a moment. "The library then? Is that it?"

"I didn't say the attic was wrong. Of course we're going to the attic. But understand, this isn't about me. This isn't about my crime; it's about yours." He stepped toward her, lowering his voice as he approached. "This is about you. This, my child, is about how you followed in my footsteps."

Somewhere up in the woods behind the Newsome's pasture, a gun was fired, and she turned toward the sound. When she turned back to Barrington, she said in a voice so tired and beaten that she barely recognized it as her own, "I didn't follow in your footsteps. I'm not . . . I'm not your child."

"Don't do this to yourself."

"I'm not . . . I'm not your child," she stammered weakly.

Barrington grasped her shoulders and bent close to her face. She could taste his breath, so cold that it was almost sweet. "Didn't you know what the girl would look like well before you saw her picture in the newspaper?"

"But I'm not—"

"Didn't you recognize this house the moment you saw a picture of it on that real estate agent's wall?"

"But I'm not—"

"You are! And now—" He took one hand away and waved it around the room, gesturing up toward the entire house surrounding them. "Now you're home. You're in the house where you and I committed two of the gravest sins imaginable!"

"No," she murmured. "I didn't kill my husband. I couldn't have. . . ."

"One moment of madness. That's all it took: for me and for you. One moment in your life when you went one step too far. One moment that forever changed—forever ruined—your life."

He took a step back and glanced up at the ceiling as if he were staring at the sky. "One moment," he repeated, his voice softening. "And even if you didn't take your own husband's life, even if he did hang himself, in the eyes of the whole world you are still a murderer. You can't escape that. Even if you too avoid prosecution, you can never escape the fact that everyone you know is convinced beyond any doubt—beyond any doubt—that you murdered your husband and then tried to convince them that he killed himself.

"Well, it hasn't worked. You've failed. Your only choice now is to stay here. Forever."

He took her fingers into his hands, squeezing them so hard that they hurt, and she found that her eyes were beginning to tear. It wasn't the pain that was causing her to cry, however, nor was it fright. It was the simple realization that Everett Barrington was right: she really had no choice. Regardless of whether she murdered her husband as he was suggesting, or Brian had killed himself, everyone she knew believed she was guilty. Deep down she knew that even her own family doubted her; even they believed she was a murderer.

And, on a level deeper than that, she was afraid they were right. Perhaps she had killed him.

She allowed herself to fall against him, quietly crying. "Where do you want me?" she asked again.

Although she was leaning against Barrington's chest, her cheeks against the coarse wool of his century-old suit, he refused to comfort her, failing either to stroke her hair or rub her back. "We'll go to the attic," he said evenly. "Everything is ready."

In the time it took Burrows to drive the half mile from the general store to Marcia's home, he had time for one thought: while he wished he had thought about the basement sooner, he wasn't surprised that he hadn't. Before Sarabeth had told him in detail about Brian's Sunday afternoon visit, there had been no reason for him to give the basement much thought.

Brian Middleton, after all, hadn't been found there. Nor had a cat been killed there.

He had been in the basement once before, when the Waterbury Crime Lab team was scouring the house for evidence, and it hadn't made a particularly strong impression on him. He recalled that a hot water heater was down there, as was the pump that drew water from the well. In the center, not far from the stairs, was a furnace.

But there wasn't much else. There weren't even any windows. Two bare bulbs hung about ten or twelve yards apart from wiring that looked as frayed as an old sweater, and provided the basement with its only light. The stones and rocks that formed much of the foundation were cold and charmless, and even the small alleys where the basement had been extended to keep up with the house's periodic extensions were uninteresting detours. Nothing more.

He turned off the Bronco's ignition in Marcia's driveway and jumped out of the car. Perhaps because it was dusk, perhaps because he was frightened for Marcia and his brother, the house looked different to him. In this light, the house became the sort of place that assaulted one by staring back. Through an unfortunate combination of windows and eaves and porches, the building returned his gaze with an expression that hovered somewhere between anger and contempt.

Moreover, it was a disproportionate house, Burrows decided. It was a Mongoloid child of a house, an architectural ogre. Burrows knew little about construction or Vermont aesthetics at the turn of the century, but he was confident that whoever had designed the house ninety years earlier had been walleyed. Everything pointed away from the building's center, tilting, climbing—crawling, if necessary—away from the house's front door.

All in all, the place made him shudder.

He zipped up his jacket and took his flashlight from the passenger seat, and then ran to the front door, pounding his feet down hard on the thin layer of snow so he wouldn't slip. He paused for one brief second before pushing open the door, thinking to himself how much he hated opening doors. He just hated it, especially this time of day.

Especially right now. He shook his head. He should have become a dairy farmer. Maybe he would have spent his life sitting on a wheezing tractor, slowly but surely going broke, but at least he wouldn't be wandering around big stupid houses, waiting for something to jump out and grab him.

He glanced around the kitchen, trying to decide which way to go. He hadn't noticed it before, but there were eight doors in the kitchen. Eight! And every single one of them was shut.

It wasn't decent to have that many doors. There was of course the front door, but there were also doors that went to the living room, a bathroom, the basement, a kitchen closet, the small glass porch, a pantry, and the front hall.

Standing alone in the middle of the kitchen he yelled once, "Simon? Marcia?"

When there was no response, he opened the door to the basement and cried their names into the dark cellar. For a split second he thought he heard something down there, a rustling perhaps, but he couldn't be sure. He stood still, hoping the noise would return. When it didn't, he turned and shut the door.

If they weren't in the basement, there was only one other spot where they might be, the spot where every other fool fox wound up in this house. The attic.

He pushed open the kitchen door and raced up the stairs to the second floor, two at a time. At the end of the corridor he tried to turn on the upstairs light, but the bulb evidently was blown. No matter. In the twilight he saw almost instantly what he was looking for. At least part of what he was looking for. Standing flat against the wall by the attic door, eyes wide and unmoving, was his brother, Simon.

"Simon," J. P. began, taking his brother's shoulders firmly in his hands, "what happened? Are you okay?"

Clearly, however, he wasn't. He was shivering, despite his heavy snow jacket, and his eyes kept darting between the attic door and the ceiling. "We got to help her," he stammered, craning his neck to look over J. P.'s shoulders, as if he expected to see someone—something—behind him.

"Is she up there?" J. P. asked, nodding toward the attic.

"Yup. But we can't get in!"

Releasing his brother, J. P. tried the attic door, and discovered that his brother was right. As it had at least twice before, the door had become a wall of sorts, as impenetrable and unmoving as a brick hearth. In frustration he kicked at the door, but it remained secure on its hinges.

"Marcia!" he screamed through the door. "Come down!"

"She won't," Simon said, shaking his head.

"How long has she been up there?"

"A couple minutes. But she wouldn't let me come with her! She kept talking to me and saying this stuff I didn't understand, and then she wouldn't let me come with her!"

J. P. tried to concentrate. "Did the Middletons have any tools? A crowbar, maybe? Or an ax?"

"I don't know," Simon answered, agitated. "But J. P., we gotta get in there!"

J. P. nodded and took his brother by the hand. "Let's go see. We'll see what's in the basement or the barn."

* * *

Images, raw but crisp memories, raced around her mind as she stared up at the noose. It dangled above her like a subway strap, the rings on the Central Park merry-go-round, perhaps even the canopy of her grandmother's four-poster bed.

It dangled above her like the rings on the Weesimmos' swing set, the bright blue swing set that had sat for years beside the barbecue in the Weesimmos' big backyard.

A noose is an odd instrument of death, she thought. It is an oddly metaphoric killer, a weapon reminiscent in shape of a wedding band, in form of a necklace. Like the drawings of the solar system that peppered her elementary school science textbooks, a noose orbits its victims, making them the center of their own little universe.

And then it literally chokes the life out of them.

Someone, somewhere, was calling her, and she almost called back that she was coming, but . . . but surely they knew that. They knew she was on her way.

Ignoring the cold that numbed her hands, she moved the old high chair from a far corner of the attic to a spot directly below the noose. Although the high chair had only two steps and a seat, it was almost the perfect height.

She then began her climb, moving slowly, haltingly, telling herself that each movement was irrevocable. It had to be. With every step that she took, there would be that much more to undo; it would be that much more difficult to turn back. At one point the high chair gave her a splinter, a sharp prick at the tip of her finger that drew blood; but splinters, she realized with an almost pleasant combination of exhaustion and relief, no longer mattered. Splinters were like everything now that wasn't the noose above her: meaningless. Pain —small like a splinter, large like Brian's affair—no longer mattered. It came and went, as would she.

It came and went, as would she.

They raced into the basement, Simon almost tripping on the top steps, and stood for a moment on the landing. Dear Lord, J. P. found himself praying frantically in his head, dear Lord, please let her be all right. Please let me get through that door in time. Please . . .

He scanned the room, finding it exactly as he remembered it: a damp, muddy place where someone might store canned vegetables, but little else. Wooden planks served as random patches over the muddier hollows and as small, thin bridges between the furnace, the water pump, and the water heater.

Without them, he might just as well have been standing in a cave. He started to ask Simon if he saw anything, his eyes darting back and forth along the walls and corners, but the words caught in his throat. Behind them, along one of the stone walls most in need of insulation, something was moving. Silently, as if it were a small eddy of wind, J. P. could sense something moving.

He turned around and sprayed the area with his flashlight, but there didn't appear to be anything there.

"See anything?" J. P. murmured, not sure whether he was referring to an ax or the breeze that had skirted the wall behind them.

"Yup." Simon smiled just the slightest bit and wandered slowly past him toward the far corner of the basement.

"An ax? A crowbar?" J. P. asked, following him, trying to see over his shoulder. "What do you see?"

His back to J. P., staring at the gray and white boulders that comprised the foundation, Simon began to speak. He spoke in a higher pitch than his natural voice, as if he were speaking to a small child, and he spoke with his eyes on a patch of wall in which the cement was cracked like a smile. The pauses suggested that Simon was having a conversation of sorts, but it didn't seem possible for Simon to pretend such a thing: he had never, as far as J. P. knew, ever had an imaginary playmate or friend.

"Hi . . . He's my brother, J. P. He's the policeman. . . . That's okay. . . . No, she's in the attic! She's by herself in the attic! . . . Yup! . . . We gotta help her!"

Simon squatted like a baseball catcher before the foundation, his head bobbing. J. P. noticed for the first time that there was a fine, powdery dirt coating some of the stones in the wall.

"We can't play now! 'Cause she's in the attic!"

J. P. placed a hand on Simon's shoulder, more to balance himself than to aid his brother. He suddenly felt wobbly, weak. He wanted to speak to his brother, ask him who he was talking to, but he was afraid to open his mouth: his own voice, he feared, would break whatever spell Simon was under, whatever link he had to the house.

"Do we need a shovel? 'Cause we could find one, maybe . . . I can get my hands muddy, it's okay." He turned to look up at J. P., asking, "Is it okay if we dig?"

Concentrating, limiting his response to three syllables, J. P. was able to ask, "You and me?"

"Yup."

He wanted to tell his brother sure, they could dig, but only if it got them into the attic. They had to get into the attic, and they had to get into the attic quickly. But Simon clearly understood this. He understood as well as J. P. the urgency of the situation and the fact they had to find a way through the door.

"Where?" J. P. asked.

"I'll see. Oh, yeah: do you still have the good luck key?"

"The good luck key. Yup, I still have the good luck key." When he thought about it, he could feel it pressing against his leg like a lit match, the pewter so cold that it actually burned.

Simon again turned away from him, and he watched as his brother listened intently to a voice only he could hear. After a moment Simon looked up and explained, "We should dig where Mr. Middleton used to dig. It's how to get into the attic."

He found himself nodding, despite the absurdity of his brother's statement. Isn't this what he had already learned from Sarabeth Nash? They should be digging wherever Brian had been digging the Sunday he died. The secret to the house didn't hang suspended from a rafter in the attic, it sat buried somewhere in the century-old rock and dirt in the basement. "Where would that be?" he asked quickly.

Simon stood up and scratched the back of his head. "In the corner, I think. By the furnace."

Carefully, because he knew his own legs were shaky, he took Simon's hand and led him to the corner by the furnace. There he moved his flashlight over the ground and then up and across each rock in the wall. Occasionally the beam would catch a small clump of dirt that looked dryer than the rest of the ground or a stone that appeared to have been removed and replaced. But each time it was nothing. There didn't appear to have been any digging by the specific clumps of dirt; and the stones, even when they looked as if they might move, were in reality still firmly attached to the rest of the wall with cement.

"Are you sure this is the spot?"

Simon paused. "I don't know."

"Did you hear . . . do you know anyplace else where Brian might have been digging?"

"By the furnace!" Simon repeated in frustration. "That's where. By the furnace!"

J. P. scanned the basement, following the walls and alleys with his eyes. Against the opposite corner, near the house's original chimney, he saw a pile of stones and boulders and bricks, a pyramid-shaped mound perhaps two feet high. It was possible—no, it was likely—that at one point the original furnace had been in that corner. He raced over to it with his brother, and with his own feet kicked at one of the rocks. It fell off the pile and rolled a yard or two toward the center of the basement.

"Start digging, Simon," he said quickly, dropping his flashlight so he could dig with both hands. "Just start heaving the rocks out of the way!"

She placed the noose around her neck, pulling the knot tight behind her. She realized she was trembling and wondered if there was something somewhere she was forgetting. Her cheeks were wet with tears, and she wished aloud that she knew how to stop herself. She wished there was some way to undo the harm she had caused, the sadness she had brought upon the Middletons and the Hamptons.

God, of course Brian was wrong, but . . . but to have killed the man.

She envisioned her cats asleep in her parents' living room, Solstice lying like a sphinx on the arm of the couch, Chloe curled into a ball on one of the cushions below it. Her father was in a boardroom, doing whatever he did behind those tremendous mahogany doors; and her mother was in all likelihood reviewing the guest list for the cotillion. Jennifer? Jennifer was fretting. She was staring at rows of numbers in tables of foreign debt and seeing only her sister. Her poor, mad sister in Vermont, a woman who had murdered her own husband.

And J. P.?

She couldn't imagine where he was. They had been together earlier that day, but she wasn't sure where or why. She couldn't even remember the last things they had talked about, the last things they had said to each other.

If she could bring Brian back to life—and oh, God, how she wished that she could—she wondered if she would ever have left him. She wondered if it would have been possible to have met and discovered a J. P. Burrows under different circumstances, whether they might have again fallen in love.

Again? Had they now? She wasn't sure, but she thought that they had. On some level, on some level that says simply, I want desperately to see this person again. I want to see this person again and get to know him better, to know all of him—despite the fact it would never work, despite the fact it would be impossible, in the long run, to find a common ground between two lives so wildly disparate.

She wiped the tears away from her cheeks and allowed herself one, long sob. J. P. She realized that she didn't even know what the *J* and the *P* stood for.

The boulders were smooth and moist, and they were much lighter than J. P. had expected. Dismantling the mound was quick and easy, and within a minute he and Simon had completed the task, littering the basement floor with a layer of small and medium-sized rocks.

"Damn it to hell," J. P. cursed softly under his breath, failing to see any sign of digging in the dirt floor. "No one dug here." He looked at his brother, frustrated. Was it possible Simon really had made the whole thing up? Perhaps he always had underestimated the man, and in actuality Simon was capable of creating an imaginary friend.

"No one dug here," he said again, louder, this time for Simon's benefit.

Simon shook his head. "See, now you gotta move the stone!"

"Move the stone?"

"Move the stone!" Simon fell onto his knees and began running his hands over the cracks between the stones along the bottom of the wall. Abruptly he found a rock that jiggled, a stone perhaps a foot wide, and he managed to slip his fingers partly behind it. Quickly J. P. joined him, kneeling beside him and using his fingers to pry the boulder loose.

All at once the stone fell away, toppling between the two brothers with a small thud.

"It's not load bearing," J. P. murmured quietly, staring at the space they had created. He turned to Simon and repeated himself, telling him excitedly, "It's not load bearing!" And while it was clear that Simon had no idea what "load bearing" meant, he smiled with J. P., understanding by the tone of his brother's voice that this was good, that he too should be pleased.

Together they pulled away stones on either side of the gap, creating a hole perhaps two feet high and two feet wide, and almost instantly J. P. saw that behind this portion of the wall was a small cavern of sorts, almost a compartment.

Or—and he wasn't sure whether the word came to him intuitively or because he had seen something for the briefest of seconds—a tomb.

They hadn't found a cavern. They'd found a crypt. In almost the same motion, he rolled aside one last rock, and then pushed his brother away. Simon tried briefly to resist him, but J. P. shrieked, "Get away! Get back now!"

He stared, only vaguely comprehending what was inside, and crawled partway between the rocks on his stomach to get a closer look. And then, when his eyes had adjusted fully to the darkness behind the wall, he shrieked again, stretching the single word *no* into one long cry. There, within feet of where he lay, were the skeletal remains of what he could only assume by its size and by the rags that clung to it, was once a little girl.

She recalled telling Brian that she hoped she would die before him; she hoped that she would die first. In the first blush of their marriage, she couldn't imagine living without him.

Within seconds after speaking, however, she had felt a tremendous pain shoot through her chest, the sort of pain she had always imagined occurred with a heart attack: sharp, throbbing, white-hot pain that cut across the chest like a drill. The pain had caused her to double over, and if Brian hadn't grabbed her by her shoulders and sat her down on the couch, she would have collapsed onto the floor.

And then, as abruptly as the pain came, it went. It just stopped. The tears that had come on with the pain went too, and she was left feeling merely drained.

She couldn't imagine that whatever pain was about to befall her could be worse than that.

And even if it were, it probably wouldn't last very long. And then, if she felt anything at all, she would just feel drained.

Behind him he felt Simon hitting the back of his leg and his ankle, and he heard his brother repeating his name over and over, asking him if he was okay. He tried to answer Simon, but he found himself merely shaking his head, as if his brother could see him through the wall. He was afraid to open his mouth, afraid that if he did, he would vomit.

He had seen skeletons before in the coroner's office, but never like this. Never buried in the basement of a poisoned old house.

The bones, more black than white, lay flat on the ground, as if the body had been placed there on its—on her—back. Her skull was resting in a pillow of mud-covered hair, matted and ratty and wild, but nonetheless hair. He couldn't be sure, but he assumed that her hands had been folded across her stomach, as if she were in an actual coffin.

He also thought that there might be something in the child's hands. It had sunk through the body into the dirt, and was covered partly by one of the remaining pieces of plaid cloth.

He wriggled closer to the skeleton on his stomach, using his elbows to slide forward, and—staring only at the object before him—he reached through the body and poked at the dirt with his fingertips. His hand hit metal. He rubbed his fingers over something flat and metal, and he realized that the child had been buried holding a steel box of some kind. Stretching his arm as far as he could, he was able to grab the box, a rectangular canister perhaps half the size of a shoebox, and pull it toward him. He then slid backward as fast as he could, emerging into the basement light that seemed now as bright as sunshine.

"What happened? What's in there?" Simon asked him, trying to peer around his brother and see behind the wall. "You okay?"

J. P. nodded, catching his breath. He held the box up before them, looking at it carefully for the first time. It was actually much flatter than a shoebox and slighter less rectangular. It was more of a square. The hinges along its back and the lock at the front were finished with ornate copper leaves, and it appeared that the box at one point had had a handle of sorts at the top.

"What's inside?" Simon asked, twisting his head like a puppy.

J. P. tried flipping open the lid, but it was locked. "I don't know," he said, "but let's see what that good luck key of yours can do to help."

He wiped the mud off his hands on his jeans, and reached into his pocket for the key. Holding both the key and the metal box in his hands, he saw that the small loops and swirls at the end of the key matched those on the box. "Let's see what we got here," he mumbled to himself, trying to fit the key into the lock.

Initially it didn't fit. Age and rust and dirt had clogged the rollers inside the lock, and for a moment J. P. feared that this too had been wasted effort, wasted time. On his second try, however, he was able to shimmy the key inside and turn it with just enough force to pry open the lid.

The moment the lid opened, the moment J. P. flipped up the top, one by one they heard every door in the house swing free, slamming into the walls behind them. Both J. P. and Simon fell against the stone wall and stared up at the ceiling above them, listening. They heard the doors opening as a rhythmic series of bangs and crashes: first the basement door, then the doors in the kitchen—every single one of them—and then the myriad doors lining the dining room, the living room, and the front hall, and finally all of the doors along the second floor. There was no doubt in J. P.'s mind what he was hearing: bedroom doors and closet doors, even cabinet doors swinging free, banging open with a series of great and small thuds. Even the door to the attic had opened, he knew it.

He took his brother by the arm, holding the box open with his free hand, and ran across the basement and up the steps, taking the steps two and three at a time. Together they sprinted through the kitchen and the front hall, up the steps to the second floor, and then down the corridor to the attic door.

The door was open, wide open. It had flung itself open with such force that it had smashed a small hole in the plaster where the doorknob had hit the wall.

"Stay here and keep this door open," J. P. told Simon, positioning his brother against the attic door. "Don't let it slam shut while I'm up there!"

Simon shook his head that he wouldn't, and stood firmly, defiantly, in the doorway. J. P. looked down once into the box in his hand, noticing for the first time exactly what was inside: a single sheet of paper, a piece of stationery.

"Just remember," he said again, "stay right here." He then ran up the steps into the attic, realizing that somewhere in the basement he had dropped his flashlight and wishing that he had it with him now.

At the top of the steps he saw Marcia immediately, lying on the floor in a small ball, curled up he assumed against the colossal cold. He rushed to her side, crouching between her and an overturned high chair, and turned her body toward him. Around her neck was a noose, the end of which looked shredded, torn.

He looked up at the beam above her, and saw where the noose had ripped free of the wood.

Marcia opened one eye, and then the other, and then said something to him in a voice so soft he could barely hear her. "I don't even know," she whispered, "what J. P. stands for."

Chapter 33

In the detectives' office Thursday afternoon, Simon Burrows threw one of his older brother's Assassins three feet wide of the corkboard target, landing it squarely in the middle of the John Deere calendar.

"Not bad, Simon," J. P. said, shaking his head. "Every bit as good as the folks from the coroner's office."

Patricia Lange glared at J. P. good-naturedly and let the remark pass. She watched in silence as Simon wandered across the room to the far wall and began to retrieve the darts, and then said to J. P., "I hear that was quite some letter you found."

"You hear? You mean you haven't read it yourself?"

"Nope. Terrance Beech hasn't let it out of the state attorney's office."

"That's typical. No doubt he thinks he's going to prosecute some guy who's been dead over forty or fifty years."

Simon returned with the darts, asking his brother, "Can we get one of these?"

"A dart board?"

"Uh-huh."

"Oh, I don't think so, Simon. Our parents and I would probably hurt ourselves real bad with something like that around the house."

"Okay. I'll use this one," Simon said contentedly, concentrating on the target.

"You got a copy of the letter?" Lange asked.

"I do indeed. I have a couple." In the pile of papers on his desk he found his Xerox copies of the note, the only item Barrington had buried in the box with his daughter. He handed one of the copies to the medical examiner and held on to the other himself. He read the note along with Lange, as astonished by it now as he had been the moment he had read it with Marcia Middleton the day before.

October 16, 1910

Everett,

What is done is done. We have sinned, we have sinned gravely.

I cannot forgive myself, and I cannot forgive you. We let things proceed apace in directions that we knew were wrong.

I don't know for sure what happened that night after I fainted, but I know what I believe happened. As bad as what we have done together, I believe what you have done alone is far worse.

Far worse.

I have considered coming forward and telling my suspicions to the pastor and the constable, but given the pain that Belle has already endured, I will not. You already have inflicted enough pain upon her, taking from the woman her only child.

Nor, however, will I ever see you again. If I should run into you in Deering or Middlebury or even Burlington, if we should find mutual cause to be in the same room, I shall do what I can to ignore you, to pretend we have never met.

I cannot abide you and I will not abide you ever again. If what I believe is true, and I believe it with all my heart, then you, Everett Barrington, can go straight to hell.

And I know you will.

Miss Constance Proctor

"Oh, God," Lange murmured, tossing the copy back onto J. P.'s desk, "it's worse than I expected. I can hardly believe it. Will you tell me, what kind of man is capable of murdering his own daughter?"

J. P. sat against the edge of his desk, rubbing the bridge of his nose. "Come on, Pat; you know how often it happens. You know the child abuse statistics. You see it every week up at the hospital. 'Accidental drowning. An accidental fall. Accidental asphyxiation.' "

"I just didn't envision it happening back then."

"Evidently, it did."

"Evidently."

Behind them he heard Simon continuing to toss his darts. "When will you and Hank be finished examining the child's bones?"

"We're still waiting on some lab work, but it's clear to me that the child wasn't hanged. I studied the vertebrae around the neck myself, and the injuries weren't characteristic of a hanging. Barrington—or someone—broke the girl's neck."

"Sounds to me like Beech has enough for a conviction," J. P. said, standing up and wandering with Simon to the dart board to retrieve the darts again. "If he thinks he can prosecute a ghost." He smiled after he said it for Lange's benefit, but enunciating the word "ghost" had given him a chill.

"You don't really believe that, do you? You don't really believe there's a ghost?"

He took Simon by the arm and led him back to his desk. "I believe there was something in the house—a couple somethings—that Brian Middleton set free when he found the little Barrington girl's bones."

"Hank told me that's what you thought. He said that's what you told Beech and Montgomery."

"That's right. I did. I told them that Middleton went nosin' around the basement the last Sunday he was alive, trying to figure out how to hitch up blue board insulation or some such nonsense, and he found the crypt. That's when he went rushing over to Josh Nash to tell the guy to stop working on his house. He didn't want anyone to know about the crypt until he understood what the heck was down there himself."

"Not even his wife?"

"Oh, God, especially not Marcia. It was only the night before that he and Marcia had discovered the noose in their attic, and Marcia was still pretty damn upset. She thinks Brian was planning to tell her, but he sure wasn't about to only twelve hours after they had found the noose."

"I didn't realize they had just found the noose."

"Yup. So Marcia thinks Brian was, well, protecting her from the crypt. Seems he had a habit of sittin' on bad news."

"What—and I want the exact words—did Gerry Montgomery say when you told him and Beech all that?"

He placed a dart in Simon's hand, reminding his brother how to grip the tip with his thumb and his forefinger. "What could he say? What could they say? It's the truth."

"They didn't flinch? Gerry didn't tell you to stay off the hard cider?"

"Oh, he got a little uncomfortable when I told him that whatever Middleton set in motion was probably finished—now that the truth was out. I said the girl was probably just trying to tell the world that she didn't really hang herself, and her old man was just trying to stop her. That's why he convinced Brian Middleton to hang himself: he knew too much. Barrington kept the noose around, and he kept ol' Constance Proctor's note around, and he even kept his daughter's body around—"

"We're going to find an empty coffin in the Deering cemetery, aren't we?" Lange said, leaning forward in J. P.'s chair.

"I doubt it will be empty. I imagine it's filled with a good forty pounds of dirt," Burrows said. "You see, this was all Everett Barrington's way of punishing himself. Evidently, he didn't want anyone else's justice—just his own."

"And Beech and Montgomery accepted that?"

"Of course they did! They're dropping the investigation into Brian Middleton's death, aren't they? The state is no longer trying to press charges against either Marcia Middleton or Joyce Renders, is it?"

"The state is no longer trying to press charges because the only conceivable—'natural'—cause of death we can find is an eighty-year-old noose, and neither Marcia Middleton nor Joyce Renders is strong enough to haul a body as big as Brian's up to an attic, and then hang it!"

"There you go!"

She waited for Simon to complete a toss, throwing the dart into the paneling beside the dart board. "Simon," she began, "tell me the truth. Where did you find that key?"

The heavier man turned toward her, scratching the side of his face. "I got it from the girl."

"You didn't find it anywhere? Like on the basement floor?"

"Nope."

"And that's what you told Mr. Beech?"

"Yup."

She looked up at J. P., smiling, and said, "God, J. P., they must think the entire Burrows family has gone squirrely."

J. P. took a breath. "You've never seen that house, Pat," he told Lange evenly. "I'll bet if you had had to spend a night in it, you wouldn't call me squirrely now."

"Oh come on! That other family, the Finches, they spent decades in that house and nothing ever happened to them!"

"They never found the bones. And . . ." He hesitated for a long moment, looking over at his sweet and simple brother. Simon. Unknowing. Unsuspecting. Unconcerned. "And the little girl never had a playmate quite like . . . my brother."

Simon looked at J. P., and nodded just the tiniest bit.

"What about your new friend? Marcia? How's she doing?" Lange asked, her voice genuinely troubled.

"Probably about as well as can be expected. Maybe even a little better."

"Where is she now?"

"With her family. Her parents and her kid sister. They arrived early this morning, and they're in seclusion somewhere up in Stowe. They're all heading back to New York City tomorrow."

"How does that make you feel?"

"I got no problem with that. Marcia's coming back."

"She told you that?"

"Nope."

"Then how do you know?"

Burrows smiled, and sat down on the edge of his desk. "I spent one fall picking apples for a fellow named Normy Oates. I guess I was nineteen. Well, the first thing Normy said to me was, 'J. P., reach for those high apples first. You can get the low ones any time at all.' That's exactly what Normy told me. So I'll tell you: If Marcia isn't coming back on her own, I'm asking her back here myself."

5.

Chapter 34

It was their first anniversary, a cool afternoon in mid October when the last of the leaf peepers had returned to New York, and once again they had their dirt road and their farm all to themselves. The sky was chalkboard gray—black, almost, the sort of ominous dark that occurs only in the hills of Vermont—and there were small, pointed waves on their pond.

But the gray didn't bother Marcia; she actually thought it looked rather pretty, gathering a measure of beauty from its simple rawness and power.

She sat silently on the steps of the front porch, as J. P. cut out the eyes of the jack-o'-lantern with his pocketknife. Marcia watched as he gently pushed the blade in and out of the pumpkin's mottled rind, oblivious of the small drawing of a face he had made on the skin.

"I have something to tell you," she said finally. She had hoped to sound mysterious, but was afraid she had sounded threatening instead.

"Oh?" He didn't look up; evidently, she hadn't sounded threatening at all.

"Yes. But you have to tell me something first." She wrapped her arms around her stomach, protecting it from a cold fall breeze. For a moment she thought she felt something—someone—move within her, but she knew it was too soon, much too soon. In time.

"A barter deal, eh?" Burrows wondered.

"A barter deal, yup."

He knew what she would ask. She would ask what he had promised he would tell her someday when they had been married a year earlier. It was to be a present of sorts, something to—as his father always said—keep the dimple on the outside, and the devil on the inside. And now it was time.

"Go ahead," he said, pretending to concentrate exclusively on the pumpkin.

Down the road she saw the Geener twins in their daddy's blue pickup, a pair of sixteen-year-old boys on their way to the Saturday football game against Middlebury. She was older now than the ages of both boys combined, perhaps only by days, perhaps only by months, but older, older for sure. The knowledge didn't bother her the way it would have once. Now it was just an observation, a random fact that grounded her, helped her to situate herself in the small town of Lincoln—the town in which she and J. P. had finally settled.

"Your name," she said to J. P. "What is it really?"

He pulled the knife completely from the pumpkin and wiped a strand of orange string on his jeans. "What do you think—J. P. is an alias or something?"

"Nope. But I think it's short for something."

He sat beside her on the steps, and put both of his hands in one of her jacket pockets. "Well," he said, noticing for the first time that three or four clapboards on the north wall would have to be replaced before the first snow came. "You saw the marriage license. It says J. P. I was born and christened and raised as J. P. Burrows."

"Your parents were thinking of something." She felt him softly massage her stomach through her jacket and her sweater, rubbing the skin just above her waist with his thumbs. Did he know? Were they already so finely attuned to each other that he knew? She hoped so. She liked the idea.

"Oh, don't blame J. P. on my mother. She was innocent on this one," he told her. Once the Geener boys were out of sight and their truck was over the hill, the farm became silent except for the wind cutting through the barn.

"Ah, but there was a plot."

"There was a plot."

"And?"

He watched the cats, Solstice and Chloe, pouncing on the dried maple leaves that blew across the yard. He could doze here, despite the chill, despite the dampness in the air. "My father's never put much stock in names. Whenever Dorothea Bartlett used to tell him that a good name was better than gold, he used to say to her, 'Dorothea, I don't think your name will buy a whole lot of feed down at Agway, but you go try.' Fact is, he used to get a little ornery with the Bartletts, and he was having a bit of a squabble with the clan when I was born. He said to Dorothea that blood mattered more than names, and he'd prove it to her with me."

"So?"

He loved to touch her, even through jackets and sweaters and shirts. He knew it was his imagination, but he could almost feel the warmth from her skin through her layers of clothing. "So, the *J* stands for Just, and the *P* stands for Plain. Though you won't see the name written anyplace official, you are spending your life with a man named Just Plain Burrows. What do you think of those apples?"

She looked into Burrows' eyes, trying to see whether he was sincere. Perhaps. She might know the answer for sure in time, but for now she would live well enough without assurance. "I think the sweetest apples fall right close to the tree," she said in the Vermont accent he had taught her. "That's what I think."